He rolled into her arms and she held him close, letting him weep in great, shuddering sobs against her breast. Her own tears flowed to join his, running down into her neck, pooling in the hollow of her throat, and she felt at last a real compassion – not the pity she had felt until now, which had begun to turn to contempt, but the empathy that was true understanding of his condition.

He's right, she thought, he can't help it. Dunkirk, the bombing, it's all hurt him somewhere deep down and we've just got to wait for it to heal. And never mind the others, who are going through worse – this is Ted, my Ted, and I can't make him any different from what he is. I've just got to wait, and be strong.

But as his body trembled and shook against hers and his tears soaked her breast, she stared into the darkness, feeling cold and bleak and lonely, and wondering how much longer her strength could last.

Lilian Harry grew up close to Portsmouth Harbour, where her earliest memories are of nights spent in an air-raid shelter listening to the drone of enemy aircraft and the thunder of exploding bombs. But her memories are also those of a warm family life shared with two brothers and a sister in a tiny backstreet house where hard work, love and laughter went hand in hand. Lilian Harry now lives on the edge of Dartmoor where she has two ginger cats to love and laugh at. She has a son and daughter and two grandchildren and, as well as gardening, country dancing, amateur dramatics and church bellringing, she loves to walk on the moors and – whenever possible – to go skiing in the mountains of Europe. She has written a number of books under other names, including historical novels and contemporary romances. Visit her website at www.lilianharry.co.uk.

By Lilian Harry

Keep Smiling Through

LILIAN HARRY

ORION

An Orion paperback

First published in Great Britain by Orion in 1996
This paperback edition published in 1997 by Orion Books Ltd,
Orion House, 5 Upper St Martin's Lane, London WC2H 9EA

Reissued 2004

A CIP catalogue record for this book
is available from the British Library.

Typeset at The Spartan Press Ltd
Lymington, Hants

Printed in Great Britain by
Clays Ltd, St Ives plc

www.orionbooks.co.uk

*For my brother Roy,
with very much love*

CHAPTER ONE

May 1941. The war that had begun in September 1939 between Britain and Germany was throwing its dark shadow over the entire world. The war that was to have been over by Christmas, was beginning to seem as if it would have no end.

The families who lived in April Grove, in the city of Portsmouth, were learning together to face the fears, the privations and the day-to-day drudgery of a war which had stormed its way to their own doorsteps. There was little history to guide them. Never before had war brought death from the skies to the ordinary homes of people who were making no attack, who had no defence. Never before had the population of the entire country been forced to burrow like moles into the earth itself for safety. Never before had a country that had not been invaded woken day after day to find its homes destroyed, its schools and churches ablaze, its workplaces gone.

It was like finding your way through unknown territory, making your own map with each painful step.

'You wouldn't know it was Pompey,' Jess Budd said sadly, when she went down to the Guildhall Square and saw the burned-out shell of her favourite store, McIlroys, the battered railway station, the gutted Guildhall. 'You wouldn't believe it had ever been a lovely city, with happy people, a place it was a pleasure to come to. It's no more than a ruin now – a horrible, dying ruin.'

It was as if the Germans had tried to blast the heart out of the city by devastating its centre, the part that everyone knew and loved. All around the whole area, streets had been bombed, houses flattened, roads obliterated by vast craters. The Madden Hotel was blown apart by a mine, Kingston Prison damaged, the main railway blocked by debris, and even the Royal Hospital struck by a mine. The Dockyard, so vital to the country's defence, was bombed again and again, and fires raged there day and night as the weary firefighters struggled to control them.

But even as she stared, her heart breaking at the sight of so much destruction, Jess felt the stirring of a determination that had been born and and was growing in the heart of every Briton during those dark months of the blitz. We *won't* be beaten, she thought. We *won't* give in. And somewhere deep inside her, like the tolling of a bell, she heard the words of Winston Churchill, spoken to hearten a nation that might otherwise have been brought to its knees.

'*We will never surrender . . .*'

'I don't know,' Gladys Shaw said restlessly. 'I don't reckon I did all that much. Not when you think about other people, people what died. They're the ones who deserve medals, not me.'

Olive Harker and her sister Betty Chapman looked at the shining silver disc in its little case. Gladys had brought it up the street to the Chapmans' house to show it to them specially. The whole of April Grove had been proud of her when they'd heard the news, and everyone would be wanting a look, but somehow Gladys didn't seem all that thrilled.

I would be if it was me, Betty thought. Or Dennis. And she knew her sister was thinking the same. Suppose she or her husband Derek had won a medal for serving their country in the war. Why, they'd be like a dog with two tails.

She looked at it again. The British Empire Medal, presented by King George the Sixth himself. Well, not handed to Gladys by him personally – she'd had to go to the Chief Constable of Hampshire to get it, and she said that she'd been more nervous about that than she'd been in any of the air-raids of the Portsmouth blitz. But the King had signed the paper, that's what mattered. He *knew* about her.

Betty shook her head, marvelling. 'It's queer to think that the King knows about people like us,' she said. 'Living in little two-up, two-down terraced houses in April Grove in Portsmouth. I mean, you wouldn't think him and the Queen knew we existed, would you?'

'They do, though,' Olive said. 'Look at the way the Queen talked to my Derek when she came last year. Asking him about me and whether we had any kids, and all that —' She fell silent and Betty squeezed her hand. She knew that Olive still grieved over the baby she had lost during one of those terrible air-raids. The words the Queen had spoken to Olive's soldier husband then had given her a lot of comfort, and she treasured them still.

'Well, that's what I mean,' Gladys said. 'There's people like you and Derek — and poor Kathy Simmons, she got *killed* that night — and all those others who did just as much as I did during the blitz, fighting fires and putting out incendiaries and getting rid of bombs, and ending up hurt or dead themselves. Why should *I* get a medal, and not them? It don't seem right.'

'Don't talk so daft,' Olive Harker said stoutly. 'You drove that old van all through the blitz, you went down that bombed cellar and saved that little girl, you went in that house that could've fallen down round your ears at any minute and fetched out that little baby, you did all sorts of things. You were lucky to get away with a broken arm. Of course you deserve a medal. You're a heroine.'

'I'm not!' Gladys said sharply. 'I'm no different to all the others. I just happened to get noticed, that's all. And don't forget there's a lot of people I didn't save.' She fell silent, biting her lip as she remembered the family of little Ruth in the cellar, staring with sightless eyes as she struggled to free the child from the rubble. The tiny baby she'd found wrapped in blankets under the stairs, its mother blown to fragments in the room above. The men and women and children she had taken in her rickety ambulance through streets of flames, to hospitals that might not even exist by the time she reached them.

And Graham Philpotts, the young sailor with the red hair and cheeky grin, who had died from the blast of a land-mine in the doorway of Portsmouth's Royal Hospital, on the night of 17 April 1941.

Betty watched her friend. She saw the tears in Gladys's eyes and knew what she was thinking. She was sad about Graham too – he'd been her boyfriend for a while, they'd even talked about getting married. But she knew it must be much worse for Gladys to feel she was responsible for his death.

'It wasn't your fault,' she said gently, as she'd already said a hundred times. 'You weren't to know what was going to happen. And you'd had enough that night. You were out on your feet. Someone had to drive the van.'

'It should have been me.' Gladys looked again at the medal. 'It was Graham should have got this, not me.'

The girls were silent for a few moments. Betty glanced around the room. It was the family living room, with the furniture her mother and father had collected over the years – a square dining-table with four chairs, a couple of armchairs for Ted and Annie, a dresser which showed off their best tea-set. In one corner was the cabinet that Betty's brother Colin had built before he joined the Navy, to house the gramophone. He'd been mad about Joe Loss and Glenn Miller, and his records were stored in the cupboard underneath the speaker.

It seemed a long time since he'd sat in this room and listened to them, winding the gramophone up after every fourth tune. A long time since he'd swung in through the door in his bell-bottoms, his face wreathed in a cheery grin. Betty missed him badly.

She missed Dennis too, and once again she wished she could bring him here. So far, she'd not said much to her family about the young man she had met on the farm where she worked as a Land Girl. Once you brought a chap home, it was considered 'serious', and although Betty and Dennis had always been very serious about each other, she knew that it would take time for her family to accept him. And the way her father was now, he might never come round to it.

'Have you made up your mind about the Wrens?' she asked Gladys.

Gladys nodded. 'I'm going down the recruiting office as soon as I can. I went before, but they wouldn't have me till me arm was better. Dad don't like the idea much but I can't help that. He's living in the Dark Ages if he thinks he can tell me to stay at home. We've all got to do our bit.'

'I know.' Olive sighed. 'I've almost decided to go for the ATS, but I still haven't talked to Derek about it. He was home on a weekend pass a couple of weeks ago, but you know how it is – we never seemed to get round to talking about things. Anyway, it didn't seem right to spoil his time at home going on about the war. All he wanted to do was – well, *you* know' – she blushed '– and go to the pictures and things like that.' She smiled. 'We went to the Regent to see Arthur Askey and Richard Murdoch in *The Ghost Train* – it was ever so funny. We nearly fell out of our seats laughing. And they've got George Formby coming to the Odeon next week, in person, to raise funds for air-raid victims. I reckon I might go – why don't you come as well? It'd do you good to have a bit of a laugh.'

'I don't know, I might.' Gladys spoke without enthusiasm. She really did seem down, Betty thought. Perhaps she'd be better once she was doing something again – either back at the First Aid Post, or in the Wrens.

The front doorbell rang shrilly and Betty got up to answer it. She came back into the room a minute or two later with Gladys's younger sister Diane behind her. Diane's face was pink and excited.

'I thought you'd be here. Guess what! I've got a job.'

'What sort of a job?' Gladys stared at her. 'You've already got a job, at the laundry. I didn't know you'd got the sack.'

'I didn't.' Diane tossed her head. She'd had her fair hair cut short lately and it clustered in tight curls round her small face. She was wearing a summer frock with short sleeves and her arms were sunburnt. 'I'm fed up with the laundry. I've got a job at Airspeed.'

'Airspeed? What, making aeroplanes?'

'That's right. I daresay I'll learn to fly them too.' Her tone was casual but the three older girls could tell that she was smouldering with excitement. 'I think that's the best thing anyone could do, don't you? Fly in a plane, up there in the sky.' She glanced towards the window, at the blue square that could be seen through the top of the pane. 'Better'n driving an old van round the streets.'

'Now just you look here, Diane Shaw –' Gladys began, but Olive stopped her with a hand on her arm.

'She don't mean anything, Glad.' She looked at Diane. 'You don't really think you'll be allowed to fly, do you? I mean, everyone knows about Amy Johnson, but they won't let ordinary girls like us fly in the war.'

'Won't they? I bet they will. Women are going to do everything in this war.' Diane's blue eyes glittered. 'There aren't going to be enough men to do the jobs, are there? We'll be doing it all, so that men can go off and join the Forces. And we'll be joining alongside 'em soon, and fighting as well. I tell you what, if we don't make up our own minds what to do they'll make them up for us. And I'm not waiting to be told – I know what *I* want to do.'

There was a moment's silence. Then Gladys laughed uneasily and said, 'Hark at you!' She turned to the other two. 'Our Di always did think she knew it all. I can just guess what our Dad'll have to say about it.'

'He's not getting the chance,' Diane declared, much as Gladys herself had done only ten minutes earlier. 'He can't stop me going to work at Airspeed, and once I'm there he won't be able to do a thing about it. Anyway, I'll probably join the WAAF in a year or so. That's where I'll get the best chance of learning to fly.'

'Learn to fly!' Gladys said scornfully. 'You've got as much chance as I have of steering the *Ark Royal*. The nearest you'll get to flying is walking past an airman in the street.'

'All the same, she's right about some of it,' Olive said.

'Women *are* starting to do all the jobs that men have been doing. And the papers are full of advertisements asking girls to join up. How do we know what we'll be having to do in a few months' time? After all, you'd never have guessed this time last year that you'd be driving an ambulance through air-raids and winning medals, would you?' She thought for a few minutes. 'I'll tell you something else. I reckon she's right about us not having the choice if we wait much longer. We're just the age to get called up, and if I've got to go I want to go into the Army, like my Derek. He'll be home again this weekend – I'll talk to him about it the minute he gets here.'

'But you're a married woman,' Gladys said. 'Surely they won't –'

'Married!' Olive said bitterly. 'You'd hardly know it, would you. You could count the nights Derek and me have had together on your fingers, and still have a few left over to mash the potatoes. I don't reckon that counts for anything these days.'

'Not even if you had a baby?'

'I'm not going to have a baby,' Olive said shortly. 'Not until the war's good and over, anyway.' She got up abruptly. 'I've got to go now, Glad. Mum and Dad are down North End with Granny and Grandpa and I promised to go and meet them so that Mum could go straight to the First Aid Post and I could walk back with Dad. He's still poorly, you know. I wonder sometimes if he'll ever get over that turn he had during the bombing.'

She walked out, and Gladys gave Betty a rueful look.

'I'm a twerp, I really am. I don't know how I could have said that to Olive about babies. One of these days I'm going to open my mouth and shove my foot so far down it I'll swallow my toes.'

'I know. I say things without meaning to as well. But you can't keep on remembering, can you – not when there's so many other things to think about all the time. And we've all got our own worries.'

'Well, we'll have to be going too,' Gladys said, getting up. She looked at her sister, who had opened the gramophone door and started to look through the records. She was humming one of the Glenn Miller tunes, and Betty felt a lump in her throat as she remembered Colin again. *String of Pearls* had been one of his favourites. 'Come on, Di. Tell us a bit more about this job of yours. You're not really going to be helping to build planes, are you?'

Betty went back to the farm next day. She'd been hoping to see Dennis while she was home, but as usual he'd been called out to help deal with some unexploded bombs that had been discovered out at Southsea. You never knew when they were going to turn up, and they always had to be disposed of straight away. The fact that they might have lain there for months didn't mean they weren't going to go off.

'A lot of them are timed,' he'd told Betty. 'Some have delaying mechanisms and their timing doesn't start until they're disturbed, or they might be set like an alarm clock, to go off after a few days – or even months. We can't take any risks with them.'

Betty shuddered. She hated thinking about what Dennis did, even though she admired and loved him for doing it.

'I don't know anyone as brave as you,' she said, and Dennis laughed and hugged her.

'Everybody's brave in this war. We just have different ways of showing it.'

He came out to the farm to see her a couple of days later and she told him about Gladys's medal.

'She doesn't seem to want it at all. I mean, she's thrilled in a way, of course she is, but she doesn't think she deserves it any more than anyone else. It's like you said – *everyone's* brave. Why should just a few be picked out?'

'Because that's the only way you can do it,' Dennis said. 'You can't give everyone a medal just for being alive now – it wouldn't mean anything. I suppose in a way, it isn't Gladys who's getting the medal, but all the ambulance drivers who do the sort of work she does. She's a sort of representative.'

'I reckon you deserve a medal,' Betty said. 'Doing what you do.'

'But I couldn't do it without the Pioneers digging the shafts and the rest of the crew. So if I did get a medal – which I hope I won't – it'll belong to them as much as to me.' He was silent for a moment, then said, 'I'm sorry I couldn't get to see you in Pompey. I wanted to see where you live – and meet your family.'

Betty bit her lip. She met his eyes. They were serious, their hazel light darkened. She sighed.

'You know what I think, Dennis. I *want* you to meet them. I really do. I want them to meet you, to know what a smashing chap I've got. But – I don't think it's a good idea. Not just yet.'

'Is it your dad still?' he asked quietly.

'Yes. He's not getting any better, you see. He's a bag of nerves. And anything that upsets him – well, the doctor says we've got to be really careful or it'll just set him back.'

'And meeting me would upset him.'

'It's not you,' she said quickly. 'I mean, it's not you as a person. It's – it's –'

'It's me as a CO,' he said. 'A conscientious objector. That's what would upset him, isn't it? Someone who refused to fight in the war.'

'You have to understand him,' Betty said. 'I mean, people like us – like him – well, we don't think that way. We think what we've been brought up to think, I suppose. Same as you.'

'No. I was brought up to think for myself.'

'Well, so was I!' she said quickly, then shook her head. 'No, maybe I wasn't. Not in the same way. But you still think the same as your dad, don't you? He was a CO in the last war. And you're one in this. So how d'you know you *are* thinking for yourself?'

Dennis smiled. 'Well, perhaps I might not have known at first. But a few months in prison would soon have told me if I wasn't. And they didn't make any difference to what I thought, did they? No, Betty, I'm pretty convinced about what I'm doing. And I feel a lot better for it now I'm in bomb disposal.' He glanced at her. 'Wouldn't that make your dad feel any different?'

'It might. Well, I'm sure it would. But – he's been through a lot, you know. The first war – and then Dunkirk. And that really was brave. He used to hate even taking the ferryboat across the harbour at night during the raids. Going all that way – and being bombed – and seeing other ships go down, and all those soldiers . . .' She shuddered. 'The doctor said it was all too much for him even though it didn't come out for months, not until that night he was firewatching on top of our turret. It was building up inside him all that time and he just couldn't take any more, and broke down. We've just got to wait till he gets better.'

Dennis nodded. 'I know. I do understand, Betty. And I'd be happy to wait, if only . . .' He took her hand and stroked it gently. '. . . If only we knew things were going to turn out all right for us. If only we could look ahead.'

Betty met his eyes and felt a deep quiver of fear. She knew what Dennis meant. If he didn't meet her family soon, he might never meet them. Life was uncertain for everyone these days, but for no one was it less certain than the members of the bomb disposal crews.

The next bomb might be his last.

'I want to marry you, Betty,' he said softly, drawing her close into his arms. 'But I want it to be with your family's blessing. I don't want anything coming between you and them – just in case . . .'

Betty stared at him, then flung herself hard against him, gripping his body against hers, burrowing her face into his chest.

'Don't say things like that, Dennis! Don't. It frightens me too much. I want to hold you tight and never let go of you. I want you to stay with me, and not go back to those horrible bombs. I don't care about my family, I don't care about anyone else – I just want *you*.'

But it wasn't true, and they both knew it. Families were important. Families, friends, strangers, people they would never even meet – all were important. That was why Betty was working on the farm, toiling until her back was almost breaking, freezing in winter, almost melting in summer.

That was why Dennis spent his days at the bottom of a deep shaft, often knee-deep in mud, working painstakingly on a bomb that might explode and shatter his body at any second.

That was what the war was all about.

'So what would you be doing in the ATS?' Derek Harker asked his wife.

They were sitting in the Chapmans' front room. It was understood that when Derek was home on one of his short leaves this room belonged to him and Olive. They'd put out a few of their wedding presents, to make it feel a bit more like their own home, and even Annie wouldn't come in without knocking. Tonight, Derek had brought Olive a bunch of flowers – big coloured daisies and a few sweet williams – from Atkinson's, the greengrocer's at the top of March Street, and she'd arranged them in the glass vase Jess and Frank had given them.

Olive sat down and snuggled into the curve of his arm.

'I don't know. But there was a bit in the paper about it last week.' She sat up and reached for a sheet of newspaper on the shelf. It was from the *Evening News*, dated 11 June, and the headline read: *War Work With A Punch In It For Girls*. Olive began to read aloud, stopping to make her own comments.

'There's ever so many different things you can do. Some of the girls are trained as gunner girls.'

'What, firing guns?' Derek interrupted. 'I didn't think they let girls do that.'

'I don't think they actually fire them.' Olive read on. 'No, it says the girls spot the raiders and direct the fire. The actual laying and firing – what's laying, I wonder? – is done by men. But it's just as important, the paper says. The girls wear battledress and work under the same conditions as the men, and share their mess and all that.' She gave Derek a mischievous grin. 'It's all right, they do sleep separate! Or I could work in Signals. That sounds interesting. It says here you're right in the "nerve centre" of the Army, replacing signals officers all over the country.

I might go anywhere!' She saw his face and added hurriedly, 'Mind, being married I expect they'd try and keep me around here. Or I might get sent down to Wiltshire. That'd be the ticket, wouldn't it, if we were in the same camp.'

'I'll believe that when I see it,' Derek said cynically, but he added, 'Go on, Livvy. What else does it say?'

'They're looking for women with a bit more schooling too,' she said, her finger on the small print. 'They train you for whatever you're going to do, of course, but they don't need any standard of education for those jobs. Just as well!' She laughed. 'But anyone who stayed on and got School Certificate or anything like that, they'll get put with the Royal Artillery on anti-aircraft and searchlight batteries, or even in gunnery research. If you're on that you have to go to a "famous army school of research" – it doesn't say where, of course – and you have a special uniform. It's a white skirt and dark blue jacket and a forage cap in pale and dark blue. Doesn't that sound nice! Better than khaki.'

'Sounds a bit conspicuous to me,' Derek said. 'You'd be seen miles away.'

'It's meant to be. It was designed in 1600. They didn't do camouflage then, they wanted to make sure everyone knew which side they were on.'

'They never had women soldiers then!'

Olive read it again. 'Well, perhaps not. It's been designed to match the men's uniforms, but they were designed then, so it comes to the same thing. Still, I don't suppose I'll be doing that. We never did science at school.'

'Is that all? What about office jobs? That's what you're good at.'

Olive didn't hear him. She was still reading the article.

'Here's something that'd suit Gladys Shaw. They have drivers too, for convoy driving. They take trucks and lorries and all sorts – even tanks, I wouldn't be surprised – all over Britain. Sometimes they're away from head-quarters for four or five nights.' She lifted her head and gazed at her husband, her eyes shining. 'Think of it. Cornwall this week, the Highlands of Scotland the next. I've always wanted to go to those places. Oh, I *wish* I'd learnt to drive when Gladys did!'

'Well, I'm not sorry you didn't,' Derek declared. 'Look, Livvy, I don't want to stand in your light, but how d'you think I'd feel, never knowing where you were? I mean, it's bad enough now when we hear there's been a raid on Pompey and I don't know if you were in it. But if you were driving all over the country, I'd be scared all the time that you'd been in some place that had got hit. And Army camps aren't the safest places to be in, you know. The Germans aim for them more than anything.'

'I know.' She laid the newspaper down and sighed. 'Don't you want me to go and register, Derek? Only I just can't stand seeing Gladys with her broken arm and her medal and thinking I'm not doing anything at all. And I think girls like me are going to be called up soon anyway.'

Derek didn't answer at once. Then he said slowly, 'I wish you didn't *have* to do it, Livvy. I don't like the idea that girls have to get mixed up in this war. But there it is, and if you've got to join up I'd rather you were doing something you enjoyed.' He repeated his previous question. 'What about office jobs? There must be plenty of those, and you've got good experience.'

Olive wrinkled her nose. 'To tell you the truth, Derek, I'd be glad to get out of the office. I've never really liked being stuck behind a desk messing about with invoices and such. Some of these jobs sound really interesting. And I'd feel I was *doing* something.' Her eyes strayed again to the headline and the photograph of ATS girls in their uniforms, lining up for parade.

'You'd be doing something in an office,' Derek pointed out, but his voice sounded half-hearted, as if he knew that she really didn't want to be persuaded. 'Well, what sort of pay will you get? I've heard it's pretty low. D'you think you'll be able to manage? I'll send you mine of course, same as I've been doing,'

Olive shook her head. 'Oh, I shan't need to use any of that, Derek. We'll put it away. I want to save up for our home, when all this is over.' She looked back at the newspaper. 'There's a bit here about the pay. Some girls only start at two shillings a day – mind, that's for Sundays as well, so that's fourteen shillings a week – but if you get promoted you can be getting nearly thirty-five bob a week. And all found. No rent or bills to pay, all your food provided, *and* all your clothes. Even your toothbrush! And they keep up the National Insurance, so there's really nothing to come out of that, it's all pocket-money. I should be able to save quite a bit.'

'You know you're going to get promoted then?' he said with a grin.

'I'm going to try my best to be,' Olive declared. She looked at him again. 'Derek, I'm sorry if you don't like it. I could always see if I can get out of it, if you really want me to. I mean, I'm working for your dad in his office – they might let me off.'

'How long for? They'd be calling you up soon anyway.' He shook his head. 'No, I reckon we've got to make the best of it, Livvy, and like I said before, I'd rather you were happy.' He reached out and drew her close again. 'Matter of fact, I think I'll be rather proud of you when you're in uniform. And I'll tell you what –' his face was very close to hers now, his lips brushing her cheek in the way that made her stomach quiver '– I've never kissed a soldier before. It'll be a new experience for me!'

'Derek Harker!' Olive pulled away, pretending to be shocked, and then laughed and let him pull her close again. 'I should just hope you haven't,' she murmured into his neck. 'So you'd better start getting some practice in now, hadn't you, for when I come home in khaki.'

With a swift movement, Derek slid her into a lying position on the settee. He lay above her, resting on his elbows, and looked down into her face. She stared back at him, her heart beating quickly, a teasing, provocative smile on her lips.

'Oh, Livvy,' he said, and his voice came out like a

groan. 'Why do we have to be apart? Why can't we be together like this all the time? This bloody, *bloody* war . . .'

CHAPTER TWO

At first, Jess Budd hardly noticed the old man, shuffling slowly along September Street on that bright June morning of 1941. There were too many like him these days – homeless victims of the blitz that had torn their city to shreds during the past few months. They were housed in church halls or schools, anywhere where a few mattresses could be spread out and people fed while the authorities tried to find them somewhere else to live. And with their workplaces destroyed too, as often as not, there was nothing else to do but wander the streets.

Jess felt sorry for him. He might have only just been bombed out, she thought, glancing at the face behind the straggling grey whiskers, the eyes peering through thick glasses. There had been a raid on Portsmouth the night before, and a huge bomb had dropped in Torrington Road. It had burrowed its way beneath the houses and failed to explode, and there were cordons around it now while they decided what to do about it.

Two nights before that, there had been a bigger raid, which had hit this part of Portsmouth badly. The Germans had dropped a number of high explosive bombs and several oil bombs which had killed some of the soldiers in the RAOC camp nearby. A few houses had caught fire, others had lost their windows. Some of the side streets were still impassable, and the dust of the blast still hung in the warm June air, the peculiarly acrid smell of explosives tingling in the nostrils.

Jess looked at the old man again, hesitating, uncertain whether she knew him. There was something familiar, a half-memory . . . And he was looking at her too, with that same tentative expression.

But no, she had never seen him before, she was sure of it. And he looked so vague and bewildered – why, he probably hardly remembered his own family, the people he lived with, let alone strangers in the street.

She could feel little Maureen tugging at her hand. Jess had let her walk up the street this morning rather than make her get into the pram, and now the little girl was looking frightened, wanting to get away from this strange, whiskery old man. Poor old chap, she thought, giving him an apologetic smile. It isn't his fault. It's this cruel war. It destroys everyone, from the tiniest baby to the oldest person. People who don't even know what it's all about.

She turned and went into the newsagent's shop. Alice Brunner and her daughter Joy were marking up newspapers. Alice smiled at Maureen and gave her a piece of string off the bales, and Joy tickled her to make her laugh.

'We're all behind like a donkey's tail this morning,' Alice said, brushing back her wispy hair. 'All the trains were late, so of course that means all the papers were too, and Joy's got to do the deliveries herself, or else people will have to come and get their own. It's always the same after a raid.'

'But what's happened to the boys?' Jess asked. 'You've still got a few doing deliveries, haven't you?'

'Oh, there's three or four who haven't been evacuated, yes. But Jacky Watson and Gerald Bone, they're both Boy Scouts and they're on message duty during raids, so they won't be fit for much, and young Curly Brown's got himself a job now and if the papers aren't here by eight he can't do it. And there's not many more boys about.' She flipped over a pile of *Daily Mirrors*. 'That Micky Baxter keeps on at me to give him a round, but I wouldn't employ him if he was the last boy on earth. Why, I daren't even turn my back when he's in the shop. You don't know what might be missing.'

Jess sighed and nodded. 'He's a real little scamp. That's about the only good thing about my Tim and Keith being out in the country – it keeps them away from him. When I think it could have been them, playing around the bombed houses and getting themselves blown up like poor little Cyril Nash, and Jimmy Cross . . .'

'And Micky Baxter gets away with it,' Alice nodded. 'It don't seem fair, does it. But then there's plenty in this war that isn't fair.'

She turned away quickly, and Jess knew that she was thinking of her husband Heinrich, interned at the beginning of the war simply because he was a German, even though he'd lived in Portsmouth for twenty years.

She glanced anxiously at Alice's back. For a long time, she and the rest of the people around September Street who knew and liked the Brunners had been afraid that Alice was going to have a complete breakdown after Heinrich had been taken away and then posted missing after the sinking of the *Arandora Star*. Other internees on the torpedoed ship were known to have died, the luckier ones had been rescued and either taken on to Canada or brought back to the Isle of Man, but there had never been any word of Heinrich. Alice had spent her days watching for him, sometimes convinced he must be still alive, sometimes miserably certain he had died, and all the time growing greyer, thinner and more bitter.

She was looking better now, Jess thought as she paid for her newspaper. And her manner was brighter too, as if she'd come to some decision. Perhaps she'd come to terms with the fact that Heinrich must be dead, and made up her mind to go on living, if only for her daughter Joy's sake.

Alice marked up the last *Daily Express* and put down her pencil with a sigh of relief. 'There, that's all done. You can start doing the deliveries now, Joy. Take the ones furthest away, anyone nearby can pop in. I'll have a cup of tea ready when you get back.' She looked at Jess. 'I don't know what I'd do without my Joy. She's a real help – a proper little godsend. Joy by name and joy by nature, that's her. Off you go, now.'

Joy nodded and shoved a stack of papers into the delivery sack. She went out to the back of the shop to fetch her bike. As she did so, the shop door opened with a little 'ping' from the bell and an old man shuffled in.

Jess glanced round. It was the old man she had seen outside. He stood at the door, staring in as if he weren't quite sure why he had come, and she looked at Alice.

There was an odd expression on her friend's face. The same feeling that Jess had experienced – that she knew the man, that he had once been familiar to her. And a growing excitement, followed swiftly by disbelief – as if she were determined not to give way to it, not to be disappointed.

'Yes?' she said, and her voice shook a little. 'What can I get for you?'

The old man gazed at her. His face was thick with grey whiskers, ragged and dirty as though they hadn't been attended to for some time. He wore an old cap that came down over his forehead, and his eyes were hidden behind the pebble-lensed glasses. But he didn't seem to be able to see very well all the same, for he took them off and Jess saw the mild brown eyes beneath, fixed on Alice, intent, as if begging her to understand.

'Alice?' he said at last, and his voice sounded rusty, as if it hadn't been used much lately. 'Alice? Don't you know me?'

Jess stared at him. She felt her heart turn over, very slowly, and her blood seemed to stand still in her veins. Then she saw Alice sway, and stepped forward quickly to catch her in her arms.

'It's me, Alice,' she heard him say, as she held her friend's quivering body. 'It's Heinrich. I've come home . . .'

'Now, that really *is* a bit of good news,' Annie Chapman said. 'Isn't it, Ted? And about time too. I bet Alice Brunner doesn't know where to put herself. She's been really down ever since Heinrich was took away.'

'I know. Mind, she's been picking up a bit lately.' Jess had come straight down from September Street to tell her sister about Heinrich's return. 'But you should have seen her face. It was like watching someone arrive at the gates of

Heaven.' She stopped, blushing a little. She didn't normally talk like that, especially to Annie who was so practical and down-to-earth. But that *was* what Alice's face had looked like. As if the sun had come out for her again.

'Well, I couldn't be more pleased,' Annie declared. She looked at the clock on the mantelpiece. 'I thought our Olive would have been home by now. She promised she'd be back in time for me to go down the Post.' She refilled her sister Jess's teacup and looked enquiringly at her husband. Ted shook his head morosely.

'You know I can't drink it if it's not sweet. And I can't stand those saccharin things.'

'Well, you can't have any more sugar. That's your ration gone for this week. It's either get used to the saccharin or go without.' Annie's voice had a sharp edge to it and she stopped abruptly and bit her lip. She bent and picked up Maureen, who was playing on the floor with a few clothes pegs. 'D'you want a sip of my tea, pet, before you and your mum have to go home?'

'I'll stop on for a bit if you like, till Olive gets back,' Jess offered. She knew that Annie didn't like to leave Ted on his own these days. Mind, this afternoon there didn't seem to be all that much wrong with him, but he was that changeable, it sometimes only needed a sudden noise from outside to set him off. And if there was a raid, like last night . . .

'It's all right,' Ted said suddenly, almost as if he could read her thoughts. 'I'm not a babe in arms. I won't start playing with the gas taps or setting fire to the house the minute you turn your back.'

Jess felt her cheeks turn scarlet. She glanced quickly at her sister and saw that Annie had gone white. *Playing with the gas taps* . . . Was that what she was afraid of – that Ted would do something really daft if he was left alone?

'I never meant –' she began, but Annie interrupted her.

'Don't be a bigger fool than you can help, Ted Chapman. Nobody's suggesting any such thing. You know you don't like being by yourself these days, and all we're trying to do is make sure you've got a bit of company. There's no need to be objectionable about it.' She tipped a tiny saccharin tablet into her tea and stirred fiercely. 'You just say, the minute you want to go back to work and I'm sure we'll all be only too pleased.'

There was a brief, embarrassed silence. Jess hadn't heard her sister speak so sharply to Ted since the night she'd come home from one of the big raids and found him curled up on the top of the little turret roof, crying like a baby. He'd been ordered to bed by the doctor and stayed there, apparently helpless, for a week or more. And when he got up, he'd been like an old man, shuffling downstairs, unable to do anything more for himself than get dressed and take himself to the lavatory.

He'd improved a bit since then, but he still spent most of the time sitting in his chair, doing nothing and hardly speaking. It was shock, the doctor had said, shock from the raids and having to ferry his boat across the harbour between Portsmouth and Gosport day in, day out, and most of all shock from the experience of Dunkirk, when he'd taken the little *Ferry King* across the Channel to rescue the battered soldiers of the BEF.

'But that was months ago,' Annie had expostulated, but the doctor had shaken her head.

'It happens that way sometimes. It must have been building up inside all the time, and that last raid was just too much for him.' She sighed. 'It was too much for a lot of people.'

'But what are we going to do? Is he ever going to get better?'

'I hope so. But it'll take time, and a lot of patience. You can't hurry these things along.'

'And what are we going to do for money?' Annie had said to Jess after the doctor had gone. 'I mean, we're all right for a while, the Friendly Society will pay out. But that only goes on for so long. Suppose he can never go back to work?'

She didn't say those things to Ted. The doctor had impressed upon her the need to be gentle with him, not to reproach him or make him feel guilty. And that was difficult for Annie, for although she was a good nurse, she was also inclined to be a sharp-tongued one, and she had never had any time for malingerers. And although she knew really that Ted wasn't swinging the lead, sometimes when she looked at him, sitting in his chair staring at nothing when other people were working all the hours God sent to help in the war effort – and when their own daughter Betty was working in the Land Army, and their son Colin risking his life at sea aboard HMS *Exeter* – well, it was hard not to say anything.

Now and then, her control snapped. She was always sorry the minute the words were out, but that wouldn't call them back. But he'd scared her, talking about gas taps like that.

'I can't think where Olive's got to,' she said at last, more for something to say than because she was really worried. 'She knew I'd be waiting.'

'She's probably gassing with Gladys Shaw,' Jess said, and turned scarlet again. She could have picked a better word! 'Or maybe she's popped up to see Florrie Harker.'

'I doubt it. She and Florrie don't see eye to eye these days. Mother-in-law trouble. Florrie seems to think our Livvy's stolen her little boy away. Well, it stands to reason he'd want to spend his time with his wife when he gets a couple of days' leave, but Florrie don't seem to see it that way.'

'Derek does go to see her when he's here, though, doesn't he?'

'Oh yes, he pops in, and he and Olive go up there for tea. But that's not enough for Mrs Harker, she wants him spending the evening there. She'd like to have him stopping the night too, but of course he won't, not when there's a nice double bed here.'

The gate clicked and Olive appeared in the open doorway. She was flushed from the sun and her eyes were bright. She looked at her parents and her aunt, and gave a queer little laugh.

'Hello! You look as if you're waiting for someone famous. Is the Queen dropping in for tea?'

'You're the most famous person we're waiting for,' Annie said tartly. 'I was expecting you half an hour ago. Where've you been?' She was already on her feet, gathering together the things she needed to take to the First Aid Post. 'And what have you been up to? You've got a funny look about you.'

'It'll be even funnier when I get into uniform,' Olive said, rather breathlessly. 'I've joined up, Mum. I've volunteered for the ATS. I couldn't sit around any longer, messing about with invoices and worksheets for Mr Harker. *She* can do that. I'm going to do my bit to help my country. And don't say I can't,' she added quickly. 'I've done it, and that's that.'

'You've joined up? Oh, *Olive*.' Annie sat down quickly, as if she were afraid that her legs would fold beneath her. Her face was white. 'But – you're a married woman. What's your Derek going to say?'

'A married woman! I reckon we can forget all about that, as long as this war's on,' Olive said sarcastically. 'What sort of a married life have me and Derek got to look forward to? A day here, a night there – and that's if he stays in England. If he goes abroad, that's it for the duration. I'm not going to sit at home twiddling my thumbs while other people win the war for me. I want to do my bit as well. And Derek agrees. We talked about it last weekend. Anyway, even if he didn't –' She shrugged. 'I'd just go and do it anyway.'

'And that's what this bloody war's doing for us,' Ted said suddenly. 'Killing all our best men, taking husbands away from their wives and sons away from their mothers, and now it's making respectable young women forget what their place really is. *Go and do it anyway!*' He glared at Olive. 'I'd like to hear your mother dare speak to me like that. A man should be master in his own house, and it seems to me you haven't even asked your husband's permission.'

'No, and nor am I asking your permission to go and do First Aid,' Annie said curtly. 'Olive's right. We've all got to do our bit, and we've got to make up our own minds about it. If Livvy thinks she ought to go, it's not for me or you to stop her.' She looked at her daughter. 'If you'd asked me, I'd have said no,' she said quietly. 'I don't want you to go, any more than I wanted our Betty to go off and join the Land Army. But everything's different now, and you've made your choice. I'll help you all I can.'

Olive's eyes filled with tears. She got up and went to her mother, laying her bright, chestnut head against the greying hair.

'I don't know if I'm right or wrong. I just felt I had to do it. We *can't* stop at home and do nothing – not girls like me. We've got to do whatever we can.' She looked pleadingly at her father. 'Can't you understand that, Dad?'

'I don't understand nothing these days,' he grumbled. 'The whole world's turned upside down, if you ask me. Young girls driving buses, talking about going in the Forces just as if they was men. Married women out at work when they ought to be home minding their babies –' He caught Annie's eye and scowled. 'All right, then, minding their own business. But ain't that just what I'm saying? Girls like our Olive, they ought to be thinking about nappies, not worrying about uniforms. Nothing's what it oughter be, these days.'

'You don't have to tell me that, Dad,' Olive said. 'Don't you think that's what I'd rather be doing?'

There was a brief silence. Annie looked at Jess and then sighed and said, 'Well, it seems there's no more to be said. Olive's joined up and that's all there is to it. And I've got to get off down to the Post. We've been busy enough lately, Lord knows what they'll send us tonight. Now, will you be all right, Ted? You know, you could always come and give us a hand.'

Once again, just as she was about to depart, the gate clicked. This time it was Rose, Jess's elder daughter, who stood in the doorway. Her dark hair was untidy, her face pale and upset.

'I've just been up to Joy's,' she said. 'I've seen her dad.'

'I know,' Jess said quickly. 'I was there when he came in. It's the best news we've had for weeks. Isn't it nice for Joy to have her dad home again?'

'I don't know,' Rose said, coming in. 'He doesn't look the same as he used to. He's grown a beard, it doesn't look a bit nice, and he's dressed in some horrible dirty old clothes. His feet were all blisters, Mum. And he looks hungry.' Her voice shook. 'He's changed, Mum. He used to smile at me, he used to be nice. He used to be so clean and tidy, and now he just looks like a dirty old tramp and he didn't want me there, he wouldn't look at me properly and his eyes were all sort of angry. He used to call me his Rosebud. What's happened to him, Mum? What have they done to him?'

Jess drew her close and looked at her sister. 'She's right,' she said quietly. 'He *is* different. I saw it too.' Her voice quickened with anger. 'They promised they'd look after the people they interned,' she said. 'What *have* they been doing to him? Where's he been, all this past year? And why have they sent him home like that now, in dirty clothes, making him walk with blisters on his feet?'

'I told you,' Ted said bitterly. 'It's this bloody war. It's turned the whole world upside down.'

The news of Heinrich's return spread fast. It was the first bit of good news for some time and was the main subject of conversation for several days. The only person not to be pleased was Ethel Glaister, from number 15 April Grove.

'They're daft, letting that lot loose again,' she said to Jess and Peggy Shaw, on the pavement. 'I mean, it's obvious they took them away for a reason. They're all foreigners – Jerries, Eyeties, they're all the enemy. They had 'em safe behind bars. Why let 'em out to roam the streets again, spying and causing trouble?'

'Heinrich Brunner's never caused trouble in his life,' Jess retorted. 'And I don't suppose the others did either. Otherwise they wouldn't be letting them go, would they? It stands to reason.'

'Stands to reason?' Ethel repeated scornfully. 'Huh! Nothing stands to reason these days. If you ask me, there's not one of 'em knows what they're doing. All running round like headless chickens, they are, not knowing what to do next. And that Churchill's no better than the rest. Sticking his fingers up in the air and trying to pretend everything's all right. Who does he think he's fooling?'

'He doesn't try to pretend it's all right,' Peggy said. 'He tells us plain – blood, sweat, toil and tears. But he puts heart into us all the same, somehow or other. I reckon we'd be in a worse state without him.'

Ethel sniffed. It wasn't often she deigned to talk to her neighbours, and even less often that they wanted her to, but she had to pass on her opinions to someone. She sought for something crushing to say, but just at that moment Bert Shaw came out of his house. He'd not been long home from work and had taken his shirt off to wash in the scullery. His braces dangled round his waist.

'I just heard on the wireless,' he said. 'They've got that Hess up at Aldershot. Tried to throw hisself down a staircase to commit suicide.'

'He never!' Peggy said. 'What happened? Is he dead?'

Bert snorted. 'No, worse luck – just broke his leg, that's all. Poor sort of a leader he's turned out to be – can't even make a job of killing hisself. I reckon old Adolf's washed his hands of him.'

'He did that in the first place,' Jess remarked, 'when Hess parachuted into Scotland on his peace mission.'

'*If* that's what it was,' Bert said. 'I wouldn't trust any of those Jerries further than I could throw 'em.'

'And that's just what I'm saying,' Ethel Glaister cut in eagerly. 'I wouldn't, either. That's why I think they're mad, letting all these aliens out again. Ought to keep 'em locked up for the duration, that's what, and I don't care who hears me say so.'

'Oh, for goodness sake,' Jess said disgustedly. 'This is where we came in. Heinrich Brunner isn't an *alien*, he's as good as you or me – a sight *better* than you, if you want my opinion – and I'm glad he's back. And I reckon everyone else round here is too – everyone with any sense, that is.' She glared at Ethel, daring her to answer. 'And I wouldn't advise you to go saying those sorts of things up round the shop, either. You'll have Alice after you. *She* won't take no nasty remarks about Heinrich.'

Ethel sniffed again and put her nose into the air. Her yellow hair had been permed again and lay in the metallic ridges of Marcel waves against her head. It looked as if she'd got a brass cap on.

'Pardon me for breathing,' she said haughtily. 'I was only trying to be neighbourly, after all – expressing an opinion. I thought we were supposed to be allowed to do that in this country, I thought that was what this war was all about, but it seems I'm wrong. And I'm sure I'd never dream of saying anything at all near Alice Brunner, or her shop. I never go in there. I don't even walk past it if I can help it.'

She turned and stalked on her high heels past Jess's front door and into her own house. The door slammed behind her.

'Nasty little cat,' Peggy said. 'I reckon the war was the best thing that ever happened to poor George. He must thank God on his knees every day for being able to join the Army and get away from her.'

'It's right, what she says,' Jess said. 'She crosses the road now, rather than walk past Alice's. I've seen her do it.'

'Oh, she's just plain stupid,' Peggy said dismissively. 'Not worth bothering about.'

'Tell you what else I heard on the wireless,' Bert said. 'They reckon Hitler's just about ready to invade Russia.'

The two women stared at him.

'But Russia's enormous. How can he ever hope to take over a big country like that?'

'Yes, but it's mostly empty,' Bert said. 'All the people are clustered up this end, see. So once he's got places like Moscow and Leningrad, he can take the rest of it easy. It'll be handed over on a plate.'

'But can't anyone stop him?' Jess asked.

Bert shrugged. 'I daresay we'll try. But Finland'll go in with him, see. That'll give him a bigger army. And he's got thousands already. The Russians'll have a fight on their hands, and *we* can't get over there, not with Jerry in the way.'

'But Finland was fighting against Germany before. It don't make sense.'

'Finland'll help anyone what fights Russia,' Bert said. 'They hate their guts.'

Jess went indoors, wishing that people could talk about something else for a change. It was war, war, war all the time, and it had been going on for two years now. Ever since before little Maureen was born. She looked at the toddler, playing on the floor with Henry the cat, and remembered the day she'd been born. Jess had had a bad time and had lain upstairs in the front room, wanting nothing more than just to go to sleep for a few hours, and they'd started delivering the corrugated iron for the Anderson shelters. The clatter had gone on for hours. And it didn't seem to have been quiet since.

She got out her writing pad and started to write to Tim and Keith. They seemed settled enough now at the vicarage at Bridge End, even though Tim had screwed up his face at first and protested that they'd have to say prayers all the time. But Mr Beckett, the thin, spidery vicar, had come as a surprise to him. The last time Jess and Frank had been there, he'd organised a tiddlywinks championship, with a pot of home-made jam as the prize. And they had company now, with the two Simmons girls staying there too. A nice little family – two boys and two girls.

Our sort of family, Jess thought, gazing at Maureen. But we're all split up. Maureen hardly knows her brothers, and Muriel and Stella Simmons are more like sisters to them now. And Rose is growing up so fast, she won't be a child much longer. We'll never have been a real family, all together.

But there was no use in thinking like that. It only made her miserable, and you couldn't afford to let yourself get miserable these days. You had to keep cheerful, or everything would seem hopeless, like it seemed to poor Ted, who seemed to be sinking into a black pit he couldn't climb out of.

Jess opened the writing pad and began to write in the copperplate handwriting she had learned at school.

'*Dear Tim and Keith . . .*'

'I didn't know who I was,' Heinrich said. He was drinking his seventh cup of tea of the day – never mind the rations, Alice said – and he was sitting in his accustomed chair by the fireplace. He still looked dirty and unkempt, but she didn't have the heart to tell him so. And she didn't care anyway. It was enough to have him there, in his own chair. It was enough to be able to reach out her hand and touch him and know that he was real.

'How d'you mean, you didn't know who you were?' she asked.

'I'd lost my memory. After the torpedo hit us, I couldn't remember anything. I didn't know my name or where I lived or how old I was – nothing.' The mild brown eyes were liquid with tears. 'I couldn't remember you, or our little Joy, or even my own *Mutter* and *Vater*.'

'None of us?' Alice said, wonderingly. 'Couldn't you even remember us getting married?'

'I did not know if I was married. I *felt* that I was – but I could remember nothing.'

'Oh, *Heinrich*,' she said softly, taking his hand in both of hers and cradling it against her.

'But you must have been saved from the ship,' Joy said. She was sitting on the rag rug at their feet, gazing up at her father. She had scarcely left his side all day, and the newspapers had never been delivered. But nobody had seemed to mind, when they discovered the reason. 'Didn't anyone else know?'

He shook his head. 'It was a very big ship. There were a great many of us aboard. When we sank, we had to take to whatever lifeboat we could find.' His shudder racked his whole body and Alice remembered how he had always disliked the water, never even paddling at Southsea beach on a summer afternoon. 'I was in the water for a long time. It seemed like many hours. I thought I would drown.' Another convulsive shudder. 'I have heard people say that when you drown your whole life flashes before your eyes. But mine just disappeared.'

They were silent for a moment, Heinrich gathering his strength to go on, Alice and Joy trying to picture the scene. Both had been to sea, across the Channel when they had visited Heinrich's family in Berlin before the war had begun. They tried to imagine being alone in the water, clinging to a bit of wreckage, feeling the waves slap against their faces and waiting for the one that would finally overwhelm them.

'But a lifeboat came along in the end,' Joy said.

'Yes, but there was on it nobody that I knew. And I had no clothes on, no papers, nothing to say who I was. They asked me questions, but I couldn't answer. I was too cold, too tired. I just lay in the bottom of the boat and waited to die.'

'What happened then?' Joy asked, but Alice shook her head.

'Don't pester your father. You don't have to talk now if you don't want to,' she said to Heinrich. 'There's all the time in the world for you to tell us about it. The main thing is, you're back and all you have to do now is get strong again.' She stroked his arm and winced at the thinness and fragility of it. Heinrich had always been so sturdy, even a little stout. 'I don't know what they did to you,' she said angrily. 'They were supposed to look after you, not starve you to death.'

He shook his head. 'We weren't starved. The food wasn't good, but we weren't starved.'

'Well, you've been ill,' she said, 'and it doesn't seem to me that they looked after you at all.'

'I don't think they thought I was ill. Just that I couldn't remember.' He thought for a minute. 'They did bring a doctor to see me a few times. An Austrian. He was what used to be called an *alienist*.' He smiled suddenly, a smile spoiled by a strange twist to his lips, and by the stained teeth showing through the straggling whiskers. 'An appropriate name, don't you think?'

'Oh, Heinrich,' Alice said again, her voice full of pity,

but Joy frowned and asked, 'What's an alienist? Is it a doctor specially for aliens?'

'Joy!' her mother expostulated, but Heinrich shook his head and smiled the strange, twisted smile again.

'No, not that. It's a doctor for the mind.'

'For mad people, you mean? But –'

'I think that's enough talk for now,' Alice said in a hard, strained voice. 'Your father needs a rest. Find yourself something else to do for a while, there's a good girl.'

Joy pouted but got up from the rug and picked up a copy of *Girls' Crystal*. She glanced at the clock. 'Can we have the wireless on? It's *ITMA* tonight.'

Alice looked at Heinrich. He was staring at the empty fireplace. He said nothing, but he seemed to shrink even further into the ill-fitting clothes. Suddenly, she longed for the Heinrich she had known, stocky and cheerful, always ready with a gentle smile and a kind word. She could not find him in this neglected figure with its matted hair and stained smile. She felt suddenly frightened.

'Let's heat up the water for a bath,' she said. 'I'll cut your hair while we're waiting. And you could have a shave. You'll feel better when you're back in your own clothes.'

'Have I still some clothes?' he asked wonderingly. 'I thought they were all lost on the ship.'

'You didn't take them all. There are still some upstairs. Your best suit and your gardening clothes.' She gave a shaky laugh. 'One extreme to the other!'

'But the air-raid warning'll be going soon,' Joy objected. The siren went nightly now, whether aircraft had been sighted or not. 'There isn't time for a bath.'

'There's time for whatever we want,' Alice said with unaccustomed sharpness. 'Your father needs to feel comfortable. He needs to feel he's at home.'

Joy said nothing, but glanced longingly at the wireless set standing on its shelf in the corner. Alice got up and went into the kitchen. She switched on the Ascot water-heater and went outside to drag in the tin bath.

Heinrich looked at his daughter. She had grown in the past year. Her figure had changed from the flat chest of a child to the rounded curves of a young woman. Her face had altered too. It was less round, a little thinner. But nearly everyone he'd seen seemed to be thinner.

'Your mother has told me what a help to her you've been,' he said gently. 'It has not been easy for you, this past year.'

Joy shrugged. 'It's been all right.' She felt oddly uneasy with her father, as if he were a stranger. He'd been through so much, so much that he hadn't yet told them, that she couldn't begin to imagine. And he looked so different. Like Alice, she felt that he had returned in a strange body, that somewhere inside her real father was lurking and she hadn't yet been able to find him.

She thought of how, in the old days before the war began, he would take her on his knee and cuddle her against him. How warm and secure his body had seemed, how strong his short, stubby fingers. Now, she looked at his mottled hands and shuddered.

At that moment, she was more aware than she had ever been of how much she had missed her father. And she was still missing him. She wanted her *father* back. Not this strange, nervous creature who stared pleadingly at her from red-rimmed eyes almost hidden in a mass of tangled whiskers. She wanted the father who had gone away.

And Heinrich, gazing at her, felt the same yearning, for the affectionate, confiding daughter he had known. He wanted to reach out to her, to make contact, but he could not do it, could not bear the thought of her recoil. And so they sat in silence, looking at each other yet avoiding each other's eyes; sharing the same memories, the same longings, yet both locked fast in their separated hearts.

CHAPTER THREE

'I never thought you'd be a bad loser, Tim,' Mr Beckett observed. They were in the vicarage garden, playing French cricket on the overgrown tennis court, and Stella Simmons had just caught him out for the third time. Tim handed over the bat as if he'd like to throw it and walked away, a murderous scowl on his face. 'As umpire, I have to say that you were out quite fairly.'

'I can't help it if you bat good catches,' Stella agreed smugly. She placed the vicar's old cricket bat in front of her legs and stood square, waiting for the ball to be thrown. Keith tossed it at her and she sent it flying high, past the edge of the court and into a clump of nettles. 'Ooh – look at *that*!'

Tim, who was nearest the clump, looked at it in disgust. 'I can't get it out of there,' he complained. 'I've only got short sleeves on – I'll get my arm all stung. I think we ought to have a new rule, anyone who hits it into the nettles has to get it out themselves.'

'Don't be a twerp,' Stella said. 'How can I get it out? I'm in.'

'Well, you ought to be out, for hitting it so far.' Tim walked over and kicked at the nettles. 'It's right in the middle.'

Muriel ran over with a stick and poked the ball out on to the grass. She handed it to Tim, who shrugged and looked towards Stella. He threw it carelessly towards her and it fell about six feet away, bounced once or twice and then stopped.

Keith picked it up and threw it again, aiming at Stella's

legs. It rolled past her and she gave it a tap as it went by, then turned to protect her legs from the new direction.

'She shouldn't have hit it then,' Tim objected. 'It didn't go anywhere near her legs. She ought to have let it go.'

Muriel immediately came to her sister's defence. 'No, she shouldn't. She can hit it if she likes. There's no rule says it's got to be near your legs.'

'There is.'

'Isn't.'

'Is,' Tim said, and caught the vicar's eye. 'Well, that's the way we always play it, anyway.'

'Is it?' Keith asked innocently. 'I don't *remember* that rule.'

Mr Beckett stalked into the middle of the hot, angry little circle. He was wearing ancient khaki shorts and looked like a spider or a stick insect, his thin, knobbly arms and legs so long and gawky that they seemed as if they must have more joints than most people's. He laid one hand on top of Tim's head and one on Stella's.

'I think it's time we all had a drink of cold water,' he said. 'Perhaps you'd like to get it for us, Tim. Muriel will help you. And then I've a little job for you in the greenhouse.'

Tim opened his mouth to argue, then caught the glint in Mr Beckett's eye. He set off towards the house with Muriel tagging along beside him. They went into the cool, dim kitchen and drew five cups of water from the tap. Mrs Mudge, the housekeeper, was nowhere in sight. She usually took her chair outside on sunny afternoons and dozed under the apple tree.

'I don't see how we're going to carry these,' Tim said in disgruntled tones.

'Use a tray, silly.' Muriel opened a cupboard door and brought out a battered tin tray. 'It's the one we used as a sledge when it snowed, remember?'

Tim looked at it. He remembered the day they'd all gone sledging, not long after the girls had joined him and Keith at the vicarage. Stella and Muriel had been open-mouthed, but Tim and Keith were just getting used to the vicar then.

34

He was, as Mrs Mudge said, just like another child. In fact, he'd fallen off the tray three times and arrived home wet through from melted snow, and Mrs Mudge had told him off just as if he really was a little boy.

'It was funny, wasn't it,' Muriel said, and Tim felt his mouth pull itself into a grin. But he didn't want to smile. He didn't want to go out into the garden again laughing, just as if everything was all right. He drew his lips back tight and pursed them up and pulled his eyebrows down as far as he could.

'It was all right,' he said grudgingly.

'Coo, you are a bear-head,' Muriel said, loading the cups on to the tray. 'Come on. I wonder what Becky's got for you to do in the greenhouse. Will you let me come and help?'

Tim had a very good idea what the vicar had in mind for the greenhouse. He was going to be Talked To. It wouldn't be any more than that – Mr Beckett never touched any of them in anger – but whenever one of them strayed beyond the lines he had drawn, he would take them aside and Talk To them. And it wasn't even that he seemed particularly angry – just sad, and disappointed. But somehow that made it worse.

'Can I?' Muriel asked again. 'Can I come and help?'

Tim turned on her. 'No, you can't! He won't want you there. *I* don't want you there. It's private business. *Boys'* business,' he added cruelly, and they went back to the lawn, Tim marching ahead and Muriel trailing behind, slightly weighed down by the tin tray.

By the time they reached the others, Mr Beckett had organised them into a caterpillar party in the vegetable patch. White butterflies had laid their eggs on the undersides of the cabbage leaves, and these must be removed so that the caterpillars wouldn't hatch out and eat the leaves. In Tim's opinion, it would be a very good thing if they were allowed to do just that, but neither Mr Beckett nor Mrs Mudge seemed to agree with him. Neither, he knew, would his mother, who seemed to have some strange way of communicating with Mrs Mudge and had told her –

before the two women had even met, as far as he could tell – that Tim was to be made to sit at the table until he had eaten every scrap of the disgusting green leaves. Even making himself sick wasn't going to be allowed to work.

He was thankful not to have to be one of those wiping the eggs off the leaves. Even if it did mean being Talked To in the greenhouse.

Keith and the two girls settled, Mr Beckett led Tim across the garden. The greenhouse was a ramshackle construction, probably as old as Mr Beckett himself, which stood in a corner of the garden. It had once been kept in apple-pie order by Mrs Mudge's husband, but Mr Mudge had died a few years ago and nobody had looked after it for years. The vicar, encouraged by all the exhortations to 'Dig for Victory' had decided to grow tomatoes in it and it had rapidly become a wild tangle of growth.

'This is what you do,' Mr Beckett said, showing Tim the plants. 'You pinch out the tops so that they'll bush out and have a lot of flowers. Or is it cut off the side shoots so that the tops will grow?' He thought for a few moments. 'Do you know, I'm not quite sure after all. I shall have to consult my mentor.'

'I know what to do,' Tim said. 'You pinch out above the fourth truss. My Dad told me.'

'Did he, indeed? He grows tomatoes, does he?'

'My Dad can grow anything,' Tim said. 'He's got an allotment. He hasn't got a mentor, though,' he added. 'Do they cost much? I could get him one for Christmas.'

The vicar smiled. 'I don't think he needs one. Tell me, Tim, do you miss your father a great deal?'

Tim considered this. It was so long since he and Keith had first been evacuated – almost two years now – that he'd got used to being away from home. And they'd enjoyed being at the Corners' house, with Reg and Edna. They would probably have stayed there for the rest of the war if Reg hadn't been called up and Edna gone to stay with her mum and have a baby. He'd thought when Mum had first told him that she'd arranged for them to stay at the vicarage that they'd hate it, but it had turned out all right. Mr Beckett wasn't nearly so impatient as Dad. You had to do what Dad said, and do it straight away, if you didn't want the rough edge of his tongue. And he kept a thin cane hanging beside the fireplace, by his razor-strop. He wasn't above using it if he thought the boys deserved it.

Mr Beckett didn't have a cane. Only that sad face, when you'd done something he didn't like.

'I don't mind,' Tim said at last. 'I miss going to the beach, though. Dad used to take us out there every Sunday in the summer.'

'And he taught you about gardening.'

'Well, we had to do that. We had to help.'

'And what about your mother and sisters?' Mr Beckett asked. 'You must think about them sometimes and wonder what they're doing.'

'Not really,' Tim said. 'I know what they're doing. Mum does the washing and cooking and sweeps the floors, and Rose goes up the street with Joy Brunner. Mr Brunner's come home,' he added more eagerly. 'It was in Mum's letter this morning. He just walked in without anyone knowing he was coming, and he had all whiskers, and Mrs Brunner didn't hardly know who he was. He got torpedoed and lost his memory and he's just been wandering about all this time, not knowing who he was or where he lived or *anything*. It must be ever so funny, losing your memory,' he added thoughtfully. 'Have you ever lost your memory, Mr Beckett? Mrs Mudge says you have.'

'*Does* she?' the vicar asked in genuine surprise.

'Yes, she told us you'd lose your head if it wasn't sewn on.' Tim glanced up under his lashes and saw the vicar's lips twitch. 'How d'you think Mr Brunner lost his memory?' he asked innocently.

'I haven't the least idea,' Mr Beckett said firmly, refusing to be diverted. 'And I didn't come here to discuss poor Mr Brunner, pleased though I am to hear that he's returned to the bosom of his family.' At the mention of bosoms, Tim turned pink. 'But surely, Tim, you must sometimes wish you were at home?'

'Well, I'd like to see our baby again. She's different every time we see her. She can talk quite a lot now, Mum says, and she can sing a bit too. I'd like to be able to teach her songs.'

'Yes,' Mr Beckett said, 'it's sad that you have to miss her baby years. And she's missing you, as well.' He paused, nipping off bits of tomato plant, and then said casually, 'But it's not making you too miserable, being here?'

'Miserable?' Tim said. 'No. I like being here.'

The vicar looked pleased. But there was still a small frown creasing his brow and after he had pinched a few more tomatoes, he said, 'You would tell me if there was anything the matter, Tim, wouldn't you? Anything worrying you or making you feel cross. Anything at all. I wouldn't want you to keep such things to yourself, especially if there were something I could do to help.'

There was a moment's silence. The vicar kept his eyes steadily on the tomatoes.

'No,' Tim said. 'I mean, yes. I mean –' He stopped, looking confused, and Mr Beckett laughed.

'I didn't put it very clearly, did I. But I think we understand each other. So – what's making you so bad-tempered lately, hmm? You're usually such a cheerful, merry little lad. But for the past week or so we've hardly had a smile out of you. It's not like you, and I don't like to see it.'

Tim pursed his lips. He'd known there was going to be a Talking To, and he'd done his best to divert it, but Mr Beckett had got there just the same.

'Don't have to smile if I don't feel like it,' he muttered.

'Of course you don't. But what's worrying me is *why* you don't feel like it. There's something wrong, Tim, and I want to know what it is.' Mr Beckett's voice was unusually firm, as if he meant to keep Tim in the green-house until he had got at the truth. Like a teacher keeping the class in after school. 'I want to help,' he added more gently. 'You're not in trouble, Tim. Just tell me what it is that's bothering you, and we'll try to sort it out together.'

Tim was silent. He rolled a tomato leaf between his fingers, turning it into a narrow green tube, then crushing it to a pungently smelling pulp. The anger that had been simmering inside him for more than a week seemed to gather itself into a hard lump inside his chest. He felt as if he might cry. He looked up at Mr Beckett, standing like a big, disjointed spider amongst the jungle of tomato plants, and felt the tears sting his eyes.

'It's not fair,' he said at last, the words bursting out of him. 'I ought to have been in the other class. I ought to have been there all the time, only no one said, no one *cared*, and now I can't take the scholarship, it's too late, and everyone else will go up without me. And I'll have to stay behind with the infants. It's not *fair*.'

He threw down the mess of tomato leaf and glared at Mr Beckett. His hazel eyes had lost their mischievous gleam, his mouth was pulled into a sullen tremble. He half turned, as if about to run, and Mr Beckett reached out a long, spidery arm and caught his shoulder.

'All right, Tim,' he said quietly. 'Now let's sit down for a minute and talk about this, shall we? What do you mean, you ought to have been in the other class? And why can't you sit the scholarship? It's not till next January, surely.'

'It was *last* January,' Tim sniffed, sitting down on an upturned bucket beside him. 'The one I ought to have taken was last January. And nobody said. All the others took it and I was left out.'

'But why? Are you sure you should have taken it?'

'Yes. All the boys in my class did. *Brian Collins* took it,' Tim said indignantly, referring to his arch-rival. 'But I was in the other class, only nobody knew because we're all mixed up together and we only go afternoons anyway. I've been doing the same work as them. I'm as old as them. I'm *older* than Brian Collins – his birthday's not till March. Just because he's bigger than me . . .' In fact, most of the boys were bigger than Tim, who was small for his age, smaller even than Keith.

Mr Beckett sighed and rubbed his hand over his face. 'Tim, I don't understand. Are you telling me that you

39

should have sat the scholarship for the secondary school last January, and didn't? And that nobody ever explained to you why you didn't?'

'Nobody ever said anything.'

'But why didn't you ask?'

'I just thought perhaps I didn't need to.'

'But, for heaven's sake –'

'Teachers don't like being asked,' Tim said. 'They're grown-ups. My dad always told me that you do what grown-ups say and don't ask questions. And now everyone else is going up to the big school and I've got to stay with the little kids.' His voice began to rise again. 'It isn't fair. I could have passed the exam, I know I could. I could've passed it better than Brian Collins.'

'I'm sure you could,' the vicar said absently. He was feeling uncomfortably guilty. 'Listen, Tim, would you like me to find out what happened? Why you got left out? There may be some quite reasonable explanation –'

'I've always been in that class,' Tim said. 'I ought to be going up with them. It's not my fault I didn't sit the scholarship.'

'No.' Mr Beckett scratched his head. 'Well, I do think I'd better ask your teacher, don't you? We really ought to find out. And your parents ought to know, as well. Do they think you'll be going up next term?'

Tim shrugged. 'Don't know.'

'Well, we must get it sorted out. Who's your teacher?'

'Mr Hodges. He's old. He's not from our school – Miss Langrish was my teacher, only she's gone now. *She* wouldn't have let me get left out.'

'I'll talk to Mr Hodges,' the vicar said, getting up from his bucket. 'And Mr Wain. He's headmaster, he ought to know what's happened. We'll find out just what happened and what we can do about it. Though I'm very much afraid you'll have to wait now, and sit the exam next year.'

'But it's not *fair*,' Tim said. 'I've *always* been in that class.'

'I know.' Mr Beckett looked down at him from his spidery height. 'All the same, Tim, it's not fair to take it out on people around you, is it? People like Stella and Muriel, I mean. It's not their fault, is it?'

Tim looked at the ground. The tears were beginning to sting again. Reluctantly, he shook his head.

'And Stella did catch you out quite fairly, you know.'

'She's a girl,' Tim muttered. 'Girls aren't any good at games.'

'And that's nonsense,' the vicar said warmly. 'You know perfectly well it is. Anyway, you've always been quite happy to play games with Stella and Muriel.' He paused. 'Does it really make you feel any better to be nasty to them? Really and truly?'

Tim looked up and opened his mouth indignantly, then saw the vicar's face and closed it. He couldn't bear to turn that gentle, inquiring look into one of disappointment. He felt his cheeks flush and said, 'No. Not really.'

'It just makes things worse, doesn't it?' Mr Beckett said. 'It makes them all go hard inside you, like a ball of lead, and you can't get rid of it. Isn't that what it's like?'

'Yes,' Tim said, astonished. 'But how do you –'

'Oh, I've felt like that too,' the vicar said, laughing. 'We all do, at some time or another, Tim. You're not the only one. And now, before we go back to the others, I've got something here you might like. Come and see.'

He went over to a corner of the greenhouse and rummaged amongst the foliage. Tim got up and followed him. After a moment, the vicar exclaimed with pleasure and withdrew his hand. There were two large, juicy strawberries in it.

'I thought they might be starting to ripen,' he said. 'Only these two so far, I'm afraid – and it's not a very big plant, so there won't be more than a few each anyway. But these are for you, Tim. Just to help melt away that horrid ball inside.'

Tim took them. He held one to his lips and bit into it. The sweet fruit was crushed between his teeth and he felt the warm, red juice fill his mouth.

The vicar was right. It did help melt away the ball of nastiness.

He looked longingly at the second one and then turned towards the greenhouse door. 'I'll give this to Stella,' he said offhandedly. 'Girls like strawberries.'

'It's horrible,' Jess said, watching Frank stick yet more pins in the map that stretched across the wall of the back room, above the piano. 'The whole world's getting swept in. They're talking about Japan coming in against us now. How can we ever win, a tiny country like us?'

It was 4 July, and Maureen Budd was celebrating her second birthday with a rag doll Annie had made her, two new pinafores cut down from one of Jess's old frocks and a bag of coloured wooden bricks that had belonged to Keith. Jess had scoured the shops for toys, but there was almost nothing to be had and in the end she'd settled for two or three rag books instead. The colours weren't very good, but Maureen seemed pleased with them.

Two weeks earlier, the Germans had carried out their threatened invasion of Russia, surprising Stalin despite the warnings he had been given by Winston Churchill. Hitler had boasted that the German army's movements were the greatest the world had ever seen, and three million troops, with thousands of tanks, guns and aircraft, were on their way to crush the people of the USSR.

'We've got allies,' Frank said, studying the map. It was covered with pins, from North Africa almost to the Arctic Circle. He had dipped the heads of some in red sealing wax to make them represent the Allies, and they stood out like brave little flames against the black plasticine he had used for the enemy. 'And we've got the British Empire behind us. We're not tiny at all.'

'Well, I know. But if Japan attacks Australia, they'll have too much to do there to bother about coming all this way to help us.' She sighed. 'If only America would help. I mean, I know they're doing a lot, what with Lease-Lend and sending us aid and food parcels and all that, but if they'd just send some soldiers . . .'

'I thought you didn't want the whole world getting involved,' Frank said, and then shook his head. 'I'm sorry,

Jess. But that's what it amounts to. Everyone getting drawn in. There won't be a safe place anywhere on earth.'

There was dismaying home news in the papers too. A shortage of tobacco – 'at least *that* doesn't worry us,' Frank commented – and a new issue of ration books coming soon. And coal was to be rationed – only one ton a month available for domestic use, and perhaps not even that much.

'One ton for the entire country? They'll be asking if we want one lump or two,' Tommy Vickers said, calling in with a present for the baby. It was a small bar of chocolate – 'and *they're* about as common as hens' teeth these days,' Tommy remarked – and because it was her birthday they let her have it there and then, sitting on the rag rug and smearing it all over her face as she chewed. She grinned up at them and pushed chocolate-covered hands into her curly fair hair.

'Look at you!' Jess said. 'And in your new pinny, too. I reckon it'll take half our soap ration to get you clean again.' She smiled, feeling the sudden burning sensation of tears in her eyes. 'I just wish the boys could be here as well.'

'Are they coming home for their holiday this summer?' Tommy asked. He was an air-raid warden and had been in the Royal Navy during the Great War. He looked a bit like the comedian Arthur Askey, and always had a joke on his lips. He liked children and missed the ones who had been evacuated. There was nobody to toss a few toffees to as he walked up and down the street. Nobody except Micky Baxter anyway, and even Tommy never thought to give him a toffee.

'I don't know. I'd like to have them home, if only for a week or two, but it depends.' Jess glanced at her husband. 'I mean, we could always send them back quick if it got bad again. Bridge End's not so far away.'

'Not as long as we're still getting the raids,' Frank said firmly. 'Look at that one we had last week. Thousands of incendiaries there were, showering down all over Portsdown Hill. The whole place was afire.'

'That was gorse, mostly,' Tommy said. 'But you're right, Frank, it could as easily have been in the town, and we'd never have been able to put that lot out. It makes you wonder about these tunnel shelters they're digging under the Hill, too. I mean, how safe are they going to be?'

'Oh, they'll be all right.' Jess had an uncle on the Council. She didn't see much of him but news occasionally came through other members of the family, and the tunnels had been a great topic of conversation. 'They're going to be deep. Too deep for any bombs. There's going to be bunks and everything down there, and people will have tickets for their own places. Not that we'll go, mind. With Frank on firewatch, I like to be here and we're safe enough in the Anderson.'

Tommy opened his mouth and then closed it again. There'd been direct hits on Anderson shelters, whole families wiped out. But it didn't do to think about that. People had to take what shelter they could, and mostly the corrugated iron huts, half buried at the bottom of the gardens, were safe enough. And none of the houses around April Grove had large enough rooms for the newer Morrison shelters, built like big iron tables indoors.

'Well,' he said, getting to his feet, 'I'd better be getting back. Freda's not so good again – keeps getting indigestion. And our Eunice is talking about going in the Wrens, and that's not helping. Any upset, and it goes straight to Freda's chest.'

'Heartburn,' Jess nodded. 'She was telling me about it the other day. I know what it's like – I was a martyr to it while I was expecting Maureen. But at least I knew it would be better once she's born.'

'Gawd,' Tommy said with mock horror, 'I hope that's not what's wrong with my Freda. I don't fancy starting sleepless nights again, not at my age!'

Jess laughed. 'You're a star turn, you are. You and Freda, starting a family again! And as for sleepless nights . . . I don't know when we last had one that wasn't.'

Tommy grinned, winked at Frank, tickled Maureen under her chocolatey chin and went out. They heard him whistling as he went off up the street.

Jess took Maureen into the scullery to wash her. She stood the little girl on the wooden draining-board and stripped off her clothes, then poured some warm water from the Ascot. Maureen stood in the enamel bowl, playing with her mother's hair as Jess wiped off the chocolate.

'That means it's all over me now,' Jess said. 'I ought to have washed your hands first, you dirty little arab. Well, never mind, you've had a good birthday.' She sighed. 'I wish we could have got you some really nice presents, though. It seems such a shame you're missing so much.'

Frank came through to the scullery and leaned against the door-jamb. 'Did I tell you we're getting women in the Yard?'

For a moment, Jess was tempted to make some saucy reply. That's Tommy Vickers' influence, she thought, trying to repress a smile as she imagined what he would say. *All home comforts provided now, Frank?* Or – *Don't they have to hang about at the gates any more, then?* But Frank wouldn't like to hear her talk like that. He had very definite ideas about the sort of jokes that were suitable for women. Sometimes, she thought, he was a bit too strait-laced.

'What d'you mean, women?'

'To help do the work,' he said. 'There's some in the canteens already, but they're putting them in the work-shops now. We're having some in the boiler-shop.'

Jess stared at him. 'But that's heavy work. Women can't do that.'

'They can't do what I do, work the steam hammer, no. But there's plenty of jobs they can do.' He sighed. 'I dunno, Jess. It don't seem right, women having to come and work in places like our boiler-shop. It's too rough in the Yard. Not that some of 'em seem to mind that!'

Jess gazed at him, trying to imagine Frank working alongside women. He had never found it very easy to make

45

friends with women, apart from the ones they knew in the family, and he certainly found it difficult to cope with women who were too forward and made up to him, like Jess suspected Ethel Glaister had tried to do once or twice when Jess was away.

Frank was too shy and reserved, that was his trouble. Not like Tommy Vickers. And he liked women to be in their place, running a home and looking after children. He didn't even talk about his work much – he didn't think Jess ought to be bothered with what went on behind the Dockyard gates. It was another world. Now that world was to be disrupted too, and he could never again feel quite so safe behind the big walls.

'I daresay it'll be all right,' Jess said. 'You probably won't have too much to do with them.'

'No, but they're *there*, aren't they,' he said, and she almost laughed. Sometimes he sounded just like Tim in one of his peevish moods.

'Well, what if they are? They're just about everywhere else, too. And you don't need to talk as if women are some sort of strange animal,' she added, remembering that they were discussing her own sex. 'We're human beings too, you know.'

'Well, of course I know that. Don't be daft, Jess.' He watched as she dried Maureen with an old towel and slipped her nightie over her head before lifting her from the draining-board. The nightie was a new one, cut down from one of Jess's, and he'd always liked the silky material. He was sorry Jess wouldn't be wearing it any more, but it was nice that Maureen could enjoy it.

'Two years old,' he said softly. 'It don't seem possible, does it. We've been at war practically all the time since that little scrap was born. She's growing up to the sound of the air-raid sirens, and planes coming over, and bombs falling. It's not right. It's not how a baby should see the world.'

Jess said nothing. Frank's words chimed exactly with her own feelings, and she was sorry she'd laughed at him over the women. She turned, still holding Maureen against her hip, and put her free arm round him, resting her head against his broad chest.

Frank held them both close. He felt Jess's hair against his chin, and the baby's cheek nuzzling his neck. It was the colour of a peach just beginning to ripen, and there was a soft, almost invisible fuzz on it, just like the bloom on the fruit.

He hadn't seen a peach for over two years. Maureen had never seen one.

All the same, they were better off in Britain than millions of others were. He thought of Russia, even now being invaded by the Germans. The poor wretches there didn't have a chance. He thought of mothers like Jess and babies like Maureen, and what would happen to them when the Nazis went marching in.

Suddenly, it didn't seem to matter so much that Maureen didn't have a teddy bear or had never tasted a peach. Nor that he was going to have to work alongside women in the Yard.

Frank wasn't the only one who didn't feel too pleased about women coming to work in Portsmouth Dockyard. Nancy Baxter, a few doors along from the Budds, was grumbling to her mother about it before setting off for her own night's work.

'You can tell just what sort of trollops they'll get in there,' she said, adjusting the neckline of her frock. It was already cut quite low, showing the tops of her breasts – not that there was much to show – but she undid another button and stared critically into the fly-blown mirror that hung over the scullery sink. 'I mean, who's going to want to work in the Yard unless they're after something else? The money's not that good – they'll be looking to make it up a bit, and they'll have all the chances too. It's not fair on the rest of us.' She fished in the scruffy handbag that lay on the table and took out a packet of Woodbines. She lit one and inhaled deeply, then broke into a hacking cough.

'I don't suppose they bothered about that,' Granny Kinch remarked from the back room. 'When's anything been fair to the likes of you and me? We just have to struggle on the best we can. Anyway, you got your regulars, and there's always plenty of sailors about.'

'Yeah, I suppose so.' Nancy smoked for a few minutes in silence, then stubbed out her cigarette in a saucer and got to her feet. 'Well, I'd better get on. Our Vera's gone to sleep all right. I dunno where Micky is.'

'Out earning a few bob, I hope,' Mrs Kinch said. 'He's making hisself quite useful these days, working down Charlotte Street. He brought home a nice bit of shin at dinner-time. I'll make a stew for tomorrow.' She followed Nancy to the door and settled herself on the chair that stood there all day. 'I'll just enjoy the sunset for a bit. It's a lovely colour tonight.'

Nancy walked up the street. She passed a few people who nodded and muttered something, but nobody stopped to chat. At the top, she met Ethel Glaister coming along September Street and said hello just for devilment, but Ethel put her nose in the air and stalked past, pretending that Nancy didn't exist.

Nancy shrugged. She'd stopped caring a long time ago what people thought of her, especially people like Ethel Glaister. What was so special about Ethel Glaister, anyway? Nancy had seen her, with her permed yellow hair and frilly blouse, trying to flirt with Frank Budd. Especially when Jess had been evacuated at the beginning of the war, leaving Frank on his own. Ethel Glaister had been sniffing round him then like a bitch on heat, until poor old Frank had hardly dared go out in his own garden.

So what made her so different from Nancy, who had to earn a living to keep her mother and her children, and didn't have any other way of doing it?

At that moment, Nancy saw her son, tearing along Copnor Road towards her on an old bike. She waved at him and he skidded to a halt.

'Where d'you get that bike? I hope you never pinched it.'

'Course I didn't,' Micky said indignantly. 'Old man Grover said I could bring it home. I can get down there quicker in the morning and do a few errands too.' He looked proudly at the big basket fixed to the handlebars. 'I'm a proper delivery boy now.'

'You'd better not let the teachers see you. You're not old enough to leave school yet.'

Micky sneered. 'I'm not going back to school. They don't teach you nothing useful. Anyway, they don't hardly know who's there and who isn't these days. If they come round again, you say I bin evacuated after all.'

Nancy laughed. 'I don't suppose they'll bother. I give that teacher the sharp side of my tongue last time. What's in them paper bags?'

'Bit of lettuce and stuff. A few veg. And I managed to pick up a pound of sausages too.' He gave her a sly glance and Nancy, who had opened her mouth to ask how he had managed to persuade a butcher to give him sausages, closed it again. What you didn't know, you couldn't grieve over, that was what Ma always said, though there was probably someone in Pompey now grieving over that pound of sausages. Still, people shouldn't leave sausages lying around where sticky-fingered boys like Micky were skulking about. 'Pick them up' was probably exactly what he'd done.

'Well, I gotta go,' she said. 'You go straight home, mind. If there's a raid tonight I want you with your gran, not roaming the streets. I'll see you in the morning, and save a couple of them sausages for me, all right?'

Micky grinned and pedalled off down the road. Nancy watched for a few moments and then turned away. She wondered if the stallholder in Charlotte Street really had said he could use the bike. Come to that, did stallholders have bikes anyway? You didn't get deliveries from Charlotte Street market. Anyway, there were never more than two or three stalls down there these days.

One of these days, Micky was going to get in trouble again, there was no doubt about it. He'd already been up in front of the magistrates twice. He was that sort of boy – the sort who got picked on and blamed for everything that went wrong. It wasn't surprising if he cocked a snook and did it anyway. But it was a shame, when Nancy knew that he was really a good boy at heart.

Like Ma said, nothing was ever fair to the likes of them.

At that moment, Micky wasn't bothered about fairness. He whistled as his feet pushed the heavy pedals round, thinking how useful it was to have wheels of his own.

Since the night when Cyril Nash had been killed and Jimmy Cross lost a leg, Micky hadn't had anyone to knock about with. Jimmy was still in hospital, and they wouldn't let Micky go to see him. Anyway, he wouldn't have known what to say, and he was scared of hospitals. And Martin Baker, who had played cowboys and Indians with them sometimes, was just a kid; besides, his mum hardly let him out of her sight now.

It was a pity Tim and Keith Budd, from number 14, had been evacuated. They were a bit goody-goody, but Tim was usually ready for some fun and where he went, Keith would follow. They'd probably have joined him in making dens in bombed houses and collecting weapons, even if they drew the line at pinching things.

Until a few weeks ago, Micky had enjoyed the war. It had been a huge game, and a boy with his wits about him could have a good time and get his mum and gran all that they wanted in the way of extra rations and stuff. But now it was different. One of Micky's own mates had been killed and another badly injured, and now he wanted to fight his own war. Drive the Jerries out. Kill the lot of 'em. He could do it, too, if he was just a few years older.

People had lied about their age before, and got into the Army or Navy. But a glance in his mum's cracked mirror in the scullery at home told Micky that he couldn't get away with it. At twelve years old, he hadn't started to shave yet and he wasn't very tall, either. But he could still do something.

He could start his own army.

The thought had struck him this morning, just as he turned the corner into April Grove. He'd stood quite still, staring down the cul-de-sac towards the wall at the end and the backs of the houses in May Street, that ran beside the railway.

His gran was sitting as usual on her chair at the door of number 10, having a yarn with Mr Slattery, who was delivering milk with his electric milk wagon. The greengrocer's cart was standing outside number 6 with Nobby, his old horse, drooping his head into his nosebag. But Micky saw none of this.

Instead, his head was filled with visions of a new army. An army of boys, gathered from all over Pompey, boys who weren't afraid of staying in the city during the raids, boys who would go into bombed buildings and down craters and collect shrapnel and bullets and guns. Boys who would fight the Germans when they invaded.

And if they didn't invade? Micky saw himself at the head of his army – his secret army. Stealing boats to take them across the Channel. Sneaking under cover of darkness into occupied France. Working like commandos, sabotaging the Germans. Winning the war.

And he, Micky Baxter, would be at the head of it. *He* would be the hero then.

That was why he'd been so pleased to find the bike, leaning against an alley wall near Charlotte Street. An army needed transport.

It also needed men. So far Micky hadn't recruited anyone to his secret army. The boys he knew were all either younger than him or older, the sort who'd want to take over. Micky wasn't going to let anyone take over. This was his army, and he meant to be in charge.

As he came to the corner of October Street, he caught sight of Desmond Cook coming along the road.

Desmond was a big boy, older than Micky, but there was something wrong with him – he had a loose, slack mouth and queer eyes, and he was slow and couldn't even read or write yet. He worked as an errand boy for his widowed mother, who had a greengrocer's shop in Copnor Road, and took his work very seriously, knowing exactly which customer preferred cabbage to cauliflower, or who had received oranges the last time they were available.

Most of the time he was amiable enough, but sometimes he seemed to retreat into a world of his own, refusing to speak to anyone else, sometimes hardly seeming to know that they were there, and now and then he was overtaken by sudden terrifying rages. The other children called him barmy and would follow him in the street, taunting him until he flew into a temper and rushed at them, snarling and flailing his fists about, but he wasn't a bad bloke if you took him the right way. Micky had befriended him sometimes in a casual sort of way, and he knew Desmond would follow him anywhere.

Micky stopped the bike and sat back on the saddle as Desmond admired it.

'Give us a ride on the crossbar?' the bigger boy asked enviously.

'All right.' Micky helped him get on and pedalled off, rather more slowly with Desmond's weight added, the front wheel wavering.

'See the raid the other night?' he asked. 'I went up the Lines to watch. It was smashing – better'n Guy Fawkes Night.'

'You're not allowed up the Lines.' Hilsea Lines was an old fort, built like the big ones on top of Portsdown Hill and around Gosport. It consisted of a long earth embankment, tunnelled inside like a rabbit warren with rooms and corridors and just a few heavily barred windows. It was grown over with brambles and trees and had been a popular picnic spot before the war, but now the military were in there and you couldn't go near without a permit.

'There's places you can get in, if you know them.' Micky had been practising for when he invaded France. He would need all the commando's tricks then of hiding from the enemy, sneaking behind their lines to spy on them, keeping out of sight. And although the soldiers in the Lines were British, they were as much enemy to Micky as Germans were. He knew very well what would happen if they caught him.

'I go up there a lot,' he boasted. 'I know the Lines like the back of me hand.'

'We used to go blackberrying there,' Desmond said wistfully. 'Before my dad went away. My mum says the soldiers'll get all the blackberries now.'

Micky shrugged and the bike wobbled. He wasn't much interested in blackberries, though he liked them all right when his gran baked them in a pie with some apple. He was more interested in watching the soldiers doing their drill, and finding out where the ammunition was stored. It was inside somewhere, but getting into the underground fort was a different matter from just wriggling through a hole in the wire. It needed someone really small to get through those barred windows.

'This bike's smashing,' Desmond said, clinging to the handlebars as they swerved their way along the road. 'Is it really yours?'

'Yeah, I can use it whenever I want,' Micky replied, but he spoke absently. For a moment, he was silent and then he said, 'D'you want to be in my gang, Des?'

The bigger boy twisted his head round to look at him. 'You ain't got a gang. You got bombed up.'

'I'm getting another one up. You could be my First Lieutenant if you wanted.'

'First Lieutenant?' Desmond repeated slowly. 'What's a First Lieutenant do?'

'Well, take charge when I'm not there, that sort of thing.' With only two of them in the gang, Micky wasn't giving much away, but he spoke as grandly as if Desmond were to be in command of thousands. 'We'll have to get a few more in,' he added. 'But we won't have just anybody, mind. This is going to be a special gang. It's going to be an army. A secret army.'

'An *army*?' Desmond's voice was awed. 'You mean we're going to fight?'

'We're going to be commandos. We're going to follow people and spy on them and do sabotage and stuff.' The front wheel wobbled again, more wildly. Micky tried to control it, failed and the cycle veered across the road, jack-knifed and deposited them both in the gutter. Desmond gave a yelp.

'Ow! The pedal's gone right into my leg.'

Micky untangled himself and dragged the bicycle off his first lieutenant, who lay with tears in his eyes, biting his lip with the pain. The pedal had dug into his calf and left a red, angry mark, but there didn't seem to be any real damage. Micky looked down at him.

'It won't be no good crying when you're being tortured by the enemy. You can't be in the army if you're going to give our secrets away.'

Desmond sniffed hard and wiped his sleeve across his eyes and nose. 'I'm not crying.' He moved his leg gingerly. 'And I don't want to be tortured.'

'Well, don't get caught then.' Micky surveyed the delivery bike. It was much more heavily built than a normal cycle and had stood up to the crash with no more than a bit more paint being chipped off. 'Are you going to be in my army or not?'

Desmond didn't hesitate. Because of his slowness, and his unattractive looks, he had no friends and was accustomed to being left out of the games the other children played. To be invited to be in Micky Baxter's gang – in his secret army – and to be First Lieutenant, was more than he would ever have dared hope for. Maybe he could even be like Micky himself, bold and cheeky and daring.

'I don't mind.' He got up and rubbed his leg.

'Actually,' Micky said, remembering something he had seen on Saturday morning pictures, 'if you aren't I shall probably have to take you prisoner anyway. You know too much now.'

'I'll be in,' Desmond said. 'And I can be First Lieutenant, can't I? You promised I could.'

'Yeah, that's all right. You got to do what I say, though.' Micky mounted the bike again. 'I'll meet you here tomorrow morning, all right? I'll give you your first orders then. And we'll decide who else to recruit.' He pedalled away. It was nearly time for the siren and he wanted to get the sausages home for Gran to cook them for supper.

He felt pleased with the evening's work. He'd got started with the army, and he had transport – a bike could substitute very well for a tank until they could lay their hands on the real thing. And even if Desmond was only ninepence in the shilling, he was big and strong and he'd do whatever Micky told him.

Micky whistled and tore down October Street and along the back alley of April Grove, narrowly missing running over the Budds' tabby cat who was watching a hole under the fence.

'Sausages for supper, Gran,' he said, bursting through the back door. 'But we got to save a few for Mum, see?'

His grandmother came through from her own sentry-duty at the front door, her metal curlers warm from the evening sun. She grinned, showing the gaps in her teeth, as Micky slapped the sausages down on the table.

'Sausages! That's a good boy, Micky. You done well. We don't 'ave much to worry about in this house with you to look after us, do we?'

The frying-pan was already on the stove, still greasy from the last fry-up they had had. Granny Kinch struck a match and turned on the gas. At the moment she did so, the siren began to sound.

'Bugger you,' she said to the approaching aircraft. 'I bin all week waiting for a few bangers. And I reckon our Micky's are going to taste a sight better'n the ones *you're* planning to drop, so just carry on past us, will you? We ain't interested.'

Micky laughed and sat down at the table. But there was a strained note to his laughter and a tightness in his face. It cost him all the strength he possessed to pretend that the drone of the aircraft didn't scare him.

The memory of that other raid, the one in which Cyril had been killed and Jimmy lost his leg, was something he tried to push from his mind. But it still came back to him with the wail of the siren, with the rattle of the anti-aircraft guns and the fury of the explosions. It came back to him in his dreams, when he could do nothing to keep it at bay.

It drove him in his desire to fight the Germans. It drove his desire for an army of his own.

CHAPTER FOUR

'Who is this bloke, anyway?' Ted Chapman asked grumblingly. 'I haven't heard our Betty mention him before.'

Annie was making a special meal. She had stood over half an hour in the queue at the butcher's that morning, hoping that Mr Hines would still have some meat when she reached the counter, but to her dismay he only had a tiny bit of beef when she got there, and that looked scraggy. She'd refused it and gone over the road to the fishmonger. After another half-hour's queueing, with no idea what might be available when she reached the counter, Annie had bought some fresh-salted cod to make a fish pie. It had been soaking in cold water in the fishmonger's big sink for almost two days and Mr Jennings had told her it should be cooked that day.

'Not bad for ninepence a pound,' Annie said now, topping it with mashed potato. 'Mind, I never think fish is as substantial as meat, but the Radio Doctor says it's good for you, and you've got to take what you can get these days. A bit of salad's not enough for a Land Girl. Our Betty's used to hard work and country food now.'

The meal was special for two reasons. Olive was leaving on Monday to join the ATS, and Betty was coming home for the day, and bringing her new young man with her.

'His name's Dennis,' Annie told Ted, 'and she's talked about him before, you know she has, only I never realised there was anything special between them. He was working at Spencers' farm when she first went there, but now he's volunteered for bomb disposal and they've sent him back to Pompey.'

'There's something queer about that,' Ted said. 'I mean, why didn't he volunteer before? Why was he working on a farm? They've got boys of their own, haven't they, the Spencers? Why send them off and then take on another bloke?'

'Couldn't say, I'm sure,' Annie shrugged. 'But he sounds a decent sort of chap and our Betty seems to like him. Anyway, I'm glad she's got someone to think about, after what happened to young Graham.'

'What's that got to do with it? They'd stopped courting months before.'

Annie sighed. Whatever you said these days, Ted seemed to have some objection to it. The doctor said it was all part of his condition – she called it an illness – but to Annie it often seemed more like sheer bad temper. And yet she had to admit he'd never been like it before the war.

'Just let's make it nice for her to come home for a couple of days,' she said. 'She doesn't get much time off, specially at this time of year.' She went out into the garden, before Ted could say that he'd never wanted Betty to go away in the first place.

Olive was picking peas to go with the fish pie. At least Ted had started to take an interest in the garden again, chivvied out there by Annie's constant remarks about digging for Victory and getting the right amount of exercise. The peas were doing well and he'd planted some runner beans and got the sticks ready for them to climb up. It was nice to have your own fresh vegetables, and even more important now there was a war on. Annie didn't think she could have borne to have to queue at the greengrocer's as well.

'I wonder when we'll all be together again,' Olive said, dropping peas in the trug. 'With our Betty out on the farm and me going in the ATS, you and Dad are going to be all on your own.'

'I had noticed that,' Annie said tartly. She wasn't looking forward to the house with no family in it. 'And we're not all together now. I'll thank you to remember you've got a brother too.'

'I know.' Olive flushed. 'I didn't mean I'd forgotten Colin. Only, it's so long since he was home ... And Derek's not here either, come to that. But after this weekend – well, it'll be just you and our Dad.'

'Yes.' Annie picked a handful of peas and dropped them in Olive's basket. 'That'll be enough for now. I expect this new young man of Betty's has got a good appetite, though they get fed well enough in the Army by all accounts.'

Olive looked at her mother, surprised by the faint note of hostility in her voice. 'I thought you were pleased Betty'd got another young man.'

'So I am. But – well, it's something your father was saying just now. Why hasn't he joined up before? Why was he working on a farm when the Spencers' own boys are in the Army? They've got three Land Girls, they could've got another one. It seems a bit funny, that's all.'

'Maybe he'd been ill or something,' Olive said. 'Anyway, we'll find out soon enough. They'll be here any minute. I'll walk up the road and see if I can meet them, shall I?'

She went out of the gate and, after a moment's hesitation, up March Street. The trouble with living at the bottom, where it joined April Grove, was that there were two ways of getting there from September Street, where the shops and bus stops were. You could walk straight down March Street to the corner where the house with the little turret stood, or you could go down October Street and then turn right along April Grove. Mostly, the family used March Street, unless they wanted to drop in on Auntie Jess and Uncle Frank on the way.

Betty and Dennis would probably come on the green Hants & Dorset bus and get off in Copnor Road. Olive walked as far as the railway line and then stopped, looking up and down the road and debating whether to go any further. She was just making up her mind to go home after all, when she saw two figures come round the bend in the road and recognised her sister Betty, swinging along in corduroy breeches and a yellow blouse. With her was a tall young man with a mop of curly brown hair, and they were holding hands.

Olive advanced, smiling rather shyly. Betty had said nothing about Dennis until quite recently, and nobody had been sure whether they were just friends, or if there was more to it than that. When she'd asked to bring him home for the day it had been obvious that there was something special about him. But even so, to be walking along holding hands, for everyone to see . . .

'Hullo, Livvy,' Betty said. Her eyes sparkled in her tanned face and her short brown curls had gone fair with the sun. Her figure had developed a bit too; she was more rounded, though her waist was as slim as ever.

She looks gorgeous, Olive thought. She looks as though she's in love.

'This is Dennis,' Betty said, keeping her hand on the young soldier's arm. 'This is my sister Olive. You're not to believe a word she says about me.'

'Go on,' he said, smiling. He was very good-looking, Olive decided – nearly as good-looking as her Derek, in a different way. He was tall but not thin, with plenty of muscle under that khaki uniform, and he had a wide, friendly smile with strong, white teeth. His hazel eyes were almost the same colour as Betty's and sparkled in just the same way. In fact, there was quite a lot of likeness between him and Betty, with the same colouring, the same curly hair and the same air of suppressed humour lurking behind their faces. Probably that was why they got on so well.

'Tell me something about Betty,' he said to Olive, 'and I'll tell you if I believe it.'

'Oh, Betty's marvellous,' Olive said. 'She's the best sister anyone could have. She does all my washing for me when she's home, she does the housework and cooks meals for our Mum, she digs the garden for Dad. And she's quite right,' she added, grinning at Betty's open-mouthed astonishment. 'I tell the most enormous lies.'

Dennis roared with laughter. 'So what am I to believe out of that? It's like the story of the black men, one who always tells lies, the other who always tells the truth. I

60

could never work that one out either.' He tucked Olive's hand through the arm Betty wasn't already clasping. 'Well, let's go and see what your Mum and Dad say about you both. I bet they'll tell me what's what.'

The three of them swung along the road, talking and laughing. Olive's brief moment of awkwardness had disappeared. Dennis was nice, she thought. He was really nice. She was looking forward to getting to know him better.

'So you're in bomb disposal,' Ted said as they sat round the table eating Annie's fish pie. 'What d'you have to do, exactly?'

'Well, what d'you think, Dad?' Betty said pertly. 'He disposes of bombs, of course.'

Ted gave her a look and turned back to Dennis. Betty made a face at Olive and rolled her eyes.

'I'm asking a sensible question,' he said. 'Though I daresay a lot of it's secret, isn't it? I mean, you probably can't talk about it too much.'

'Not too much, no, Mr Chapman,' Dennis said easily. 'Seems a bit daft here, I know you don't have any fifth columnists hiding behind the furniture –'

'They'd have to be pretty small ones,' Betty put in, looking round the crowded room.

'But it's best not to say too much all the same,' Dennis went on, giving her hand a squeeze under the table. 'What you don't know, you can't pass on.'

'I hope I'd not pass on anything I was told anyway,' Ted said stiffly. 'But you're right, the girls might say something they didn't mean to. And with our Olive going in the ATS –'

'Our Olive will get to know her own secrets,' Olive said sharply. 'And keep them, too. We're not all tittle-tattlers, Dad.'

'All right, all right.' Ted looked at Dennis again. 'What I'm curious to know is why you didn't get called up sooner? Why were you working on a farm? I thought all your age group would've gone by now.'

'I was given exemption,' Dennis said quietly.

There was a sudden tension in the room. Betty found his hand again and held it tightly. She had dreaded this moment and knew that the dread had made her act differently, making silly jokes and being cheeky to Dad. And that had made the others uneasy – Mum and Olive had both kept looking at her as if wondering what was wrong, and she knew Mum thought she was going to tell them something they wouldn't like – that Dennis had got her 'into trouble', or they wanted to get married. Or both!

She wished it was true. But Dad would never allow them to marry, not until he knew Dennis a lot better – he'd only given in to Olive and Derek because of Dunkirk, and they'd known Derek and his family all their lives.

'Exemption?' Ted repeated, frowning. 'What, because of farm work being a reserved occupation? But the Spencers have got two lads of their own, haven't they?'

'That's right. They're in the Army. That's why I was drafted to the land.' Dennis paused for a moment. Betty might have thought he was nervous, but she knew that he was proud of his beliefs. He could only be uncertain because it was her dad he was talking to, and he didn't know how Ted might react.

'I was given conditional exemption as a conscientious objector,' he said at last, quite calmly.

The room was suddenly silent. Betty sat very still, only her eyes moving as she looked at each face in turn. Dennis looked composed enough, but a tiny muscle ticked in his cheek. Olive was staring at him as if he had suddenly changed into some kind of alien being. Her mother's hand moved slowly to her mouth, as shocked as if he had announced that he was Hitler's brother. And her father had drawn his brows together in a heavy frown.

Oh dear, she thought, he's going to take this really bad. 'A *conchie*?' Ted said at last, spitting out the word as if it were something evil. 'You're a *conchie*?' He turned on Betty, his fury erupting. 'You've had the brass neck to bring home a bloody –'

'Ted!' Annie was on her feet, moving quickly round the

table to lay her hand on her husband's arm. 'Now, don't get yourself all excited, you know what the doctor –'

'*Bugger* the doctor!' Ted shook her off. The shock of the word he had used, so seldom heard in this house, struck them all into silence. 'If I want to get excited, I'll *get* bloody excited. I reckon there's something to get excited about.' He turned on Betty again. 'You'd better take this – this *filth* out of my house, before I throw him out myself. I warn you, I'll do it if I have to – and I might not be a young man any more,' he added, his eyes raking Dennis's lean, muscular body, 'but I can still give a good account of meself, same as when I took my ferryboat to Dunkirk, to fetch home better men than you'll ever be!'

'Dad, listen –'

'I'll not listen to nothing while that dirty conchie's in the house,' Ted snarled. 'Look, my girl, I've *seen* it – I've seen what war's about. I've seen men standing up to their necks in the sea, waiting for boats to take 'em off the beaches – and all the time there were German planes flying overhead, backwards and forwards up the beach, dropping bombs on 'em, strafing 'em with machine-guns, mowing 'em down like you been mowing hay in the meadows. Think of that, girl – think, for every blade of grass you cut, that's a soldier's life slashed away while the poor bugger's stood there in the water, helpless. And stood there for *hours*, for a *whole night*, a *day* and a night, some of 'em *three* days, with nowhere else to go – Germans at the back of 'em, Germans overhead, and only our little boats to fetch 'em off, packing 'em in as best we could, pulling 'em on board out of water that wasn't much more than running blood, and them covered in their own blood, and shit, and other blokes' guts and brains what had been sprayed over them when the bombs and bullets got 'em . . . And all the time we was doing that, blokes like *him* – he jerked a contemptuous thumb towards Dennis '– were sitting safe at home, cutting a bit of grass, milking the cows, collecting the eggs from under the hens . . . Real dangerous work *that* is – I don't think! And you've got the cheek to bring him here, with our Olive sitting at the same table and knowing her man was one of the last out from Dunkirk, and could've been left there to rot and moulder on the beach . . .' He spluttered and floundered into silence, his face crimson, his eyes no more than reddened slits.

'*Ted* . . .' Annie whispered, appalled. She laid her hands on his shoulders again and gripped them hard, and this time he did not shrug her away. Instead, he sat breathing hard, and his big hands, clenched into fists, trembled on the table in front of him.

Annie looked at her daughters. Olive was sitting like stone, her fingers twisted together in her lap. Her face was white and her eyes bright with tears. Until now, Annie knew, Olive had understood little of what went on at Dunkirk. Neither Ted nor Derek had told anyone much. She herself hadn't realised the full horror until Ted's outburst.

Betty, too, was pale and shocked, but there was anger in the tight compression of her lips and her eyes were defiant. She jumped to her feet, facing her father.

'That's not fair! None of it's fair. You're calling Dennis a coward, and he's not. He never was. D'you know what it takes to be a conscientious objector? It takes a lot of thought and a lot of guts. You have to go to a tribunal and have people pull you to pieces for what you believe in. You have to go to *prison*. Dennis spent months in jail, just because he doesn't think it's right to kill people, because he doesn't agree with what went on at Dunkirk or what's going on anywhere else in this horrible war –'

'Pity he didn't stay there,' Ted said brutally. 'Then we wouldn't have to sit and listen to filth at our own dinner-table.'

'You're the one talking filth, not me,' Betty flashed. 'Anyway, what does it matter now? Dennis isn't working on the farm. He's not milking cows and collecting eggs – he's working in bomb disposal. Going down holes where bombs have landed and making sure they won't blow up. And that's a bloody sight more than most people are doing.' She turned to Olive. 'I'm sorry, Livvy, but it's more than your Derek's doing just now. *He's* only building huts down in Wiltshire. Dennis is putting his life at risk every day.' And, looking again at Ted, 'Anyway, since when have you had room to talk? It takes you all your time these days to go out in the garden and plant a few beans. D'you know how many of Dennis's mates got killed last week? *Do* you?'

Ted flushed and started to get to his feet, while Annie glared at her daughter and tried to hold him in his chair.

'There's no call for that, Betty. Your father's been ill –'

'Ill,' Betty sneered. 'He's not ill. He's just plain terrified. He always has been. And he talks about *Dennis* being a coward!'

'That's enough!' Ted tore himself from his wife's grasp. 'It's all right, Annie – I'm not so ill I can't chastise my own daughter when she's saucing me. And you're not too big to be chastised either,' he said to Betty, 'for all you think you're so independent in your trousers and cowboy hat.'

'Go on, then,' she said, standing her ground. 'Go on and hit me. I warn you, if you do I'll walk out of this house and never come back again.'

'*Betty!*' Annie's cry was agonised. She caught again at Ted's sleeve, imploring him to stop. 'Don't let's argue, Ted, for God's sake. Isn't there enough fighting going on in the world, without us adding to it? Look, why don't I make us all a cup of tea and let's sit down and talk about it quietly. And let's listen to what Dennis has to say. We've all been shouting so loud the poor chap hasn't had room to get a word in edgeways.'

Ted hesitated. He was still breathing hard, as if he had run all the way down March Street, and his face was suffused with blood. His eyes, when he looked at Betty, were murderous. He did not look at Dennis at all.

'I won't sit at a table with him,' he said belligerently.

'All right then, you sit in your chair.' That hadn't been what he meant and Annie knew it, but she had been badly frightened by the row and was determined not to let it go any further. 'Betty, you take Dennis out in the garden for a few minutes and Livvy, you can help me make the tea.' She watched as the three younger people got up and left the room, then turned to Ted and laid her hand on his arm again. 'Sit down for a few minutes, Ted, and get your breath back. You've got yourself all upset, but it won't do no good getting yourself at odds with our Betty. You know what she's like. If she walks out of here in a temper, she's just stubborn enough to stay out.' Her voice trembled for the first time. 'We don't want to lose her, now, do we?'

Ted set his jaw and pushed out his lip, but after a moment or two he glanced at Annie's face and gave in. He sat down in his armchair by the fireplace.

'All right, Annie. I won't do nothing to upset the applecart. But she oughter know better than to bring a bloke like that here. With our Olive and all –'

Olive poked her head round the kitchen door. 'Don't you drag me into it, Dad. I've got nothing against Dennis. He seems a decent chap and he's fond of our Betty, anyone can see that with half an eye, and he is in bomb disposal now. She's right, you can't get much more dangerous than that.'

'Maybe so,' Ted said grudgingly. 'But he didn't volunteer, did he? He tried to get off.'

'I'm not so sure about that,' Annie said. 'I thought once people like that had got exemption it carried on.'

'All the same,' he said, changing tack, 'I still think she oughter've had more sense than to bring him here, after what our Olive's been through. And she might have known *I* wouldn't want him under my roof.'

'You've always told us we could bring our friends home, Dad. You said you wanted us to, so you could see what they were like.'

'I didn't need to see *him* to know what he's like,' Ted declared obstinately. He sat down in his chair and shook out the pages of the *Daily Express*. Annie gave him an exasperated glance and went out into the kitchen, where the kettle was just coming to the boil. She swished a drop of water into the teapot and rinsed it out, then added four spoonfuls of tea from the caddy. Lord Woolton had been encouraging everyone to drink weaker tea – 'one per person and *none* for the pot' – but Annie had taken this a step further. If anyone objected, she said that it was her spoonful she'd left out, so it was her business, and none of the family had the courage to suggest that she kept her hot water separate too.

'Call Betty and Dennis in,' she said to Olive. 'We ought to give that young man a chance to speak for himself. Betty wouldn't have brought him home if she didn't think a lot of him.'

The family gathered again round the square dining-table. Ted remained stubbornly in his chair. Betty was looking pink and there was still a flash of anger in her hazel eyes, and even Dennis's calmness seemed more fragile. Annie glanced from one to the other and then spoke quietly.

'All right. Let's get things straight.' She addressed herself to Dennis. 'I think my husband's right. Betty ought to have told us about you before she brought you here. Not that we'd have refused to let you in,' she added with a warning glance at her husband, 'but we would at least have known where we were right from the start.'

'I don't see as that would have made any difference,' Betty objected. 'It's Dennis I wanted you to meet, not a military rank or a uniform. Though he's got both those now,' she added, 'so I don't see what you've got to complain about.'

Dennis laid his hand on hers. Annie looked at it. It was a strong hand, with long fingers that looked as if they had a firm grip, and his wrist was well muscled. And his nails were clean. Annie did like clean nails, and Ted never managed to keep the oil and grease out of his for long, somehow.

'I think it's time I said something,' Dennis said quietly. 'I didn't butt in before because – well, you all seemed to have plenty to say.' His eyes crinkled with a smile that Annie was hard put to it not to return. 'And I don't like rowing any more than I like fighting. But that doesn't mean I won't stand up for my opinions,' he said to Ted. 'I just do it in a different way, perhaps.'

Ted said nothing. He picked up his teacup and sipped

noisily. Dennis waited for a moment and then went on.

'I didn't refuse to fight because I was afraid of being killed. We all have to die some time and that doesn't worry me at all. I believe in God, you see, and I believe in his justice and love, so why should I be afraid of dying?' He looked at them with calm eyes and Annie felt embarrassed. Talking about God like that was almost as bad as talking about death and sex. She cleared her throat and offered Olive the sugar, forgetting that they had all given it up in favour of saccharin.

'What I was afraid of was killing other people,' Dennis continued. 'I just don't believe we have the right to do it. We're told *Thou shall not kill*. I believe that. And I won't do it.'

He made his statement very quietly, but there was a quality in his voice that left no one in any doubt that he meant it. Almost unwillingly, they lifted their heads and gazed at him.

'But that doesn't stop me wanting to help my country. Or my fellow-men.' He paused, and added even more quietly, '*All* my fellow-men.'

'You mean you'd help a Jerry?' Olive asked incredulously.

'In some circumstances, yes. If I found a parachutist, say, hurt, I'd do what I could for him. I wouldn't help him escape, or anything like that – but I wouldn't leave him to bleed to death, either.'

'Well, nor would I,' Annie exclaimed. 'I mean, that's just common humanity, isn't it.'

'I think so, yes.' Dennis smiled at her. 'And I can't see the sense of shooting a man down if you're going to do your best to save his life afterwards. Anyway, that's what I believe in. So I refused to join up and was sent before a tribunal. And as I've already told Betty, they gave me exemption on condition I stayed in my job – the only snag was, my employer, who happened to be Portsmouth City Council, refused to employ me.'

'First bit of sense I've heard all day,' Ted muttered.

'Now look, Dad –'

'All right,' Annie said, raising her voice above Betty's. 'All *right*. We won't start that again, if you don't mind. So that's why you went to work on the farm.'

'After a few months,' Dennis said. 'As Betty told you, I had to serve a while in prison first.'

There was another brief silence. Annie could feel what Ted was thinking. *So she's brought a jailbird into the house as well as a conchie.* Swiftly, before he could utter his thoughts, she said, 'But how is it you're in the Army now? Did you change your mind after the blitz?'

'Not exactly,' Dennis said. 'The blitz helped, of course. Seeing the fires over the hill, hearing the explosions, knowing what you were all going through here . . . But I'd been worrying about it long before that. And when people I knew started getting killed – those airmen that used to come out to the farm and see the girls – specially Geoff, the pilot poor Erica was engaged to – well, I knew it wasn't right to stay safe. So I volunteered for a non-combatant role.'

'There you are,' Annie said to her husband. 'He did volunteer.'

'Did you actually choose bomb disposal?' Olive asked. 'I mean, that's really dangerous, like Betty says. Or did they say that's what you had to do?'

'Oh no, I volunteered.' He smiled faintly. 'We're all volunteers. It's no use having men who aren't keen on the work.'

Betty shuddered. 'I don't see how anyone can be keen on work like that. Knowing it could blow you to smithereens any minute.' She moved closer, her eyes challenging her father to object. 'I don't care what anyone says, I'd rather you stayed safe on the farm.'

There was a short silence. Then Annie said, 'Well, I reckon that clears that up. It don't seem to me that Dennis has got anything to be ashamed about, and as far as I'm concerned he's welcome in this house any time he cares to come.' She looked at Ted. 'You can always go out if you feel like it.'

Ted opened his mouth, then closed it again. Like many

of his mates, he liked to believe that he was master in his own house, but when it came to the point it was more often Annie who had the final say. He glanced at Olive and then at Betty, and knew that he was beaten.

'Pity our Colin ain't here,' he muttered. 'Chap could do with another bloke around with all these women ruling the roost.'

Dennis laughed. 'My father says just the same. I've got three sisters – against them and Mum, we don't have a chance.'

Ted looked at him. Dennis was smiling, his face open and friendly. But Ted could not respond. He still could not forget the men standing up to their necks in blood and salt water at Dunkirk. He could not forget his own son, Colin, at sea aboard HMS *Exeter*. He could not forget the bombs raining down upon Portsmouth during the blitz, and his own shame as he crumpled on top of the turret where he had been firewatching, his nerve broken at last, leaving him sobbing like a baby under the blazing sky.

Betty and Dennis left that evening. Dennis had to go back to Fort Widley, on the Hill, but he took Betty to Bishop's Waltham on the bus first. They had to walk from the middle of the village out to the Spencers' farm near Stephen Castle Down, and twilight was falling as they strolled through the quiet lanes and beside the watercress-filled stream, their arms around each other's waists.

Despite her defiance, Betty had been shaken by the row with her father. The Chapmans were a close family, not given to rowing, although there had been inevitable grumbles from the girls as they grew up and Ted tried in vain to exert the authority he thought a father should have. They'd won a series of small battles, over lipstick and what time to come in at night – well, that was more a compromise than a victory, for Ted had steadfastly refused to allow either of his daughters to stay out later than ten o'clock, with eleven as an occasional and reluctant concession. But they'd never come as close as this to a real showdown.

It had been sunny and warm all day, and the heat hadn't yet died away. It seemed to rise up from the road and burn her face. She touched her cheek and felt tears against her fingertips. She had hardly known until then that she was crying.

Dennis noticed the movement and stopped. He drew her into his arms and they stood close to the hedge as he kissed her and tasted her tears.

'Sweetheart, don't. He'll come round.'

'It's not just that,' she said, letting the tears come more freely now. 'It's you. When he was talking about Dunkirk – it made it all so real. And when I think of what could happen to you, any day . . .' She looked up at him. 'I feel so scared, Dennis. It's like living in a nightmare.'

'Everyone lives in a nightmare these days,' he said soberly, his hand stroking the back of her neck. 'It's no different for anyone else.'

'I know. And I know what it's like to have that nightmare come true. Think of last summer – first it was poor Erica's Geoff getting shot down, and then Sandy and Duff. And that girl from October Street, Kathy Simmons, and her baby getting blown up, and Olive having a miscarriage. And God knows how many others . . .' For a moment the tears overwhelmed her, and she put her fists against her cheeks and took a deep, shuddering breath.

Dennis held her close. There was no easy comfort to offer her. No platitudes, no murmured 'there, there, it'll all be all right'. It wasn't all right. People were being killed, all the time. Sailors, soldiers, airmen like the ones she had mentioned, who had been such regular and welcome visitors to the farm. Old people, young children, mothers and babies, fathers who had been forced to fight when all they really wanted was to be at home . . . The pain was there all the time, an ache with no cure.

And it wasn't any the less because you'd felt it before, or because everyone else was feeling it too. It made it all the worse, because you couldn't let it out. You could grieve for a while, but then you had to pull yourself out of it and go on with your life. Hardest of all, you had to keep a smile on your lips while you did so.

Dennis hadn't talked much about his work. A lot of it was secret, but Betty knew that as a Pioneer his job had been to dig down to the bombs that had torn their way into the ground, sometimes twenty feet or more down, and lay there unexploded. Nobody knew whether they were still live, and the men had to work with as much care as archaeologists sifting for fragile remains, excavating cautiously and shoring up the walls of the pit as they did so; knowing all the time that the bomb somewhere beneath their feet might even now have begun to tick and so started its progress to explosion.

And nobody ever knew how long the delay might be. It could be a matter of seconds from the moment when the timing mechanism began, or it could be days. It might be even longer than that. And the bombs were changing all the time. You never knew whether this one might be different – and even more deadly.

It was bad enough, Betty thought, when Dennis had been one of those digging down through the ground. But it was even worse now that he had been transferred from Pioneers to Bomb Disposal itself.

'Oh, Dennis,' she said brokenly. 'How long have we got to go on like this? Only seeing each other once or twice a week – wasting so much time. I want to be with you every minute I can. I want to be *married* to you.'

'I know. I want that too, you know I do. But we've got to think of others, Betty. Your dad –'

'I'm not letting him spoil my life!' she broke in. 'He just doesn't want me to do *anything* I want to do. I wouldn't be in the Land Army if he'd had his way. I wouldn't have gone to dances or had any boyfriends or nice clothes, or *anything*. I'd have been still in ankle socks, sitting at home with my knitting and learning to cook. He just doesn't want me to grow up, that's what it is.'

'He's ill,' Dennis said quietly. 'You can tell what Dunkirk did to him. I can understand the way he feels about me, after going through something like that. And all the bombing –'

'There's plenty of people been through the bombing. They don't use it as an excuse to ruin other people's lives.'

Dennis sighed. Gently, he pulled her hands away from her face and held them against his shoulders. He kissed her lips.

'Let's be patient, Betty. We love each other, and nothing can stop that. But I don't want to do anything that'll cause trouble with your family. Your dad thinks the world of you, anyone can see that. It'd break his heart if you stopped going home. And your mum – she's got enough on her plate. She doesn't deserve more worry.'

'But I don't *want* to cause them worry,' Betty said. 'I just want to get married to you. And it'd be all *right* – you're just the sort of chap they'd want for me – if only – if –'

'If only I weren't a CO,' he said as she stumbled into silence.

'Oh, Dennis,' Betty said, in tears again, 'why does everything have to be so *complicated*?'

He laughed. 'Life *is* complicated, sweetheart. And it's usually unfair as well. It's just something we have to put up with. And it helps if we can keep cheerful about it. Don't let it get us down, eh?' He kissed her again and turned to walk on, keeping her hand firmly tucked into his arm. 'Just remember, Betty, we've got each other. That's a lot more than plenty of other people have. And I don't even have to go away. We can be together a lot of the time. Your Olive doesn't see Derek once or twice a week, now does she?'

Betty shook her head, feeling ashamed. Dennis was right. Everyone had something to put up with, and at least they could be together out here on the farm, where everyone knew and liked Dennis. Even Erica, who'd been so much against him to begin with.

If Erica could come round, perhaps Dad would too, when he was better. Perhaps Dennis's way was the right one after all – just waiting, just giving him time.

They were almost at the farm. The flint walls of the long, low building stood before them, shadowy in the gathering darkness. The warm scent of roses wafted across the yard from the thick, tangled bush that climbed beside the front porch to the bedroom windows. Over in the orchard they could hear the murmurings of a mother hen settling her brood.

Betty stopped, her hand on the gate, gazing at the dark bulk of the farmhouse. Even here, the blackout was strictly observed and it was impossible to tell whether there were any lights on indoors. Most likely, everyone was in bed and fast asleep, gathering their energy for the next day's toil.

She and Dennis had met here, they had grown to know and love each other in the fields and meadows that surrounded the farm. They had worked side by side, cutting corn, bringing in the hay, milking the cows and a hundred other jobs. She would have been content to have gone on like that for ever.

But Dennis possessed a conscience that would not allow him to rest while others fought and died. A conscience that might very easily take him to his own death.

'Let's say goodnight now,' Dennis said quietly. 'No use brooding. There's work to do tomorrow.'

'I know.' Betty took one last look at the stars and the moon above. It struck her suddenly that there had been no raid tonight, not even a warning. It was one of those rare nights when it was possible to remember peace.

Peace.

She took a deep breath, drawing in the scent of the roses, and offered her lips to Dennis for his kiss.

CHAPTER FIVE

Annie told Jess about the scene with Betty as they walked up March Street together on Monday morning, after Olive's departure for her new life in the ATS. They'd had a cup of tea in Annie's kitchen before setting out, to give Annie time to get over Olive leaving, but the daily work still had to be done. Shopping took so long these days, with all the queues, and you had to get out early or there'd be nothing left. Often enough, Jess had come home after nearly two hours' queueing in different shops, with barely half a shopping-bag to show for it.

'And it takes as long to queue for two people as for three or four,' Annie remarked. 'It'll seem funny just cooking for Ted and me after all these years.' Her lip trembled a little. 'I dunno – I thought with our Olive married, she'd be stopping at home. But they don't seem to take much account of that these days.'

'It's a pity she lost the baby,' Jess agreed. 'I mean, it was a shame anyway, but it would have kept her at home too. I wouldn't like the idea of our Rose going in the Forces. You don't know who they're going to meet, do you? There's a lot of rough girls going in now they're conscripting.'

'Well, we done our best to bring 'em up decent, we just have to hope they'll remember all they've been taught.'

They came to the top of March Street and made their way along to the shops. Ethel Glaister was waiting at the bus stop. She nodded at them and said, 'There's not a thing worth having round here. I'm going down to Fratton. Smarts have got some lovely autumn coats at their shop.'

'I didn't know Smarts had a shop at Fratton,' Jess said, and Ethel looked impatient.

'Well, it's their blitz address, of course. And I know a really nice greengrocer there, he always keeps something special for me. Not *black market*, of course,' she added, lowering her voice to a whisper, 'but very good value.'

'Well, you're welcome,' Annie said. 'I'd rather support local shops myself. I think we all ought to do what the Government says and not travel any more than we've got to, even if it is only down Fratton.'

Ethel sniffed, but the bus came along and she said no more. She climbed aboard, her tight skirt showing a lot of leg.

'I know we're supposed to save material when we have anything new,' Annie remarked, watching her, 'but Ethel's had that blue costume since well before the war and the skirt never used to be that short. I wonder what George would say if he saw her flaunting herself like that.'

'I sometimes wonder where she goes of an afternoon,' Jess said. 'She's always out, you know, in her best clothes and those high heels. She likes to pretend she's better than the rest of us – too good to shop round here. And that hair! My Frank would kill me if I dyed mine yellow like that. Well, here are the queues. I wonder what we'll be able to get today.'

Desmond had not arrived at the corner when Micky cycled up October Street, so he shrugged and pedalled away. That was the trouble with Desmond, you couldn't rely on him. He probably couldn't even tell the time. It wasn't much use having a First Lieutenant who couldn't tell the time.

However, by the time Micky had reached the point where September Street joined Copnor Road, he had almost forgotten Desmond. His mind was racing ahead to Charlotte Street, the market in the city centre where he could usually manage to pick up an odd job or two.

He'd have to hide the bike somewhere nearby, so that it would be handy for later. Nancy had been quite right to suspect that he hadn't been given permission to use it; he'd noticed it in the alley for two or three days and since nobody seemed to be using it, he'd decided he might as well borrow it. It was a long way to Copnor, unless you could jump a ride on a bus without the conductor noticing. And the basket was useful for bringing home all the bits and pieces he was either given or could help himself to as he scurried between the shops and stalls, running errands.

Some of Micky's wealth was come by honestly enough. More of it was collected by what Nancy called his 'sticky fingers'. But the traders in Charlotte Street weren't like the shopkeepers in September Street. They knew a boy was going to take advantage of any opportunity that came his way, and they just made sure there weren't too many opportunities. And for the most part, they were willing enough to chuck him a halfpenny to run an errand, or give him an apple or a couple of spuds.

Micky parked the bike in an alleyway, hoping it would still be there when he came back, and strolled round to Alf Reckitt, the stallholder who usually had a job or two for him to do. It wasn't really a stall, just a big barrow filled with odds and ends of vegetables and whatever the man could pick up cheap. Before the war, the narrow street had been crammed with barrows like this, or bigger carts with horses still in harness, their heads buried in nosebags. But now there were only a few, selling local produce or stuff they had grown themselves. Once, Alf had brought in a load of cherries and the queue had stretched right out into Commercial Road.

This morning, to Micky's surprise, the road was running with dank, smelly water. Alf Reckitt was staring at it, his long face even more melancholy than usual.

'Look at that,' he said to Micky. 'Bleedin' drain's blocked. And will anyone do anythin' about it? In a pig's eye, they will!'

'Why's the drain blocked?' Micky asked. 'D'you think there's something down there?'

'Well, of *course* there's summat down there,' Alf said irritably. 'Gawd knows what it is. Bleedin' body, I wooden be surprised.'

'A body? *Bleeding?*' Micky gazed at the murky water with awe. 'You mean someone's got bombed, and they're all in bits, and the bits –'

Alf raised his eyes to the sky. 'Gawd give me strength! *Course* I don't mean that. I dunno *what's* down there. Jus' muck, thassall. It wants clearin' out, it does, but *they* won't do nothin' about it. Got too many more important things to worry about than us poor bleeders down Charlotte Street.'

'I'll clear it,' Micky offered. 'I don't mind. You'll have to give me summat for it, though.'

Alf looked at him. 'I'll give yer a penny.'

'Not on your nellie. That's worth a bob any day, that is.'

'A shillin'?' Alf repeated. 'You'll be lucky, mate! I could get a mudlark ter do that for tuppence.'

'You got me,' Micky said, grinning, 'an' I used ter go mudlarking at low tide every Saturday, picking up pennies what folks chucked off the ferry pontoon. But I wouldn't walk down the Hard just for tuppence.'

'Thruppence,' Alf said, making to turn away. He stepped in a wet, soggy mess and swore as it soaked through his shoes.

'Ninepence.'

'You gotta nope. Thruppence, an that's my last word.'

'Tanner, and that's mine,' Micky declared.

There was a moment of silence as their eyes met and locked. Micky held the gaze for about ten full seconds and then let his eyes slide sideways. The water was almost surrounding Alf's barrow now. It had an evil smell which rose and seemed to hang over the collection of battered vegetables like an acrid cloud. Micky wouldn't have been at all surprised if it was oozing from a dead body.

'I'll do it for thruppence and a bag of spuds,' he offered at last.

'You know I can't sell potatoes off ration.'

'I'm not askin' you to sell 'em to me.'

'You know what'd 'appen if a copper caught me,' Alf said, but his voice was wavering.

'Okay,' Micky said, turning away with a swagger. 'I'll go an' see who else needs a bitta help. If I see any mudlarks, I'll tell 'em you've got a job for them.'

'Oh, all right,' Alf said with exasperation. 'But mind you do it proper, see? I don't want it floodin' again. It's losin' me a lotta custom.'

He handed Micky a galvanised bucket, and Micky got down on his knees. The draincover was choked with rubbish and it was easy to see why the drain was flooding. There was certainly something down there, stopping the flow of water. The funny thing was, it hadn't rained for days. Probably a burst waterpipe somewhere, he thought, flooding into it.

The draincover was hard to remove. It probably hadn't been touched for years – Alf was right about the Council, who never seemed to bother themselves about Charlotte Street. Micky got his fingers round the bars and tugged. It didn't move. He tugged again and again, without result. Breathing hard, he sat back on his heels, then leaned forward and gave another mighty heave.

The draincover came away as if it had just been lying there all the time. Micky fell over backwards and heard Alf laughing.

'Gawd, look at you! Covered in muck from 'ead ter foot. I wooden wanna be in your shoes when you gets 'ome, I reckon your gran'll skin yer.'

Micky scowled at him. 'She won't, not if I got a bag of spuds to give her. You stick to your part of the bargain an' I'll stick to mine.'

'Awright, awright,' Alf said, turning away. 'I won't say another dickybird. You just get on with it an' let me know when you're finished. An' keep an eye on the barrer while I goes an' sees a man about a dog.'

He walked off in the direction of the shack that was used by stallholders and barrow-boys as a lavatory. Micky turned back to the drain and started to fish out the muck that was choking it, piling it up beside the hole. It was impossible to tell just what was in the stinking mass, but some of it looked and smelt like rotting meat.

Bodies . . .

'Oy! Ain't there no one servin'? Or is it all free today?'

Micky looked up. The voice came from a fat woman standing by the barrow. She was dressed in a cotton frock that had seen better days and a man's jacket. Her hair was covered with a grubby scarf, wound into a turban, and underneath it he caught a glimpse of metal curlers like the ones his gran wore.

'Where's Alf?' she demanded. 'I ain't got all day.'

'Gone for a pee,' Micky said, turning back to the drain. 'I 'spect he'll be back soon.'

'Well, it'll be too late for me,' she said irritably. 'My old man'll be 'ome at twelve and he don't 'alf create if 'is dinner ain't ready. Can't you take me money?'

Micky hesitated. He glanced at the few piles of vegetables on the barrow, most of them close to rotting. The barrow-boys in Charlotte Street only ever got the worst these days, especially with so much food being controlled, but it was cheap and all that some people could afford. This old woman probably came from Rudmore or somewhere like that, where they lived ten or fifteen to a two-roomed hovel.

All the same, she had money in her hand and who was to know just how much she handed over?

'All right,' he said. He stood up, wiping his filthy hands down his grey shorts. 'What d'yer want?'

The fat woman had a shopping bag with her. He filled it with potatoes and carrots and took the coins she held out. She turned away and he dropped threepence in Alf's tin and a penny in his own pocket.

Well, that would buy him a bag of chips for his dinner. And as soon as Alf came back he'd –

The air was split by a sudden scream, and Micky whirled round. At his feet, sprawled in the pile of debris he had dragged out of the drain, was a woman in a pale blue suit. Her hair was yellow and carefully waved, her face artificial with make-up. She was screeching and clutching the leg that she had caught in the hole that Micky had left uncovered.

It was Ethel Glaister, from number 15 April Grove.

'I'm taking him to court,' Ethel declared as she gave her children their tea. 'I'm getting him prosecuted. Leaving a drain all uncovered like that. My leg's proper bruised. And all that muck! My blue costume's ruined, and my last pair of silk stockings are torn to shreds.'

'I don't suppose he meant it as a booby-trap,' Joe said, reaching for the dish the shepherd's pie had been in. He scraped at the crispy bits of potato around the edge. 'Anyway, what were you doing down Charlotte Street? I never knew you went down there shopping.'

'That's because you never take an interest,' Ethel said sharply. 'And you might leave a bit of enamel on that dish, Joe, if you don't mind. As it happens, I spend most of my day shopping, cooking and running around after you two, not that I expect any thanks for what I do.'

Joe and Carol glanced at each other. Mum was off again, their looks said, going down the same old track like a train that didn't have anywhere else to go. It had been bad enough when Dad was home and she nagged him all the time, but now that he was away she turned all her attention to them.

'They're calling up all the nineteen-year-old men now,' Joe said, trying to change the subject. 'I reckon it won't be much longer before my lot go.'

'You're not nineteen!'

'I know,' he said patiently, 'but I'll be eighteen in September and the rate we're going there just aren't going to be enough men. They're saying Japan'll be in soon. They're going for China already.'

'I wish you wouldn't talk about it at the table,' Ethel said crossly. 'You know I like mealtimes to be nice.'

Joe and Carol glanced at each other again and Joe lifted his eyes briefly to the ceiling. Carol stifled a sudden giggle and her mother glared at her.

'I don't know what you find so funny about that. Someone has to keep up standards.' She frowned. 'Here, what have you done to your ears? Push back your hair.'

She reached across the table and Carol leaned back, but Ethel was too quick for her. One hand thrust back the roll of hair that hung down fashionably over Carol's right ear, and Ethel stared.

'You've had your ears pierced. Who said you could do that?'

'I didn't ask,' Carol said defiantly. 'They're my ears.'

'And you're my daughter! You're not sixteen yet – you ask permission before you start acting like a grown-up. I suppose you got it done in your dinner-hour.'

'Yes, I did. *Last Friday's* dinner-hour.' Carol stared back at her mother. 'And this is the first day you've noticed it.' She jabbed her fork into the shepherd's pie and Ethel flushed.

'Are you trying to make out I'm a bad mother? Haven't I just told you I went all down Charlotte Street to get a few extra potatoes and things for you two? I don't know why I bother, I really don't. *You* could be bringing me back a bit of shopping to save my legs, but no, you're off with the rest of the trollops from Littlewoods, prancing round the shops and making yourselves up like tarts and getting your ears pierced.' She was breathing quickly, her pale blue eyes snapping with rage. 'Well, I'll tell you something now, my girl, and we'll see how you like this. If you can afford to do that sort of thing, you've got more money in your pocket than's good for you, and you're not giving enough to help here. I'll have another two shillings a week out of your pay packet, and you'll hand it over to me before you open it, so there's no temptation for you to spend on the way home, is that understood?'

'Another two bob! But that'll only leave me enough for my fares and lunches –'

'You'll have as much spending money as a girl your age needs,' Ethel stated. 'There'll still be enough for a few sweets and your Saturday night pictures, and that's all you want.'

'It's not. I want to be able to buy things. I want to be able to get my own clothes.'

'*I'll* see to your clothes. Just because you're out at work,

doesn't mean you can start acting like a young woman.'
Ethel snatched the dish away from Joe. 'I told you not to
scrape that dish bare! D'you think I'm made of money?'
She stormed out to the scullery and they heard her clatter
the bowl into the earthenware sink.

'I bet that's chipped another inch of enamel off,' Joe
muttered, and winked at his sister. 'Cheer up, kid. When I
go in the Forces I'll see you right for an extra bob or two.
And you might be able to volunteer yourself before long,
the way this war's going.'

'She'll never let me,' Carol grumbled. 'Anyway, why
shouldn't I get my ears pierced and wear make-up? *She*
does.'

'Maybe that's why,' her brother said shrewdly. 'She tries
to look young, but when people see you they know she's
not, any more. But she can't keep you in ankle socks for
ever.'

Carol looked gloomy. For ever was a long time away,
and she wanted to wear lipstick and earrings now. She'd
been experimenting with her mother's make-up and
jewellery for weeks, and was looking forward to trying on
her earrings as soon as she could take the sleepers out.
There was one pair she specially liked, dangly ones with
stones in that looked like real diamonds.

'I wish I was old enough to leave home,' she said. 'I'm
fed up with being treated like a kid.'

Ethel came back with the pudding. It was made from
custard poured over stale breadcrumbs with a couple of
spoonsful of jam stirred in. On top, she'd put a dollop or
two of mock cream, made from sugar and marge and dried
'household' milk powder.

Carol stared at it and made a face. But she was still
hungry, and it was all there was to eat. She took the bowl
her mother gave her and swallowed the mixture, grimac-
ing at the feel of the breadcrumbs mixed with the thin
custard.

The sudden hammering at the front door came as a
welcome respite.

*

83

'I'll get my own back, see if I don't,' Micky raged. 'Doin' a good turn, I was – clearing out that mucky drain, serving at the barrow – and she has to come along and fall in! I mean, she just wasn't looking where she was going. The drain had to be cleared, there was muck pouring out of it, the road was stinking. I reckon that's why she slipped in the first place, in them daft shoes she had on.'

'She was all right, though, wasn't she?' Nancy asked. 'I mean, she wasn't hurt or nothing.'

'Scraped her leg a bit, that's all, and tore her fancy stockings. Alf offered her the money for 'em, but she wouldn't have it. Just stood there screeching at him. And then a copper come along, of course, just like they always do when you don't want 'em, and she told 'im she wanted me charged.' He stared indignantly at his mother and grandmother. 'All I was doing was trying to help! It ain't fair.'

'It ain't,' Granny Kinch declared. 'And I'm going down there to tell 'em so. First thing tomorrow morning, I'm going down the police station, and you can come with me, Micky. And you, our Nance.'

Nancy looked dubious. She had been to the police station more than once on what she termed 'official business', and liked to stay clear as much as possible. Most of the regular bobbies knew her anyway. 'I dunno as that's a good idea, Ma,' she said.

'Well, *I'm* going anyway. And I'll tell you what I'm going to do this minute.' Granny Kinch thrust her misshapen feet into the pair of broken-down old shoes that stood by the door. 'I'm going down to give that Ethel Glaister a piece of my mind. Taking her bad cess out on our Micky when he was doing an honest job.' She didn't add 'for once', but the words seemed to hang in the air. 'I'll make her sorry.'

She shuffled to the door and they heard it slam behind her. Nancy glanced at her son.

'She's not worth bothering with, that Mrs Glaister. I seen her down Charlotte Street a time or two now. I don't reckon it's the shopping she goes for, neither.'

84

Micky turned away. He wasn't interested in why Ethel Glaister went to Charlotte Street. He wasn't even all that bothered about being taken to court, except that it would probably mean a fine. But he was filled with all the righteous indignation of a young ruffian who has got away with more misdemeanours than he can count and is then arraigned for something he either didn't do, or intended as an honest job. His grandmother's unspoken 'for once' still hung in the air.

I'll get my own back, he swore again vengefully. See if I don't.

The whole street heard the row as Granny Kinch stood at Ethel Glaister's front door, shouting and haranguing. Twice Ethel tried to shut the door but the old woman's foot was firmly stuck in the way. In any case, Ethel couldn't resist yelling back, and Jess, who happened to be outside talking to Peggy Shaw, hustled Rose inside quickly, afraid of the language she might hear.

'You've always had it in for our Micky,' Granny Kinch raged. 'You're just like the rest of 'em – never give 'im a chance. Don't matter what goes wrong round 'ere, it's always our Micky what gets the blame. What d'you 'ave to go down Charlotte Street for, eh, lookin' for trouble? Why did it 'ave to be *you* what fell down the drain?'

'D'you think I did it on purpose, or something?' Ethel screeched. 'D'you think I *want* to go all that way to do a bit of shopping, just so I won't meet any of you lot, and then run into '*im*? Isn't nowhere safe? That was my best stockings ruined this afternoon, and my nice skirt all covered in muck. And what d'you think I felt like, coming home looking like a scarecrow? I could've died of shame.'

'Pity you didn't. I reckon the whole street would've put our Micky up for a medal if he'd rid us of your sour face.'

'*Oh!* You old *bitch*! That's incitement to murder, that's what that is. I could have the law on you, saying things like that.' Ethel glanced around for witnesses, but everyone had disappeared behind their front doors, though she had no doubt that every ear in the street was flapping to catch every word. 'It's no wonder your Micky's turned out the way he has,' she said haughtily to Granny Kinch. 'With a grandmother like you it's a wonder he hasn't finished up in prison before this.'

'With neighbours like you, he'd probably be better off,' the old woman retorted. 'Anyway, you're doin' your best to see he gets there, aincher? Gettin' 'im charged over a simple accident. He was only doin' a good turn, too. It was your fault you fell down that drain, not his. You oughter bin lookin' where you were goin', instead of struttin' along with yer nose in the air.' Her lip curled with scorn. 'One of them stallholders is goin' to take you for a chicken one of these days, the way you walks about.'

'Well, at least they'll never take me for a common *tart*,' Ethel flashed.

There was a tiny silence. Then Granny Kinch said with quiet venom, 'You'll be sorry you said that, Ethel Glaister. You'll be really sorry. Don't forget, I knew you when you lived down Fratton. I knew your ma and I knew about all the dance you led 'er. It wasn't till George Glaister come along that –'

'Shut up!' Ethel screamed, stamping her feet on the doorstep. Her face was scarlet with fury. 'Shut up, shut up *shut up*!'

'No, I won't. I won't shut up. It's time people knew the truth about you and your fancy ways. Settin' yourself up to be Someone when all the time you're nothin' but a dirty little –'

'I won't listen to you. I won't.' Ethel turned and addressed Joe, who was lurking behind her in the passage. 'Go and fetch a policeman this minute, Joe, and tell him this old faggot's causing a breach of the peace. Slandering me, she is. You can go to prison for that, you know,' she added to Granny Kinch. 'And a good job too. Good riddance to bad rubbish, that's what that'll be.'

'That's enough!' Tommy Vickers was on the scene, dressed in his ARP uniform and brandishing a truncheon for all the world as if he were a copper himself. He put a hand on each woman's shoulder, holding them apart.

'Stop that screeching, you two. You're like a pair of alleycats tied to a clothes-line. This is a decent street –' he glanced at Granny Kinch '– well, as decent as we can make it anyway, and we don't want none of your caterwauling here. If I hear any more of it *I'll* be the one fetching a policeman. And I'll be charging you *both* with a breach of the peace.'

'You get out and mind your own business, Tommy Vickers,' Ethel retorted. Her face was scarlet. 'This old cow hasn't got a leg to stand on and she knows it –'

'I thought it was you didn't have a leg to stand on, down Charlotte Street this morning,' Granny Kinch cut in swiftly, and Ethel's face turned even redder. 'All this is just because my Micky was doing someone a good turn and Lady Muck here come along with her nose in the air and fell down the drain.' She sniggered. 'Lady Muck! I reckon that was a good name for you this afternoon, an' all!'

Ethel quivered with fury but before she could retort, Tommy spoke again. He gripped each woman's shoulder firmly and shook them a little.

'I meant what I said. Any more noise and I'll call the police. And it won't be just a court case in front of the magistrate – it'll be a night in cells for both of you, to give you time to cool off.'

Ethel stared at him for a moment, then jerked away and flounced back into the house. She slammed the door so hard that the entire terrace seemed to shake. Granny Kinch shrugged.

'Good job my foot wasn't still in that doorway, I'd have had her up for damages. All right, young Tommy, you can let go now. I ain't goin' ter smash the windows in. Not that it ain't what she deserves, stuck-up bitch.' She turned and shuffled away up the street, back to number 10.

Frank had been working overtime as usual, and had missed the excitement. It wasn't until they were in the shelter that Jess had a chance to tell him. The siren had gone off as usual soon after dark, and they were huddled on the benches with Rose and Maureen. Rose was pressed

87

close against Jess, flinching at every explosion, while Maureen played unconcernedly with her rag doll.

'She never said anything about Charlotte Street when Annie and me saw her, she said she was going to Fratton to look at new coats.'

'I don't reckon you want to believe too much of what Ethel Glaister says,' Frank remarked. 'She's always putting it on. She probably does all the shopping she can in Charlotte Street to save a few coppers for more make-up.'

Rose looked up. The bombing had stopped for a while and they were beginning to think the raiders might have gone.

'Joy Brunner's got a lipstick,' she said. 'I had a go with it. It looked nice.'

'Rose –' Jess began in dismay, but Frank cut angrily across her voice and Rose shrank back, surprised by his sudden sharpness.

'Well, you'd better not have another go with it, my girl. Dolling yourself up at your age! If I catch you wearing lipstick I'll put you over my knee, big as you are.'

'Joy's allowed to wear it,' Rose said in an injured tone. 'I'm fourteen, Dad.'

'Fourteen's fourteen,' Frank said unarguably. 'You're still a child. And what Joy Brunner does is up to her parents. It doesn't mean you can do the same.'

There was a brief silence. Rose glanced at Jess, who tried to make her eyes convey that she sympathised but nevertheless sided with Frank. After a moment, Rose spoke again.

'Joy's leaving school. She's going to work properly in the shop.'

'Joy's hardly been to school since the war started, from what I can make out,' Frank said. 'Why, she practically ran that shop till Mr Brunner came back.'

'Yes, but she's leaving properly now,' Rose persisted. 'I wish I could leave too.'

'Well, you can't.'

'But what's the use of it? I mean, we hardly ever do any proper lessons, just those in people's houses a couple of times a week. I could get a job –'

'You'll get a better job if you stay on at school and do a typing and shorthand course,' Frank said firmly. 'They're starting them after the summer. You can do a year, and then leave and get a decent job in an office like your cousin Olive had.'

'Or even better,' Jess added. 'You might even get into the Civil Service.'

'And what if the war's still on?' Rose asked. 'I'll be getting called up. What use is typing and shorthand going to be then?'

'Qualifications are always useful,' Frank stated. 'There's office work to be done in the Forces same as everywhere else. I wish I'd had your chances when I was a boy . . . Mind, it's more important for a boy – that's why I'm so annoyed over our Tim getting left out of the scholarship. It's put him a year behind, that has.'

'I can't understand why he never said anything,' Jess said wonderingly. 'I mean, he's a bright enough little boy, he ought to have realised. Now he's just fed up. I wouldn't be surprised if he gave up working properly at school.'

She stopped as the drone of enemy aircraft sounded overhead again, and they all crouched and bent their heads in an effort to protect themselves from the detonations. But tonight it didn't seem so bad. Most of the bombs seemed to be dropping with a dull thud in the harbour. It was low tide and they were falling mostly in mud. For some reason, they didn't always seem to go off then, or perhaps you just didn't hear it so much.

Maureen had fallen asleep and Rose's eyelids were drooping. Jess settled the two of them on the other bunk and cuddled up against Frank. Normally, he would have been firewatching, but Bert Shaw and Tommy Vickers and some of the other men were taking their turn tonight, and he was allowed a rest.

'How are those women getting on in the Yard, Frank?' Jess asked after a while.

'Oh, they're all right. There's a few I wouldn't give you tuppence for, but what d'you expect? And some are no more than bits of girls anyway. But most of 'em seem decent enough.' He spoke in a tone of some surprise, as if he had had the same expectations as Nancy concerning the women who were being employed in Portsmouth Dock-yard. 'We've got a few in the boiler-shop.'

'I don't suppose you have much to do with them, do you?'

'Oh, I've got a couple working alongside me,' he said, surprising her. 'Doing riveting and things like that. One of 'em's quite a character. Her name's Cherry. Got an answer for everything.'

'Cherry?' Jess imagined a fluffy young girl with yellow hair. Or maybe red. She'd have saucy eyes and a flirty way with her. 'Doesn't sound your sort.'

'Well, they're not there for my entertainment. But we get a few laughs. It helps the work along.'

'I suppose it does.' Jess spoke a little doubtfully. She had never thought of Frank having 'laughs' in the boiler-shop. Still, if it made his day easier . . . She knew that his work was very strenuous and the conditions unpleasant in the hot, steamy atmosphere. She couldn't begrudge him a few moments of relief during the long days.

Frank seemed to have accepted the fact that women were now working in his once all-men domain, more easily than she'd expected. She wondered how much this was due to a saucy little 'character' called Cherry.

CHAPTER SIX

The heat continued throughout August. A few years ago, the people of Portsmouth would have spent their spare time on Southsea beach, or swimming in whichever parts of either Portsmouth or Langstone harbours were nearest their homes. Now most of the coastal strip was surrounded by barbed wire, and there were rumours that mines had been laid beneath the shingle.

The war was spreading like a black, evil wave over the whole world.

Japan had invaded Indochina, and as a result America and Britain had both imposed trade embargoes. Japan must either yield or go to war. And it seemed that their preference was for war, because their next action was to begin bombing China.

The situation in Russia was going from bad to worse, despite Mr Churchill's promises of aid. A Second Front was being called for, but where were the men to come from to hold it? Already the Forces were being sent all over the globe to answer one threat after another. There just weren't enough, unless the Americans came into the war or the Government started calling up old men and little boys.

The sirens were still sounding every night, and by mid-August there was talk of opening the tunnel shelters which had been dug deep into Portsdown Hill. Admission was to be by ticket, with priority given to mothers with children and those who had no shelter of their own. There was to be room for at least three thousand people.

'They're talking about that tunnel under the harbour again too,' Jess said. She had heard this on the family grapevine, through her parents Arthur and Mary, at North End. Arthur was getting more forgetful and difficult these days, but Mary's mind was as sharp as ever and she relayed all the news. Her cousin John Bellinger, who was on the City Council, still visited her regularly and had told her about the Kearney tunnel.

'It's a sort of tube,' Jess told Frank. 'It'll go to Gosport. It's going to be paid for by America and our people won't have to pay a penny. They'll be able to use it as a railway tunnel after the war.'

'That'll please the ferry,' Frank remarked. 'They get a lot of custom from dockyardmen who live in Gosport.'

But the plan was turned down by the council – by only one vote, it was rumoured – and there were other things to worry about. By the end of August Winston Churchill was accusing the Nazis of the wholesale massacre and 'merciless butchery' of Soviet civilians. Already millions were starving and Leningrad was threatened with a full siege.

'They can't let it go on,' Jess said. Nobody could stand by and let such atrocities happen. But where were the fighting men to come from?

Everyone felt that America must come in soon. Food parcels and Lease-Lend were no longer enough. American Navy ships were being attacked too, off Iceland and in other waters. What more must it take to bring them in as Allies?

Accommodation in the tunnel shelters was increased to five thousand.

'They're expecting it to get worse,' Jess said, and made no demur when Frank allowed the boys to come home for only a short summer holiday.

Late in September, one of the Southern Railway paddle steamers which plied across the Solent between Portsmouth and the Isle of Wight, hit a mine and was blown up just off Southsea. It sank at once, losing all eight of the crew. Nobody knew how many passengers were on board.

'That's one of the worst things about this war,' Jess said, reading the newspaper headlines as she walked down the street. 'People go out of the front door in the morning and never come back, and you might never know what happened to them. Got caught in a raid – blown up by an unexploded bomb –'

'Run away from home,' Bert Shaw put in lugubriously. He had had another row with Gladys over going into the Wrens. She'd grown tired of waiting for her papers and gone down to the recruiting office to ask if they were ever going to call her up. 'Seems to me some people can't wait to get away. Look at your Olive. Nothing would do for her but getting married, and now she's off joining the Forces. I mean, what must her bloke be thinking, never knowing where she is or what she's getting up to? What sort of a way is that for a young married woman to behave?'

'That's an awful thing to say,' Jess said sharply. 'The young people just want to do their bit, that's all. They're being patriotic. What's wrong with that?'

Bert snorted. 'They want to cut loose, that's what they want. Get away where no one'll curb them. I know what they're like.'

'You know what *you* were like,' Peggy said, coming out to the doorstep to join them. 'Proper young monkey you were, before you took up with me. My dad went on at me something terrible when he saw us out together.'

'Your dad would've gone on at you if he'd seen you out with the Prince of Wales,' Bert declared, and grinned unwillingly as the women laughed. 'Well, at least I never got a girl into trouble. I had a bit of respect for young women, and they had a bit of respect for themselves. Not like now. Doing men's jobs, getting into all sorts of places a young woman wouldn't have been seen dead in a year or two back – I dunno what the world's coming to.'

Jess was half inclined to agree with him. She knew Annie was anxious about Olive, and she still felt uneasy herself about the women working in the Dockyard, alongside Frank. He'd mentioned that Cherry more than once now, describing things she'd said and done. A proper saucy little piece she sounded, always cheeking the foreman and standing up for her rights – not at all Frank's cup of tea, Jess would have thought. But he sounded as though he admired her, and his serious face broke into a smile when he told Jess of her exploits.

'You can't get anything past her,' he said. 'Sharp as a needle, she is, and got an answer for everything. Don't care what she says or who she says it to.'

She didn't sound a bit the sort of girl Frank would take to, though he'd always admired spirit and told Rose she must always stand up for what she thought was right. But this Cherry seemed to go a lot further than that. Jess imagined her flouncing into the boiler-shop of a morning, all ringlets and hair-ribbons, her mouth red with lipstick, cheeking the men left, right and centre and turning the heads of steady chaps like Frank.

There was something in what Bert Shaw said. You couldn't get away from it. The boys living out in the country, away from her and Frank. Young Betty on a farm, going steady with a man who'd been in prison. Olive joining the Army, just as if she wanted to be a soldier like Derek . . .

The war was turning everything upside down.

It took Olive some time to get used to being in the ATS.

After parting from her family at the bus stop in September Street, it was as if she had simply handed her life over to others. From the moment the conductor had pushed her along to the front seat of the bus, to the orders snapped out by the non-commissioned officers who took charge when she finally arrived at Queen's Camp, just outside Guildford, she had no choices to make, no decisions. Worse still, her most intimate decisions were being made by men.

Still dressed in civilian clothes, the girls were herded into a long shed to be issued with their uniforms. They looked at the tables, piled high with khaki garments, and at the brawny soldiers standing behind like shop assistants, their faces red and surly.

'Strewth,' said the girl behind Olive, 'we ain't going to have to tell them our vital statistics, are we?'

'I hope not,' Olive said, but she knew that her hope was

a faint one. The NCOs were already barking out orders to the girls to hurry up, and the first in the queue were being questioned loudly about their sizes.

'*E* cup?' Olive heard a sergeant repeat derisively. 'Blimey, we ain't got anything that big. You'll 'ave ter make do with pillowcases.'

The girl, who was blonde and blowsy, flushed scarlet and swore at him. The sergeant's eyes narrowed.

'Say that again, and you'll be on a charge before you're even in uniform. 'Ere, take this one – a week or two on Army rations and you'll squeeze into it all right.'

'I'll die if he says anything to me,' whispered the girl behind Olive. She was shorter than Olive and rather plump, with tangled black hair. 'I mean, fancy having to tell a man your brassiere size. It's not even as if he was your boyfriend!'

The girls passed slowly along the row of tables, collecting their uniform. Some of the items were men's, and Olive looked at her jacket with some dismay.

'The buttons do up the wrong side. And we can't put our passbooks in the breast pocket, it'll be uncomfortable.'

'Look,' the sergeant said, 'you didn't join the Army to be comfortable. And it ain't my fault if you're built a different shape. That's an Army battledress and if you can't get into it you'll 'ave ter make yer own arrangements. Strap 'em down with elastoplast or summat.' He turned to the man beside him and said, just loudly enough for Olive to hear, 'I dunno what they think they're doin', lettin' this lot in. They might be all right for a bit of snoggin' behind the canteen, but Gawd knows what good they'll be else.'

Worst of all was having to ask the last man in the row for sanitary towels. Every girl who came to his table looked ready to burst into tears. But there was no escape. Nobody could pretend that they wouldn't be needing them, and when they finally emerged from the hut, each clutching a brown paper package along with her uniform, they were all cringing with embarrassment.

'We're going to have to do that *every month*,' the dark girl said. 'I'll never get used to it.'

'Still, at least they've had to get these in specially,' Olive remarked. 'They can't fob us off with men's!' The two girls giggled, feeling the mild hysteria of sudden release from tension. They walked across to the hut where they were to sleep.

'They've even told us what kind of knickers to wear. D'you think they want us to melt away?' she asked as they spread their new acquisitions out on their beds. 'I mean, look at this thick skirt, and this tunic. It's the middle of summer, haven't they noticed? And these awful stockings!'

'Think yourself lucky to have them,' the girl replied. Her name was Brenda Wilson and she came from Gosport. She and Olive had already discovered that they'd both known Graham Philpotts, the young sailor who had been killed while helping Gladys Shaw with her ambulance. 'I ain't seen a pair of stockings in months.'

Her legs were stained brown, with gravy browning or shoe polish, Olive thought. A lot of girls had been doing that, but the summer had been so fine that most of them now had suntanned legs. Drawing the black line down the back of the legs to look like a seam was still tricky, though. Olive had given up trying.

She looked at the rest of the kit she'd been issued with. Everything was khaki – battledress, blouse, trousers, skirt, leather jerkin, anklets, brown boots and tin hat. There were also a gas mask and a water bottle.

'I thought they didn't send women fighting,' she said. 'We've got everything here but guns and bayonets.'

The other girl shrugged. 'Look at these bloomers. Proper passion-killers they are! I wonder the Jerries don't use 'em for parachutes.'

'They probably would,' remarked a fair-haired girl on the other side of Olive. She was called Claudia Stannard and her father was a doctor in Fareham, about five miles west of Portsmouth at the head of the harbour. 'But parachutes have to be made of silk, not this stuff that looks as if it was meant for Army blankets.' She held up a pair of regulation knickers. They were thick and voluminous, and the same drab khaki as the rest of the uniform. 'We can't wear these horrible things in this weather. We'll never stop itching. I've never been able to wear anything but silk next to my skin.'

'I don't suppose you'll go short of volunteers to help you scratch,' Brenda observed. She looked enviously at the other girl. 'I wish I had a figure like yours. You'll look smashing whatever you wear.'

Olive had laid out all her kit on the bed and gazed at it, feeling suddenly depressed. She ought to have been used to uniform, with Derek coming home in his, but the impact of having to wear it herself had not struck her until this moment. She looked regretfully at the summer skirt and blouse she had come in.

'If only we could have had a bit of colour. Or something pretty. It's going to be like wearing mud.'

'You're in the Army now,' Brenda said. 'We're not here to admire each other's outfits. And at least it makes us all equal. I mean, it's bad enough at school or out at work, when some people can afford nice clothes and the rest of us have to make do.' She fingered the battledress jacket. 'I've never had nothing as good as this before.'

Olive felt ashamed. Brenda was right, this wasn't a fashion parade and her own clothes looked worn and old. Claudia, on the other hand, was dressed in a frock that looked brand new and as if it had come from one of the best shops.

Olive came somewhere in between, with the skirt and blouse Auntie Jess had made her last year. Auntie Jess had been a professional dressmaker and the things she made always looked nice. But once in uniform, there would be nothing to tell them all apart.

'I suppose we'd better change,' she said uncertainly, wondering where to go. She looked up and down the hut, which was filled with girls all laying out their uniforms. The beds were only two feet apart and there were no screens or curtains around them. One or two girls had already started to undress.

Claudia unbuttoned her dress and began to pull it over her head. She didn't seem in the least self-conscious. Olive stared at her silky underwear and then turned and caught Brenda's eye. The Gosport girl shrugged and rolled her eyes.

'You might as well forget about being modest,' she said, pulling off her crumpled blouse. 'We're all in this together and there ain't going to be no secrets.'

Her words were proved right over and over again during the four weeks' training at Guildford. Life in the hut was communal; the only privacy was in the lavatories. Baths had a head-high screen between them, but nothing more. As for dressing and undressing, within a few days they had all forgotten their shyness and would sit on their beds or wander about with little or nothing on, chatting while they did their hair or nails.

Homesickness was a greater problem. As Olive lay awake that first night, missing Derek desperately, she heard muffled sobs coming from more than one bed. Almost in tears herself, she pulled the rough blankets over her head to shut out the sound and lay counting the hours until at last she fell into a deep sleep, only to be sharply awoken at 6.30 a.m. by the harsh trumpeting of reveille.

The days passed in a blur. Breakfast was porridge – either lumpy or too slack, with no in-between – followed by parade for inspection and drills. On the first few mornings almost every girl was picked out for having something wrong with her appearance – shoes not shiny enough, buttons dull, collar crooked, hair untidy – and few of them could march in step. Olive, Claudia and a few others had been in the Girl Guides so were a little more practised, but it seemed that nothing would satisfy the drill-sergeant, a hard-faced woman who seemed to take pleasure in keeping them standing for hours under the hot sun.

After lunch, it all began again. More drills, lectures and then 'fatigues' – commonly known, Claudia remarked sourly, as skivvying. Washing dishes, scrubbing floors, cleaning the 'ablutions', preparing vegetables – it all had to be done. And all, it seemed, by the new recruits.

'I don't think much of this as a way of winning the war,'

Brenda grumbled as they sat 'spud bashing' in the big kitchen hut. 'Anyway, spuds don't need peeling, we always has them in their jackets at home.'

'My father says they're better for you that way,' Claudia agreed. Different though their backgrounds were, the three girls had drawn together on the first day and stayed friends. Maybe it was the uniform after all, Olive thought, for it was certain that the 'posh' Claudia would never have become friendly with shabby, down-at-heel Brenda in the ordinary way.

'Well, they've got to be done,' she said, dumping yet another peeled potato in the big pan. 'I'll tell you one thing, though, I'm not volunteering to be a cook, not after this.'

Towards the end of the second week, they went on their first route march, Already exhausted by their strenuous new life, they found themselves ordered to pack almost everything they owned into huge rucksacks and carry them on long treks across the countryside. They arrived back at camp tired out, many with blisters, the packs apparently weighing at least twice as much as when they had set out. They flung themselves on to their beds and Brenda dissolved into tears.

'I'm just worn out,' she sobbed as Olive and Claudia tried to comfort her. 'I don't reckon I can take no more. And I've never bin out in fields with cows in – I mean, they're so *big*. And their horns! And the way they follows you around. I was scared stiff.'

'Those weren't cows,' Claudia said. 'They were bullocks.'

'*Bullocks?*' Brenda squealed. 'But they could have gored us to death.' She dropped her head on her arms. 'I tell you, I can't take no more. I've had enough.'

Olive felt much the same way. She was missing Derek more than ever, and lived for his letters. Somehow, living in a Nissen hut on an army camp seemed to have taken her further away from him rather than brought her closer. She had thought that to be living the same kind of life would tighten the bond between them. Instead, because Derek had never been to the camp and because she found it so difficult to write to him about the life, it seemed to have created a gulf.

It had been so much easier to write letters that were filled with the ordinary, familiar things he knew. The office in his father's yard, the men who came in and out, the things his mother had said and done, the life that went on at home in April Grove. All these were things Derek would recognise, things he wanted to know about because they would bring home closer.

Now, Olive too was starved of news from home, and all she could pass on to Derek were the odd scraps of information contained in her mother's short weekly letters. And Annie was no letter-writer. You had to go to Auntie Jess for that.

Claudia came round the bed and put her hand on Brenda's shoulder. 'Come on, Bren. Dry your eyes and have a wash. You're not going to let them get you down, are you?'

Brenda shrugged. 'Why not? It's what they want, isn't it?' She rolled over and stared at them both. 'It wouldn't be so bad if it wasn't for that old cow of a sergeant. She's always on at me. If it's not my shoes it's my hair, and if it's not that it's my belt or my stockings or my fingernails, or anything else she can think of. She picks on me the whole time. She's sent me to the nit-shed three times this week, and she knows they never find any. She just likes being mean.' The tears welled up in her eyes again. 'She's been trying for the past fortnight to make me cry and now she's bloody done it! Why don't you fetch her in to see, give her the satisfaction, then maybe she'll leave off.'

Claudia stared at her and then laughed. 'Picks on *you*? I thought it was me. She never leaves me alone, haven't you noticed? I thought it was because of the way I speak. She's always making some nasty comment about my voice.'

'I think she does it to everyone,' Olive said. '*I* thought it was me, because I'm married!'

They looked at each other and began to laugh. Brenda wiped her eyes and sat up.

'She's just a nasty old bitch who's never been young, never had a bloke and never will. You're right, Claud, we don't have to let the likes of her get us down. Anyway, we'll be out of here in another couple of weeks.'

'And she'll be stuck in Queen's with a new lot of recruits,' Olive said, grinning. 'Maybe we ought to leave them a few notes around the place, warning them.'

At the end of the month, the girls were posted to their units. By this time they had forged bonds of close friendship and were almost as upset to part as they had been to leave their families – more so in the case of some of the girls. They held a party in their hut on the last night, sipping ginger beer and lemonade from the NAAFI and singing the latest songs, and finished up by dancing a conga in a long line through the hut and outside, where they met lines of girls from the other huts doing exactly the same thing.

The officers, who would usually have been on the alert and put a stop to any such goings-on, were conspicuously absent.

'We'll keep in touch, won't we?' Olive said to Brenda and Claudia as they waited in a dejected little group for their transport next morning. 'Write and let us know how you get on, Bren.'

'You write to me too,' Brenda responded. She was looking miserable, although she had got the posting she wanted – she was going as a driver to the RASC Transport Workshop at Camberley. Olive, who had read about the work ATS girls did there, was faintly envious, imagining Brenda driving lorries, Lister platforms and even parts of tanks all over the country. But she remembered Derek saying how he'd never feel safe if he didn't know just where she was. He wouldn't have liked her to be doing that kind of work.

She looked at her own posting, wondering if he'd be any better pleased about that. With Claudia, she'd volunteered for a training course in Wales, learning aircraft recognition and height-finding, and then working alongside soldiers on anti-aircraft guns. There was a good chance she'd be posted back to the Portsmouth area – but what would he say about the danger she'd be in?

I can't help that, she thought. We've all got to face danger these days. I can't hide myself away in an office while girls like Gladys Shaw are out in the raids driving ambulances, and Brenda's driving trucks like a man. Maybe it's not what we wanted – but nobody's getting what they want these days.

The secret, she told herself, is to want what you get and make the most of it. Even if there is a war on.

Micky Baxter's private war continued. He hadn't had much luck with forming his army, but he'd carried out his threat to get his own back on Ethel Glaister. The drain incident had led to a court appearance and a fine of two shillings and sixpence. Nancy had to go to court and pay the fine, and Granny Kinch went too, taking her curlers out for the occasion. She looked unfamiliar with sparse grey curls over her head, wearing a brown felt hat and the shapeless brown coat that did duty during her doorstep vigils in winter. She was incensed by the fine and grumbled all the way home, but Micky said nothing. He was too busy planning his revenge.

Two days later, he forced open the Glaisters' back window, having got in through the unlocked conservatory. He had watched Ethel go out and knew there would be two clear hours before she came back. He was carrying a brown cardboard box under his arm and when he was inside he stood for a moment, looking round the room. Then he grinned, put the box on the table and set to work.

Ethel came home a little later than usual and walked down the road with her son Joe, who had got on the same bus. Joe was an apprentice in the Dockyard. Like Frank Budd, he did a lot of overtime these days, but this afternoon he'd clocked off at the normal time.

'I might go swimming after tea,' he said as they came round the corner of October Street into April Grove. Mrs Seddon had just closed her little shop and the street was quiet and warm in the early evening sun. 'It's been sweltering in the Yard today.'

'Well, you watch out,' Ethel told him. 'You're not supposed to go down the beaches now, you know that.'

'Oh, there's places along Langstone where it's all right.' He waited while his mother fished out her key and unlocked the front door. 'And it's high tide tonight, should be good.'

Ethel went ahead of him into the little passage. She paused and sniffed. 'There's a funny smell.'

'I can't –' Joe came in behind her and stopped abruptly. 'Yes, I can. It's something gone bad somewhere.'

'Don't be daft,' his mother said sharply. 'There's nothing could've gone bad.'

'Something dead, then. A mouse. It must've died in a corner –'

'Are you saying my housework's so scamped I wouldn't notice a dead mouse?' she demanded. 'Anyway, we don't have mice. It's only dirty houses have mice.' She opened the door into the back room. 'I – *oh*!' Her voice rose to an outraged screech. 'Oh, my *God*!'

'What? What is it?' Joe pressed close behind her, craning to see over her shoulder. His glance took in the scene before them and he drew in an awed breath. 'Coo!'

'Coo?' Ethel repeated wrathfully. '*Coo?* Is that all you can say – coo? Someone's been in here, in *my house*, some *vandal*, chucking the furniture about and smashing things up and leaving *filth* behind – and you know as well as I do just who *that* was – and all you can do is stand there and sound like a bloody *pigeon*? Do something, for God's sake. Go straight up to number 10 and get that Baxter boy down here.' She stared round the room. 'Oh, if only your father was here. I'd give him such an earful! Why couldn't he find us somewhere decent to live? Why do we have to mix with people like that?'

Joe stared over her shoulder. Whoever had been in here had done a thorough job. Every piece of furniture except the heavy sideboard had been turned upside down. The square dining table lay with its legs in the air. The contents of the sideboard and wall cupboards were spread around the room and Ethel's best tea service had been laid out on the underside of the table, as if for a party. In the middle, where a cake might have taken pride of place, was a large meat plate. It was piled with a mass of stinking rubbish, and the rubbish looked as if it might have come out of a drain.

'It's horrible,' Ethel said in a trembling voice. 'Oh, it's horrible. It's *evil*.' She turned on her son, almost beside herself with rage. 'Go and get him! Bring him here. I'll wring his neck. I'll tear him limb from limb, that's what I'll do. Oh, the little devil, the little *devil*!' Tears began to stream down her face, her mascara making black runnels in the heavy make-up.

'You don't know it was him,' Joe said, his lips twitching as he looked at the devastation. 'It could have been someone else.'

'Of course it was him!' Ethel advanced into the chaos. 'Who else would do a thing like this? He ought to be sent away, that's what, he ought to be locked up, and so he will be, if I have anything to do with it.' She turned again, stamping her foot. 'Well, what are you waiting for? Go and fetch him along this minute, and bring that slut of a mother of his as well, *and* that old witch of a grandmother. They were all in it together, likely as not, and they can all give a hand to put it right!'

Joe had been having trouble keeping a straight face ever since he saw the confusion of the room, but the thought of Nancy and Granny Kinch helping Micky turn the furniture upside down and arrange the teacups on the upturned table was too much for him. He broke into a snort of laughter. He tried to smother it at once but Ethel, who had bent to pick up her best teacups, heard and straightened, glaring at him.

'Well, I don't know what you find so funny about this! Don't you realise how serious it is? That little villain's been *in* here, messing about with *my* things and leaving his filth behind to stink us out. I suppose you realise he broke in? And I don't suppose for a minute that he went out empty-handed – oh no, he'll have pinched whatever he could pick up. Why, he's probably been into every room – ransacked the entire house. And it's not just that,' she continued, glowering at her son. 'Now he knows how to get in, he'll be back. I'll never dare go out again!'

'Don't be daft, Mum. Of course he won't be back. That'd be asking for trouble –'

'*Asking for trouble?* Oh, he's going to get trouble, don't you make any mistake about that.' She surveyed the disorder again and then put back the teacup and saucer she was holding. 'I've changed my mind. Don't bring him down here. Go and fetch a policeman instead.'

'A policeman?' Joe echoed. 'But –'

'You heard what I said. Go up the phone box and get one along here at once. Tell 'em there's been a burglary.'

'But we don't know he's taken anything –'

'He's broken in, hasn't he? That's a criminal offence. You can be put in prison for breaking and entering. You don't have to have pinched anything.' Ethel's eyes glittered with angry satisfaction. 'He won't get away with a half-a-crown fine this time. I'll see that young scoundrel in jail yet, you see if I don't.'

The police took Micky's escapade at number 15 April Grove seriously, and the constable who was sent to investigate the 'burglary' looked gravely at the chaos and went straight up to number 10 to interview him.

'Our Micky wouldn't do a thing like that,' declared Granny Kinch, who had been at the door when the policeman cycled down the street and watched with popping eyes as he propped his bike up on the kerb outside number 15. 'He's a good boy. He wouldn't go breaking into people's houses.'

'Go out Eastney and tell it to the Marines,' the constable said wearily. 'You know as well as I do he's bin in and out of trouble since he was five years old. Anyway, who else would have done it, eh? There ain't hardly any other kids around here.'

'So it's got to be our Micky, ain't it. You always got to

pick on him. And you'll believe that Ethel Glaister before you believes him. Just because she wasn't looking where she was going and tore her fancy stockings, she has to go and take it out on our Micky. And where she get stockings these days anyway, have you asked her that? There's more'n one sort o' market down Charlotte Street.'

'I'm not here to investigate the black market,' the policeman said. 'Your scallywag of a grandson broke into a house and did damage. That's a serious matter and I'll have to talk to him about it. Mrs Glaister wants to bring charges.'

'I didn't do no damage!' Micky burst out, tumbling into the room from where he had been listening behind the scullery door. 'I never broke nothing and I never pinched nothing either. I just moved it about a bit. There's no law against moving stuff about.'

'There is when it's in someone else's house.' The policeman looked sternly at him. 'So you admit you were there, then.'

Micky opened his mouth to deny it, then realised that he had walked into a trap. He shut his mouth again and glowered sullenly. His grandmother gave him a look of exasperation.

'You little twerp. She couldn't never have proved nothing.'

'She wouldn't need to,' the constable said. 'His finger-prints would have been all over the place. Well, it saves us the trouble of taking them.' He gave Micky another stern look. 'You're in real trouble this time, young man. It's not only Mrs Glaister. We've had complaints from the local cinema manager about you too.'

'The pictures?' Granny Kinch echoed. 'Why, what's he supposed to have done there?'

The policeman consulted his notebook and began to speak in a monotone, as if he were reciting dull poetry. 'According to the manager, a number of his female customers have complained that their handbags have been rifled. They put them under their seats while they were watching the film and when they went outside their purses were empty, even though they knew there was money in them when they went in.' He glanced at Micky again. 'The usherettes were told to keep an eye open and they've noticed this young gentleman several times, on occasions when these thefts have been reported. One of them saw your grandson crawling along empty rows of seats. Obviously, it would be a simple matter for him to reach underneath, pull out the bags, empty them and replace them without being detected.'

'They didn't never actually see him do it, though, did they?' Granny Kinch said sharply. 'There's no proof.'

The policeman sighed. 'Circumstantial evidence –'

'That ain't proof. You needs either proof or a confession. You got no proof and Micky ain't going to confess to summat he never done.' The old woman stared at him with triumphant black eyes. 'Are you, Mick?'

Micky shook his head and the policeman sighed. 'All the same, he's going to have to come down the station about Mrs Glaister's bother. He's admitted he did that.'

It meant another trip to the court for Micky. The cinema manager and usherette came too and made as good a case as they could about the plundered handbags but Micky stuck firmly to his denials and, as his grandmother had said, there was no actual proof. Nevertheless, the magistrate ordered that he should be banned from all the cinemas in the city for a month and Nancy had to promise to send him to Sunday School. Worse still, he was given six strokes of the birch and put on probation.

The sentence was carried out immediately. Micky came home furious, humiliated and crying, one hand rubbing his backside. His grandmother was red-eyed and indignant, hardly knowing whether to stay inside for the next three days or take up her usual position at the front door and accost everyone who went past. Nancy, parting from them outside the court, added to her son's punishment with a cuff on the ear.

'That'll learn you to do daft things,' she said brusquely. 'You'd better keep your nose clean in future, young Mick, or you'll be getting evacuated out to the country with the rest of the kids. I can't be doing with this going to court every five minutes. It's gettin' me a bad name. All them coppers knows our faces now, and they knows just who to pick on every time they wants a scapegoat. I don't want to end up behind bars on account of you.'

'I'm *not* going to Sunday School,' Micky said furiously. 'It's a lot of cissies. I *won't* go.'

'You'll do as you're told for once,' Nancy told him sharply. 'The probation officer'll see to that. And you'll keep out of trouble from now on, see?'

Micky went home with his grandmother. They had baked beans and sausages for dinner – Micky's favourite meal – but he ate them without comment. His heavy dark brows were drawn together as he plotted his next move.

CHAPTER SEVEN

For the children at the vicarage, life continued to be sunny. Mr Beckett cycled round the parish like a creaky spider on his old bicycle, and became a sort of honorary child when he was at home. Stella and Muriel Simmons, apparently not too badly affected by the loss of their mother and baby brother, collected rose petals to make scent and strung together immensely long daisy chains which they wore round their necks till the flowers withered. Tim and Keith, scorning these as girls' games, kicked a football around the old lawn and went fishing for sticklebacks in the little stream. For the time being, Tim had stopped worrying about school and given himself over to enjoying life.

Mike Simmons, his ship docking for a few days in Southampton, came out to Bridge End to see his daughters and found them in the shaggy grass, holding a teaparty for two dolls and a battered teddy bear that Mr Beckett had resurrected from the attic.

He stopped at the gate, watching unseen. The sun was warm and the leaves were tinted with autumn. A few dahlias made a patch of bright colour at the edge of the lawn and the gnarled apple tree was heavy with fruit. There was a hum of late bees in the air, a sound as warm as the day itself.

Mike had walked from Eastleigh railway station. He was hot, and wanted a drink of water. But he stood for a few minutes, gazing at the little girls, his heart aching with love and grief.

Only a year ago, his Kathy had been still alive, expecting Thomas. She hadn't wanted to be evacuated – like Mike, she believed that families ought to stay together, and she'd been determined to keep their house in Portchester Street nice for him to come home to. But the house had been destroyed by one of the first bombs to fall on Portsmouth, and she'd had to move to October Street.

Mike had changed his mind about evacuation then. He'd been frightened by the complete demolition of their home and wanted her to come out to the country. He hated the thought of her having to go down to the dank little Anderson shelter night after night, and he'd been horrified when he heard that Thomas was actually born there, in the middle of one of the worst raids of the blitz. But Kathy had steadfastly refused to leave. 'I want to be here when you get home, even if it's just for a few hours,' she'd told him. And then there'd been another raid, another direct hit, and she'd been killed, with the baby in her arms.

Mike had been stunned with grief. If it hadn't been for Jess Budd, he didn't know what he would have done. But Jess had taken in the two girls and looked after them, she'd even arranged for them to come out here to stay with Mr Beckett and her own two boys. And now here they were, playing in the sunshine as if they hadn't a care in the world.

Didn't they miss their mother at all? he wondered, suddenly angry. And then turned his anger on himself. Of course they missed her. And they'd suffered too – they'd been bombed out, endured the raids, been frightened and homeless. But they could still have a bit of pleasure, couldn't they? It was the only childhood they would have – let them enjoy as much of it as they could.

Stella glanced up and saw him leaning on the gate. For a moment, she sat quite still, her eyes huge. Then she jumped up and ran towards him, shrieking at the top of her voice.

'Daddy! It's *Daddy!*'

The others stopped what they were doing. Muriel abandoned her dolls and ran after her sister, hair blowing round her face. The boys stopped kicking their ball and stood a little awkwardly, unsure whether to greet the stranger or melt away. Mrs Mudge appeared at the kitchen door, wiping her hands in her apron, and Mr Beckett popped out from the shed, where he had been mending a puncture in his bicycle.

Mike held out his arms to his daughters and they scrambled up the gate and flung themselves at him. He held them close, half laughing, half crying, and Tim and Keith glanced at each other and turned their backs, studying the grass with sudden attention.

Mrs Mudge watched, her own eyes damp, and the vicar came along the garden path to stand at her side. He smiled and spoke quietly.

'A cup of tea, I think, don't you? And some of your lemonade for the children. It's good to have something to celebrate, for a change.'

For a change! the housekeeper thought as she went indoors to put the kettle on. Celebration was one of the guiding principles of Mr Beckett's life. Few were the days when he did not find something, however small, worth celebrating – the first touch of autumn, the first leaf of spring, the first winter fire, the first warm day. But this was something special.

Mike Simmons came home all too rarely from his Merchant Navy ship, and for the two motherless girls he was their only true family. Hard as she and the vicar might try, they could never really make up for all that Stella and Muriel had lost. Brief though his time might be, it must be made as memorable as they all knew how, to give him and the girls something special to remember.

Mrs Mudge put on the kettle and delved into the back of a large cupboard to find the tin of ham she had put away from the last American food parcel that had arrived at Bridge End. It was supposed to be saved for Christmas. But what better time to have it than now, with a few of the vicar's own tomatoes, to show Mike Simmons just how pleased they all were to see him here?

Mike Simmons' few days at Bridge End were soon over and he went back to sea, feeling an ache in his heart that was even worse than when he'd had to part with Kathy. He took the girls to Southampton to show them his ship, and borrowed an old van to take them for a run in the New Forest. There were still a few places where you could get down to the shore, and they sat on the beach gazing out to sea.

'Are you going away again soon?' Stella asked wistfully, and he nodded.

'Tomorrow.' He felt the tears gather in his throat, thinking of the last time he had said goodbye to his family and feeling a bitter longing for Kathy and their baby son.

The girls said nothing. A convoy was leaving Southampton now, merchant ships surrounded by a protective flotilla of destroyers bristling with guns. They watched as the ships steamed away down the arm of the Solent.

'I expect there's a lot of daddies on those ships,' Muriel observed. 'It's a pity their boys and girls aren't here to wave to them.'

'We could wave for them,' Stella suggested, and stood up, barefoot on the stony beach. 'Let's do that, and perhaps someone will wave for us when our Daddy's sailing away.'

Muriel jumped up beside her sister and together, hand in hand, they made their way down the beach to the edge of the water. They stood, their backs to their father, waving at the ships that were steaming slowly towards the horizon. Stella took a handkerchief from her pocket, and it fluttered in the breeze.

They stood for a long while, watching until the convoy had finally disappeared, and then they turned and came back to where Mike sat, his arms looped around his knees, his eyes dark.

'There,' Stella said in a tone of satisfaction. 'Now they've been waved to, properly.' She wound her arms around her father's neck. 'When you go away, you'll be able to imagine us here waving to you. We thought of you all the time we were waving, didn't we, Mu?'

Muriel nodded. And Mike, looking at them through a sudden blur of tears, knew that he would indeed, as his ship sailed down the Solent next morning, be able to look back and see the figures of his two daughters, waving to him from this small and lonely beach. As if they had left some imprint of themselves in the air; as if their presence here could not be erased.

He shook his head and scrambled to his feet. 'I'll do that,' he said. 'And I'll wave back, all right? And now we'd better get back to Bridge End. Mrs Mudge said she was going to make something special for tea, and I don't want to miss it. And I promised Tim we'd have a game of cricket before bedtime.'

With long, swift strides, he set off up the beach, before the girls could see the tears on his face.

The sirens continued to sound. The blitz was over – for the time being, it appeared, anyway – but there were still minor raids almost every night. One of them dropped its bombs close to the Spencers' farm at Bishop's Waltham. The explosion uprooted trees and flung them into the next field, terrifying the cows and disrupting milk production for the rest of the week. The hens, fastened into their coops for the night, had hysterics and flung themselves at the walls, bruising their wings and feet. In the house, an old grandfather clock which had not worked for years, suddenly chimed twelve and began to tick steadily, keeping perfect time.

One of the cows was badly injured and had to be put down. Betty, Yvonne and Erica mourned her as if she had been a personal friend.

'She was the first cow I ever milked,' Betty said. 'Dennis showed me what to do.' Her eyes filled as she thought of that first morning, with Dennis close to her in the byre. 'It doesn't seem fair,' she said fiercely, dashing the tears away. 'They're making war on *cows* now.'

The aircraft was shot down over Bridge End. It crashed in one of Mr Callaway's fields and the children dashed out to see it. Brian Collins swaggered by the gate, taking a proprietorial attitude because he lived on the farm.

'You can't come into the field,' he said bossily. 'There's a policeman here guarding it till the soldiers get here.'

'Can't we have a bit as a souvenir?' Tim asked longingly.

'I'd like a bit with a swastika on it.'

'I'm having that bit,' Brian said instantly. 'Anyway, I don't suppose they'll let people have bits. It's secret.'

'Why? Why is it secret? It's a German plane. Anyone can see it, anyway.'

'You can only have it if Mr Callaway says so,' Brian said, changing tack. 'It's his field so it's his plane. Anyway, if you come in you're trespassing.'

Tim wandered away. He had never got on with Brian Collins and didn't feel like arguing with him now. He climbed up a wooded slope and sat on a tree-stump, his chin in his hands, staring down at the scene below and imagining the excitement of the chase the night before. He and Keith had heard the planes overhead and longed to be outside, but Mr Beckett had forbidden them. He had made everyone go down into the old cellar, and had sat with his arms around Stella, while Muriel crouched close to Mrs Mudge.

I wish I was old enough to join the Air Force, Tim thought. I could have been up there, flying a Spitfire, shooting down the enemy. I could win medals. I could help win the war.

It didn't seem fair that Brian Collins would get first pick of souvenirs from the wrecked aeroplane.

There were more people in the field now, policemen and soldiers from a nearby camp. They approached the wreckage cautiously, as if expecting someone to open fire on them. But Tim could see that there was no one in the mangled cockpit. The plane must have exploded when it landed, for there was twisted metal everywhere. Probably the pilot had baled out, he thought, and felt a sudden nervous excitement. He might be lurking in these very woods, waiting to pounce.

Tim got up quickly. He felt as though there were eyes on him, watching from the undergrowth. He looked all around, forcing himself to keep still and listen as Reg had taught him when they were looking for birds' nests. His heart was thumping.

Something rustled high in one of the trees. Tim gasped

and jumped, feeling as if his heart had leapt right into his throat. He stared upwards, peering through the brown and yellow leaves, and then relaxed as he saw a squirrel gazing down at him. It chattered angrily, and an acorn fell at Tim's feet.

There's no one here, he thought. Any parachutist would have gone by now. He wouldn't have waited to be caught.

But suppose he was injured? Or caught up in a tree? He might be lying somewhere quite close, waiting to be discovered. *Tim* might be the one to find him.

A parachutist. A prisoner. That would be better than any old bit of a plane.

His nervousness only partially replaced by excitement, Tim began to creep cautiously through the trees, his eyes moving from side to side. He kept along the side of the hill, within sight of the field where the wreckage lay, feeling a kind of comfort in the presence of the soldiers down below. They were clustered round the plane now, examining it, picking amongst the bits of wreckage that were flung all over the field. One of them was standing by the gate, keeping out the villagers and children who had gathered to stare.

Tim thought of his triumph as he led his prisoner down the hill towards them. He was convinced now that the pilot had parachuted out of his plane moments before it landed, and was hiding in this very wood. It stood to reason, after all. There was nowhere else for him to hide. He must be here.

Suppose he was armed. Tim hesitated, then shrugged the thought away. Pilots weren't armed, what would be the point? Pistols were no use when you were up in the sky. They had machine-guns in their planes. Besides, once they'd landed in enemy territory they were bound to be caught and taken prisoner. Resistance, he thought grandly, would be useless.

The phrase, gleaned from a Biggles book he had been given one Christmas, struck his imagination and he repeated it several times as he crept through the trees. It would be exactly the right thing to say to the pilot when he discovered him.

Something fluttered from a tree ahead of him, and he stopped, his heart bounding again. It looked like a piece of cloth. He approached cautiously, and stopped about two feet away, staring at it.

It was a bluish grey. The sort of colour a British airman wore, only slightly darker. Tim gazed at it and swallowed. Maybe the pilot really was in these woods. His heart raced and he felt suddenly frightened. Suppose the German wasn't injured after all. He'd be a lot stronger than Tim. He might not *want* to be captured.

Nervously, he glanced again from side to side. The impulse to run was almost too strong to resist. He looked down into the field again, watching the figures of the soldiers as they moved about. They looked very far away.

Suddenly, it didn't seem such a good idea after all to try to take a prisoner.

There was another rustle from the trees and Tim gave a frightened little half-scream and turned to run. Maybe it was just a squirrel, but he wasn't staying to find out. He was going to go straight down to the field, tell the soldiers he was sure the airman was in the woods, let them capture him. Tim would still get the credit for finding him. He could still hold up his head in front of Brian Collins and the others.

He scurried down the slope, his legs shaking, tripped over a twisted tree-root and fell flat on his face in a pile of leaves.

For a few moments he was too winded to move. He shut his eyes tightly, half expecting to feel a heavy hand on his shoulder, convinced that he had been pursued. But nothing happened, and as his breath slowly returned he opened his eyes and turned his head.

There was no one near him. But lying on the ground, quite close to his face, there was a glove.

Tim stared at it. It was a brown leather glove, quite large, the sort a soldier might wear.

Or an airman.

His certainty that the pilot had parachuted into the woods returned. Still lying on the leaves, he reached out a hand and touched the glove. If it really was German, it would be a smashing souvenir. As good as a bit of plane, any day.

With two fingers, he pulled the glove towards him. And then stopped, his heart jittering all over again, a sick bile rising in his throat as he stared at what he had found.

There was no doubt that it was the German pilot's glove. His hand was still inside.

'Poor little chap,' Mrs Mudge said. 'What a thing for a little boy to find. He was sick three times in the night and when he did go to sleep he dreamt that hands were coming after him.'

'The pilot must have been blown to pieces when the plane exploded,' Mr Beckett said. 'The soldiers found most of the remains but there's still a chance that parts will be found by children. They'd better not go near that field for a while.'

For Tim, the war had abruptly stopped being a game, an adventure, and become horribly real. When the other children, their ghoulish imagination protected by not having seen the reality, demanded details, he turned on them in fury and then ran away. He threw Keith's souvenir – a fragment of twisted metal with sharp edges – out of the window, where it landed in the cabbages Mrs Mudge had planted in what had once been a flowerbed. He lay awake at night, listening to the distant wail of sirens over Southampton and Portsmouth, to the *crump* of exploding bombs.

He began to worry about his parents and baby sister. 'How do you *know* they won't get hit?' he asked Mr Beckett, echoing Rose's own tormenting doubts. 'God isn't looking after other people. How do you know he's looking after *my* mum and dad?'

Mr Beckett shook his head. 'We can't know, Tim, I'm afraid. We just have to trust – to have faith.'

Tim stared at him. He thought of all the people who had

trusted, and found their trust betrayed. People in Portsmouth who had been bombed out or killed. Stella and Muriel's mother and baby brother. Some of his own friends in the village, who had been called out of class to be told that their fathers had been lost in action.

'I don't see what good faith does,' he said flatly. '*I* don't trust him, not a bit.'

The vicar sighed. He looked at Tim's white face and haunted eyes and longed to give him comfort. Faith in a higher being – call it God, or what you would – could be such a strength at times like this. It kept you bolstered against the terrible things that were happening. But once shattered, it left you very small and defenceless, without hope in a world that was tearing itself to pieces around you. He had to pray hard, night and morning, for strength to keep his own faith. What chance did a boy like Tim have?

'Try to hold on,' he said, putting his hand on Tim's shoulder. 'I know it's hard – but don't turn your face away just yet. You feel as though you're falling the dark, and the rope you were holding is falling with you. But keep your hands tightly around it, Tim, and you'll find it *will* hold you up, in the end.'

Tim let his eyelids droop, veiling his glance. He did not want Mr Beckett to know that he was right – that Tim felt exactly as if he were falling down a long, dark hole, with nothing to stop him. His fingers moved, as if he were indeed reaching for a rope. But in the darkness of his mind, there was nothing there, and he turned away abruptly.

'I wish I could go home,' he said, his voice angry. 'I'm fed up with being here.'

Mr Beckett sighed again. He watched Tim walk away across the old lawn, his shoulders hunched miserably. He felt the weariness of disappointment and failure weigh down on him.

I'm too old to be in charge of children, he thought. I imagined I could win their trust by becoming one of them, by entering into their world. I imagined I could be a buffer between them and the war, help them to enjoy their precious childhood, and grow strong and healthy in mind and body in my care.

I thought I knew best. And now Tim has shown me the arrogance of my thoughts. How can I, an old man, expect to win the heart of a child? How can I hope to show him the love of God, when every day he sees before him the face of evil?

Tim's sister Rose, too, was feeling restless.

Now that she was back at home, she found life different from what she had expected. Somehow, although she knew that the boys wouldn't be there and baby Maureen would, although she knew very well that there would be air-raids and sirens and nights in the shelter, she hadn't fully realised any of these things. She had come back unconsciously expecting home to be as it had been before the war, before Maureen was born, when it had been just her and the boys and Mum and Dad. She had somehow expected that she herself would be as she had been then, the twelve-year-old Rose still enjoying her childhood. Instead, she was fourteen and had lost interest in dolls and skipping games. And she did not know what to be interested in in their place.

Even her desire to look after the baby was beginning to leave her. Maureen was no longer like a living doll, to be bathed and dressed and pushed in a pram. She was an active toddler, her fingers into everything, and she never stopped talking or asking questions. Rose would play with her for a while, but then she grew irritated, and she resented having to take Maureen about with her.

Worst of all, and making everything harder to bear, her life was overshadowed by the dread of air-raids, of bombing, of invasion.

'They're not coming here,' Jess said. 'We've kept them out so far and we'll go on keeping them out. How could they land? All the beaches are mined. And the RAF won't let them get their planes in.'

But planes did come, night after night. The blitz had abated but there were still plenty of raids. You could never be sure it wasn't going to start again.

School was erratic. There were lessons for Rose and other girls of her age, held in people's front rooms. You went once or twice a week and had homework to do the rest of the time. Rose was bored with them and impatient to leave. Her friend Joy was officially at work now, in her parents' shop, and it had already made a difference. She seemed more grown-up, sure of herself.

'You take that shorthand and typing course,' Frank said to his daughter. 'I don't want you working in a shop. It's all right for Joy, it's her family business, but we've got nothing like that. An office is what'll suit you, the Civil Service.'

The Civil Service would keep her out of the Forces, but he didn't tell her that. Girls of Rose's age were unpredictable and obstinate and if she thought that was what he had in mind she'd be just as likely to fail her exams on purpose.

Still, she enjoyed the typing and sat by the wireless every night taking down the News in shorthand. Perhaps working in an office might not be so bad after all.

There were bright spots amongst all the talk of the Malta convoys, British restaurants, and Russia. There were still cinemas to go to, and Frank allowed his daughter to start attending church dances with Joy, although he still forbade the use of lipstick. And on the last Saturday in September, the famous actress Anna Neagle came, in a drift of silk and perfume, to open the RAOC fete at Hilsea.

'Anna Neagle!' Rose exclaimed when she heard the news. 'She was Queen Victoria in that film we saw. She's gorgeous.'

She and Joy went down to the main railway station and joined the huge throng gathered to see the film star arrive. They tried to get her autograph, but the crowd was too big and they watched instead as the actress drove off in an Army car to have lunch at the officers' mess. By the time she reached the fairground in the afternoon, the girls were there to listen to the speeches and cheer as she told them how pleased she was to be in Portsmouth, and to coax them to spend as much as they could afford that afternoon 'to help get the war over as soon as possible'.

'I'd like to be a film star,' Joy sighed. 'Better than marking up newspapers. I'm fed up with the shop.'

'Well, at least you've got a job,' Rose said. 'My dad hits the roof if I talk about leaving school.'

'My dad hits the roof if I talk. He's an old misery these days and all Mum says is I've got to make allowances because of what he's been through.' Joy scowled. 'I know it was awful, what happened to him, but he's alive, isn't he? He's home again. I'm fed up with making allowances. I've got a life too, haven't I?'

There had been yet another row with her father that morning, when she and Alice had been marking up newspapers. He'd come downstairs, unshaven and bleary-eyed in his pyjamas, to complain that the papers weren't ready, that the boys would be here soon to start their deliveries, that it had never taken so long when *he* had done it. Joy, exasperated and indignant, had turned on him and said he was welcome to do it again, she wouldn't mind staying in bed for a change.

She'd slammed out of the room then and stormed up to her bedroom, trying not to feel guilty at leaving her mother to finish the work, trying not to hear her father's voice as he wept in the room below, trying not to see the pictures his broken words conjured up in her mind.

'What am I to do? How can I find my way back? I feel a part of me is still out there, lost in those black, stinking waters, when all it wants is to be here with you and Joy, happy together as we used to be. Oh, my liebchen, *what is to become of us? Where is it all to end . . .?'*

Joy had pushed her head under her pillow. She couldn't bear the despair in her father's voice. She couldn't bear the anguish it aroused in her own heart. Instead, she took refuge in anger and disappointment, and found a wilful pleasure in the bright red lipstick she smeared across her mouth, and in marching out of the house that afternoon to go to the fair with Rose.

The two girls wandered amongst the sideshows. The RAOC, which was raising money for its Comforts Fund, had devised a number of ingenious methods of parting them from their money, and the young soldiers called out to invite them to patronise their particular stalls.

'Have a go on the Hoopla, sweetheart?' 'Bowl for a pig, come on, you never know your luck.' 'Try your luck with me, ducky, we've got some smashing prizes today.'

The two girls threw hoopla rings without success but got a bar of chocolate each from the Lucky Dip. At the next stall, they found Carol Glaister rolling pennies. You set the little wooden ramp at the edge of a board marked out in numbered squares and hoped your penny would roll down to land in one. If the penny did not touch the sides of the square, you won that number of pennies back. Most people instantly played them again and lost, but a few canny ones collected up their winnings and went off in triumph to spend them on another attraction.

It didn't really matter. One way or another, all the money was spent at the fair and went into the Comforts Fund. Nobody went home with more money than they'd come with.

'I won sixpence just now,' Carol said. She had a glass vase under one arm. 'And look what I got on the lucky dip. Mum'll be ever so pleased.'

Rose and Joy eyed the vase. It was a virulent shade of green, with crinkly edges. It would just suit Ethel Glaister's front room.

For quite a long time, Carol Glaister and Joy hadn't had much to say to each other. There were almost two years' difference between them, a long time when you were under twelve, but the difference didn't seem so much now. But mostly their constraint was caused by Ethel's antagonism towards the Brunners. It was difficult for the girls to be friends when their mothers were such bitter enemies.

But on this sunny September afternoon, with people milling about all over the field laughing and enjoying themselves, war and bitterness seemed very far away. Carol and Joy looked at each other and smiled, a little uncertainly, and after a moment's hesitation Carol fell in beside them as they sauntered through the fair.

'Have a go at the coconut shy?' a cheeky-eyed young private suggested. 'There's a special prize if you knock one off.'

'Oh, and what's that?' Carol challenged him. She was wearing a pink blouse of her mother's and looked older in it. And she'd rolled her fair hair into a bang at the front. 'Anyway, they're not proper coconuts. They're just balls with bits of matting stuck on them.'

The soldier grinned again. 'Can't help that, darling, the monkeys were on strike. Come on, have a go and I'll give you a special prize anyway.'

Carol gave him a saucy look. 'I want to know what it is first.'

'It comes better as a surprise.'

'Pooh,' she scoffed, 'I can guess just what sort a surprise *you'd* give me! No thanks, we'll spend our money somewhere else. Come on, Rose.' She linked one arm through Rose's and the other through Joy's and stalked off, her nose in the air. The soldier laughed and Rose heard a wolf-whistle float through the air behind them.

'They've got swinging boats over there,' Joy said. 'Real big ones. Only you need two, and Rose says they make her feel sick.'

'I'll come with you,' Carol offered. 'Tell you what – there's going to be a dance tonight. I've got tickets. D'you want to come?'

Joy accepted eagerly. But Rose shook her head. She knew that Frank would never let her go to a dance with soldiers, and in any case she wasn't sure she wanted to go. She was enjoying the fete but felt nervous at the way some of the young men were looking at her. Just lately, her figure had started to develop and she felt embarrassed by it, convinced that everyone was staring.

She watched as Joy and Carol, laughing now like old friends, climbed into the swinging boats. And she felt suddenly lonely, as if she were being left behind.

Ethel Glaister made no demur when Carol announced that she was going to the dance. She simply shrugged and said,

'Don't you go pinching my stockings. Bare legs are good enough for a girl like you. Anyway, I'm going out myself.'

'Where?' Carol asked. She had given her mother the green vase and Ethel had been grudgingly pleased with it and stood it on the little table in the front window so that the neighbours could see. 'Are you going to the dance too?'

'Not likely. And it's none of your business where I'm going. Just out with a friend.' Ethel extracted two pilchards from a tin and laid them on Carol's plate. 'And I shan't be late back, so don't think you can hang around the streets afterwards. I want you back here at ten o'clock on the dot, see?'

'Ten o'clock?' Carol wailed. 'But the dance doesn't finish till eleven.'

'Never mind that. Ten o'clock's your time. It'll be dark by then as it is. Mind you walk home with Joy, and don't let no soldiers bring you back.'

'Why not?' Carol had half made an assignation with the soldier on the penny-rolling stall. The thought of being walked home after the dance had brought a peculiar, tingling excitement.

'Never you mind why not,' Ethel said sharply. 'Just do what I say, or there won't be no dance for you. Do you want some beetroot?'

'No thanks,' Carol said in a sulky tone, but she dared not say any more. Her mother was quite capable of refusing to allow her out, despite the green vase. And she desperately wanted to go to the dance.

She dressed carefully, in a pink crocheted jersey with a frilly neckline and a short, swirling skirt. Her bare legs were tanned and looked better without stockings. Her hair, naturally fair as Ethel's had once been and without the brassiness that her mother's had now, curved in a bob under her ears. She had a stub of lipstick that Ethel no longer used, and she smeared it thickly on her mouth.

'How do I look?' she asked Joy when she reached the newsagent's shop. It was closed now, so she went round to the back door and found the Brunners just finishing their tea.

'Smashing.' Joy had curled her hair again and borrowed one of Alice's blouses. It was made of green satin and looked very sophisticated. Carol gazed at it with envy. Mrs Brunner had probably brought it home from Germany on one of their visits to Mr Brunner's family before the war.

Alice Brunner felt a touch of the same awkwardness that her daughter had experienced with Carol Glaister. She wondered what Ethel had said when she knew that the two girls were going to the dance together. But Carol seemed perfectly natural, and Joy was happy enough about it, especially as Rose Budd couldn't go.

She watched them set off, chattering excitedly, and turned to her husband with a wistful smile, hoping to coax him into a better mood.

'Our Joy's first dance,' she said. 'She's growing up, Heinrich.'

'This war is making everyone grow up,' he replied. 'How can children be children when they are surrounded by hatred and destruction?'

Alice sighed. Heinrich was taking such a long time to get over his experiences. Sometimes, she wondered if he would ever completely recover.

'Well, they enjoyed this afternoon,' she said. 'It seemed like peacetime again, having a fete and someone like Anna Neagle to open it. And then a dance to go to this evening – it's time Joy started to have some fun.'

'And if there's a raid? What then?'

'There's a shelter there,' Alice said firmly, quelling her own fears on that account. 'They'll be looked after all right. It's a properly organised dance, Heinrich. And we can't keep Joy in all the time. She's got to be allowed a bit of independence.'

She got up to clear the table. If there was one thing she'd learned during those difficult months while Heinrich had been lost, it was that you had to keep busy, or your thoughts could drive you mad.

'So what's your name, then?' the young soldier asked, whirling Joy on to the floor.

'Joy.'

'That's a nice name.' He was holding her close, his uniform scratchy against her jersey. 'Mine's Artie. I come from Kent.'

'Kent? Isn't that where they grow hops?' She was feeling slightly breathless, squeezed up against him.

'That's right. Garden of England. Best place in the world.' He grinned down at her. 'Mind you, it's not bad in Portsmouth tonight. Bit hot in here, though. How about going outside for a bit of air?'

'All right,' Joy said, and when they came to the doorway they stopped dancing and he led her through the blackout curtain and outside the hall.

'Over here.'

There were quite a few couples outside the hall in the darkness. Joy could just see their dim outlines and hear their whispers. They were all very close together, and she felt suddenly nervous.

'Look, I don't want –'

'This'll do.' He pulled her into a shadowy corner and put his arms round her. The buttons on his tunic pressed against her breasts. 'How about a little kiss?'

Joy tried to wriggle free. 'I told you, I don't want –'

'Yes, you do.' His face was very close, his breath hot on her cheek. 'It's what you come to dances for, innit? Come on, purse up.'

'No.' She ducked her head. 'Let's go back inside.' One of his hands was moving over her body, feeling the shape of it. 'Don't do that.'

'Like playing hard to get, do you?' He squeezed her breast and Joy gave a little squeak. 'Oh, you like that, don't you.'

'No. No, I don't. It hurts.' Joy's figure had only lately developed and her breasts were tender. 'I don't like you touching me there. I want to go back inside.'

'Now look,' he said, 'you was pleased enough to get the tickets. What did you expect?'

'I came to dance.' She pulled herself out of his arms. 'I'm going back.'

'There's a name for girls like you,' he said angrily, but Joy was already on her way inside. She pushed through the thick curtain, her face hot, and looked around for Carol.

Carol was dancing with a sailor. He had tousled brown hair and looked about eighteen. He had approached her shyly when Joy had gone to dance with the soldier. He had a Scottish accent, which Carol found intriguing.

'I'm no' much of a dancer. You'll have to teach me.'

'Oh, it's easy.' Carol loved dancing. She had been taught several steps by her mother and always went to the church dances, where several of the older men had taken her as a partner. She showed the sailor how to hold her and then explained the steps.

'You have to listen to the music. You're supposed to dance in time with the beat, see? *One*, two, three, *one*, two, three – and you're supposed to guide me so that I don't bump into anyone.' She giggled. 'I haven't got eyes in the back of my head.'

'I havenae got eyes in my feet, either,' he said. 'How'm I supposed to see what they're doing and steer at the same time?' But he was picking up the idea. 'Och, that wasnae bad, was it? We got all the way round!'

'You'll be a second Fred Astaire.' Their feet suddenly became tangled and they tripped and almost fell. 'Whoops – spoke too soon there, didn't we! It's all right. Just stop and wait for the music.'

The tune came to an end just as they reached the seats where Joy and Carol had been sitting. There was no sign of Joy and as the sailor hesitated, Carol sat down and patted the chair beside her. She gave him a friendly smile.

'What's your name? Mine's Carol.'

'Roderick MacPherson. My mates call me Mac but at home I'm called Roddy.'

'Have you been in the Navy long?'

He shook his head. 'I've only just finished my training on Whale Island. I'm waiting for a ship.'

'I bet you can't wait to get to sea,' Carol said. 'My brother wants to go in the Navy. I daresay he'll be called up soon.'

The sailor said nothing. She glanced at him and was surprised to see a look of misery on his face. He was staring at the floor and kicking a scrap of paper about with his toe.

'I didnae want to join up, not really,' he burst out suddenly. 'I was supposed to be going to university. I never wanted to be in the Navy at all.'

'Oh.' Carol felt nonplussed. She remembered her mother talking about Betty Chapman's young man, Dennis. 'You mean you're a CO? A pacifist?'

'No, I'm not. I just don't want to fight. I won't be any good at it. I know I won't.'

'Well, you won't have to. You're not in the Army.'

'I'm a gunner,' he said flatly, and she was silenced. 'I'll be shooting at other ships. And aircraft. Why should I have to do that? I was supposed to go to university.'

'Yes, but everyone's having to help the war effort,' Carol said. 'Lots of people have had to give up their jobs to go into the Forces. They're even calling up women.'

Roddy shrugged. 'And how many of them want to go? Tell me that.'

'Well, probably a lot of them don't, but they haven't got any choice, have they? I mean, even if you are a CO, you still have to go in front of a board, and they don't always –'

'They havenae got any choice,' he repeated. 'That's just it.' He gave her a desperate look. 'I *wanted* a choice, just to live my own life. I want to do something I'd be good at. What's so wrong with that?'

'Nothing. Nothing's wrong with it.' Carol felt a sudden huge sadness and pity for the boy beside her. Until now, she had only known people whose lives were accustomed to adapting to circumstance, who had ordinary jobs and ordinary lives, who had drifted automatically from school into the first job that came along, into the first marriage that came along, and had never had the chance to make choices. They might grumble at the direction their lives were taking now but they wouldn't seriously complain, because they were accustomed to being told what to do.

'And now I've got to go to sea and shoot guns,' he said. 'I never wanted to do that.'

'Why did you become a gunner?' she asked. 'Wasn't there something else you could have done?'

'Och, there were a thousand things I could have done, but they don't ask you that. They give you eye tests and medicals and they look at your records and see what your education is, and then they decide. Or maybe they just pick it out with a pin. And once they've decided, you don't argue. It's lesson number one, that is: never argue. You can forget having a mind of your own.'

The music was beginning again. Carol glanced around, wondering where Joy was. She felt sorry for the sailor but she didn't want to sit here listening to his moans, she wanted to dance.

'Look, I'm sorry,' he said. 'You're fed up with me. I'll go away.'

'No – no, don't do that.' She caught his sleeve. He was wearing a matelot's thin white summer shirt with a square neckline and short sleeves. His arms were brown. 'Let's try this one. It's a rhumba.' The hot South American rhythm was already catching her mind and she grinned at him and jiggled her body. 'Come on.'

Roddy got up. He watched her and watched the other dancers. Then he took a couple of experimental steps.

'That's it! That's right!' Carol laughed and grabbed his hand. 'I thought you said you couldn't dance.'

'I canna. Not this sort, anyway – I can do Scottish dancing.' There was nothing wrong with his sense of rhythm, she thought, letting herself go in the elation of the dance. 'Hey, it's nae so bad, is it?'

'Not so bad at all.' She swung close and then let him catch her in his arms. 'You know, I reckon you're a natural. We could be good partners.'

'Aye,' he said, holding her close and looking down into her face, 'I reckon you're right.'

Carol danced all the way home that night. Hardly noticing Joy's silence, she floated along the moonlit streets, her arms lifted as if the young sailor were still within their embrace. She chattered dreamily.

'I didn't even like him all that much to begin with. I mean, he looked all right but he's only eighteen, just a boy really, and when we got talking he seemed so miserable. Homesick, I reckon. He lives near Edinburgh. I thought he was just sorry for himself. But he turned out really nice. He's got lovely eyes. They're a really dark brown, like velvet.'

Joy said nothing. After coming in from her encounter with the soldier, she had hidden for a while in the ladies' cloakroom, soaking lavatory paper in cold water and pressing it to her eyes. An ATS officer had come in and glanced at her curiously, and Joy had bolted into the cubicle and stayed there until the woman had gone again. After a while, she put on some more lipstick and came out but although Carol had waved and beckoned her over, she hadn't felt like dancing again. She sat on the chair and watched, waiting for the time to pass until they could go home.

'Did you enjoy yourself?' Carol asked, noticing her silence at last. 'I saw you with that soldier. What happened to him?'

Joy shrugged. 'Dunno. Went off.'

'Didn't anyone else ask you?' Carol asked. 'There was plenty of blokes there.'

'I didn't feel like it.'

Carol shook her head. 'What's the matter with you? I thought it was smashing.'

'It was all right,' Joy said, determined not to tell the other girl of her humiliation. 'I just didn't feel like dancing any more, that's all.'

'Oh well,' Carol said, shrugging, 'so long as you enjoyed it. Here, there's another one on in a fortnight. You'll come with me, won't you?'

'I might.' Just at the moment, there was nothing Joy felt less like doing, but having professed to have enjoyed herself, she could think of no excuse not to go again. 'I'll have to see what Mum and Dad say.'

'Roddy says he'll get the tickets,' Carol said. 'And guess what – he's asked me to go to the pictures with him.'

'The pictures?' Joy stared at her friend. She could see her smiling in the moonlight. 'But that's like a – a proper boyfriend.'

'Well, so what? I can have a boyfriend, can't I? I'm nearly sixteen.' Carol lifted her nose, looking suddenly very much like her mother. 'We're going to see *Pimpernel Smith*. It's Leslie Howard – you know, the one who was in *Gone With The Wind*. I think he's smashing.'

'I liked Clark Gable better. When he said "Frankly, I don't give a damn".' Joy shivered and giggled. 'His eyes make me feel all funny.'

'Roddy's eyes make me feel like that,' Carol confided. 'Did that soldier try and kiss you?'

Joy nodded. Her mood, which had begun to lift, was deflated again. Carol eyed her for a moment, then slipped her arm through Joy's.

'You don't want to take no notice of that. They all try it on. It don't mean nothing.'

'I didn't like it,' Joy said. 'He was too rough. I don't want boys pawing me.'

'Well, don't go outside with 'em, then,' Carol said bluntly. 'You don't have to let it stop you having fun. Just say you'd rather dance, and have a good time.' They were almost outside the shop now, and paused. 'You will come to the next one, won't you?'

'I don't know. It's all right for you, you've got a proper boyfriend now. I'll be on my own.'

'No, you won't. I'll ask Roddy to find you a partner. Anyway, you'll never have a boyfriend if you don't go out and find one.'

Joy sighed. For most of the evening she had been wishing that she hadn't dressed up in Alice's blouse and come to the dance. She'd been looking forward to her first time out as a young woman, instead of a girl, but the episode with the soldier had undermined her confidence. She was no longer sure she was ready, and yearned to be indoors with her parents, or playing Ludo with Rose.

But even as she thought of it, she knew that it was no longer enough. Home was no longer the comforting place it had been. And she had crossed some invisible dividing line tonight, had entered a different world. Like it or not, it was the world she would live in from now on, and she could not slip back into childhood.

'Say you'll come,' Carol urged.

But Joy would make no promises. She shook her head and said, 'I'll see', and then slipped down the little side alley to the back door.

Carol looked after her for a moment. Then she tossed her head so that her hair flew round her face, and danced all the way down October Street.

CHAPTER EIGHT

Olive returned to Portsmouth in late November, having completed her training as a gunner girl. To her delight, she was posted to the anti-aircraft battery on Southsea Common.

By that time, the war had moved on. In Russia, Leningrad was still under siege and Moscow battling for its life. The onset of the cruel Russian winter seemed to be the city's only hope, for despite Stalin's pleas there was no chance yet of a Second Front. Germany was still too great a threat to Britain and the RAF was fully occupied in attacking the major cities. In one night, nearly four hundred aircraft flew to bomb Berlin, Cologne and Mannheim. One in ten did not return.

There had been a thousand air raids on the island of Malta when the *Ark Royal*, one of the Navy's proudest ships, which carried load after load of Hurricanes there in its defence, was finally sunk off Gibraltar, thus bringing true at last one of Lord Haw-Haw's constant jibes. The only consolation was that almost the whole crew was saved.

The world's attention was turning also to the threat of Japan against America. War between the two countries seemed almost inevitable; it was little more than a matter of when and how it would begin. Winston Churchill announced that such an involvement would be followed 'within the hour' by a British declaration of war against Japan. To many people, it could come only as a relief to have America fighting beside them, even though it meant yet another enemy to be confronted. With the sinking of the first US Navy ship off Iceland, war against Germany too seemed to come closer and the anxiety increased.

The tension spread everywhere. It was like a creeping fog, slithering into the most private places, the most intimate situations, and it cast a deep chill over everyone's lives. Nothing seemed to be the same any more.

But there were still things to be cheerful about, Jess observed. 'Potato Pete' had arrived, easing the shortage of potatoes, and now they were plentiful enough to be used all the time. The price was fixed at a penny a pound and Lord Woolton was recommending that they be used to make pastry, and even mashed potato sandwiches! He also extolled the virtues of carrots and swedes. Carrots were supposed to help you see in the dark, which would help in the blackout, and it was said that they were eaten in huge quantities by night-flying pilots. And tinned food was put on 'points' rationing, and everyone got sixteen points a month, to use as they wanted.

Derek managed to get a weekend pass when Olive came back to Portsmouth, and they had a passionate reunion in Olive's bedroom. But even their lovemaking seemed tainted somehow by fears and anxieties that could not be escaped.

'Oh Derek, I feel as if I've been away for years,' Olive said, pressing herself close against him. It didn't seem possible that he was actually here, in her arms, that she could look into his eyes and run her fingers through his hair. 'I thought the time was never going to pass.'

'North Wales is a hell of a long way away,' he agreed. 'It could have been the North Pole, as far as I was concerned. What was it really like, Livvy?'

Olive had tried to keep her letters as cheerful as possible, but now that she was with him she couldn't pretend any more. She turned down her mouth and wrinkled her nose.

'It was horrible. There's nothing much there, you know – just sea and cliffs and awful black rocks. Might be all right in summer, I suppose, but it's not nice beaches like it is here. And they all speak Welsh, did you know that? It was like being in a foreign country.'

'Didn't they lay on anything for you? Dances and things?' There was a slightly over-casual note to Derek's voice, as if he hoped they hadn't, and Olive felt a faint twinge of resentment. They had dances at the camp in Wiltshire, didn't they? Why shouldn't she have a bit of fun as well? Didn't he trust her?

She shook her head. 'They didn't seem interested. Probably thought we'd attract the Germans and get them all bombed! There were a few dances in the camp but us girls weren't allowed to dance with the officers, even if they asked us, so it wasn't much good. You soon find out who counts for anything in the Army.' She looked at his face and felt ashamed of her sourness. 'Anyway, I didn't want to go, not without you.'

Derek hugged her. 'You poor thing. You've had a miserable time.'

'Well, it was quite interesting, all the same,' Olive said. 'The work, I mean. We did aircraft recognition and we learnt to work out what height the planes were flying at.'

'You did that? I didn't know they trained girls for that sort of thing.'

'Why shouldn't they?' she challenged him. 'We've got brains as well, you know, just the same as the men. We aren't made of cotton-wool.'

'All right, all right, no need to be so touchy. How did you do it then – how did you work out the height?'

'Well, they used to fly across the sea, pulling a big sleeve behind them. You take bearings, see, and work it out with maths. It's not that hard. And once we'd got their height worked out, we'd tell the gunners and they'd fire.'

'Trying to hit the planes?' Derek asked in surprise, and Olive laughed and shook her head.

'Don't be daft! They were aiming at the sleeves. It was awful at first – they didn't hit a single one the whole week. I kept thinking, suppose it was Portsmouth we were defending, and we'd let all those planes get through. It was our fault, you see, the gunner-girls, for not giving them the right directions.'

'But you were all right in the end.'

'Oh yes,' Olive said proudly. 'I passed out top in our group. We hit every one.' Her face grew sober again. 'I just hope we'll be able to do it when it's real.'

'You'll be all right,' Derek said, stroking her neck. 'Just don't expect to be perfect. We all make mistakes, can't help it.'

'That's all right when it's just a matter of burning the dinner or forgetting some shopping. But when it's planes getting through and bombing Portsmouth – perhaps killing your own family –' Olive's face was white. She stared at him with huge brown eyes. 'I don't know how I'll be able to live with myself if anything like that happens.'

Derek was silent for a minute or two. Then he said,'Look, Livvy, some of them are going to get through. They're bound to. You can't shoot down every plane in the sky. And the ones that make it will drop their bombs, we all know that. You don't have to blame yourself for that. You just have to be thankful for the ones you do hit. It's better than nothing. It's lives saved. Just think of that, see?'

'Yes,' Olive said, a little waveringly. She gave him a watery smile. 'I suppose you're right. It just seems – well, such a responsibility.'

'It is,' Derek said, 'but it's not so much responsibility as the people who got us into this. We can't none of us do any more than our best. And now come here and let me do what I do best. I've been starving for you all these weeks, Livvy.'

He began to caress her with more ardour, unbuttoning her pyjama jacket and spreading the cotton fabric aside so that he could bury his face in her breasts. Olive lay back, waiting for the familiar excitement to sweep over her, waiting for her body to be taken over by the sensations she had learned to love so much.

But they were slow to come, and she found herself consumed by anxiety more than by passion. Her thoughts were still circling round the conversation they had had, disturbed by the hint of disapproval in Derek's voice and the touch of resentment she had felt in response.

He never said he didn't want me to go in the ATS, she thought huffily. Maybe it's just dances and things he doesn't want me to go to. And again, she wondered – didn't he trust her?

But that was men all over, wasn't it – one rule for them and another for their wives. And when it looked like this war was going to show them something different, they didn't like it.

'Livvy.' Derek's voice whispered in her ear. 'Livvy, what's wrong? You don't seem to be with me. What's the matter?'

Olive looked up into his face. He was gazing at her with puzzled eyes, as hurt as a puppy who doesn't understand what he's done wrong. She felt a sudden surge of love and caught him hard against her.

'Nothing's the matter,' she said. 'Nothing – only that you're going away again, and I want this horrible war to stop so that we can settle down properly and live our lives the way we wanted to. Oh, *Derek* –' her voice quivered and broke '– oh Derek, make love to me. Make love to me all night and don't ever stop. Don't ever, *ever* stop . . .'

Olive returned to camp after Derek had gone back to Wiltshire, feeling as if she had had her right arm torn off. She went into the hut and found Claudia sitting on her bed, painting her toenails.

'So how was married life?' Claudia enquired. 'You know, I'm not sure I like this colour after all. It's too dark for my toes.'

Olive glanced at it. 'I don't see what difference it makes. No one's going to see them.'

'That's not the point. We've got to do something to keep up our morale. They won't let us varnish our fingernails. A girl's got to take a pride in herself.' Claudia frowned. 'All the same, I think I prefer something more *pink*, don't you?'

Olive sat down on her bed. It was hard and narrow, not like the wide bed she shared with Derek in her room at home. She wondered how long it would be before they managed another weekend together, and her eyes filled with tears.

'Now look,' Claudia said, still staring at her feet, 'you're not going to start weeping, I hope. Otherwise I'll have to have a talk with Hatchetface. "We can't have you gels coming back from weekends and flooding out the camp."' Her imitation of the officer's accent was so accurate that Olive had to laugh, despite her tears. 'You must learn to leave your marriage outside the wire fence, Harker. In here, you're a soldier.'

'You're a fool,' Olive said affectionately. 'And I'm not going to flood the camp.' She sighed. 'Heaven knows, I ought to be getting used to saying goodbye to Derek by now.'

'We're all getting used to saying goodbye,' Claudia said soberly, and swung her feet to the floor. 'Well, they'll have to do. I'd rather have pink but since I haven't got it, I'll make do with red.'

'You'll have to take it off the minute Hatchetface spots it. You're not supposed to do your toenails any more than your fingernails.'

'I know. It's because it's inflammable. They're afraid we might burst into flames.' Claudia padded over to the stove. A few girls were sitting round it and there were enamel mugs standing on the top. Claudia reached across to take two and brought them back to the beds.

'Good old Army cocoa, you can't beat it. I bet you've been just longing for this all weekend, haven't you?'

'Haven't I just!' Olive accepted a mug and blew on it before taking a cautious sip. 'Claud, you wouldn't go through my recognition with me again, would you?'

Claudia nodded. All the girls had left their training well able to identify any aircraft in the sky, but they were all terrified that they would let a German go through, to bomb the city. Or, worse still, mistake an Allied one for a German and cause one of their own pilots to be shot down. They went over their recognition again and again.

'Spitfire. Hurricane. Halifax. Lancaster,' Olive recited. 'Boeing B-17 Fortress. Junkers Ju88A, Dornier Do17, Heinkel.'

'Perfect,' Claudia announced at last. 'There won't be a plane in the sky that we can't identify at a glance. We'll be the best gunner-girls the Army's ever had.'

'I hope so.' Olive looked nervously at the pictures again. 'I think I ought to go over them once more, just to make sure.'

'You'll do no such thing.' Claudia removed the booklet and placed it firmly under her pillow. 'You can't know them any better than you do now. Anyway, it's nearly time for lights out.'

Olive washed, undressed and got into her narrow bed. She lay in the darkened hut, listening to the other girls breathing, to the odd snore, and longing for Derek.

She could not forget what had happened during their lovemaking last night. It was the first time in their marriage that anything had gone wrong with the passion that had seemed so secure between them. Now, although in the end they had both cried out in the climax of their loving and had slept with their bodies closely entwined, ready to love each other again with their awakening, there had been a hint of discord which she could not dismiss.

We need to be together, she thought. We need to be together properly, day after day, night after night, like a proper married couple. That's the only way we can build a real marriage, one that'll last us all our lives. You just can't do it with the odd weekend here and there.

It wasn't just her and Derek, either. It was all the girls and men who'd got married only to be torn apart by the war. It was girls like her sister Betty, still waiting, not knowing when they would even be able to get married. Not knowing *if* they ever would . . .

Bugger Hitler, she thought, turning over and thumping her pillow. Bugger, bugger, *bugger* Hitler.

Out at Bishop's Waltham, the Spencers had received a telegram. Gerald, their elder son, had been wounded in the fighting in the Western Desert and was being sent home. Mrs Spencer hardly knew whether to be anxious or relieved.

'They don't say what's happened to him,' she said, scanning the telegram. 'It must be pretty serious if they're sending him home. What d'you think they'll do, Jack?'

'Send him to an Army hospital, I suppose.' The farmer looked almost as anxious as his wife, but he put his big arm round her thin shoulders to comfort her. 'One thing, Ada, he'll be out of the fighting. It's our Dick you ought to be worrying about.'

'D'you think I'm not?' she asked sharply. 'There's not a day goes by when I don't think of 'em both a hundred times. First thing when I opens me eyes in the morning, last thing when I says me prayers at night. And you can't say our Gerald'll be any safer. They've got to get him back to England first, and then you don't know where he'll be in hospital.'

Jack Spencer sighed and nodded. Being brought home was no guarantee of safety, he knew that. But it must be safer than fighting in the African desert.

Jonas, the ancient farmhand who had hobbled out of retirement when the war began and boasted that he could still work any of the 'youngsters' off their feet, said, 'Pity he can't stop at home. Plenty of work on the farm and then we could send these bloody Land Girls back where they come from.'

'Jonas!' Mrs Spencer exclaimed, and Jack Spencer frowned.

'That's enough of that, Jonas. You know as well as I do, the girls do a good job. We'd be in a pretty poor state without 'em.'

'Be in a better one with the men back where they belong,' the old man muttered, and stumped out of the kitchen. The farmer and his wife looked ruefully at the three girls.

'He'll never change,' Mrs Spencer said. 'He don't mean half he says, you know.'

'Oh, we don't take any notice,' Betty said cheerfully. 'We all know Jonas by now. We're all really sorry to hear about Gerald,' she added. 'I hope he isn't too badly wounded.'

'Yes.' The farmer's wife looked down at the telegram again and sighed. 'You think you know all about the war until it hits you in your own family, and then somehow it seems different.' She glanced up at Erica. 'I'm sorry, love – that must sound hard, when you've already lost your young man.'

'It's all right,' the blonde girl said gently. 'I know what you mean. You think you really feel it for all the others, and it's still a terrible shock when it happens to someone you love. But Gerald's going to be all right. They'll bring him home and he'll be as good as new again.' She went over to the sink. 'I'll make you a cup of tea while Betty and Yvonne see to the milking.'

The other two girls went outside. November mist lay like an old grey Army blanket across the yard. The cows had walked through three times already that day and had trampled mud and dung through on their hooves. They were standing in the byre waiting to be milked, their breath steamy.

'Erica's changed a lot since she first came,' Betty remarked as they settled down beside the cows. 'She's nicer, somehow.'

'I know.' Yvonne coiled her lanky legs around her low milking-stool. 'She thinks about other people more. Feels for them, too. She was really good to Mrs Spencer just now.'

Betty giggled suddenly. 'Remember when we first arrived and she wanted a room to herself? I thought she'd have a fit when she saw the attic! We thought she was a right toffee-nosed little squirt.'

'So she was. But I reckon Geoff was good for her. It's a shame he was killed.'

They were silent for a few moments, thinking of the laughing airman and his two friends Duff and Sandy. The milk made a steady hissing sound as it squirted into the pails. One of the cows shifted suddenly and uttered a low moo.

'All the same,' Yvonne said at last, 'I don't reckon Erica would've been so nice now if it hadn't happened. I mean, I know that sounds awful but it was losing him that changed her, somehow. Don't you reckon so?'

'Yes, I think I do,' Betty said thoughtfully. 'Before that, she was against everyone. Especially Dennis. And afterwards too, for quite a while. But then she seemed to gradually change. And she doesn't paint herself up the way she used to. She was a real glamour queen when she first came.'

'Wasn't she just!' Yvonne agreed. 'But it would be a shame if she forgot about being pretty. I mean, she can look gorgeous but she hardly ever bothers now. It's as if she's decided it's not worth bothering.'

'She hasn't got over Geoff yet. Maybe she never will.'

Yvonne shrugged and moved on to the next cow. 'You can't go all through your life hankering after someone who's not there any more. Erica'll find someone else when she's ready. Or someone'll find her.' She glanced across the byre at Betty. 'How's your Dennis, anyway?'

'Oh, he's fine.' Dennis was still at Fort Widley, so he and Betty were able to meet quite frequently. 'He's coming over on Sunday. He's taking me to meet his mum and dad.' She stretched her arms and then shivered. 'I'm scared to death!'

Dennis's parents lived in Portchester, but Betty hadn't met them before because they had been in Somerset, looking after Dennis's grandmother. After a long illness, she had died and now they were back in Portchester where Mr Verney was a librarian.

'I hope they'll like me,' Betty said nervously as she walked beside Dennis along the little road near the old castle. 'They won't think I'm common, will they, because our house doesn't have a bathroom or anything?'

Dennis laughed. 'Of course they won't! We're Friends, remember? Everyone's equal. They won't take any notice of things like that.'

'All the same, they might not think I'm good enough for you.'

Dennis stopped and put his arms round her. He kissed her firmly on the lips.

'Dennis! We're in the middle of the street –'

'I don't care. I love you, Betty, and even if my parents hated you on sight it wouldn't make any difference to that. But they won't. They'll love you, just like I do.' He grinned. 'Well – maybe not *quite* like I do . . .'

'Dennis, you're awful sometimes. Nobody would think you were religious,' Betty said, blushing, and he laughed again.

'What's wrong with liking one of the best things God made for us? Loving's right, Betty, it's good and natural, and we ought to enjoy it.' He let her go and tucked her hand under his arm. 'Come on, they're not ogres. You'll be all right.'

The house was on a corner. It had a semi-circular bay window in front, and a small conservatory behind. The front garden was a square of grass with plants all around it in a border, some green, some purple, some feathery, some with broad, furry leaves. Betty looked at them, puzzled. They weren't flowers but they certainly weren't vegetables.

'They're herbs,' Dennis said. 'Mum grows them for flavouring and medicines. She's a great one for making medicines.'

Betty had never heard of anyone making their own medicines, or using herbs. Her own mother made a lovely mint sauce to have with roast lamb – when she could get lamb – and Aunt Jess mixed up honey and lemon juice for coughs, but any more than that sounded a bit like witchcraft. She looked doubtfully at the little bushes and followed Dennis round the side of the house.

The back garden had been dug up for vegetables. Betty looked at the neat rows of cabbages, turnips and onions and felt happier. A tall man with silver hair was digging potatoes at the end, and Dennis waved at him.

'That's Dad.'

The man came up the garden path, still holding his fork. He was well over six feet tall and looked rather like Betty's idea of Moses coming down from the mountain – except that Moses wouldn't have been carrying a hoe, she thought with a nervous inward giggle – but he was smiling, and he had warm hazel eyes just like Dennis's. He took Betty's hand in his, and she felt the warm, gentle strength in his fingers . . .

'So you're Betty.' His voice was deep and strong. 'Welcome, my dear. We've been waiting a long time to meet you.' He turned and leant the fork against the fence. 'Come in and meet Cicely. She's making a special soup.'

An appetising scent wafted from the kitchen window and Dennis grinned. 'I always know I'm home when I smell one of Mum's soups. Come on, Betty.'

Dennis's mother was as short as his father was tall. She couldn't have been much more than five feet, and she had grey hair, cut short to curl around her face. She was wearing a dark brown skirt and a cream jumper and her face was a mass of wrinkles, all smiling. She had very bright blue eyes that sparkled with energy.

'Dennis! You're looking well. And this is Betty.' She held both Betty's hands, gazing at her with as much pleasure as if Betty were her own daughter. 'Oh, it's so good to see you.' She let go and reached up to kiss her son. 'I've missed you so much while we've been with Granny.'

'I wish I could have come down to Taunton,' he said. 'But they wouldn't give me time off until she'd died. Grandmothers' funerals are allowed – but I told them I'd rather have seen her while she was still alive.'

'She would have liked you to have been there,' his father said quietly. 'But she was proud of you. We all are.'

Cicely Verney turned to the stove and took the lid from a large saucepan. The appetising scent drifted out, more strongly than ever, and Betty felt her saliva begin to flow. She looked around the kitchen.

It was larger than her mother's, with a big, scrubbed wooden table in the middle set for the meal. It was quite plain – just brown soup bowls and plates, with a big platter of bread in the middle. There was a jug of water and four glasses, and at one end Mrs Verney had put a little pottery jug filled with leaves from the herbs Betty had seen in the front garden.

'Sit yourselves down,' Dennis's mother said, taking the pan from the stove and turning off the gas. She tipped the soup into a large bowl and Betty looked at it. It was rich and brown, and thick with vegetables.

'It looks lovely, Mrs Verney. And smells delicious.'

'That's Robert's home-grown vegetables and my herbs,' she said. 'Nothing from the shops at all. And please don't call me Mrs Verney. We like to be addressed by our first names.'

Dennis had already told Betty that Quakers – or Friends, as they preferred to call themselves – disliked the titles Mr and Mrs, but she still felt awkward using the Christian names of people she had only just met – especially when they were her sweetheart's parents. She would have to try to get used to it though – you couldn't go through your whole life addressing your in-laws as 'you'.

The thought of Robert and Cicely Verney being her in-laws gave her a little quiver of excitement. That would mean she was well and truly married to Dennis! She sat quietly beside him, eating her soup and listening to the conversation.

Dennis was talking about his training for bomb disposal work. He made it sound easy, but Betty felt the tremor of fear that she always experienced when she thought of what Dennis did, and wished again that he'd stayed on the farm.

Robert Verney listened gravely.

'I'm thankful that you're treated better than I was,' he said at last. 'The Government has a more civilised attitude these days. The pity is that it doesn't extend to preventing war altogether.'

'But Dennis had an awful time,' Betty exclaimed. 'He went to prison.'

Robert smiled and said nothing, but Cicely said fiercely, 'They nearly tore poor Robert to pieces in 1914. They were barbarians in the Great War, as they like to call it.'

Betty stared at her, then turned to Robert. He was looking serious again and he caught her eye and nodded.

'It's true. Pacifists were very badly treated then. If you weren't in uniform, women – perfect strangers – would come up to you and give you the white feather, for cowardice. And if you refused to join up you were arrested and put into the army anyway.'

'But you – ?' Betty said, and stopped, unable to think of a way of asking how he had been nearly torn to pieces.

'I refused everything. I wouldn't even put on the uniform. So they roped me to a gun-carriage, harnessed the horses and drove them away.' He gave a wry smile. 'It took me quite a long time to recover, and of course I was useless as a soldier. But I was luckier than some of the others.'

'Some people were shot,' Dennis said. 'They had plenty of ways of persuading people to fight. You have to be pretty strong to watch your mates being executed and know it's your turn next if you don't cave in.'

There was a short silence. Betty thought of Erica, who had been so hostile towards Dennis, and of Mrs Spencer's sister Iris, who had hated him with a viciousness that was quite frightening. She looked at Robert Verney, imagining him tied behind a gun-carriage and dragged across the ground. He could have died.

Robert Verney was eating his soup. Betty looked at him, thinking how tall and strong he seemed. And yet she could still sense that gentleness which she had felt when he held her hand. A gentleness and belief in God and man which had compelled him to refuse to fight, coupled with the courage which had given him the will to resist even when tortured.

He looked up suddenly and met her eyes. Betty blushed, certain that he knew exactly what she was thinking, and he smiled again.

'Tell us when we're going to have the pleasure of welcoming you as our daughter,' he said. 'We've longed for a daughter for years. We're both so pleased to have you.'

Betty looked from him to his wife. She thought of her own family and the way her father had reacted to Dennis and the tears came to her eyes.

'I don't know,' she said, feeling suddenly miserable. 'You see, my Mum's all right, but Dad –' She stopped, ashamed to go on, and felt the tears brim over.

Dennis put his arm round her. 'Betty's Dad isn't keen on me being a CO. I keep telling her, he's got a right to his opinion and we'll just wait until he comes around, but it's hard for her.'

Robert nodded. He didn't seem at all embarrassed by Betty's tears, but he didn't ignore them either. He gave her a friendly smile, while Cecily put both her hands over Betty's and held them warmly. 'Dennis is right. Your father deserves his respect. And this is the way Friends work. We don't always agree with one another, you know – we have our problems and our disputes. But when we can't agree, we simply wait. We discuss the matter again. And wait. And slowly, gradually, one by one, those in dispute will begin to change their minds. And when we're all in accord, we act.'

'But that could take years,' Betty said despairingly.

'Years that are well spent. But I know that's hard for you to accept.'

'We're not waiting years,' Dennis said firmly. 'We're going to wait until the summer, or maybe the spring, and if he hasn't come round then . . . At least we'll have given him the chance. But we don't want to wait any longer than that.'

'A spring wedding,' his mother said softly, and took Betty's hand. 'I'm so glad, my dear. So very, very glad.'

Betty's anxiety about the work Dennis was doing had never disappeared, but since nothing had yet happened to him, she tried hard to persuade herself that nothing would. Dennis, however, knew that he was in danger every minute.

He had now finished his training and, having been promoted to Lieutenant, was working full-time on bomb disposal. And there was plenty of work to be done. Of the bombs that had fallen during the blitz, many still lay unexploded at the bottom of craters or beneath buildings.

Some were still being reported by people who had not at first realised they had fallen – people who had come back to their homes from evacuation and discovered a strange, sinister cylinder nestling in their coalshed or under an outside wall; people who had re-opened a disused building to find a bomb staring them in the face.

All these must be dealt with as they came to light. And there were still fresh bombs being dropped which might be even more urgent.

The day before he was due to come out to Betty at the farm, Dennis was sent to deal with a bomb which had been discovered in a garden at Cosham. Nobody knew quite when it had fallen, for the occupants had been away since April. It might be from one of the last great raids of the blitz; it might be much more recent, perhaps from one of the swift hit-and-run forays which were often made by lone pilots, perhaps jettisoned by a plane which had been on a mission further up the country and turned back.

'They think it's a five-hundred-pound bastard,' Captain Anderson told him as they drove to Cosham. 'Not all that big, but the sort that the Jerries like to fit with a nice little surprise for us. Wonder what it'll be this time.'

Dennis knew all about the 'surprises' that the enemy liked to attach to their bombs. For some time, the Germans had been using timing devices which could delay a bomb's detonation for days, or even months. And others were booby-trapped, to appear safe until the bomb disposal experts actually began to work on them. Then the slightest vibration could set off the explosion.

The whole street had been evacuated and the Pioneers were already digging the pit when the team arrived. This was the job that Dennis had first volunteered to do – the careful uncovering of a bomb that had buried itself perhaps twelve or twenty feet below the ground. The pit itself must be made safe as it was dug, with a wooden shaft being built to make it possible for the disposal team to climb in and out without risk of crumbling earth and to enable the bomb to be hoisted out after it had been defused.

Every movement must be made with care, for although the bomb had obviously suffered considerable impact when it fell, the devices with which it was fitted might yet mean that the slightest disturbance would trigger its explosion. Or the clock mechanism might have been set to begin on impact, and time even now be running out.

Men were killed every day doing this work, and Dennis knew that his chances of coming unscathed through the war were slim.

He walked to the edge of the pit and looked down. It was about fifteen feet deep. The nose of the bomb was showing and one of the sappers was gently removing the wet earth around the body.

'That's not a five-hundred-pounder,' Dennis said quietly. 'That's a thousand if it's an ounce.'

'Reckon you're right, sir,' the sapper agreed. 'Make a bloody big bang when it goes off.'

'Well, we're not going to let it.' Dennis walked back to Captain Anderson. 'We'd better get the steam steriliser along.'

One of the staff sergeants went off to telephone for the equipment. The sappers continued their work. As well as the wooden shaft, a tripod had to be erected above the pit with pulleys which would drag the bomb up from the depths after it had been made safe. Nearby, a pump was sucking water from the bottom of the shaft. Another staff sergeant was listening from behind a wall on an electrical stethoscope, and Dennis went over to him.

'Any sign of life?'

'No ticking yet, sir. Going to steam it out, are you?'

'If the equipment arrives in time.' Dennis walked back to the pit. The bomb was almost completely exposed now. He stared at it uneasily, then turned to the Captain.

'I'm not sure we ought to wait for the steriliser. I think there are two fuses there. We ought to dismantle them as quickly as possible.'

Anderson nodded. 'I agree. Are you ready to start?'

Dennis nodded. His heart was beating quickly and he felt the familiar tension grip his stomach, but he knew that this initial apprehension, which could if allowed turn into real fear, could be harnessed and channelled into the precise use of skill which gave him such satisfaction.

A quiet excitement flowed in his veins. This was the seventh large bomb he had tackled, and he had never known anything quite like the sense of exhilaration that caught him when he knew that he had succeeded in making them safe.

But he could not allow that excitement to affect him. The job he was about to do demanded total concentration and steadiness of hand and brain. Dennis had already witnessed several incidents in which men had been killed while trying to dismantle unexploded bombs. There were so many things which could go wrong. During his training, he had been watching from a distance when a large UXB was being hoisted with extreme care from its pit to be dealt with at ground level, on the supposition that after a few days the time fuse was no longer dangerous. Just as it reached the surface, one of the men had put a hand on it to stop it swinging. It had exploded at once, killing all eight men in and around the pit.

That was when the Army had begun to realise that timing devices could be set months, rather than days, ahead.

Then there had been the time when a corporal had died at the bottom of the shaft from the effects of ammonia fumes. And the man who had been badly scalded as the explosive was being steamed out of the bomb casing. And the numerous occasions on which an officer, in the act of dismantling a fuse, had set it off by too sudden a movement or by coming across a device not previously encountered. Sometimes, simply turning a screw the wrong way was enough.

For this reason, the officer working on the bomb talked quietly into a telephone headset, narrating every movement he made so that those on the surface knew exactly what was happening. And if his final remark was accompanied by an explosion, the survivors would know what had caused it.

'We'll use the Q-coil,' Captain Anderson said as they prepared to climb down the ladder into the shaft, now vacated by the sappers. 'If there is a clock there, that should stop it and we can get the thing out.'

The Q-coil was a fairly new device, developed to stop the clock by magnetising it. This would deal with the Type-17 fuse. The other – suspected to be a Type-50 – was even more dangerous. This was designed to delay the detonation until the bomb was moved or tapped, and was the one which had killed the eight men during the earlier operation.

To make this fuse safe, a man had to work on the bomb while it was still in its shaft, operating with the utmost care as any slight jarring movement could trigger the explosive.

Dennis and the Captain reached the bottom of the shaft. They studied the bomb, noting every detail. The slightest difference in its construction must be reported, so that the Unit could keep up with the developments and modifications the Germans were constantly making. You could never assume that you knew everything about the deadly weapon facing you. There might always be some new trick, an innocent-looking button or screw, placed to trap the man working on it.

Bombs did not always fail to go off because they were defective. Many of them were designed to explode later, so that an air-raid of a few hours could extend its powers for many weeks afterwards. And even a 'dud' could never be declared safe until it had been completely dismantled. Deteriorating explosives could be the most unpredictable. Sometimes a clock which had been set in motion would stop, and then re-start. There was no way of knowing how long it had left to run. It might be several days; it might be less than a second.

Dennis began to scrape away the remaining earth from around the bomb. The Type-17 fuse was already partially exposed, but it was also partly underneath the bomb. He dug with his bare hands, trying not to brush against the casing or to let earth fall against it as he scrabbled a little pit under the fuse, large enough to get the clock-stopper over it. The sappers at the top lowered down the device, which weighed about seventy pounds, and Dennis and the Captain manoeuvred it over the fuse.

It was in place and the current switched on. That was the clock made safe, although only for a limited time – to make it permanently safe, a much heavier stopper must be used. But at least they were given some time to work on the even more sensitive Type-50.

'God almighty,' Anderson said in disgust, 'it's right underneath the bloody thing.'

Dennis stared at it. To work on the fuse in the pit was impossible. The bomb must be lifted clear.

He remembered that other bomb, swinging into view. The sergeant's hand, barely touching it. The huge explosion that had blown every man in the team to pieces and shattered every window for half a mile.

'We could dig underneath,' he suggested dubiously.

Anderson shook his head. 'The slightest jarring – just a small stone knocking it – could set it off. You know that as well as I do.'

'So how do we raise it without jarring it?' Dennis asked. 'We've got to get the strops underneath for a start. We're going to have to shift a bit of earth to do that.'

Captain Anderson considered. Dennis watched him, knowing that what he had said was true. But whoever took on the difficult and delicate task of scraping earth and mud from underneath the bomb without giving it the smallest jolt was putting his life at serious risk.

Their lives were already at serious risk, he thought, just standing there. What difference did a little bit more make?

It might make the difference between marrying Betty and living their lives together, and never seeing her again.

'You're right,' the Captain said at last. 'There's not a lot needs shifting. But it's a job only one man can do. You get back up top, Verney, and I'll do it.'

Dennis shook his head. 'I think it should be me, sir. It's my idea.'

Anderson looked faintly exasperated. 'This is no time for grabbing kudos –'

'I'm not interested in kudos. I just think if anything goes wrong, you're more use to the Unit than I am.'

'Nor heroics,' the Captain said sharply. 'A man who wants to be a hero is a dangerous man. You need to be cold steel for this job.'

'And so I am. That's the way I'm looking at it.' Dennis faced his superior steadily. 'I don't want to be a hero, sir, dead or alive. But I'm here to do a job to the best of my ability, and to serve mankind and my God in the best way I can. And I reckon that if only one of us is to come out of this alive, it ought to be you. You're the leader here. I'm not, and never will be.'

Captain Anderson stared at him. Then he said abruptly, 'Very well. We certainly don't have time to stand here arguing about it. That fuse has had five minutes already.' He gave a sharp nod and set his foot on the bottom rung of the ladder. 'Give me three minutes and then start work. And – good luck.'

Dennis nodded back, unsmilingly. The two men's eyes held for a few seconds longer and then the Captain began to climb.

Dennis stood quite still until he had disappeared over the rim of the shaft. He heard the voice above, ordering everyone out of range of the hole. Then he knelt in the damp earth and began, slowly and carefully, to dig away the soil.

CHAPTER NINE

The shaft was now a tangled cat's cradle. The clock-stopper's wires were straggling down the side of the shaft from its two batteries and switch-box, and there were balloon cables ready to lift the bomb out when it was finally made safe. Dennis crouched at the bottom, trying not to get himself entangled or to catch and jerk one of the wires. He talked quietly into his field telephone as he worked.

'I can see the fuse pretty well now. It's definitely a fifty. I've got it almost clear. I'm scraping away the last few bits of earth.' A tiny pause, and those above held their breath. 'It's been damaged,' he said quietly. 'I don't think we can do anything to it.'

Damaged! Then why hadn't the bomb already exploded? The men above ground looked at each other and shook their heads. Captain Anderson walked back to the top of the shaft.

'You'd better come up right away.'

Dennis looked up. The Captain's face looked odd, hanging above him in the circle of light.

'I think I ought to stay here, sir. I'm safe enough so long as nothing jars it, but if we keep climbing in and out . . .'

'Bugger it, man!' the Captain exploded. 'Don't you *ever* obey orders?'

Dennis grinned. 'All the time, sir. And if you order me to stay here I'll obey willingly.'

The Captain snorted. Then he said, 'So what do you propose to do? Spend the rest of your life down there?'

They both knew that this might well be exactly what Dennis was going to do, and that the rest of his life might be short indeed. But Dennis shook his head and said cheerfully, 'I think we can steam it out, sir. Then we'll detonate both fuses. The steamer ought to be here soon.'

'It's arriving now,' Anderson said, glancing over his shoulder to where an Army truck was pulling in at the end of the street. Soldiers jumped out and one of the officers came down the back alley towards him. He joined the Captain at the rim of the shaft and Anderson gave him a quick briefing on what was happening.

'You reckon it'll steam?' the newcomer said, peering down at Dennis.

'It's our only chance. I can't touch this fuse. But if we can get the TNT out . . .'

The officer nodded. 'Right. Let's get moving. You've had that stopper on it a while already.' He set off back to his truck at a run.

Anderson looked down the shaft again. 'You don't have to do this, Verney.'

'But someone does,' Dennis answered. 'And I'm here.' He paused and added, 'And I won't come up unless you specifically order me to.' He was quite sure that Anderson would not do that now. For one thing, the task they were about to do needed two men and the Captain would probably come down again himself.

He was right. After a few minutes – with the clock-stopper's time steadily running out – Anderson climbed down again and the steamer was lowered into the pit. By now, Dennis had very gently unscrewed the bomb's base-plate. He removed it with a tiny sigh of relief, and Anderson positioned the steam-jenny.

The shaft filled with steam. It billowed about them in a great scalding cloud, hissing in their ears. The humidity soaked into their clothes and filled their nostrils with the smell of hot, wet earth.

TNT began to flow out of the bomb in a wet stream, solidifying as it met the floor of the pit. Even though it was less dangerous in that state, the bomb was far from safe, for even without its explosive the fuses still carried a charge powerful enough to kill them both if they fired. And as more and more steam gushed out, the shaft became hotter and hotter. Dennis found himself taking short, shallow breaths, unable to draw the hot air deep into his lungs. His head reeled but he dared not take his attention from the steam-jenny. Once started, this was a job that had to be finished.

It was two hours before they could declare their task complete. By that time, both were sweating and almost unconscious with the heat, but they channelled every scrap of concentration into what they were doing. Their world narrowed to the inferno of the little pit, and for all they knew time could have become eternity.

'D'you think it's happened?' Anderson muttered once. 'D'you think the whole bloody caboodle's gone sky-high and we've got to Hell?'

Dennis shook his head. 'You haven't got a tail.' He saw the other man's teeth flash briefly in the glimmering light and felt cheered. Not much of a joke, perhaps, but who could be Tommy Handley in a situation like this?

The bomb was empty at last. The floor of the pit was covered in several hundred pounds of solidifying TNT. Three sappers climbed down into the pit and began to carve it into blocks, which were sandbagged and raised to the surface. Nothing more could be done to the bomb until every scrap of explosive had been removed to a safe distance.

It was dark when Dennis and Captain Anderson finally emerged from the hole. They were both filthy, covered in mud, earth and the dank water that had seeped from the walls of the pit or condensed from the steam. They had attached charges to each of the fuse-pockets and timed them to go off after half an hour. There were only a few pounds to detonate, but the restricted area and the steel cases in which the pockets were housed would make a fierce enough explosion.

They climbed wearily out of the pit and went with the rest of the team to take cover.

Twenty minutes later the two charges blew. Every window in the street shattered.

Huddled in their temporary shelter, the men grinned at each other and gave the thumb's-up. Once again, they had challenged death. Once again, they had won.

In early December, the King and Queen made another visit to Portsmouth and lunched in the Dockyard on board HMS *Victory*. Afterwards, the King visited the Gunnery School while Queen Elizabeth toured the city. She visited one of the British Restaurants, St Mary's Hospital and the Dockyard, where Frank Budd saw her. She passed close to the boiler-shop on her way from the *Victory* and they all came out and lined up to be inspected. He told Jess about it that evening.

'She's got the bluest eyes I've ever seen. Cherry said they looked just like robins' eggs.'

'So Cherry was there too?' Jess said.

'Oh yes, men and women alike, we all lined up together.'

Jess sniffed. She'd been hearing a bit more than she wanted to about this Cherry just lately. The girl seemed to worm her way into almost everything Frank said these days. Cherry this, Cherry that – he'd never talked about what went on at work so much before, nor had he ever seemed to find so much to enjoy while he was there. Why, his serious face proper lit up when he was recounting the latest exploit, and made him look quite young again. It's me that ought to be putting that look on his face, Jess thought, me that ought to be making him laugh.

But Frank didn't seem to find much else to laugh about when he got home. He'd come in of an evening – invariably late, because of the overtime – and go straight to the big map on the wall to figure out the latest positions, with the *Daily Express* and the *Evening News* spread out on the dining-table in front of him. Then, having moved all the little pins with their red and black heads, he'd do it all again after the Nine o'Clock News on the wireless. He always looked grave while he was doing this, and no wonder, with the way things were going, but the trouble was that was his evening almost gone. By then it would be time to be out on firewatching duty, or going down to the shelter, or trying to get an early night because he had to be up at five-thirty next morning . . . It didn't give him and Jess any time at all to be together, to be themselves and enjoy each other's company.

It was the people at work who got the best of him, she thought uneasily. And that hadn't worried her when it was chaps like Dick Foster or Harry Banks. But when it came to flighty young girls like this Cherry . . .

I shouldn't worry about him, she thought. I ought to trust him. I do, really – I've never had a moment's doubt over him before, never. I know he loves me, and I know he'd never do anything wrong. But all the same – when a chap's working hard, and worried half out of his mind over what's going to happen next, and he hardly sees his wife and then they stick a saucy little piece like that right under his nose for eight or ten hours a day . . . Well, he's only human, after all.

And so am I. I can't *help* worrying!

Peggy Shaw had seen the Queen too. She told Jess about it next day, full of excitement because Her Majesty had actually visited the First Aid Post where she and Gladys worked as volunteers, and had spoken to them.

'She saw Gladys's BEM. She'd got it pinned on – she didn't want to really, but the Super told her she ought to. The Queen was really pleased – well, it was her hubby what'd give it to our Glad, wasn't it, when you think about it – and she asked what Gladys was going to do and our Glad said she'd volunteered for the Wrens, only they didn't seem to be in any hurry to have her and she was thinking of going for a nurse instead, and the Queen said she thought Glad'd make an *excellent* nurse. That's what she said – excellent.' Peggy stopped for a moment, almost breathless. 'And then she asked me if I had any more children and I said yes, a boy in the Army and another girl working at Airspeed waiting to be old enough for the WAAFs, and guess what she said then, she said I'd done a wonderful job and people like me – and my Bert too, I suppose – were bringing up just the kind of young ones who were going to win the war for us. Me and *Bert*! And she said it was hard for us all but sunshine *would* come again.' Peggy paused again, gazing at Jess with shining eyes. 'Fancy the Queen saying all that to me and Glad. It don't seem possible, does it.'

Jess smiled at her. 'You are lucky, Peg. I wish I'd seen her. It seems as if everyone in the street's talked to the Queen except me. She spoke to Derek Harker last time she came to Portsmouth, you know, after Olive lost the baby. Said much the same to him. It really put heart into Olive.'

Peggy nodded. 'It's made a difference to our Glad too. She's made up her mind she's not waiting any longer for the Wrens to make up their minds. She's going to see about training as a nurse. I think she'll be good at it. She's done really well with her First Aid, driving that ambulance.'

Jess went back indoors. It really was a wonder, the way a few words from someone like the Queen could make such a difference to people who were feeling down. It was as if she had a special, magic touch, as if she knew just what you were feeling and wanted to share it with you. And in a queer sort of way, that made you feel better.

It was a pity she couldn't talk to a few more people. People like Ted, for instance. Poor Annie was nearly at her wits' end over Ted.

'I feel so *ashamed*,' Annie said, brushing tea-leaves up from the carpet, where she had scattered them to pick up the dust. 'I mean, there's all the other men working all the hours God sends to try to win the war, and you just sit there feeling sorry for yourself. There's nothing wrong with you. You're fit and healthy. You've got your strength. But have you gone back to work? No, you haven't – you just whine about what it's like to take the ferryboat across the harbour at night.'

'I've told you time and time again,' Ted said, 'I'll go back to the ferry when I'm ready. The doctor says I've got to take me time. It won't do no good to force it.'

'Well, I don't think you'll feel any better till you *do* go back,' Annie said. 'All this sitting about feeling sorry for yourself isn't doing you no good neither. There's nothing wrong with you. You've never been hurt. There's plenty worse off than you.' She knelt on the floor, her brush in one hand, the sheet of newspaper into which she was sweeping the tea-leaves in the other, and looked up at him. 'Just as if there weren't any others every bit as scared, only *they're* not giving in to it. And then you've got the nerve to sneer at Betty's Dennis and say *he's* a coward!'

'I've told you before, I don't want that chap's name mentioned in my house,' Ted retorted. 'He's not a coward, I'll give him that, and I never said he was, but he still won't fight for his country. That's what sticks in my craw. There's lads like our Colin, and Derek and Bob Shaw and all the others, all doing their bit, and he'd rather go to jail than do what they're doing. *Doesn't think he has the right to kill people!*' he snorted. 'What makes him think he's got the right to decide? World 'ud be in a fine pickle if everyone thought that way.'

'The world's in a pickle as it is,' Annie said sharply. 'Maybe it'd be better if everyone did think his way. It couldn't be any worse, at any rate. But I'm not talking about Dennis, I'm talking about you. What about you getting up off your backside and doing *your* bit?'

'Don't you think I've done my bit?' he demanded. 'Don't you think Dunkirk was enough? I told you, I saw more there in those few days than I ever saw in the first war. More than enough to last me. There's not a day goes by when I don't remember, when I don't see it all again, when I don't hear the screams . . . What I saw at Dunkirk –'

'What you saw at Dunkirk was just the same as what thousands of others saw,' Annie said sharply. 'And a lot of them were wounded, and some still haven't got over *that*. And the rest have gone back to fighting. You done well at Dunkirk, Ted, I'm not denying that, but you've been playing on it ever since.'

'*Playing on it!* Now look here, Annie, I've been up on the roof firewatching more times than you've had hot dinners. I've taken the *King* across the harbour hundreds of times since Dunkirk. I was there the day they bombed the harbour station, thought the boat was going to go up in flames with it. You can't say I've been playing on Dunkirk, because I haven't.'

'And what did you do when we had to call the doctor to you?' Annie demanded. 'You were nothing but a jelly that night, and all you could babble about was Dunkirk and planes and machine guns and bombs.'

'Shock. She said it was delayed shock.'

'All right, all right, I know what she said. You don't need to go over it all again.' She brushed fiercely. 'But there were others at Dunkirk too, Ted, and they haven't just sat back and said they're not doing no more. Soldiers –thousands of them – who've *had* to go back. Sailors who just did it as all part of the day's work and had to go back to sea again. Yes, and men like you, older men who don't have to fight but have still gone on with their own war work – firefighting, ARP and all the rest of it. You weren't the only one there.'

'I know I wasn't,' he muttered. 'And I wish you wouldn't go on about it all the time. It doesn't do any good. I can't help how I feel, don't you understand that? The doctor told you, it's like an illness. I'll get better in me own time, if you'll only leave me alone.'

'Oh, yes?' Annie said sarcastically. 'And just when d'you think that'll be? When the war's over? When there's no more need to worry about bombs dropping? I should think we'll all get better then, Ted Chapman. It'll be easy, won't it. But it's *now* that matters – now, when we all need to pull together. When we all need to pull our own weight.'

'And I'm not, am I,' he said sullenly. 'That's what you're saying, isn't it?'

Annie got stiffly to her feet and stood looking down at him. He was a big man, her Ted, but this morning, sitting in his chair by the empty fireplace, he looked somehow shrunken, as if the heart had gone out of him. She felt a pang of pity, and thrust it away quickly. She'd had enough of feeling sorry for Ted.

'No, you're not,' she said bluntly. 'In fact, if you ask me, you're not pulling any weight at all. What you're doing is more like *pushing*.'

She turned and marched out through the kitchen into

the garden. She tipped the contents of the newspaper into the dustbin and then stood there, leaning on the fence, trembling a little.

She hadn't ever spoken to Ted as sharply as that, not since he'd first been taken ill with this nervous trouble of his. The doctor had told her it was depression, brought on by his experiences, and that time was the only cure. But time had passed – it was a year now since Dunkirk – and he seemed to be getting worse, not better. And to Annie, who had always been a believer in getting on with things, it didn't seem right to see a grown man with all his health and strength and a job to do, just sitting there in a chair day after day feeling sorry for himself.

'Fat lot of sympathy I get from you,' he'd said to her one day and she'd answered him sharply.

'You don't need my sympathy. You've got enough of your own.' And immediately she'd bitten her tongue, feeling angry with herself because that was just what the doctor *hadn't* ordered. But maybe the doctor was wrong. Treating Ted like a piece of Dresden china didn't seem to be doing any good at all. Perhaps it was time to start treating him like a sulky child instead. Time to ignore his tantrums and tell him to get on with it. There were plenty worse off in the world, after all, and she had the rest of the family to think of. Betty, out on the farm. Olive, in the ATS. And Colin, somewhere at sea on HMS *Exeter*.

Dennis himself wasn't feeling very brave as he went off duty that night. He'd noticed it before – this reaction that set in after a particularly tricky job. There wasn't so much as a tremor at the time, yet afterwards – hours later, sometimes – he'd start shaking, his body shivering, teeth chattering as if he was freezing cold, and nothing he did seemed able to stop it. He just had to wait for it to pass.

What he'd have most liked to do at such times was go and have a deep hot bath, just lie there and soak the reaction away until his body relaxed. But you couldn't relax much in five inches of water, tepid water at that as often as not. So he usually tried going to bed with a book, or lying there listening to the wireless going in the corner of the hut. A Glenn Miller concert, perhaps, or one of the comedy programmes like *Much Binding in the Marsh*, or *Stand Easy*.

Whatever he did, it wasn't long before his thoughts drifted away to the subject that occupied them most, whenever he wasn't concentrating on dismantling a bomb.

Betty.

At twenty-nine, Dennis knew that he was deeply in love with Betty Chapman, and committed to her in a way in which he had never been committed to any other girl. Brought up as the eldest in a family of devoted Quakers, he had always taken relationships with the opposite sex seriously, and never taken part in the coarse jokes or crude attitudes towards women in which some of his school-friends and, later, workmates had indulged. With the example of his gentle father's never-failing courtesy towards his mother always before him, he had grown up believing that marriage should be a haven of loving security, a home for the spirit where none might batter down the door.

He knew, of course, that many marriages were not like that. He had seen his friends' parents spitting at each other like cats, snarling in bitter argument or – worse still, it sometimes seemed – living together in icy silence. One or two had even separated and lived apart, to the shame of their children, and he knew one boy whose parents were divorced and had no more to do with each other.

Divorce was like a dirty word – something you just didn't speak about. You had to go to court to get a divorce, and give evidence about how badly your partner had behaved, with details of what they had done that were reported at length in the newspapers and pored over by strangers. It was almost as bad as committing a crime, and your life afterwards might not be much better than if you'd actually gone to prison.

Dennis did not want a marriage that ended like that, nor one that struggled on with quarrelling or long, cold silences. He wanted a home like the one he had grown up in, with a family whose members loved each other – scrapping from time to time, that was only normal, but never letting their differences get out of hand. Respecting each other as people. Loving both their faults and their virtues.

With Betty, he believed that he could have such a marriage.

Betty wasn't the first girlfriend he had had. There had been a few others, mostly casual affairs that went no further than a Saturday-night outing to the pictures and a goodnight kiss at the front door, and there had been one he'd thought might go deeper. Jean, her name had been, and she'd had long brown hair and slanting eyes. She lived in Fareham and Dennis had met her at Hilsea Lido, where she came swimming on Saturday afternoons. There had been a crowd of them, all in their early twenties, stretching themselves out on the square flagstones to sunbathe or climbing up to the high diving-board that was the best showing-off point in Portsmouth.

Dennis remembered his first sight of Jean, standing like an Amazon against the blue sky. She'd been wearing a scarlet bathing costume which showed off her figure almost as if she'd been naked, and he'd felt his body stir as he gazed at her.

She was the best diver he'd ever seen. He could remember still the shape of her as she spread her arms and floated out in a swallow-dive. He'd almost believed she could really fly.

Looking back, he could see that that was really all there was to his passion for Jean – a desire for that perfect body, a lust he had later been ashamed of. He wasn't ashamed now – it was part of the normal male reaction to a female who offered herself to both his gaze and his touch as readily as Jean had offered herself to him. But after it was over, when he had realised that there was no more between them than an animal attraction, he had been more cautious in his responses. Sex was, he knew now, a powerful driving force that could carry a man into a world he might not want to enter. He was careful not to let it overwhelm him again.

Until Betty. And even then, when he had first known her when she had come to the Spencers' farm as a Land Girl, he had held back. Different though she was from Jean, with her short, naturally curly hair and her laughing eyes, he had felt her attraction at once. But he'd soon discovered that Betty already had a boyfriend, and that they were more or less engaged. It was only later, when their friendship had ripened and he knew that it was more than a sexual attraction that drew him to her, when she'd told him that it was over between herself and Graham, that he'd allowed that deep need in him to begin to surface.

Now, he could not imagine life without Betty and the love they shared. More than anything in the world, he wanted them to be together, to be married and sharing a home as his parents did, bringing up a family in their turn. He longed for the life of 'every day' – the life of an ordinary married couple in a simple home, with a baby or two crawling on the floor and no fears of war to darken their existence.

It would come one day. He was sure of that. Provided he could keep his steady coolness when dealing with bombs that might explode beneath his fingers at any second. Provided he could stay alive.

Richard Murdoch and Kenneth Horne were singing the signing-off tune of *Much Binding in the Marsh*, with their witty commentary on the events of the past week. Dennis hadn't heard a word of it. But his shivering had ceased and he was able to turn over and go to sleep.

In the house with the little turret at the corner of April Grove and March Street, Annie and Ted were also lying in bed. But the closeness they had once shared seemed to have gone and they lay apart, not touching. Since their argument that morning, they had scarcely spoken to each other, and they were too miserable to be able to go to sleep.

Never let the sun go down on your wrath, Annie's mother had always said, and Annie had tried to follow that advice. She remembered it now. I wish I could say I was sorry, she thought. But I can't. I *am* sorry we quarrelled,

I'm sorry he's upset, but I still think it's been going on too long. He's got to pull himself together some time, and giving way to it just isn't doing any good. And there *are* people going through worse – much worse – and not complaining about it. And besides –

'Look,' Ted said suddenly, breaking the day-long silence, 'I can't *help* it, Annie. If I could get over it, I would. D'you think I *want* to be like this, old before my time, sitting in a chair and mumbling like a ninety-year-old.' The desperation in his tone was something she had never heard before, and it ran like cold water into her veins. 'I *want* to get back to normal. D'you know something? I hate myself, some days. I look in the mirror and I think, Ted Chapman, what use are you to man or beast? You ought to be out there, doing your bit, helping the war effort like everyone else. And if you can't, you'd be better off making an end of yourself.' His voice sank to a whisper. 'Sometimes, Annie, that's just what I feel like doing. It'd be the best thing all round. You'd all be much better off without me.'

Annie could not reply. She rolled over towards him and felt for his hand. His fingers were stiff and unresponsive. She felt suddenly frightened.

'Don't talk like that, Ted,' she said shakily. 'You mustn't say such things. It's wicked even to think them.'

'It doesn't feel wicked to me,' Ted answered, and the energy had drained from his voice, leaving it flat and hopeless. His hand relaxed suddenly, turning limp and flaccid. 'It feels like the only thing to do.'

'It's not. It's not.' Her fingers tightened around his, trying to find some response, some sign of strength. 'Ted, there's enough tragedy in this world without us adding to it. You've got to think of other people. Think how upset everyone would be if anything happened to you. Think about me. What would I do?'

'You'd be all right. You can cope with anything. I've never known anyone as good at managing as you.'

'Well, I couldn't cope with *that*,' she said vehemently. 'I couldn't manage at all without you, Ted, and don't you forget it. You're all I've got now. Our Colin's at sea, our

Betty's on the land, Olive's married and in the ATS – we've got to look after each other, you and me. That's what we got married for in the first place, remember? Not because we wanted kids. Because we wanted *each other*.'

'Oh, Annie,' he said, and she could hear the tears in his voice, the difficult tears of a man who had been unused to weeping for over forty years and was now overwhelmed by the need to cry. 'Annie, I don't know what I'd do without you, I really don't.'

He rolled into her arms and she held him close, letting him weep in great, shuddering sobs against her breast. Her own tears flowed to join his, running down into her neck, pooling in the hollow of her throat, and she felt at last a real compassion – not the pity she had felt until now, which had begun to turn to contempt, but the empathy that was true understanding of his condition.

He's right, she thought, he can't help it. Dunkirk, the bombing, it's all hurt him somewhere deep down and we've just got to wait for it to heal. And never mind the others, who are going through worse – this is Ted, my Ted, and I can't make him any different from what he is. I've just got to wait, and be strong.

But as his body trembled and shook against hers and his tears soaked her breast, she stared into the darkness, feeling cold and bleak and lonely, and wondering how much longer her strength could last.

CHAPTER TEN

Since the night of the dance, Carol Glaister and Roddy had spent every spare minute together. At least two nights a week, they went to the cinema and sat in the back row. It took quite a long time on the first evening for Roddy to pluck up courage to slip his arm around Carol's shoulders, even though she was snuggling invitingly against him, but he managed it halfway through the big picture and they sat cuddling close together, watching Leslie Howard in *Pimpernel Smith*. Afterwards, they shared a pennyworth of chips wrapped in newspaper and walked slowly home.

Roddy kissed Carol goodnight just outside her front door and she felt, as she told Joy Brunner afterwards, as if she was drowning. Joy listened, half envious, half unconvinced, and when Carol suggested again that she come to the next dance she shook her head.

'I don't like the soldiers. I don't want to be kissed and pawed about.'

'Go on, it's just a bit of fun. You've got to do it some time.'

'I don't see why.'

'Don't be daft. Everyone's got to do it. You've got to do a lot more than that when you get married.'

Joy wrinkled her nose distastefully. 'I shan't get married, then.'

'You won't have any kids. Not unless they're – you know – *illegitimate*.' Carol lowered her voice to speak the word, glancing over her shoulder as she did so. 'Mind you, you'd still have to do *it*, even then. There's no other way. Your mum and dad did it.'

Joy thought of Alice, with her stringy grey hair, and her father, no longer the neat, dapper little man he had been but carelessly dressed, with stains on his pullover and his moustache turning yellow, and felt revolted. She turned away.

'I don't want to talk about it. And I don't want to know about you and Roddy. I think it's all horrible.'

Carol laughed. 'It's not horrible, it's lovely. Not that we've done anything,' she added quickly. 'Only kissed and held hands in the pictures. There's nothing wrong with that.'

It was at the cinema that they saw most of the war news. *Pathe Pictorial* always came on between the big film and the small one, and a series of images filled the screen, with a commentary told in a hard, hurrying voice. It was much more dramatic than hearing it on the wireless, and they sat staring at film of soldiers out in the deserts of Africa, of Hitler's troops advancing through terrible blizzards on Moscow, or ships like the *Ark Royal* being blown up at sea. Roddy clutched Carol's hand tightly when such pictures appeared and she squeezed back, then lifted her free hand to her mouth and bit her knuckles. When it got too bad she looked down at her lap, trying to shut out the loud, hectoring voice of the commentator.

It wasn't so bad when they showed pictures of people at home. It didn't matter what happened, the film photographers could always find shots of smiling faces, of people 'taking it' as they dug out the rubble of their homes or queued cheerfully for scraps of fish or meat or a handful of sausages. They saw queues of another sort, too – single women in their twenties, being called up to serve in the police, the fire service or the Forces, all women under forty being registered as 'available labour'. That'd give Mum a turn, Carol thought, she was always making out she was still in her thirties when Carol knew for a fact (having come across her marriage certificate in a drawer) that she was forty-two.

'A lot of them women must be fed up at having to go out to work in factories,' she whispered to Roddy. 'But they all look as pleased as if they're going to a party.'

He didn't answer. She glanced at him and saw that even in the darkness his face looked pale. He was still thinking about the pictures of ships being blown up and sunk. They didn't ought to show such things, she thought indignantly. It's not fair.

The next day was a Sunday. Roddy came round after dinner and they went on the ferry to Gosport, just for the ride, and walked up the High Street. There wasn't much there, but it made a change from Pompey and Carol had always liked the short boat trip across the harbour, seeing all the ships, even when the weather wasn't up to much. They walked slowly, pausing to look in some of the shop windows – the little Woolworths and Littlewoods down by the Hard, not a patch on the ones in Pompey, Carol thought, and the sweetshop halfway up, and Nobes, the toyshop in Stoke Road. They passed the Forum cinema and the White Hart.

'I've got something to tell you,' Roddy said at last.

Carol stopped dead in the middle of the pavement. 'You've got a ship.'

He nodded. 'HMS *Cadover*. She's in for repairs. We'll be sailing pretty soon.' He looked at her miserably. 'I'll be going away, Carrie.'

'Oh, Roddy,' she said, and buried her face against the blue serge of his tunic.

He put his arms round her and held her close. Then he turned her face up to his and kissed the tears. 'You know I don't want to go,' he said. 'I canna face leaving you, Carol.'

'I don't want you to go either. But what can we do? Like you said – we don't have any choice.' She drew herself out of his arms and they walked on in silence. They reached Foster Gardens, a little ornamental corner of paths and shrubberies, with a pergola and a round pond in the middle. It was damp and misty, and they were the only people there. They sat on a seat in a small wooden shelter and gazed at the silent pond.

'This is a really pretty place in summer,' Carol said.

'There's all roses over those trellises, and lilies on the pond, and the rockeries are lovely.' Her voice trailed away. 'It's going to be awful without you, Roddy.'

'I know.' He put his arm round her shoulders. 'I don't want to go to sea. I never did, but now I've met you . . . Och, I might never come back, Carrie. I might never see you again.'

'Roddy, don't.' Once again, the tears began to flow. 'I can't bear it.'

They clung together in the quiet garden. A woman came in with a small terrier. She let it off the lead and it rushed up to them and sniffed their ankles. The woman called it away and it gave a yelp, put its head on one side to give them a last, bright-eyed glance, and rushed off.

'I wanted to court you properly,' Roddy said at last. 'I wanted to ask you to marry me, and give you a ring and all that. And now there's nae time.'

Carol lifted her head and stared at him. 'You wanted us to get engaged?'

'I want to be with you all the time. I want you to be my wife.'

'But I'm not old enough! I'm not even sixteen till next month. And Mum would never let us get married.'

'We're never going to get the chance,' Roddy said. 'This war'll finish me, Carrie, I know it. I'm going to be killed, and never have a chance to live my life.' His eyes were desperate. 'I canna go away without loving you just once,' he said. 'I canna just leave you like this.'

'I can't bear you to go.' She felt the roughness of his serge tunic under her fingers, tried to imagine the moment when he walked away from her and she could no longer touch him, see him, hear his voice. The pain of loss filled her already and she gripped his arms convulsively and pulled him hard against her. 'I can't let you go – I can't.'

The short December afternoon was drawing in, the low mist bringing darkness early. The garden was growing dim. The woman with the terrier had gone and there was nothing to be heard but the soft drip of condensation from the leaves of a few evergreen shrubs.

Roddy pressed his face against Carol's cheek. She could feel the faint roughness of his chin against her smooth skin. She turned her face so that their lips met, and stroked her fingers on the back of his neck.

He pulled her coat open and touched her breast. He had done this before, and always Carol felt a surge of excitement at his touch, a need to be closer. She made a tiny, soft whimpering sound and moved her body so that she was half-lying on the bench.

'Oh, Carol,' he whispered in her ear. 'Carol, my sweet, lovely Carol . . . I love you. I love you.'

'I love you too, Roddy.' His lips were warm on hers, on her neck, on her small, growing breasts. Something was fluttering deep inside her, beating butterfly wings against her heart. Her head was spinning. She had forgotten everything except her need to be closer to him, to be somehow merged with him, to keep him with her always. She felt her body become soft and pliable, her bones melt, as his hands touched her and stroked her and caressed her into a daze of need. His fingers brushed her thighs, drawing up her skirt, and she could feel his own skin against hers, his flesh warm and cool, smooth and rough. Her body was liquid. It parted for him and closed around him, and she folded him deep within her and clasped him in a gentle, pulsating rhythm that quickened and soared, sweeping them at last with sudden devastating power to a momentary peak, and holding them there for a breathless instant of eternity before dashing them into the valley below.

They lay in each other's arms, bemused, only half aware of where they were or what had happened.

'Carol . . .' Roddy whispered at last. 'Oh, *Carol* . . .'

'Roddy.' She turned her head. His face was close to hers, his eyes half shut, his lips parted. She kissed them softly. 'Roddy, I love you so much.'

Only a day later, the news came through that the Japanese had attacked Pearl Harbour. America was at war.

Frank added a new section to the big map that now covered the living-room wall. Pearl Harbour was in the islands of Hawaii, deep in the South Pacific. He stared at the unfamiliar territory, fixing in his mind the shapes of China, Japan, Borneo and North Australia. They all looked frighteningly close to each other.

'But Japan's such a little country,' Jess said. 'How can they beat somewhere as big as America?'

'By taking them by surprise,' Frank said soberly. 'It says in the paper they sank nearly twenty warships, destroyed nearly two hundred aircraft and killed two and half thousand men. Just in a couple of hours! And all they lost was five midget submarines, one ordinary one and about thirty planes. They just about wiped out the Pacific Fleet in one go.'

'The aircraft carriers weren't there, though. They didn't get hit.'

'Just as well,' Frank said. 'I bet the Japs were disappointed. If they could have got them as well . . .'

'It's the whole world now, isn't it.' Jess stared at the map with its black and red pins stuck in all over it. 'It's spreading like some horrible disease. Europe, Russia, Africa, Japan, America, Australia – everyone's mixed up in it. I don't see how they can ever sort it all out, Frank.' She bent and picked up Maureen, who was clinging to her skirt and grizzling. 'Poor little mite. What sort of a world have we brought you into?'

A state of emergency had been declared in Singapore and the forces in Malaya stood at battle stations, with the warships *Prince of Wales* and *Repulse* already on their way to give aid. Britain had declared war on Japan, Finland, Hungary and Romania. China also declared war, on Japan, Germany and Italy. It was, as Jess said, like a disease spreading all over the world. And how could anyone keep up with it all? How could you know who was fighting who?

Moscow's torment was eased at last by the bitter winter, which struck at the German troops and forced them to retreat. The Russian army, equipped for the cruel weather that only they understood, drove them across the frozen plains. The Germans announced that they had 'no reason' to expose their troops to the rigours of the Russian winter; they would wait and take Moscow in the spring. But it seemed clear that this offensive had failed and would not be recovered.

Boys and girls of sixteen were now told they must register for service, and the boys encouraged to join the Home Guard. 'We must see that our *boys do not run loose*,' Winston Churchill said as the announcements were made.

'He must be thinking of brats like Micky Baxter,' Frank commented. 'But I wouldn't have thought they'd want his sort in the Home Guard.'

'He's too young, anyway,' Jess said, thankful that the same applied to her own boys. She was still anxious about Tim, who wasn't enjoying the repetition of his last year at junior school. But at least he'd be taking his exam soon. He'd probably feel better then.

Mr Churchill also warned of a '*very hard period*' ahead, but believed that the flow of aid and arms from America would '*vastly exceed anything that could have been expected on a peacetime basis*' and prophesied that together Britain, America and the Soviet Union would teach the '*gangs of wicked men*' a lesson they would not forget in a thousand years.

'He knows what he's doing,' Frank said. 'If anyone can steer us through this mess, he can. And with Roosevelt on our side as well . . . It'll all come out right, Jess, you'll see.'

But for thousands – millions – of people it would not come out all right. They would die, never knowing if their sacrifice was in vain.

The news grew worse. Both *Repulse* and the *Prince of Wales* were sunk by Japanese aircraft as they steamed towards Singapore – another thousand men lost, and each of them some mother's son. It was enough to break your heart.

And there must be thousands of broken hearts, in homes all over the country, as families grieved for these and for others, their lives wasted in a cause that was now irretrievably lost in the muddle of hatred and brutality that the world had become.

Every day the horror grew. Hong Kong, abandoned by the British, Canadian and Indian troops who had been stationed there, lay under siege. More vicious attacks by the Japanese destroyed half the American Far East Air Force, and half the British air strength in northern Malaya. Only a week before Christmas, the British Mediterranean Fleet was torn asunder, with the Malta convoy sailing into a minefield and the battleships *Queen Elizabeth* and *Valiant* destroyed along with several other ships in Alexandria. It began to look as if the Mediterranean would have to be abandoned.

'God knows what would happen then,' Frank said gloomily. 'It's vital, the Med is.'

Frank was gloomy most of the time these days, and Jess hardly dared ask if Tim and Keith could come home for Christmas. There hadn't been so many air-raids lately, but the warnings were still sounding regularly and you never knew when another blitz might start. Why, last year they'd had that terrible raid down in Conway Street on Christmas Eve itself. And the blitz had started not long after the boys had gone back. Who was to say what Hitler had up his sleeve for 1942?

But to her surprise, Frank declared that the boys could come for three days – Christmas Eve, Christmas Day and Boxing Day. Not only that, they'd have Stella and Muriel as well. He would ride his bike over and bring them on the train and take them back.

He hesitated. 'Matter of fact, there's something else I want to talk to you about, Jess.'

'Talk about?' Jess stared at him, feeling a sudden sinking in her heart. 'What's that? Is it about this Cherry?'

'Well, yes.' Frank looked uncomfortable. 'It's just – well, you know I've been talking about her quite a bit –'

'Quite a bit?' Jess said before she could stop herself. 'You haven't stopped these past few weeks.'

'Oh come on, Jess. It's not that bad. You get plenty of chance to put your five eggs in.'

Jess bit her lip. Frank had been touchier lately, answering her sharply and snapping at Rose and even the baby. She'd talked to her sister about it and Annie had given her opinion that everyone was on a short tether these days, what with being up half the night with air-raid warnings and firewatching, and never knowing what was going to happen next. But Jess hadn't been able to suppress an anxious feeling that in Frank's case there might be more to it than that.

Suppose there really was something in her fears about this Cherry. She would never have believed that a steady chap like Frank would ever let a slip of a girl turn his head, but everything was turning upside down these days and you just didn't know. Strain made people do some funny things, and when you got saucy little flirts dancing around a place like a boiler-shop with a lot of men –

'All right, then,' she said, more sharply than she meant to, 'what about this Cherry, then? What's she been up to now?'

'She hasn't been up to anything. I just thought – well, here she is in Pompey with none of her own family around, nothing much to do when she's not at work – I thought we might just ask her over for Christmas dinner or something, that's all.' He looked at Jess, an odd, half pleading expression on his face, and she was reminded suddenly of Tim. 'Only if you want to, mind, but I know she'd like to meet you.'

'She'd like to meet *me*?' Jess stared at him. It was the last thing she'd expected. Not that she knew really just what she did expect, but if anything *was* going on between this Cherry and Frank – not that she'd ever suspect Frank of such a thing, not in a million years, but all the same, men were men, couldn't help it, and some of these young girls these days, nothing but brazen hussies they were, you couldn't get away from it, and . . . She caught up her floundering thoughts and tried to get them into some sort of order. Would Frank be asking to bring this girl home if there was anything – well, not quite right?

'What d'you think?' he asked, a shade anxiously. 'It's for you to say, Jess.'

Suddenly, Jess knew that there was only one thing she could say. Like it or not, she'd have to meet this Cherry, if only so that she could picture her when Frank mentioned her name. And once I see her, I'll know, she thought. I'll know if there's anything to worry about.

She shrugged and spoke offhandedly. 'Tell you what. Ask her for dinner next Sunday, if you want, then if we get on all right we can think about Christmas. Can't promise anything special, mind, we're on rations, visitors or no visitors.'

'That's all right.' He looked relieved. 'Cherry knows all about rations. I don't reckon she gets more than bread and scrape in her lodgings. Canteen dinner's the only cooked meal she gets. She'll appreciate whatever you provide.'

I just hope she does, Jess thought. And I hope she realises that I'm not going to provide anything apart from a meal. My Frank's not there for the taking.

Perhaps it was a good idea after all to bring her home, so that Jess could size her up and see just what it was about this girl that was fascinating her husband.

Cherry Buckley came to dinner with Frank and Jess the following Sunday. She was coming by bus from her lodgings in Portsea, and Frank walked up the street to meet her.

Jess fussed about the little terraced house, telling herself that it didn't matter two hoots what the girl thought of her home, yet at the same time anxiously determined that there wouldn't be a thing out of place, nor a speck of dirt to be seen. She washed Maureen's face three times in a quarter of an hour and told Rose to dust the ornaments on the mantelpiece half a dozen times before the girl rebelled.

'There isn't any more dust on them, there can't be. Why do we have to do all this anyway? We don't bother when it's Auntie Annie or Mrs Shaw popping in.'

'That's different,' Jess snapped, though she would not

have known how to explain the difference if Rose had asked. She glanced at the clock. 'Your father's been gone nearly twenty minutes. Whatever can they be doing?' Her imagination showed her Frank doing something totally uncharacteristic – taking this Cherry into a pub, for instance, which he would never normally dream of. 'I'll walk up the street and see if I can meet them,' she said, removing her pinafore. 'You stay here with Maureen.'

Rose pulled a face, but Jess ignored her and marched out of the front door and over to the corner of October Street. The street was empty, with the quiet of a November Sunday drifting in the mist. There was no sign of Frank, nor of anyone who might be called Cherry.

Jess started to walk up the street. She didn't really want to be introduced to this girl in public, but neither did she want to stay in the house any longer. And she didn't want Rose's sharp eyes observing this first meeting. The girl was getting altogether too knowing just lately. Only the other day, when Jess had told her that a young neighbour had just had a baby, Rose had replied that she'd already known it was on the way, and when asked how had retorted 'Because she got fat, like *you* did.' Jess had been shocked, not least by the resentment in Rose's tone. Maybe we were wrong to keep it from her when Maureen was on the way, she thought. Maybe she would have enjoyed helping to get things ready, sharing it all.

She was halfway up to September Street when two figures came round the corner and approached her. Jess stopped and stared.

One was unmistakably Frank. She could even see the expression on his face – smiling, laughing a bit, walking easily and assured like a man who had nothing to hide, nothing at all to feel uneasy about. But the other . . .

Cherry Buckley – if that was who this was – was no saucy young woman, not long out of school, with flirting eyes and a pert, too obvious figure. Instead, she was almost middle-aged – at least in her late thirties, Jess thought – and short. No more than five feet, probably. And she was plump too – a little round body with a little round head stuck on top, for all the world like a cottage loaf. Her face was round and quite plain, with a distinct resemblance to Winston Churchill, and she had very short, thin hair with almost no colour to it.

This wasn't the sort of person to turn men's heads.

Jess forced herself to step forwards again. They had seen her at once and were approaching quickly. On Frank's face she saw a look of pride and he reached out a hand and laid it on her shoulder, drawing her close.

'This is Jess,' he said, and there was no mistaking the affection in his voice.

Cherry held out her hand. Her round face had split into a thousand beaming creases, her small blue eyes almost disappearing in their folds. Dazed, Jess took her hand and Cherry enveloped it in both of hers.

'Eh, I'm right glad to meet you,' she said in a broad Birmingham accent. 'It's ever so nice of you to ask me over. Frank's told me such a lot about you. Is it all right if I call you Jess? I feel like we're old friends already.'

'Yes – yes, of course it's all right,' Jess stammered. Why hadn't Frank told her Cherry had a strong Birmingham accent? Why hadn't he told her what Cherry *looked* like? 'I'm glad you could come,' she added warmly, feeling relief flood through her body. 'It must be awful being away from your family and having to live in lodgings.'

'Eh, that don't bother me,' Cherry said cheerfully as they started back down October Street. 'I'm used to it. I was a housekeeper when all this lot started, in a big house. Worked me way up from scullerymaid. Went into service when I was fourteen and never lived at home since. The place I've got now isn't much cop, but I've had worse.'

'So you've been in domestic service,' Jess said with interest. 'My sister Annie did that. She was a cook.'

'And a lot of fancy ideas it gave her too,' Frank said from Cherry's other side. 'Jug of water on the table. Rice with meat. Bits of this and bits of that. At least she's had to tone it down a bit since the war started.'

'Oh aye, they likes their bits and pieces, folk with a bit o' money,' Cherry agreed. 'Were you in service too, Jess?'

Her easy use of Jess's first name was slightly startling. Most people gave you your proper title until they knew you really well. But Cherry didn't seem to have any shyness or reserve, she just came straight out with whatever she wanted to say. Perhaps that was why Frank liked her.

'I was apprenticed to a dressmaker,' she said. 'Our mother wanted us to learn things that would always be useful to us. I make nearly all my own clothes, and the girls' too. I can't do so much for the boys now they're bigger, tailoring's not my line.'

'I don't mind a bit of sewing,' Cherry said. 'Or knitting. I knit all me own jumpers and things.'

They reached number 14 and Frank opened the door. Jess led the way in. She'd intended to keep Cherry in the front room, with its three-piece suite and little polished table that Frank had made, but it seemed more natural to take her on into the back, where the fire was burning brightly because it was a Sunday, and Maureen was playing with some coloured wooden bricks on the rag rug.

'Ooh, so you're the baby,' Cherry exclaimed, bending down at once. 'Eh, you're a little beauty an' all.'

Maureen looked up, startled. She was going through a shy phase and Jess wondered if she would burst into tears at this sudden intrusion. But instead, after staring for a moment or two, her face broke into a smile and she reached up a hand and patted Cherry's cheek. Jess noticed the warts on Cherry's skin, but they didn't seem to bother the baby.

'Well, you've scored a hit,' Jess said as Maureen scrambled to her feet and held up her arms. 'And this is Rose. Rose, say hello to Miss Buckley.'

'Eh no, call me Cherry,' the little woman said, beaming at Rose. 'Everyone does. If anyone says "Miss Buckley" I have to look round to see if someone's standing behind me.'

'Sit down,' Frank said, gesturing towards Jess's armchair. 'I daresay the dinner's nearly ready, isn't it, Jess?'

'It won't be long.' Jess watched as the visitor settled herself in the chair and lifted Maureen on to her lap. She had taken off her brown winter coat and was dressed in a grey jumper, obviously handknitted in a rather loose stitch so that it hung baggily on her round little body. Her skirt was a plain, muddy tweed and she wore thick lisle stockings and heavy shoes. Jess had a sudden vision of the Cherry she had expected to see, and felt her lips pull themselves into a smile.

'Well, you are a little duck, and no two ways about it,' Cherry said to Maureen. 'And is this your big sister, then? I bet you did everything for her when she was a little mite, didn't you, Rose?'

'Rose was like a little mother to her,' Jess said warmly. 'No one ever had a better little helper. Mind, she's not always so keen to look after her these days.'

Rose scowled. 'I do a lot to help.'

'Of course you do. She's a lovely little cook,' Jess told Cherry. 'Bake a cake, cook a roast dinner – that's if we ever had such a thing these days – our Rose can turn her hand to anything. She was just learning when the war started – did some lovely little fancy cakes, but now you're not allowed to do icing, she's had to stop. And she does a lot around the house.'

'That's right,' Cherry said. 'It's all good training. Me mum made sure we could all do a bit of cooking and sewing and cleaning before we left school. You can always find a job if you're handy in the house.'

Rose settled down on a stool beside her. 'I'm going to work in an office. I'm learning typing and shorthand.'

'Typing!' Cherry said. 'Eh, that's grand. So you're going to be a secretary, are you?'

'Yes,' Rose said. The idea of being a secretary had never actually occurred to her, but it certainly sounded more impressive than 'working in an office', which her cousin Olive had done in Harker's builder's yard. 'Or a Civil Servant,' she added, remembering what her father had said.

'My godfathers! A Civil Servant. That'll please your dad.'

Frank had gone out to join Jess in the kitchen. The square dining-table that stood in the middle of the room had been laid for four, with Maureen's high chair next to Jess's place. A smell of stew wafted through the door.

Cherry sniffed appreciatively and went on talking to Rose about what she was doing at school and when she would be leaving. She nodded sympathetically when Rose told her that all her friends had already left and got jobs. She was especially interested to hear about Joy Brunner.

'Your dad told me about her. Poor little soul, she's had a rough time. Still, her father's home now and she's working in the shop, she'll be all right.'

'Yes.' But Rose didn't sound too sure. There had been something odd about Joy just lately. She seemed uneasy, sometimes snappy, at others almost in tears as she begged Rose to assure her that they were still 'best friends'. It was as if they had quarrelled, yet Rose couldn't think of anything that had gone wrong between them. It was ever since the day of Hilsea Fair, she thought. The day when they'd met Carol Glaister and Carol had got tickets for the dance.

Rose had asked Joy once how she'd enjoyed the dance, but Joy had just shrugged and said it was 'all right'. But she hadn't gone to any more.

'Dinner's ready,' Jess said, coming back into the room with a large bowl of stew. 'It's not a proper Sunday dinner, we can't often get meat for a roast these days. But I thought on a day like this, a good beef stew with plenty of vegetables would warm us up.'

'Eh,' Cherry said, lifting Maureen into her high chair and settling down beside her, 'that looks right good. Better'n canteen dinners in the Yard, eh, Frank?'

'I should hope so,' he said, bringing in a bowl of mashed potatoes. 'You know I never eat 'em meself, Jess gives me a dinner to heat up. Now, you just have a good plateful, Cherry, it's all homegrown veg and there's some of our own fruit for after. Jess bottles it and we has it stewed all through the winter.'

'That's what I don't make into jam,' Jess said. 'Frank

grows a lot of fruit over on the allotment. We wouldn't live half so well if he didn't keep us provided.'

Cherry pointed her fork at Frank. 'I want to see this allotment of yours after. We'll walk over soon as I've helped Jess with the pots.'

Rose gaped at her. She had never heard anyone – not even her mother – talk to Frank like that, as if they were giving him orders. Half afraid of his reaction, she swivelled her eyes round to her father. But he was just helping himself to mashed potatoes and grinning a bit, as if he rather liked being ordered about by Cherry.

During dinner they discussed Jess's methods of bottling fruit and making jam, an argument one of Frank's workmates had had with the foreman and the new tunnel shelters which were being built under Portsdown Hill. They were almost complete and were expected to open after Christmas.

'I don't know that I fancy them much,' Jess said. 'I've never much liked being in caves. I went to Cheddar once and the stalactites were lovely, but I kept thinking about all that rock up on top of us. I mean, what's there to stop it falling in? I knew a little boy once, got buried in a sandpit, he was choked to death before they got him out.'

'Those caves have been there for millions of years,' Frank said. 'They've never fallen in all that time, why should they now?'

'Why shouldn't they?' Cherry asked. 'The world don't stand still. It's all moving a little bit, all the time – you just want one little stone to move and the whole lot'll come tumbling down. Like those bricks your Maureen was playing with just now.'

'Well, anyway, these tunnel shelters aren't the same – they're properly built. There's nothing to worry about there.'

'People are going to have tickets for the shelters,' Rose said. 'There's even going to be bunks with your name on them. It'll be your own special place. And there'll be canteens and First Aid and all sorts down there.'

'I don't know,' Jess said dubiously. 'It sounds all right,

but it all depends on the other people, doesn't it? I mean, you can't choose who's going to be in the next bunk. It might be anyone. I think I'd rather stay in our own shelter.'

Frank pushed his pudding bowl over for another helping of stewed gooseberries. Jess might say that she couldn't present such a good table with all this rationing, but today's dinner had been as good as any peacetime meal. Not as much beef as he'd like in the stew, it was true, but plenty of other good things, with the added satisfaction that he'd grown most of it himself.

Later, he and Jess and Cherry walked over to the allotment. Rose had gone up to September Street to spend an hour with Joy and they were able to talk more freely. Jess took the opportunity to mention her worries about their daughter.

'It's nothing you can really put your finger on. She just seems different, somehow. I mean, she's never been one to sulk or answer back, but just lately she's been quite sharp when I've told her to do something. And she seems to be turning against Maureen for no reason at all.'

Maureen was toddling along the narrow paths leading between the allotments. She was wearing a pair of gaiters Jess had made from an old pair of corduroy trousers of Frank's, and she kept stopping to peer down at her legs with a funny little smile of pride crinkling her lips.

'She's growing up too fast,' Frank said. 'They all are these days. Why, I saw that Carol Glaister from next door walking down the street with a sailor the other day, bold as brass, her face all made up and arms round each other's waists. I don't want our Rose getting those ideas.'

'I don't think any of them knows *how* to grow up,' Cherry said. 'I mean, a few years ago it was all plain and easy. Young girls waited till they were sixteen or seventeen before they even thought about walking out with a boy, and then they'd bring him home first for Dad to look over. Now they're getting called up and going away to work on the land or in munitions and all, and they just run riot. We've got a few in the Yard, haven't we, Frank? Saucy little bits of nonsense, wants their bottoms smacked for them.'

And that's the sort of girl I imagined Frank bringing home today, Jess thought. She looked at Cherry's cottage-loaf body, stumping along the path holding Maureen's hand, and wanted to laugh again. But not at Cherry. Her laughter was directed at herself.

Late that night, when Cherry had gone back to her lodgings and she and Frank were in bed, Jess lay in her husband's arms and smiled at him. She knew that her smiles and kisses were different now, just as their lovemaking had been different – lighter, more joyous, more as it used to be. And she knew that this was because a weight had been lifted from her heart that she hadn't even realised was there.

'What are you laughing at?' Frank asked lazily. He too felt more relaxed, his recent tension eased. He did not know why; he only knew that when Jess was happy, he was happy, and when she was miserable, he was worried. 'Tell me the joke.'

'It's not a joke. I was just wondering – why did you make friends with Cherry?'

'Don't you like her?' he asked in surprise. 'I thought the two of you got on really well.'

'Oh, we did. I like her very much. And I'll be glad to have her here for Christmas. But what do *you* like about her, Frank? What made you like her in the first place?'

He considered. 'I dunno, really. I don't think it was so much a matter of *liking* her exactly, not first off. I suppose I felt sorry for her, mostly. I mean, she's no oil-painting, is she, with that funny little face and all those warts and everything. It can't have given her much of a chance in life. But it don't seem to bother her. She's always cheerful, always got something to say, and yet she don't let anyone trample over her. I reckon I just liked her spirit, once I got to know her.'

You felt sorry for her, Jess thought. And she remembered her uneasy suspicions, and felt ashamed.

'Give me another hug,' she said, tightening her arms around him, 'and then we'd better go to sleep.'

On Christmas Day, Hong Kong surrendered to the Japanese. A week later, on January 1st, 1942, the four great powers – Great Britain, the United States, the Soviet Union and China – and 22 other countries signed a solemn agreement, as the 'United Nations', to fight to the utmost against the Axis. They accounted for four-fifths of the world's population.

'That gives us a bit of hope,' Frank said. 'We won't get countries agreeing to peace in dribs and drabs. It's one for all and all for one now.'

But the enemy were still attacking on all fronts, and Japan had embraced war with total dedication. Now they had taken the Malayan capital, Kuala Lumpur, and Singapore itself was under grave threat. They spread across the Pacific like a tidal wave.

Roddy's ship, HMS *Cadover*, had sailed only to be damaged in the North Atlantic by a mine. She wasn't badly damaged and managed to limp back to Portsmouth, where she went into dock again for repairs.

'It was the worst thing I've ever seen,' Roddy told Carol. 'I thought we were a goner. Tore a great hole in the bulkhead and the water just came gushing in. They managed to seal it off but we had a turrible list on all the way back.'

'You could have died,' Carol said, hugging him tightly. 'Oh, Roddy, I don't want you to go away again.'

They were sitting in the front room of number 15. Ethel was out but might come back at any minute and they dared not take the chance to love each other as fully as they longed to do. Roddy slipped his hand inside Carol's blouse and she closed her eyes, ecstatic and yearning.

'I wish we could be married,' she murmured. 'At least we could be together when you came back. We'd have a right.'

'Are you sure you mother wouldnae let you?' Carol had had her sixteenth birthday now and Roddy had given her a tiny pearl pin which she considered her engagement 'ring'.

'Not in a million years. There's no point even asking.'

'If we were in Scotland,' Roddy said, 'we wouldnae have to ask. People can get married there at sixteen without anyone's permission at all.'

'Can they? Really?'

'Aye. There's no harm ever came of it that I've been able to see.'

'If we were in Scotland . . .' Carol repeated dreamily. 'Oh Roddy, just think. If we lived near enough, we could just slip over the Border . . . Isn't there somewhere special you have to go? Gretna Green – I've heard of that.'

'You don't *have* to go there. It's just that it's the nearest place to the Border. There's a tradition that people can get married in the blacksmith's forge.'

'The blacksmith's forge!' Carol giggled. 'What a place to get married. You wouldn't want to wear a white frock, would you.' She thought for a moment. 'All the same, I wish we lived a bit nearer. We could go there and no one could stop us – and once we were married, we could do what we liked.'

'I'd still have to go away,' he pointed out. 'That's the worst of it, Carrie.'

'I know.' She was silent again, then she suddenly drew in a breath and turned to him, her eyes bright. 'Roddy, why don't we do it? Why don't we go to Gretna Green and get married? And then we could just go and live somewhere together, where nobody'd ever find us. You don't have to go back to your ship. You don't have to fight. We could just be together – somewhere nobody will dream of looking. Scotland –'

'That's the first place they'd look. That's where I live.'

'Wales, then. Or London. There are millions of people in London, it'd be like looking for a needle in a haystack. Or *anywhere*.' She gripped his sleeve and gazed at him. 'Let's do it, Roddy. Let's just go away.'

He stared at her, biting his lip, his brows drawn together. His chin had a soft fuzz on it; he had been shaving ever since he joined the Navy, though as yet there was no real need. He'd told Carol he wanted to grow a beard but you had to ask permission and if the growth of hair wasn't very strong they wouldn't let you.

'That's deserting,' he said at last. 'I could get shot.'

'Only if they find you. They'll never find you, Roddy, not if we're careful. We'll change our names. I'll dye my hair. We can get jobs –'

'How? You have to be registered. And what about our ration books?'

'We'll manage somehow.' Carol swept his doubts aside. 'People lose their ration books all the time. We'll say we've been bombed out, got nowhere to go. They'll never check up, they don't have time. We'd be *together*, Roddy.'

'That's all I want,' he said. 'Us to be together, and out of all this fighting.'

'What right do they have to tell us what to do with our lives?' Carol demanded. 'What right do they have to send you away to be killed?'

The sound of Ethel's key in the front door made them spring apart. When she came into the room, wrapped in the astrakhan coat she'd bought in Bulpitt's last winter, they were sitting decorously on the settee, their faces still a little flushed.

Ethel gave them a sharp glance. 'I hope you two haven't been up to anything you shouldn't be.'

Roddy stood up, his flush deepening, but Carol answered pertly, 'We haven't if you haven't.'

'And that's enough of your sauce, miss.' Ethel reddened with anger. She looked at Roddy. 'Time you were out of here, young man. I won't have the neighbours talking about my daughter the way they do about young Diane Shaw.'

'Why, what's Diane been doing?' Carol asked with interest. 'I haven't heard nothing.'

'Never you mind what she's been doing, but when a girl goes out night after night and comes back in the dark with a different bloke every time, it doesn't take many guesses to get it right. She's always been a flighty piece, that Diane, and I'm not having you causing gossip, all right?'

'Let us get married then,' Carol said daringly. 'Doesn't matter what we do then, does it.'

Ethel swung her hand at Carol's cheek, but the girl stepped back quickly and she missed. Roddy stepped forward in dismay.

'Och, there's no need to go hitting her, Mrs Glaister –'

'You mind your own business,' she snapped. 'Carol's my daughter and under my control since her father's gone gallivanting off playing soldiers. I'll discipline her as I see fit. I told you to get out.'

'I was just going to make a cup of cocoa,' Carol said, her voice trembling slightly. 'He can stop for that, can't he?'

'I said *out*,' Ethel repeated, and held back the blackout curtain that hung at the front door.

Roddy gave Carol an agonised glance but she shrugged and turned down the corners of her mouth. 'It's all right,' she said, 'you get back now. I'll see you tomorrow, like we said.'

'We'll see about that,' Ethel began, but Carol met her eyes coolly.

'You can't stop me going to work, Mum. And if I want to see Roddy, I will. He hasn't done anything wrong.' She stepped past her mother and gave Roddy a quick kiss on the lips. ''Night, sweetheart. I'll see you tomorrow and we'll talk about – *you know what*.' And she gave him a quick flicker of a wink and pushed him gently out of the front door.

'And what was all that supposed to mean?' her mother demanded as soon as the door closed. 'What have you two been cooking up between you?'

'Nothing much,' Carol said airily, keeping out of range of Ethel's arm. 'We're just trying to decide which film to go and see, that's all. Roddy wants to see *In Which We Serve* but I'd rather see Leslie Howard again, in *First of the Few*. Which d'you think would be best?'

'I think it'd be best if you stopped going about with sailors,' Ethel said acidly. 'You've been a different girl since you met that young man. I've told you already, I don't like him. There's a look in his eye . . . If he hasn't taken advantage of you already, he'll try soon.' She eyed her daughter. '*Has* he done anything he shouldn't't?'

'No, he hasn't,' Carol said emphatically. 'And nor have I. We haven't done anything at all we shouldn't.'

And that was absolutely true, she thought as she climbed the stairs to go to bed. There hadn't been anything happen between her and Roddy that wasn't completely right and natural and good. All they had ever done was love each other.

She undressed and got into the cold bed, longing to feel Roddy's warm body beside her. She lay in the darkness, waiting as everyone always did for the wail of the siren, and thought of him going away, perhaps never to return.

We can't let it happen, she thought. We can't.

CHAPTER ELEVEN

The tunnel shelters were open now and Granny Kinch went along to have a look, with Nancy and Micky.

There was room for five thousand people in the deep caverns in the chalk. Clutching their tickets, the three entered through the big iron gates and walked down the passages as if they were in church. The walls were lined with corrugated iron, with concrete floors, and in the long dormitories were bunks in tiers of three, stretching away into the hill.

'It ain't a bit like being in a cave,' Micky said, disappointed. 'I thought it'd be all big and dark, with stally-whatsernames hanging down and bats with big wings.'

'Don't be daft,' Nancy said. 'These ain't real caves. They're tunnels what've bin dug down here. Stands to reason they'd make a proper job of it.'

'There's a canteen,' Granny Kinch said, looking at the piece of paper they'd been given. 'And a place for people to have a fag – you're not allowed to smoke in the bunks – and a place for entertainment. I wonder what sort of entertainment there'll be?'

'Tommy Handley,' Micky said gleefully. 'And Arthur Askey, and Enoch and Ramsbottom. It's going to be smashing.'

'They won't have none of them,' Nancy said. 'They'll have Vera Lynn and Anne Shelton. It's singsongs you want in a shelter.'

Micky made a face. Vera Lynn and Anne Shelton sang soppy girls' songs like *White Cliffs of Dover* and *As Time Goes By*. He thought jokes were better any day.

'There's a hospital too,' Granny Kinch said. 'A First Aid room, a sick bay, why there's even an isolation hospital for infectious diseases. You could *live* down here.'

'You could die here too.' Nancy shivered. 'I don't like it. It's not natural, being underground. I mean, suppose they bombed the place where you come in. We'd all be buried alive down here. We'd suffocate, like those poor sods in submarines.'

'Well, I reckon it's smashing,' Micky declared. He looked around the corridors and the long dormitory, his eyes gleaming, and wondered if the tunnels led into the other mysterious places under the Hill, the forts and ammunition dumps that everyone knew must be there.

He thought of all the people here, asleep, their belongings on the floor, the lights dim. And there'd be other boys too, boys he could recruit into his secret army.

He started to go to the tunnel shelters every night. At first, his mother and grandmother came with him, but Nancy soon drifted back to her usual haunts and Granny Kinch began to complain about the conditions down under the Hill. 'I'd rather be in me own place,' she said. 'Have a fag when I feel like it, and nobody around kicking up a din or telling you what to do. It's like being in the army down here. And they've never got Tommy Handley, nor Vera Lynn.'

Micky continued to go alone. He preferred it that way. There was no one to keep an eye on him, no one to question where he went as he roamed the crowded tunnels. People were supposed to stay in their own places, in the bunks that had their name and number on, but for the first few hours at least they were more inclined to go wandering, visiting friends and relatives in different sections, or going to the smoking area or the entertainment room. They brought their knitting and flasks of tea or cocoa and sat nattering, wondering what was going on outside. As often as not, there was no raid, but you could never be sure. Down here, all you'd hear would be the occasional rumble of a really big bomb. The sound of planes going over and the rattle of ack-ack fire was deadened.

And people were careless. They brought in great, sagging bags containing their knitting, magazines, books, newspapers, and strewed them about on the floor. Nagged by the wardens to keep the place tidy, they said there was nowhere else to keep their stuff. They piled it on their narrow bunks and it fell off when they turned over in their sleep. It got pushed and kicked underneath, and all mixed up together.

It was easy for a boy, wandering casually along the aisles as if looking for his own place, or for a mate, to help himself to a few oddments here and there.

So far, Micky hadn't had much luck with his army. He'd managed to gather a few more together, but the trouble was, round Copnor most of the kids at home were quite a bit smaller, like Martin Baker or Alan and Wendy Atkinson – not that he wanted girls in, anyway. There weren't many of about Micky's size. Younger ones were just kids, and bigger boys would want to be in charge.

Desmond, however, had no qualms about recruiting younger children. He felt more at ease with them, as if they were nearer his age than Micky. He had roped in Martin and Alan at once, though even he had had doubts about Wendy.

'You've got to let girls in,' Wendy said. 'Girls are going to be in everything. They're going to be policemen and firemen and soldiers and –'

'Go on,' Martin said derisively. 'How can a girl be a police*man*?'

'Well, they are. My Mum read it out of the paper. Anyway, you can't have Alan without me, he's not allowed out by himself.'

Given a choice between two recruits and no recruit at all, Desmond didn't have much option. He shrugged and hoped Micky wouldn't throw Wendy out straight away. She could climb trees and fight, after all. She was almost as tough as a boy.

'There's Susan Cullen, too,' Wendy said. 'She'll be in it.'

Desmond began to feel dimly alarmed. One girl was bad enough, but two . . .! However, Martin knew Susan Cullen. He had met her when he was running away from Bridge End, and she'd come with him. They'd been found wandering hand in hand on the Southampton road, lost, hungry and exhausted, and Martin had been taken straight to hospital to have his appendix out. They'd been friends ever since. Desmond knew that he wouldn't be in the army if she was turned out.

Micky was disgusted when he discovered that Desmond had allowed little kids like Alan Atkinson in, and even more when he found out about Wendy and Susan.

'I'm not having girls. Girls can't keep secrets.'

'I can't tell them they're not in now. I've said.'

'Well, say I won't have them. Otherwise you'll have to have an army of your own. A *girls'* army,' Micky sneered.

Wendy, however, was quite amenable to this idea. 'Girls are as good as boys any day. We'll be the Junior ATS. We'll have our own den and if you come round we'll fight you.' She eyed Micky, who was several sizes bigger, and poked out her tongue.

'Garn,' he said, turning his back. 'You'd never be able to get me down.'

For answer, Wendy shot out her foot and placed it between Micky's ankles, tripping him neatly. He lay on the ground, winded, and glared up at her.

'You're asking for it, Wendy Atkinson.'

'Pity you ain't got it,' she retorted, and skipped out of his reach. 'Come on, Alan – Susan. *We'll* show him who's the best army round here.'

'Alan can't be in your army,' Micky called, desperate for the last word. 'Not if it's a girls' army. He's a boy.'

Wendy turned and stuck out her tongue again. 'Think I don't know that? He's my brother, isn't he. He'll be our mascot. Every army has to have a mascot. You can't be a proper army without a mascot, so there, Micky Baxter.'

Micky scowled. The idea of a mascot had never occurred to him. He swore and gave Martin a push to relieve his feelings.

'All right,' he said reluctantly, 'but no more girls, see? This is going to be a fighting army, with real guns and grenades and things, and girls aren't allowed to use them, even in the real army.'

'Where are you going to get guns from?' Wendy asked interestedly, but Micky shook his head.

'That's secret. Only us officers knows that.'

So far, no weapons had been collected. But Micky, walking home from the tunnel shelter, was already turning over a few ideas in his mind. He had a new henchman now, too – Jimmy Cross who had lost his leg but now stumped cheerfully about on a wooden one. Jimmy was scornful of some of the members of the army, especially Desmond.

'I dunno why you want him in,' he said. 'He's barmy.'

'Yeah, but he knows a lot about aeroplanes, and guns and stuff like that,' Micky said. 'He's in the ATC and he goes up the airfield every week, trainin' and learnin' to shoot. You ask him anything about aeroplanes and see.'

Jimmy was sceptical, but the next time the boys met, in the den that Micky had established in the ruins of a bombed house, he listened open-mouthed as Desmond recited a list of the names of Allied aircraft, from the old Sopwith Camels and Tiger Moths that had been famous in the 1914–18 war and were still occasionally used as spotter planes, to the newest Hawker Hurricanes and Typhoons. He knew their weights, their airspeeds, the details of their engine power and their markings. He even knew the different kinds of sound they made.

'I never knew he knew all that,' Jimmy muttered. 'I always thought he was batty.'

'He is,' Micky said. 'He just knows a lot about some things. He don't know nothin' about others. He can't *think*. It's just like people knowin' a lot of poetry, it don't really mean nothin' to him.'

Desmond seemed to think it meant a lot, however. The sight of a home-made model aeroplane with some of the details missing upset him, although he could not explain what was wrong. Jimmy, who had spent a lot of his time in hospital and at home chipping away at bits of wood to make models, slipped the one he had brought back into his pocket. He didn't want to risk one of Desmond's sudden tempers.

As a member of the Air Training Corps, Desmond went to the local airfield on Sunday mornings for drill and rifle practice. He wore a uniform that was modelled on the RAF and although he still looked gangling and awkward in it, he seemed to stand up straighter, as if he was proud of himself. He towered above the other boys.

'It's not fair,' Micky said enviously. 'I ought to be in the ATC. I'd be as good as Des. Better.'

'You're not old enough,' Wendy said unnecessarily. She never missed an opportunity to take a dig at Micky. 'They don't let little boys play with guns.' She dodged expertly out of the way of Micky's foot.

Micky glowered, but said nothing. Wendy was smaller than he was, and a girl, but she could still hold her own in a scrap. And he was surprised to find that he was beginning to develop a grudging sort of liking for her. She didn't kowtow to him like the others did. It made her more interesting. Sometimes he thought it was a pity she couldn't be his Lieutenant instead of Desmond.

But he had other things to think about just now. Watching Desmond shamble away along the street on his way to Sunday morning drill, his mind drifted ahead to the airfield.

Just because of his uniform, Desmond was allowed through the strictly guarded gates. He could wander about amongst the aircraft, see into the hangars. He could use a rifle, handle ammunition.

He knew where everything was and, because of the peculiarity of his mind, he would never forget a single detail of what he had seen. If anyone could help Micky to get weapons for the secret army, Desmond could.

In the middle of January, it began to snow. It covered the ground thickly but soon melted away in the city once daylight came. Out in the country, however, it whipped itself into a blizzard and lay twelve inches deep, with drifts of three or four feet.

Farm work was almost impossible. There was little that could be done other than feed and milk the cows and see to the other animals. Yvonne spent a couple of hours sawing logs for the fires, and Betty and Erica helped Jonas patch up a few weak places in the barn.

Gerald Spencer came out to watch them, his arm in a sling. As well as his injuries, Gerald had been suffering from dysentery and was finding it difficult to regain his strength, so he'd been sent home to rest for a few weeks. After the initial strangeness, he'd slipped easily back into the old life at home and treated the three Land Girls with a teasing familiarity, as if they were his sisters. Though Betty couldn't help noticing, as they all sat round the big kitchen table of an evening playing cards or talking, that he looked at Erica rather a lot. But that was natural enough, seeing how pretty Erica was.

'You don't think he's getting sweet on her, do you?' she asked Yvonne one night as they got ready for bed. Erica was still downstairs, drying her hair in front of the fire. 'It wouldn't be surprising. I mean, he's been away a long time and he doesn't seem to have any girlfriend round here.'

'I dunno, I reckon that Maisie from the pub's got her eye on him.' Yvonne pulled off her vest and wrapped herself swiftly in flannel pyjamas. 'She's been up here three times this week on one excuse or another. Anyway, Erica's not interested in another bloke. She's still got Geoff's picture beside her bed.'

Betty glanced across the attic to the third bed. The face of the young airman laughed out at her from the little wooden frame on the box that served as a bedside table. She bit her lip, feeling the sadness that washed over her every time she thought of the three young men – scarcely more than boys – who had spent all their spare time at the farm almost two years ago. Shot out of the sky, one after another, to plunge to their deaths in flames above the cruel sea. She remembered Sandy's remark – '*It's pretty lonely up there in the sky . . .*' And the day he and Duff had come to tell Erica that Geoff had been killed, with doom in their own haggard young faces.

It almost put you off falling in love, knowing the pain of that sort of loss. It wasn't surprising that girls like Erica refused to take the chance again.

It was bitterly cold in the barn. Gerald sat on a bale of straw, looking as if the walk from the farmhouse door had been almost too much for him.

'You ought to be still in bed,' Betty said. 'You look as white as a sheet.'

'I'm all right. I'm fed up with being in bed. Besides, I'll never get my strength back if I don't exercise.'

'You'll get pneumonia, sitting out here,' Erica said. 'It's freezing. Go back in, Gerald, for heaven's sake.'

'Leave the lad alone,' Jonas growled. 'Fussing over him like a pair of old hens. He's a soldier, he knows how to look after hisself.'

'Matter of fact,' Gerald said, 'I don't think I could walk back at the moment. I feel a bit sort of . . .' His voice trailed off and he slipped sideways on the bale. Erica and Betty rushed to catch him and propped him between them. Erica pressed his head gently down between his knees.

'You shouldn't have come out here,' she scolded. 'It's bitterly cold. You've been in a hot country for months and months, you've been ill and wounded . . .' Her voice shook suddenly and Betty glanced at her in surprise.

Erica was staring down at the bent head, the thin, bony shoulders, as if she had been struck. Her fingers rested on the curling dark hair at the nape of the neck. She moved them very slightly, almost tenderly, and then she withdrew them. Her eyes were filled with sudden tears.

She's thinking of Geoff, Betty thought, and wished the other girl could get over her loss. 'We'd better get him back indoors,' she said. 'Give us a hand, Jonas. You can see he's not fit to be out here.'

Between them, they got Gerald to his feet. He gave them a shaky grin and draped his arm across Betty's shoulders. He glanced round for Erica, but she had moved hastily aside and Jonas took her place.

'Bloody fool,' the old man muttered. 'Shouldn't never have gone for a soldier in the first place. Shoulda stayed on

198

the farm, and then we wouldn't have to have bloody women messing about scared to get their hands dirty. And you wouldn't be in this state.'

Gerald shook his head and tried to speak, but he was clearly exhausted. He gave Betty a glance of apology and she laughed.

'It's all right. We don't take any notice of this old windbag. He knows we can run rings round him any day. Now, you just let us get you back indoors and *stay* there this time, in the warm, see?'

The three of them moved slowly out of the barn and across the snow-covered yard. Erica came to the door to watch them go. She stood just inside, her face shadowed, out of sight of anyone watching.

She looked down at her fingers and tried to understand the sudden tingling they had felt as she stroked the back of Gerald Spencer's neck.

The snow was even deeper out at Bridge End, where Tim was to sit the scholarship examination at last. All around the village, children looked hopefully out of the windows, hoping that the examination would be postponed, but they stumped through the snow to school to find everything laid out ready.

'Sit here, Tim,' Mr Hodges said. 'You've got everything you need – pencil, ruler, a bit of rubber, plenty of paper. If you need to use the pencil-sharpener you'll have to ask, but apart from that you mustn't speak at all. Do you understand?'

Tim nodded a little sulkily. He still hadn't got over his misery at having been left out of the examination a year ago, and he'd spent the intervening months bored and angry. He didn't see why he had to sit in a class with children younger than himself, learning the same things all over again, and he blamed Mr Hodges and the other teachers for missing him out.

'You ought to have said,' Mr Wain, the headmaster, told him, but he knew that the responsibility wasn't really Tim's. But schooling was so difficult these days, with the little village school being shared turn and turn about by the village children, it was a wonder they hadn't got into an even bigger muddle.

The examination started. Tim sat at his desk and stared at the questions.

A weight of 56 tons is carried 200 miles for £12; how far should 70 tons be carried for the same amount?
Divide £837.19s.4 ¼d by 56.
Divide .04006 by 3.75. Multiply together the same two numbers.
Find the amount of £1520 for 3½ years at 4¾ per cent per annum simple interest.
A bankrupt owes £515.12s.6d to one man, £407 to another, and £293.6s.8d to another; his estate is worth £911.19s.4 ½d. How much can he pay in the £?
A man leaves £5000 to his wife, and the remainder to be divided equally among his four children. It is found that each of his children has one-seventh of the whole. How much did he leave altogether?

There were sixteen arithmetic questions altogether, although only four of the six most difficult ones had to be answered. Tim did the easy ones and then struggled with the 'problems'. He had never been quite sure what a 'bankrupt' was and had difficulty in understanding how anyone could have the vast sum of £5000 to leave his family. Some of the other questions – about grocers buying huge quantities of sugar or water running into and out of a bath – were equally beyond his comprehension. It wasn't that he couldn't do the arithmetic, it was just that the questions didn't seem to have any relevance to life as he knew it. Water didn't run in and out of baths. You dragged in the tin bath from the yard on Saturday nights and filled it from the tap at the sink, helped out with kettles. Even at the vicarage, they did that. And nobody had thousands of pounds. It would take you a whole lifetime to save up that much.

In the afternoon they had English. A stern warning at the

top of the paper said that writing would be taken into account throughout. That meant you had to write slowly and carefully, however little time you had.

Tim started with composition. This was his favourite subject and he had soon covered the requisite page and half with an anecdote about an animal. He chose the big tabby cat, Henry, who was still at number 14 with Mum and Dad and Tim's sisters, and wrote about the time when he was a kitten and had fallen into the lavatory. After that, they'd had to make sure to keep the door closed until he was old enough to know better.

Analysis wasn't nearly so much fun. Tim stared at the rhyme *'In the castle, weak and dying, Was the Norman baron lying.'* Which were the subject and object, and what was the predicate, and what did it matter anyway? He left a space and went on to the next question, which was to parse the words underlined in the rhyme. He left that, too.

The last two questions consisted of several pieces of poetry with long words, to be rewritten so that they meant the same but were easier to understand, and an exchange of conversation between two sailors which had to be punctuated. Tim did the last one but he couldn't make head or tail of the poetry. He always went to sleep or daydreamed during poetry lessons. He chewed his pencil and stared at it, then went back to the analysis, but that made him feel sick. He looked out of the window and wished the exam was over so that he could go and play in the snow.

I bet last year's exam was easier than this, he thought. I could've passed last year, easy as winking. Reg would've helped me with the problems when we got them for homework, and then I'd have known about bankrupts and baths and things. And I bet they used easier poetry then, too. They must have, or Brian Collins wouldn't have passed.

He sat staring at the paper, filled with misery and anger at his wasted year, and when the teacher announced that time was up, he had completed only half the questions. He handed it in, avoiding Mr Hodges' eye, and ran out into the snow, holding his arms straight out sideways and pretending to be a Spitfire.

The next day they had Geography, History and General Knowledge. By now, Tim was almost past caring. He scribbled a page or two about the St Lawrence River and Great Lakes, named several of the chief coalfields in Great Britain, and described a voyage from Southampton to Melbourne. The question about the chief vegetable products of the Punjab, the Sunderbunds and the Deccan completely floored him, as did the chief mountain ranges of South Africa, the difference between the ports of Vancouver and Quebec and a deceptively innocent question about the importance of six of the world's major cities or canals.

History was as bad. Tim knew quite a lot about Julius Caesar but nothing about the Danes. Asked to write a life of Simon de Montfort, he had only the haziest idea of who the man was. He enjoyed telling the story of the Spanish Armada but was stumped by the South Sea Bubble. The Indian Mutiny was exciting but took too long, so that he didn't have time to decide which question to choose last. Dithering between the Crusades and the Wars of the Roses, he had only just written the number of the question when time was called, and then found that he hadn't answered the one question which everyone was supposed to have tried, about Acts of Parliament.

I knew all those things last year, he thought resentfully, handing in the mass of scribblings and crossings-out – he had forgotten all about careful handwriting by this time. I know I'm not going to pass, and it isn't my fault. It's theirs, for forgetting about me.

He plodded slowly home to the vicarage, ignoring the other boys' calls to join a snowball fight, and when he got back Mrs Mudge looked at his face and sat him by the fire with a big mug of cocoa and a slice of cake, which they normally only had on Sundays.

'It's not the end of the world if you don't pass, Tim,' she said. 'There's other things as important as being clever.'

'I *am* clever,' he stated. 'I know I am. I *ought* to be going on to the Grammar School. And I won't be, and it's *not fair.*'

Mrs Mudge sighed. She knew that there was some justice in what he said, but what could you do? You couldn't wind back the clock or make things all right with the wave of a wand.

'Well, you just drink your cocoa and then go out and build a snowman,' she said. 'Or go and talk to Mr Beckett. He's over in the church, looking at the bells.'

Tim liked the bells. They weren't allowed to be rung now, because that was the signal for invasion, but he knew that Mr Beckett and the head bellringer kept them in good condition for the time when they could be rung again, and he was hoping that when that time came he'd be allowed to pull one of the ropes. He finished his cocoa and cake, and pulled on his wellington boots again.

The bells were reached by a spiral staircase, leading up from the ground floor of the tower where the ropes hung with their coloured 'sallies' looped together. There were six of them, hanging in the dim bell-chamber, each in its own frame with a big wheel to make it turn. The ropes came up through the floor and wound round the rim of the wheel. Mr Beckett had told Tim that if the ringer pulled too hard and broke the wooden 'stay' that prevented the bell from turning right over, the whole length of rope would shoot up and wind itself round the wheel, and the ringer would have to let go quickly or be dragged up with it.

The bellringing captain was in the tower with Mr Beckett. They were greasing the bearings and talking about ringing. Words like 'Grandsire', 'Stedman' and 'Treble Bob' floated around the chamber and Tim, his head poking up through the trapdoor from the ladder that led from the top of the spiral staircase, got the impression that the bells were listening and yearning to make their music again.

'The war's spoiling everything,' he said to Mr Beckett when the head bellringer had gone and the two of them were sitting on the top of the frame, gazing down at the big metal bodies. 'I'm fed up with it. Nobody can do what they want to any more.'

'I know. But that's life, Tim. We can't always do what we want to do.' The vicar looked down at the boy's bent head. The fair curls were turning darker. He was still small for his age, but had filled out quite a lot since coming to the country, and his arms and legs were sturdy. How that poor mother must miss her sons, he thought sadly. How all the mothers must be missing their children.

'Shall I tell you a secret?' he asked, and Tim looked up, momentarily bright-eyed, then drooped his head again and shrugged. 'It's the secret of being able to do what you want to do.'

'How?' Tim asked suspiciously. 'I don't see how you can, unless it's magic, and I don't believe in magic any more.'

'There's nothing magic about it. It's just a matter of seeing what you *can* do, and finding something you want in that. And forgetting about the things you know are impossible.'

'But *they're* the things I want,' Tim said, feeling let down. 'I don't think much of that for a secret.'

'It doesn't sound much to start with,' the vicar agreed. 'But if you think about it, you'll see what I mean. For instance, we can't ring the bells now so I can't teach you how to pull the rope and hear the sound. But I could tie up one of the clappers so that it didn't make any sound, and you could learn that way. And you could learn to ring the methods, like Grandsire and Plain Bob, on handbells. Then, when peace comes, you'll be ready to join the team.'

Tim turned his head and stared at him. 'Could I? Could I really learn to ring?'

'If you want to. That's what Mr Enfield and I were talking about just now. That's why we were greasing the bearings. We're going to tie up all the clappers and get the ringers together – those that are still in the village – and start practising again. And teach some new ringers.'

'Reg was a bellringer,' Tim said, thinking of his former foster-home.

'Yes, and a very good one, too. It's a shame he can't be here, he could help teach you. But there are a few old bellringers still in the village, and with you young ones we'll soon have a good team again.'

Tim looked down at the bells. They hung silent in their frames. He thought of them ringing, each one swinging round full circle, its clapper striking against the rim. They wouldn't be doing that, of course, but still . . . The idea of learning something new, something that grown-up people did, made his blood tingle and the misery of the scholarship examination was forgotten.

Brian Collins can't ring the bells, he thought. But Reg could. And I could too. And when peace does come, I'll be here, ready to ring the bells out loud so that everyone can hear them and know we've beaten Hitler.

That's something I can want, he told himself. Something I can want and something I can *do*.

Who cared about silly old school examinations?

CHAPTER TWELVE

The bitter weather continued. February was even colder than January, with the temperature never above freezing and often down to 11 degrees of frost. More snow fell, but the newspapers never reported it until at least ten days had passed, by which time everyone knew about it all too well.

Annie was desperately worried about Ted, but even more now about their son Colin on HMS *Exeter* somewhere out in the Far East. The Japanese, entering the war with fresh energy and brand-new equipment, were scoring terrifying victories. Daily reports told of their approach to Singapore, of their dive-bombing of the beleaguered island and, finally, of its fall as thirty thousand troops landed and forced back the Australians struggling to hold it. Days later, nearly two hundred aircraft flew in an attack on Darwin, bringing the war into Australia itself.

'If only we knew just where the ship was,' Annie said to Jess. 'But of course they don't tell us. Anyway, I expect she's dodging about all over the place. But when I think of the ships they've already sunk – the *Prince of Wales*, the *Repulse* . . . Even the *Ark Royal*'s gone. All the time old Haw-Haw kept telling us it was sunk and we knew it wasn't, we could laugh at him. But now . . .'

Jess sighed. They were hearing almost every day now of people they knew who had been killed or were missing. The sight of the telegram boy, coming down the street on his red bike, was almost as frightening as the sound of the air raid warning, until you knew where he was going. And if he came to *you* . . .

He hadn't come to Annie yet, but the dread was always in their hearts.

'How's your Betty?' she asked, changing the subject. 'Has she brought that young man of hers home again?'

Annie nodded. 'I must say, he does seem a nice young chap. I'd give 'em my blessing, but Ted just can't seem to accept him. I tell him, the boy's doing a good job now, he's risking his life every day, but Ted can't see past the fact that he's a pacifist and won't fight. Pity there aren't more like him, I said the other day, and you know, I thought Ted was going to hit me, I really did.' She sighed heavily. Ted was still as depressed as ever, and although she could feel for him more sympathetically since his outburst in bed after their quarrel, she found it hard to keep cheerful herself in the face of his continuing gloom. She wondered sometimes if he was ever going to get better.

'Betty must worry about him being on bomb disposal,' Jess was saying now.

'She does. But she don't say much about it. She's changed a lot since she was out on the farm. Grown up, like.'

'Well, she had her twenty-first birthday a couple of weeks ago,' Jess said. 'She can get married if she wants without her father's say-so.'

'I know. But Dennis wants them to start off on the right foot. He says they'll wait till the spring, and if Ted still won't see reason they'll go ahead.'

Wait till the spring. But with a job like Dennis's, would spring ever come for him?

Annie and Jess were on their way to North End to see their parents. They were both anxious about Arthur, who had been growing increasingly forgetful lately. He'd left the gas on twice and one day he'd accused the next-door neighbour, who'd called in with a few potatoes from the garden, of being a burglar.

'He just didn't seem to know who Bill was,' Mary told her daughters. 'He remembered after a few minutes and we passed it off by saying the light was bad, but I don't mind telling you, it frightened me. I mean, he was just like a stranger, not like your Dad at all.'

Arthur was upstairs having a nap. He came down when Mary made a cup of tea and asked for one of the chocolate biscuits they had in the tin.

'Chocolate biscuits!' Mary said. 'I haven't seen a chocolate biscuit for over two years. You're dreaming, Arthur.'

'I'm not. You brought them home yesterday.' He stared at her aggressively. 'You're keeping them all for yourself, that's what it is. You don't want me to have any.'

'Arthur, don't be so daft.' Mary cast a frightened look towards Jess and Annie. 'Of course I wouldn't keep them for myself. We haven't got any. There weren't any.'

'Yesterday,' he repeated. 'You got them in the Co-op. I carried the bag home.'

The three women gazed at him. The Co-op had been bombed and moved to Fratton. Mary never went that far to do her shopping.

'You see what it is,' Mary said in a trembling voice. 'He's in a world of his own half the time.'

Arthur was staring out of the window. He turned back to them and said in a perfectly ordinary, matter-of-fact voice, 'It's a bad job about the Japs. You must be half out of your mind over Colin, Annie.'

The conversation about the chocolate biscuits might never have taken place. Arthur drank his tea and re-counted stories of the Boer War – which all of them had heard before – and remained perfectly lucid. For the rest of the afternoon the four of them sat chatting normally about the war, grumbling about the new soap rationing ('How am I ever going to keep Frank's working clothes clean on four ounces of soap a month to go round all of us?') and the bitter weather. Coal was so scarce now that nobody could afford to light a fire before evening, and the house never seemed to get warm, apart from the one room where the whole family gathered.

'It's not right, all the same,' Annie said as she and Jess walked home. 'You could see he wasn't with us over those biscuits. And he nearly drifted away again a couple of times, did you notice?'

Jess nodded. 'Mum told me he sometimes forgets what time of day it is. Says they haven't had their dinner when they have, and sulks if she won't cook again. He accused her of trying to starve him the other day. And when he is all right, he's worrying about the war, fretting because he's not doing his duty to help.'

'Poor Dad,' Annie said. 'And poor Mum.'

They walked on in silence and then stopped as two men, walking the other way, called out their names.

'Mrs Chapman! And Mrs Budd, isn't it?' One of the men was stocky, with grizzled hair and a creased face. The other wasn't much more than a boy – no more than nineteen, Jess guessed. Their faces were vaguely familiar but she couldn't place them. I'm getting as bad as Dad, she though wryly.

Annie knew them, however. 'It's Sam. And Ben.' She smiled at them both. 'I'm pleased to see you. How's the *King* doing these days?'

So that was who they were. The crew of the *Ferry King*, the ferry boat which Ted had skippered across Portsmouth Harbour for years and had taken to Dunkirk. They were working under a new skipper now, but didn't think much of him.

'It's not like being with Ted,' Sam said. 'He let us get on with our own work. This bloke's always breathing down your neck, thinking he can do the job better himself. I nearly gave him a handful of cotton waste the other day and told him to polish up the bilges while I went and steered!'

Annie laughed, but there was a wistful note in her voice as she said, 'I'd be as pleased as you if Ted would go back to work. It'd do him good, instead of moping round the house. It's as if he needs something to jerk him out of himself.'

'Well, we were thinking of calling round one day,' Sam said. 'Young Ben here's got his papers. He's off into the Navy soon. I've been telling him, he ought to go up and say cheerio to Ted.'

'So he should.' Annie looked at the young man. He was tall and thin and lanky. A couple of yards of drainwater, she'd heard Ted describe him as when Ben had first joined the ferry service, but he'd turned out a useful engineer. 'How are you looking forward to going into the Navy?'

'Oh, it'll be all right. I'm going in the engine-rooms – I've finished my apprenticeship now. I'm looking forward to working on really big engines.'

His bony young face had a slight sheen to it, as if he were sweating. But it was too cold for that. Annie looked at the flickering eyes and wondered if he were looking forward to going to sea as much as he said. She wouldn't blame him if he was scared stiff.

He and Sam had both been at Dunkirk with Ted. It might do Ted a bit of good to know that this boy was going off to sea, having been through the same experience.

'Come up and have a cup of tea some time,' she suggested. 'I know he'd like to see you both. And you can tell him all what's been going on down the ferry lately.'

'It's going to be this weekend,' Roddy said. 'We're sailing Friday night. I'm not supposed to tell you that. And I cannae tell you where we're going, because we dinnae ken.'

'We're going to have to do it, then,' Carol said. 'We're going to have to run away. Go to Scotland.'

'Och, you know we cannae do that. It's a crazy idea.'

'Crazy? What's crazy about it? We want to be together, don't we? We want to get married? Well, all we have to do is go to Scotland. They'll let us get married there, you said so.'

'No.' He shook his head. 'It's not that easy, Carol. They'll ask for papers – birth certificates and that, to prove who we are. And by then I'll be posted as a deserter and your mother will have set the police after us. We'd be caught right away.'

Carol scowled and thought for a few minutes. Then she looked at him and said, 'All right, then. We won't get married. We don't have to. All we need do is *say* we're married. I'll call myself Mrs MacPherson. No, I wouldn't, we'd have to change our names. I'll be Mrs – Mrs MacGregor. Or Mackintosh. Something Scottish anyway, because of your accent.'

'Och, if only we could,' Roddy sighed. 'It'd be a grand thing, right enough. But we'd need money. We'd need to get right away from Portsmouth and go somewhere where nobody would hear of us, and we'd need money to pay our fares and rent and food and all sorts. All I've got is a few shillings I've managed to save out of my pay.'

'That's all I've got,' Carol said. 'But my mum's got plenty.'

'Your *mum*?'

'Yes. It's in a drawer in her bedroom. I was looking for some earrings and I found it under her jumpers. A big thick envelope full of pound notes.'

'Where did she get that from?' Roddy asked. 'She's always havering on about how hard up she is.'

'I know. I don't know where it came from. But she takes enough off me and Joe, so I reckon I'm entitled to some of it back,' Carol said determinedly.

Roddy shook his head. 'She'll never give it to you. She'll go mad if you ask.'

'I wasn't thinking of asking,' Carol replied, and looked him in the eye.

'But that's stealing,' Roddy said after a moment. 'Stealing from your own mother.'

'Only if it's really her money. And I don't see how it can be. It's money she's had from me and Joe, that's what it is, and she hasn't used it so it's ours. And I know Joe wouldn't mind if I took it.'

'Are you sure that's what it is?'

'What else can it be? There's only the money Dad sends her, and she spends that on the house and stockings and make-up and stuff.'

'Perhaps she's got a wee job. She's out all hours, you told me.'

Carol snorted. 'Mum with a job! She'd never do that – thinks she's too good. Anyway, she obviously doesn't need that money and we do.' She caught his hands and gripped them tightly, gazing into his eyes. 'Roddy, there's enough there to take us anywhere we want to go. Scotland, if you want to. Or London. Anywhere. We can find a room somewhere, get jobs, who's going to know we're not married? If anyone asks, we'll tell them we got bombed out, like I said before, and lost our certificates and everything. And you won't have to go away. You won't have to *fight*.'

Roddy looked at her. He thought of the ship, which still seemed so huge and alien. He knew he would never get used to the grey steel bulkheads, the stark, narrow gangways, the cramped mess, the bare, spartan hardness of it all. The thought of going into action made him feel sick.

'We'd be together,' Carol said. 'We'd have our own little home. You'd come home at night and I'd have your supper cooking and we could listen to the wireless and go to bed whenever we felt like it. We could forget about this horrible war.'

Roddy didn't think it would be possible to forget about the war. But he'd heard that there were places in the country where they hardly knew it was happening. Places where there were still milk and butter and eggs, where people didn't spend night after night in an air-raid shelter.

'I don't like the idea of taking that money, all the same,' he said. 'Suppose your mum told the police? We could go to prison.'

'She won't do that. Not to her own daughter,' Carol said confidently. 'Anyway, we're not going to get caught, are we? We're going to just disappear. We'll be in hiding, like spies.' She looked critically at his matelot's uniform. 'We'll have to get you some different clothes, mind. I wonder if our Joe's things'd fit you.'

'We cannae steal your brother's clothes,' Roddy said, outraged.

'Why not? He's not going to need 'em much longer. He got his own papers this morning. Anyway, it's just to get started. It's only *borrowing*.'

'No. I'll not pinch Joe's clothes. I'll go to a second-hand shop and get fitted out.' At some point, he realised, he seemed to have agreed to this crazy scheme of Carol's. But he couldn't go back now. The thought of going to sea was too hideous. *I wouldn't be any good to them as a gunner anyway*, he thought. *I'd miss everything. They'd be better off without me.*

'Will you? Will you really?' Carol's face was alight. She pulled him against her and kissed him enthusiastically. 'Oh Roddy, it'll be all right, I know it will. It'll be lovely. Just think – the two of us in our own little home.' She sighed ecstatically. 'It's better than *Gone With the Wind*.'

'We'll have to make some plans,' Roddy said. 'We'll think about where we're going first. We'd better go on Thursday night – maybe they'll not discover I'm missing till the ship's at sea. And if your mother's out, she won't know you're not there till morning.'

'I'll have everything ready,' Carol promised. 'I'll take my things up to Joy and ask her to look after them for me. Mum never goes into their shop, so no one'll tell her. We can be miles away before anyone realises we've gone!'

She flung her arms around his neck again and he held her tightly. He was scared about what they were doing, but being scared had become a normal part of life for Roddy since he had joined the Navy. And nothing scared him as much as the idea of going to sea.

Friday, he thought. *On Friday we'll be away together, starting a new life. Carrie's right, it doesn't matter that we won't be properly married. It'll feel like that to us, anyway. That's what really matters.*

'Och, Carrie,' he said. 'I really do love you.'

Snow and ice turned the roads into skating-rinks, but somehow the buses and trains kept going. The *Evening News* reported stories of dockyardmen having to dig their bus out of a deep snowdrift before it could take them to work early in the morning. One man said the road was so slippery he had been forced to crawl on his hands and knees to reach the stop. Scores of cars were stranded one day on Portsdown Hill, and their drivers had to walk down to Cosham and continue their journey from there. Farmers had to take their milk round by tractor, and in some places they simply left churns at a local pub or accessible house so that their customers could collect it themselves.

On Thursday afternoon, the weather was slightly better and Ethel Glaister went out as usual to have tea with her friend Violet Mitchell, in Kingston. That was the night Carol and Roddy usually chose to go to the pictures, so Ethel wouldn't be surprised when Carol wasn't home that evening. She'd start to worry – or get annoyed – when Carol didn't come in at ten o'clock, but she probably wouldn't go into Carol's room until well after eleven, and by then she and Roddy would be well away. And when she did go in, she'd find the note, pinned to Carol's pillow, telling her not to worry. She might even think Carol was home first and not go in until next morning.

'Have you got everything?' Roddy asked when Carol met him near the railway station. They had agreed it was better not to be seen together where they might be recognised. He had slipped into a public lavatory and changed his uniform for the second-hand clothes he had bought, and he looked strange and unfamiliar in grey flannel trousers and a brown overcoat.

'I've got as many clothes as I could carry.' Carol looked him over and giggled. 'That coat's about three sizes too big for you. We could both get into that.'

'It was all I could find.' He sounded affronted, but inside he was shivering with fear. Suppose someone saw them and reported them? Suppose a redcap were to realise he was a sailor on the run? I've done it now, he thought, looking at the brown sleeve. I've deserted. 'Let's get away from here, Carrie. I feel as if everyone's staring at us.'

They got on the first train that came along and sat in a third-class compartment. It was already dark and there was only a dim blue light showing in the train. Outside, the streets looked dark and gloomy, and when they got out into the countryside the white fields looked hostile.

The train was filled with people. Some of them were going home from work, others were going further afield. The corridor was packed with luggage and there were soldiers sitting on kitbags, smoking. Carol and Roddy were squeezed tightly against each other. They held hands, wishing they could talk.

'Where are we going?' Roddy whispered at last. He had left the buying of tickets to Carol. He knew that she had taken the money from her mother's drawer but he didn't know how much she had. He wasn't really sure if he wanted to know.

'London, of course.' Carol's eyes were bright with excitement. She had had no qualms about taking the big envelope of money. To her mind, it was probably mostly hers anyway, and Joe wouldn't mind her having his share. *Borrowing* it, she corrected herself. She could feel it now in her pocket, a thick wad of paper. She hadn't had time to count it properly but she reckoned there was at least fifty pounds. Fifty pounds! It was a fortune.

'We'll go to an air-raid shelter tonight,' she said. 'And tomorrow we'll find ourselves somewhere to stay. Somewhere cheap but decent. And then we can look for jobs.' She squeezed his arm. 'We could have a couple of days' holiday first, though. See the sights, eh? St Paul's Cathedral, and Westminster, and the Houses of Parliament. I'd like to see the Tower of London too.'

'You cannae go there now. It's all closed.'

'I know, but you can still *see* it, can't you? I've never been to London.' She shivered with excitement. 'It's going to be gorgeous.'

Roddy wasn't sure that blitzed London would be at all 'gorgeous'. But he was too thankful to be away from the ship, and with Carol, to say so. I don't care where I am, he thought, so long as we're together and I don't have to go and fight.

As Carol had hoped, Ethel did not discover her absence until next morning.

She had come home later than usual the evening before and assumed that Carol was already in bed. Joe was asleep on the sofa in the front room downstairs and didn't stir as she passed the door, and there were two cups on the draining-board in the scullery. Ethel washed her face quickly and went straight upstairs to bed.

The next morning, she came down to find Joe already gone to work and no sign of her daughter. It was Carol's job to make tea and start the porridge. Outside, the garden was white again with a fresh fall of snow and she could hear the scrape of a shovel as Jess Budd cleared the pavement in front of the house.

Clicking her tongue with annoyance, Ethel stood at the foot of the stairs. 'Carol! *Carol!* It's time to get up. You've overslept.'

There was no reply. Ethel gave a sharp exclamation and shouted again. Then she stamped quickly up the stairs and flung open Carol's bedroom door.

'Carol! I've called you twice already. When are you going to . . .' Her voice trailed away and she stared, half frightened, half unbelieving, at the empty bed. '*Carol!*'

Jess Budd had just finished scraping away the snow when the door of number 15 burst open and Ethel appeared, her face scarlet and her eyes wild. Jess looked at her in surprise and concern.

'What's the matter? What's happened?'

'It's my Carol. The little slut. The little hussy.' Ethel waved a piece of paper under Jess's nose. 'Look at that. *Look* at it. See what she's done.'

Jess took the note and read it, her eyes widening. 'She says she's run away with Roddy. Is that the sailor she's been going with? But they can't. He's on a ship.'

'Not any more,' Ethel said grimly. 'He's scarpered, that's what he's done. And taken my Carol with him. That's desertion, that is, and he can be shot for it.'

'Oh, no.' Jess gazed at her. 'He's only a boy. And he looks such a nice young chap.'

'So nice he runs away with my daughter. God knows

what he's doing to her now.' Ethel clenched her fists and shook them. 'I just wish he'd come walking round the corner now, I'd wring his neck for him, that I would. Oh, I shouldn't never have let her go out with him. I shouldn't never have let her go to that dance up Hilsea. That's what started it all. She hasn't been the same girl since she met him.'

Jess didn't know what to say. She'd never liked Ethel much and there had been quite long periods when they didn't speak to each other, but she was a neighbour all the same and you helped neighbours when they were in trouble. But what could you do when a girl had run off like this? And she couldn't help feeling a sneaking sympathy for Carol. What she'd done was wrong, of course, no two ways about it, but when you looked at her mother and thought what sort of a life she must have had . . .

And youngsters could do some silly things when their heads were turned by being in love, especially the first time. Even more especially these days, when nothing was what it ought to be.

'I'm really sorry,' she said at last. 'What are you going to do about it?'

'What d'you think? I'm going to the police, of course. Carol's only just sixteen, she's under my control, and I want her brought back. I'll tell them what ship that young man's on, too. They'll send the military police after him. I tell you, he's going to find himself in real trouble.'

'Why not wait a day or two?' Jess suggested. 'They'll probably come back of their own accord. Once they run out of money –'

'Money!' Ethel exclaimed. She stared at Jess, then tore the note from her fingers and rushed back indoors. 'If I find that dirty little trollop's been in my drawer – if she's *dared* –'

Jess stood uncertainly on the frozen pavement for a few moments. Then, from the window above, she heard a scream of fury and a stream of swearwords that shocked her. And the tone of Ethel's voice turned her cold.

I wouldn't like to be Carol or Roddy when Ethel Glaister

catches up with them, she thought. And, feeling shaken and upset, she turned and went indoors to where Rose was giving Maureen her breakfast.

For a few days, Carol's elopement with the young Scottish sailor was the talk of the street. But it was soon overshadowed by greater events.

On the last day of February, Ted came in from the garden to find Annie standing white-faced by the wireless, a duster screwed up into a tight ball in her hand. Quickly, he crossed the room and put his arm round her shoulders while she blurted out the news that had just been given out.

'There's been a big battle in the Java Sea. They said the Dutch had been told they could fight for the East Indies – you know they've got a lot of territory out there – and they've lost any amount of ships, and there've been two British destroyers sunk.' She stared at him. 'They're calling it a major disaster.'

'Destroyers,' Ted said, knowing what was in her mind, almost as frightened as she was. 'Destroyers. The *Exeter*'s a cruiser, Annie. It can't be her.'

But Annie was almost frantic. 'The *Exeter*'s there, though. Our Colin's out there. He could be next. He might even be hurt or dead now. Those awful Japanese, Ted – they're just murdering everybody.'

'It's war,' he said bitterly. 'It doesn't count as murder when it's war. You know what they say – *all's fair*.'

'It's not, though. It's not fair. Why did the Japs have to come in anyway? Nobody was hurting them. The war was nothing to do with them. Why did they have to start?'

'They just saw their chance to grab the Pacific,' Ted said wearily. 'Like a kid, pinching apples when the grocer's back's turned. At least it brought America in on our side.'

'Yes, but it means we've got to send more forces out there, instead of beating Hitler. I don't see how they'll ever sort it out.'

'Look, Annie, there's no use meeting trouble halfway. You know what they say. No news is good news, and there's been nothing said about the *Exeter* yet.'

It was the most positive thing he'd said for months, but before Annie could reply there was a ring on the front doorbell. She went to answer it and came back looking a little more cheerful.

'It's Sam and Ben come to see you, Ted. Ben's got something to tell you. I'll make a cup of tea.'

Sam came in and sat down on one of the chairs round the dining-table. Ben stood just inside the door, looking gawky and self-conscious. Ted looked at them. He felt pleased that they'd taken the trouble to come, but he also felt awkward. He wondered if they thought he was skiving.

'Well, come in properly and sit yourself down, boy,' he said to Ben. 'You make the place untidy standing there . . . How's things on the ferry, then?'

'Oh, much as usual,' Sam answered. 'We'd be better set if you were back. I don't get on with old Len Barber. And what with young Ben here off on his travels –'

'Travels?' Ted said. 'What travels?'

'What d'you think?' Ben asked. 'Been called up, of course. I'm off next week – Royal Navy. Engineer.'

His voice had been late breaking and was still a little squeaky. He looked at Ted with his mouth set, trying to pretend he was pleased to be going. But that boy had seen Dunkirk, Ted thought. He knows what it's going to be like.

'You'll be all right,' he said. 'You know your job. Had a good master.' He glanced at Sam.

'Had a good skipper,' Sam said. 'We made a good team, the three of us.'

And now there would be only one of them on the old *Ferry King*. Ted looked away, unable to meet their eyes. His heart was thumping in his chest. I don't want to do it, he thought. I don't want to go back.

Annie came in with the teapot and a jug of milk. It didn't matter who was there or how urgent it was, she would never bring the milk to the table in a bottle. She poured four cups of tea and handed round the bottle of saccharins.

'It's time for the six o'clock news,' she said. 'Turn on the wireless, Ted, will you?'

They sat drinking their tea and listening, the four of them. And then they heard it.

'*It has just been announced that the British cruiser HMS* Exeter *was sunk in yesterday's fighting in the Java Sea. She was fighting north of Java with four Japanese cruisers. The British destroyer* Encounter *and the US destroyer* Pope *were sunk in the same action. HMS* Exeter *had already been hit in earlier fighting and was facing two enemy ships on the port quarter and two in the starboard beam. She lost all power and sank soon after coming under fire. It is not yet known how many men survived.*

'*The Japanese victories in the Java Sea are presenting a grave danger to Madagascar, at present controlled by the Allies. Enemy control of this island would threaten the western entrance to the Indian Ocean, cutting off the vital supplies of oil from the Persian Gulf and causing a breakdown in communications with the Far East.*

'*Prime Minister Mr Winston Churchill has said –*'

'Turn it off, Ted,' Annie said, her voice trembling. 'Turn it off. I don't want to hear any more. I don't want to hear any more about the war, *ever*.'

Ted snapped the wireless into silence. They sat staring at each other, barely able to take in the news they had just heard.

'*Exeter* sunk,' Ted whispered at last. 'Oh God, Annie . . . the *Exeter*'s been sunk . . .'

'Oh Ted,' she breathed, staring across the table at him. She wanted to be in his arms, feeling his strength, she wanted to hear his voice telling her it wasn't true, it was a dream, a nightmare. 'Ted, what's been happening to our Colin?'

Neither of them could move. They sat rigid, frozen, paralysed. Their need for each other was palpable but neither could stir. Their eyes met, helpless, anguished, and their faces slowly crumbled into despair.

Sam looked slowly from one to the other. He felt their shock as his own. He had known Colin all his life, seen him grow from a lively toddler to a mischievous boy, always up to something – shooting arrows at the neighbours' cats from the top of the turret, coming down to the *Ferry King* and poking about in the engine-room, demanding to be allowed to steer. He'd seen him in his first Naval uniform, swaggering and proud in bell-bottoms.

'They don't know how many's been lost,' he said at last. 'The BBC just said so. There could be a lot saved.' But he knew that this could be of little comfort until they knew that Colin was amongst the survivors.

He poured another cup of tea and pushed it across the table to Annie. She looked at it as if she did not know what it was. He stirred in two saccharins.

'Drink some, Mrs Chapman. It's good for shock.'

Annie shook her head slowly, still gazing at her husband. 'Ted. *Ted* . . .'

With a sudden, violent movement, Ted pushed back his chair. He stumbled to his feet and round the table to his wife. He gripped her in his arms and pulled her out of her chair, hard against his chest, and she burst into sudden, noisy tears. They stood together, clinging, weeping, and Annie clenched her fists and beat them against him.

'Why? Why, Ted, *why*? Why are all these terrible things happening, all over the world – thousands, *millions*, of people being killed, slaughtered like animals, and what's it all for, eh? We went into this to help the Polish – and what have we ever done for them? They're no better off – and now it's spread everywhere, *everywhere*, and nowhere's safe, there's nowhere in the whole world that's safe any more. And where's it all going to end? How *can* it end, until we're all dead, every last one of us, and there's no one left to kill?' Her weeping increased and her words were barely coherent, but each of the men in the room heard her repeat her son's name, over and over again, and heard all the bitter anguish of a mother who has lost her child and knows him to have died in pain.

'Colin. Oh Colin, my little boy, my dear, dear little Colin . . .'

CHAPTER THIRTEEN

Carol and Roddy had been gone for almost a month, and nothing had yet been heard of them.

Ethel was furious, humiliated and bitter. And her temper was not improved by George's arrival home soon after she had sent him the news.

'You mean she's been gone *three weeks* and you never saw fit to let me know!' he shouted. 'What in God's name have you been playing at, Ethel? Didn't it strike you I had a *right* to know? I'm her father, ain't I?'

'I didn't see what you could do about it,' she said sullenly. 'All them miles away. I mean, you're too busy fighting a war to bother about your family, aren't you.'

'And there's no call to get sarky. That ain't going to help. I joined up because I had a duty, as you know perfectly well, and it ain't my fault if they never sent the Unit off to get killed in France or somewhere. That'd please you, wouldn't it – but I daresay we'll go soon enough.' He glared at his wife in a way quite unlike his usual mild manner. 'You oughter got in touch right away.'

'I told the police. And the Navy. There's nothing you can do that they can't.'

'That's not the point. I'm her father. I ought to know what's happening to my kids.' He was angrier than she had ever seen him. 'Seems to me you're not fit to look after 'em on your own, Ethel. Look what's happened since I went away. Our Shirley, torpedoed and nearly drowned because you would have it she was sent off to Canada. And now Carol, getting into God knows what sort of trouble with a sailor. I mean, whatever got into you to let her go about

222

with him? He musta been a bad lot, surely even you could see that.'

Ethel flinched. George had never spoken to her like this before, never shouted at her and laid down the law. It's this Army training, she thought resentfully, it's making a brute out of him.

'You're a fine one to talk,' she retorted. 'You never had a word to say when I was worrying about Shirley being evacuated. Left it all to me, didn't you. *I* make the decisions and *I'm* the one to get blamed when things go wrong. It's always been the same. I have to take all the responsibility and then you can turn round and say it's my fault.' She glowered at him. 'So I'm not fit to look after my own children, am I? Well, maybe *you'd* like to take a turn and I'll go off and fight the war. I'd soon give Hitler a bloody nose, I can tell you!'

'And that's just about all you could give him. There's bloody little else you're prepared to give a bloke!'

Ethel gasped and swung her hand at him. George caught her wrist. She lashed out with her foot, the pointed toe of her high-heeled shoe catching him painfully on the shin, and he gave a howl, let go of her wrist and slapped her hard across the side of the head.

'You bitch! You nasty, spiteful bitch!' Enraged by pain and years of humiliation, he struck her again and she stumbled, tripped over a chair and fell, catching at the tablecloth and bringing all the tea things with her. She lay in an ungainly heap, crying noisily amongst the wreckage.

'You brute, George Glaister. You vicious brute. You've been working up to that, haven't you. You've been working up to it for years.' She sat up, feeling first her elbow, then her head. 'I'm bruised all over. I always knew there was a violent streak in you. My mother warned me. I should have listened to her and taken Bert Spedding. He was after me too.'

'He had a lucky escape, then,' George said. 'I'll remember to congratulate him next time we run into each other.' He looked down at his wife. 'Get up, Ethel.'

'Just so you can knock me down again? No thanks.' But

she moved away across the floor and began to gather up the broken cups and saucers. 'Look at all this,' she said, breaking into fresh sobs. 'My second-best teaset, all smashed. And jam all over the rug. And that's all the milk we've got left. I just hope you're proud of yourself.'

George bent to help her. His rage was already evaporating and he was beginning to feel ashamed. He had never touched Ethel in anger before, never been able to understand men who knocked their wives about. He couldn't understand what had got into him. It was as if he'd turned into another person, he thought, just as if someone else had taken charge.

All the same, she ought to have let him know about Carol. How did she think it made him feel, knowing she just hadn't bothered?

'Come on, Ethel. Perhaps I shouldn't have done that. But it just got me on the raw, knowing you didn't think I was worth being told about my own girl. I'm still her dad, after all. And I'm still your husband, too.'

Ethel bit back the retort she wanted to make. She scrambled to her feet and sank into a chair, keeping a wary eye on George in case he suddenly went mad again. She felt scared and bewildered, but she wasn't going to let him get the upper hand, not after all these years.

'Don't you dare do that again,' she said, her voice trembling. 'Don't you dare ever lay a finger on me again. I swear if you do, I'll go to the front door and I'll scream blue murder. I'll get the police round, that's what I'll do, if you ever attack me again like that.'

'I didn't attack you, Ethel. You hit out at me first, and you kicked me. I'm surprised you never broke my leg. Anyway, the police won't interfere between man and wife.'

'More's the pity. There's a lot of women would be a lot happier if they did.'

George sighed. 'This isn't getting us anywhere, Ethel. It's Carol we ought to be thinking about. She's what's important, not bickering like a couple of kids. That's why they've given me a pass, to try and get things sorted out.'

'There's nothing to sort out. They've run off, the pair of them, and haven't even had the common decency to let me know they're all right. The police are looking for them, and so's the Navy. That boy's been posted as a deserter, and serve him right. He'll be for the high jump when they catch him, and no mistake. There's nothing you can do.'

'But what are they living on? Our Carol never had any money, and he wouldn't have been paid much.'

'They took my savings,' Ethel said angrily. 'Searched through my drawer and took out the money I've been putting by for new furniture. I want a new three-piece suite and carpet and some decent curtains when this lot's over. And a new bed for my room. The whole place'll want decorating then, and you can be sure nobody else down April Grove will have thought of that. They'll all be living in hovels while we've got the smartest place in Copnor.'

George stared at her. 'You've been saving up for new furniture?'

'And why not?' she demanded. 'There's nothing wrong with taking a pride in your home, is there?'

'But you always say how hard up you are. You're always complaining about my Army pay. How much d'you manage to save?'

Ethel's eyes shifted. 'A bit. Not that it's any use thinking about it now. That daughter of yours –'

'How much?' George demanded suspiciously.

'Ten pounds. Eleven, something like that.'

'Go on,' he said disbelievingly, 'you've always known to the last penny what money you've got. How much?'

'Fifteen pounds,' she said reluctantly, and then, 'Oh, all right, twenty-one pounds fourteen and a penny, if you must know! Enough to keep those two little thieves comfortable for a few weeks. And my new three-piece gone.' Tears welled up in her eyes again and rolled down her cheeks. 'I'll have to start all over again now, and if they stop this war too soon I'll never be able to get it.'

George sat down on a chair as if his legs had given way beneath him. He felt his anger return and fought to control it.

'Ethel, I just don't understand you. Your daughter's gone missing, run off with a sailor, and all you can think about is your new three-piece suite. Can't you see, none of that matters? It's Carol what matters. What's happening to her, where is she? She might be dead, for all you know – bombed, or strangled. We might never find out. Don't you *care*?'

'Of course I care,' Ethel snapped. 'I'm her mother. I carried her for nine months, I went through hell giving birth to her. Why don't you ask her if she cares about me? Does it look as if she does?'

'I wish I could,' George muttered. 'I only wish I could.'

He got heavily to his feet. 'I'm going down the police station, see what they've got to say about this. I haven't got much time – got to be back Monday morning. And listen to this, Ethel – if you hear *anything*, anything at all, from our Carol, or if she comes back home, you let me know straight away, understand? I'm not going to be kept in the dark again.' He surveyed the mess on the floor. 'You'd better get this lot cleared up. And get something hot on the stove for my supper. I've been travelling all day and had nothing but a bully-beef sandwich. This is still my home, and I'm master in it, whatever you like to think, all right?'

He pulled open the door and stamped out, slamming it behind him. Ethel sat for a moment on the chair, staring at the broken china and shaking with anger and fear.

George had never, in all their marriage, spoken to her like that. He had never dared order her about. She had had the upper hand ever since the day they'd met.

Ethel did not know what to do. But she found herself on her knees, picking up the broken cups and mopping up the spilt milk. And when she had finished, she went out into the kitchen and started to fry some sausages and onions and some leftover potato, for her husband's supper.

Betty shared her family's worries about her sailor cousin, and her anxiety added to her fears for Dennis. There seemed to be more and more unexploded bombs turning up all over Portsmouth, and miles out into the countryside, and they were often reported in the local paper. Sometimes, inevitably, the reports told of people being killed by them.

'It seems as if everyone you know's in danger these days,' she said to the other Land Girls. 'There isn't anyone I can think of who's really safe.'

'We're all in it together,' Yvonne agreed. 'Even out here on the farm – remember that bomb that killed the chickens and started the grandfather clock ticking?'

The clock was still keeping perfect time. The only good thing the Germans ever did, Mr Spencer had commented. Pity they didn't stick to mending clocks.

'A good kick would've got it going just as well,' Betty said. 'It didn't have to be a bomb.'

They were sitting in the barn, having a short break. A shadow loomed up in the doorway and Gerald came in.

Gerald had improved a lot. His arm was still giving him some trouble – chipped elbow bones, the doctor said – but the effects of the dysentery had almost gone and he was slowly building up his strength. It wouldn't be long before he had to go back to his regiment in Africa. Meanwhile, he was able to do some work on the farm, and both Betty and Yvonne had noticed that as often as not, this meant sharing in whatever job Erica was doing.

'Thaw's setting in,' he said. 'We'll be able to get on with that ploughing. Top three fields never got done last autumn, did they?'

The girls shook their heads. Jonas, who had been sitting at a short distance chewing a Marmite sandwich, said, 'Tidden the only job wants doing. We only got half the bloody corn threshed when the team was here. The stack'll be riddled with rats an' mice, an' we're running short of hay to feed the flickin' beasts. Wants someone in there with a couple of terriers, flush out the bloody lot.'

Yvonne shuddered. She wasn't afraid of much, but rats always turned her sick. She glanced appealingly at Betty and Erica.

'I can't stand them. I think it's the way they stare at you with their little eyes. And the way they run – as if they'd got

227

wheels instead of feet. And then having to hit them.'

'Well, someone's got to do it,' Betty said, and glanced mischievously at Jonas. 'You're the one with the terriers.'

'You're the ones with the young legs,' he retorted. 'I can't skip about like you can, don't mind admitting it. Rats needs someone quick an' nimble.'

'So what job d'you want to do, Jonas?' Gerald enquired. 'Seems there's more than enough to go round.'

Jonas glanced at him. 'Ploughing's my job, allus has bin. I'd hev finished them fields last November if I hadn't bin laid up with that flickin' bronchitis. Time I was about again, bloody ground was frozen. I'll carry on with that.'

'Sorry,' Gerald said. 'Dad's already told me to get on with that. I can drive the tractor one-handed –'

'You never can! You need two hands for that job. How d'yer think you can steer the tractor an' pull the levers to lift the plough an' all the rest of it with that gammy arm of yours? Don't talk bloody daft.'

'I'll have one of the girls to help me,' Gerald said. 'They need to learn how to plough anyway. We can't always rely on you being able to do it.'

The old man's face darkened. 'An' what d'yer mean by that? I always bin reliable enough in the past. Over fifty years I worked on this bloody farm, man and boy, worked for your grandad I did when farming *was* farming, none of this fancy modern stuff –'

'Like tractors,' Gerald put in, grinning.

'All right, you can laugh. Yes, we used to plough with horses, *an*' do a damn sight better job'n you young ones ever could. We were using horses till five years back, still do when we needs. I could've done all the lower fields with the horses last autumn if Boxer hadn't gone lame.'

'Seems everything went wrong last autumn,' Gerald observed.

Jonas glared at him. 'So it did. There's a war on here, as well as in bloody Africa.'

Gerald shrugged. He looked at Erica. 'How about it, then? Want to help me on the tractor and learn to plough?'

Erica jumped up and brushed her palms down the seat of her dungarees. 'Yes, *please*.' She blushed, as if surprised by her own enthusiasm, and glanced at the other two. 'Sorry, but I'm not too keen on rats either. I promise I'll take my turn later.'

'You bet you will,' Yvonne said, but she spoke in a resigned tone. The girls had quickly learned that on a farm there was no room for squeamishness. 'I'll be along later to see how straight you've ploughed.'

'It'll be just as if we'd done it with a ruler,' Erica promised, and hurried out of the barn after Gerald.

Betty watched them go and then looked at Yvonne with raised eyebrows. 'Keen, isn't she?'

'Yes,' Yvonne said slowly, 'I reckon she is.'

The two girls smiled at each other. And Jonas snorted.

Gerald and Erica went straight to the tractor-shed. The tractor was a Fordson, bought second-hand and liable to be temperamental. Jonas treated it with as much care as if it had been a living animal, murmuring to it in an unusually gentle voice as he greased and polished.

'He thinks it's his,' Erica said, laying her hand on the mudguard. 'He looks after it like a baby.'

'Or a horse. Jonas was senior horseman when we were still using them for the plough. As soon as the tractor came in, he switched over but secretly I think he still wishes we were using horses.'

'Why does he love it so much, if he'd rather go on in the old way?' Erica asked.

'Because of his position as ploughman. It might sound pretty ordinary to someone from the town, but on the farm the ploughman's top dog. Everything depends on him getting his job right. And he's generally more of a farm foreman for all the other jobs – takes charge.'

'So if Jonas refused to use the tractor and stayed with the horses, your father would have employed someone else as ploughman and Jonas would have taken second place.'

'That's right,' Gerald said, smiling at her. 'Unfortunately for Jonas, that happened anyway because Dick and I ranked higher than him. If we wanted to drive the tractor, we did!'

'Still, he would accept that because you're the farmer's sons. He couldn't grumble about that.'

'Don't you believe it. He might accept it but that wouldn't stop him beefing. He never stopped. If Dick or me did a bit of ploughing, Jonas would be out there walking the furrows, pointing out all the rough bits or the bits we'd missed. Jonas doesn't let anything come between him and his moaning, it's his favourite pastime.'

They laughed. Gerald turned away to reach down the paraffin can and Erica looked at him affectionately. During the few weeks Gerald had been home, she had grown very fond of him. She wasn't looking forward to his going away again.

Nevertheless, she always tried to keep a little distance between them. The moment when he had almost fainted in the barn, and she had found her fingers stroking the back of his neck, had shaken her. For the first time since Geoffrey's death, she had experienced the tingling of desire, and the feeling left her guilty and disturbed. I shouldn't be feeling like that about another chap, she thought. It's disloyal to Geoff's memory. Yet she could not resist the temptation to spend her time with Gerald whenever possible. So long as it doesn't go any further than that, she thought.

Gerald turned suddenly and caught her glance. They stared at each other and Erica felt her face grow hot.

'Show me what to do,' she said hurriedly. 'What's the paraffin for?'

'To get the engine started. Once it's running, we can switch in to normal fuel.' He gave her a comical look. 'Oh, lor'.'

'What? What's wrong?'

'We're going to have to get old Jonas along after all. You have to crank the engine to get it started, and it's a real brute. I can't do it with one arm, and you certainly haven't got the muscle. We need him to give it a swing.'

'I'll go and fetch him,' Erica offered, and ran across the

yard, glad of the cold air on her cheeks. She had seen the darkening of Gerald's eyes as he met her look, and knew that he was talking to cover his own feelings. This is getting serious, she thought. Another couple of minutes in there, and he might have kissed me.

Jonas sneered when she asked him to come over and give a hand with the tractor. 'Two of you on the job, and can't get the bloody thing started! What flickin' use are you going to be out in the field? If the pair of you got no more strength than a couple of kittens, better if you came in here and chased rats.'

'Gerald wants to do the ploughing,' Erica said firmly. 'He wants you to come and give the cranking-handle a swing, that's all. He's not asking you to sell your soul.'

'Always did want to rule the roost, that one,' Jonas grumbled. 'Pair of 'em trying to run before they could walk, and the boss letting 'em.'

Erica stopped in the middle of the yard. She planted her legs apart, put her hands on her hips and faced him.

'Just what's the matter with you, Jonas? Why is it that nothing's ever right? When we first came here, you never stopped grumbling about us taking the boys' places. You never let a day go by without telling us how much better at everything they were. Well, maybe that was true, but it wasn't our fault and we did our best. Now Gerald's back and you grumble just as much about *him*. What is it you're so afraid of? That someone might actually be better than you at something? And why would that be so terrible, anyway? It's the *job* that matters – the *bloody, flickin' job*!'

Jonas stared at her, his eyes narrowing, his mottled lips pushed out. She saw a dark flush rise in his weatherbeaten cheeks and knew that something she had said had scored a hit. For a moment, she wondered if she had gone too far.

The she heard a burst of applause and looked past him to see Betty and Yvonne at the barn door, clapping their hands together. Behind her, Gerald was leaning against the tractor, grinning broadly. And over at the open farmhouse door, Mr and Mrs Spencer were standing open-mouthed.

Jonas saw her glance and followed it. His face reddened deeper yet. He muttered something Erica couldn't hear, and pushed past her.

'All right,' he growled, 'let's get at it. Well, don't just stand there staring! There's bloody work to be done, ain't there?'

Annie had been awake almost all night and then fallen heavily asleep towards dawn. That was how it was now – for hours every night she lay stiff and still in the bed, staring into the darkness and imagining Colin's last hours on the *Exeter*, the ship already damaged and threatened on all sides by the enemy. And then the final attack, guns blazing from every quarter and the brave British ship returning fire, defending herself until those very last minutes when the damage became too great to be borne and she disappeared beneath the waves . . .

They hadn't had a chance, she thought. And still nobody knew how many had really survived.

It was thought that a large number of the men had survived the sinking, that they might even have reached land, but nothing had been heard of them since. They might have wandered off into the jungle and starved to death, or been savaged by wild beasts – though nobody was quite sure what kinds of wild beasts roamed the jungles out there. Anyway, according to the conventions of war, the Japanese should have taken them prisoner and then notified the British of their names. But no such notification had been received. It was as if the men had disappeared off the face of the earth.

'They'll let us know soon,' Ted said when they discussed it. 'They'll have to. It's all a bit of a muddle out there, that's all. They'll get it sorted out.'

'A bit of a muddle! It's blooming chaos,' Annie said. But she knew he was as worried as she, and all they could do was give each other what comfort they could.

Annie turned over in bed and found herself alone. Ted

must have got up early. As she realised this, the bedroom door opened and he appeared with two cups of tea. Annie stared at him in astonishment.

'You're in your working clothes –'

'Yes.' He sat down on the bed. 'I'm going down the ferry. I don't know if they'll let me back on the *King* straight away, but whatever they want me to do, I'll do it.' He looked at her gravely. 'I'm ashamed of myself, Annie. The way I've been – well, I dunno how you put up with me, I really don't. Whining and moping round the house all this time when there was work to be done. And young Ben going off to sea. And our Colin . . .' His voice shook a little. 'Well, I been thinking and I reckon it's time I pulled meself together and got back to work. That's all.'

'Oh, Ted.' Annie laid her hand on his arm. 'Ted, I know I've been hard on you these past few weeks –'

'No harder than you should be. You were right to go on at me, Annie.'

'Well,' she said, 'let's not argue about that. But you're not to go back unless you really feel like it, Ted. I mean, there's no use forcing yourself.'

'I'm not forcing myself. I want to.' He set his jaw, looking more determined than she had seen him in months. 'I won't pretend I'm not still scared of the bombs, but I reckon most people must be the same, and if they can carry on, so can I. I'm not letting it beat me again.'

He drank his tea and then gave her a crooked grin. Annie felt the tears in her eyes. She wanted to hug him, but sensed that this was not the moment. Let him stay in charge.

'Right,' he said, putting down his cup and smacking his lips. 'That's it, then. I've had me breakfast, so there's no need for you to get up just yet. I'll get me bike and go.'

He leaned forwards and kissed her. And Annie, unable to restrain herself any longer, threw her arms round his neck and held him tightly. They stayed together for a long moment and then he drew away.

'You're a good wife, Annie. I dunno what I'd have done without you.'

'And you're a good husband. And a good skipper, too.

They'll be pleased to see you back on the ferry, I know that.'

She lay back and heard him clump down the stairs and out of the back door. A few minutes later, she heard him wheel his bike along the side of the house and give a cheery ring on the bell.

For a few moments, she had been almost able to forget Colin. Now the remembrance rushed back, almost overwhelming her with fresh pain. But somehow it was just a little easier to bear, now that the worry about Ted was over.

I hope this isn't just a flash in the pan, she thought. I hope he really *is* better.

CHAPTER FOURTEEN

As the spring evenings drew out, Micky's army was able to forage more for weapons. Micky still spent a good deal of time on his own, but he was now often accompanied by Desmond, who followed him like an adoring puppy. He would do anything that Micky asked him, and had brought out several handfuls of live bullets from his Sunday morning firing practice.

'You mean you just carry the boxes of ammo yourselves?' Micky had asked incredulously when he first discovered the routine. Desmond never volunteered information – you had to drag it out of him, though he was willing enough to give it once you asked the right questions. 'They just give you the boxes to carry, and they're full of bullets and not locked or anything?'

Desmond nodded. 'Bullets aren't any good without guns.'

Micky rolled his eyes. No good without guns! 'But they're full of explosive,' he said. 'Gunpowder. We could make bombs.'

'Bombs aren't any good without aeroplanes,' Jimmy Cross said. 'Des is right. Ammo's no use without guns.'

'All right, so we get guns too, don't we. But we can start off by collecting live ammo.' Micky looked at Desmond again. 'You could get some, couldn't you? Take a few out of the box when nobody's looking?'

Desmond's face didn't change. He had very little expression – sometimes he laughed, sometimes he scowled furiously, but mostly he just looked blank. It was difficult to know if he was thinking about Micky's order, picturing himself stealing some bullets, or whether it meant nothing to him. But the following week, after dinner on Sunday afternoon, he turned up at the den with a handful of live bullets.

'Cor, look at that,' Micky breathed rapturously as Desmond dropped them in his hand. 'Just *look* at that.'

The bullets were about two inches long, with shiny caps. They felt smooth and heavy in Micky's palm, and he turned them over and stroked them reverently. He longed for a gun so that he could fire them, and imagined himself lying on his stomach, aiming at the invading Germans. Saving Portsmouth. Saving England.

That would show all those stupid magistrates and the probation officer he had to go and see every week, who just talked to him like a kid.

It wasn't fair that Desmond could be in the ATC and learn to fire guns, and he couldn't.

'Can't you get a gun out?' he asked. 'Stuff it under your jacket? We got to have guns.'

'Have to give the guns back,' Desmond said. 'They always ask for the guns back.'

Well, it stood to reason that they would. Micky looked again at the bullets in his hand and felt his longing increase. There had to be a way.

'Can't you find out where they keep 'em? Are they locked away?' He knew they must be, but people weren't always as careful as they ought to be – look at the way Des had managed to get the bullets. 'Don't they ever leave the guns out anywhere?'

'Not our guns,' Desmond said. He took one of the bullets back and cuddled it in his big hands. 'My bullets.'

'No, they're mine now. You can keep that one but the rest are part of our arsenal. And you got to find a way of getting some guns.' Something Desmond had said struck him. 'You said they didn't leave *your* guns out. Does that mean they leave others around?'

'In the repair shops.' Desmond slipped his bullet back into his pocket. Micky stared at him.

'The repair shops? What d'you mean?'

236

'Repair shops in the hangars. They've got all old planes in there – Tiger Moths and Camels. They mend them.'

'And they got guns?'

'Yes, they got guns. I seen 'em, on the benches some of them.' He held an imaginary machine-gun in his arms and aimed it around the basement of the bombed house. 'Rat-at-at-at-at! You're all dead.'

The others backed away a little. Desmond might be only pretending, but there was something chilling in his blank eyes. They felt glad he hadn't got a real gun.

'But that's just what I bin *asking* you,' Micky said, exasperated. 'Time and time again I asked you if there was guns left out anywhere. You said there wasn't.'

'You asked about *our* guns,' Desmond said, looking hurt, and Micky reminded himself that there was no use in getting annoyed. Desmond answered the questions he was asked, and that was all. It wasn't his fault if you didn't ask the right questions.

Now that Micky knew what to ask him, the information came out quickly enough. Some of the old aircraft that had been used in the Great War were used now for 'spotting' and brought to the airfield for maintenance. Some that were found to be past help were taken to a 'graveyard' at the outer edge of the aerodrome and dumped there, and you could pick up some useful bits and pieces. One boy had a pilot's seat which he'd taken home, and several had smaller souvenirs – bits of engine, scraps of wing, a battered wireless set which might just be able to be mended.

The other aircraft were taken to a big hangar, where repairs and maintenance were carried out, and there they might be partially dismantled. That was when a gun might be removed and put on a bench, out of the way, while the work was being done. Desmond had seen several.

'You mean they just let you wander in and out whenever you like?'

Desmond nodded. 'If we're in uniform we can go in any time. I talk to them. I like looking at the Tiger Moth. They know me.'

Micky could believe that. Desmond would talk to anyone, especially if he could talk about aeroplanes. People were often surprised at how much he knew, yet it was quickly obvious that there were strange, huge gaps in his knowledge and that his actual understanding was very limited. Micky could imagine him wandering in and out of the hangars and maintenance sheds, tolerated by the men working there because they knew that he could never be any threat.

'So you could get a gun,' he said.

Desmond looked uneasy. 'They'd see me. They wouldn't let me.'

'Anyway, how'd he get it out?' Jimmy Cross demanded. 'He'd never get it past the guards. You know their orders – shoot first and ask questions after.'

'Don't want to be shot,' Desmond said, looking frightened.

'You're not going to be.' Micky frowned heavily. 'This is something that's got to be properly planned. We'll have to go in during the night.'

'Don't be daft,' Jimmy said, 'they'd never let you in then. I bet they wouldn't even let Des in. They know the ATC don't go there night-times.'

'There's a way through the fence,' Desmond said suddenly. 'By the graveyard. Nobody else knows it. It's my secret way.' He looked pleased and crafty. 'I could show you. We could go in and I could show you the Tiger Moth.'

'Never mind the Tiger Moth,' Micky said, but his eyes were gleaming. He looked at Desmond speculatively, wondering just how much of what the bigger boy said was true. Last week, Desmond had seen a lion walking down Copnor Road, large as life. He had been present when a barrage balloon collapsed on a house at the end of Tokyo Street. He had helped put out the fire when the Guildhall had been bombed last year. He had jumped from a ferry-boat and saved a woman from drowning.

Only one of those incidents – the one with the barrage balloon – had actually happened, though he might have been near the Guildhall during the blitz. But you never knew when he was telling the truth or when he simply thought he was. Lions and acts of bravery on the ferry could be dismissed. But a way into Airspeed? An aeroplane graveyard, where you could pick up real souvenirs? A hangar full of aeroplanes, with machine-guns left lying about on benches?

'Show me,' Micky said decisively. 'Show me where it is.'

The secret army was becoming a real possibility.

Shocked by the damage and the depression they found in London, Carol and Roddy had got on the train again. This time they'd gone to Bournemouth.

'It's a seaside place, there's bound to be lots of cheap places to stay,' Carol said. 'And it hasn't been bombed like London and Pompey. It was horrible up there, wasn't it?'

'Och, it was miserable,' Roddy agreed. 'All those bomb sites. And folk trying to be cheerful but you could see they were feeling awful underneath. And all crowding into the Underground stations at night, like rats in a hole . . .' He shuddered. 'I cannae stand being in places like that, Carol. It gives me the creeps.'

It wasn't as easy as Carol had expected to find somewhere to live; all the rooms seemed to be taken by soldiers and airmen for their wives to stay in. But at last they found a small backstreet boarding house and asked for a room, telling the thin-faced landlady they'd just got married. She looked at them sceptically but showed them up to a room which looked out on the tiny backyard. There was a small air-raid shelter there, built against the garden wall, and a clothes-line. A weary-looking shrub wilted sadly in an old, broken chimneypot.

Carol and Roddy looked at the room. There was dull green linoleum on the floor and one armchair, covered with worn American cloth. The double bed was iron and pushed into a corner to make enough room. A small kitchen table served as a washstand, and there was a chest of drawers and a cupboard built into the fireplace alcove. The fireplace itself had been removed and a small gas fire put in its place.

'Ten bob a week, with breakfast,' the woman said. 'You'll 'ave to find yer other meals yerselves, but no cookin' up 'ere, mind, I couldn't be responsible. The gas fire's on a meter, shillin' in the slot.'

Ten shillings a week. They could afford that, for a while anyway, till they both got jobs. Carol nodded.

'Do you get many air-raids?'

The woman shrugged. 'We gets a few. Mostly lookin' for the aeroplane factory at Christchurch. There's bin a few bombs.' She looked at them shiftily. 'The shelter's a shillin' a night extra, else you'll 'ave to go to the public.'

She took them downstairs and showed them the lavatory, outside the back door. Carol peered inside the shelter and wrinkled her nose.

'It smells as if something's died in there,' she told Roddy when they were back in the room. 'I wouldn't want to spend the night in it even if it was free.'

'Old skinflint,' Roddy said. 'She'd charge for the air we breathed if she could measure it.' He looked dispiritedly at the little room. 'It's no' the sort of place I wanted to bring you to, Carrie.'

'It doesn't matter.' She hugged him. 'It's our room – our private room. We can do just as we like in here, and nobody to interfere –' She stopped abruptly as the door opened without warning and their landlady came in, staring at the two standing there in each other's arms. They stepped apart quickly, blushing.

'I 'ope everythin's above board with you two,' Mrs Higgs said suspiciously. 'You sure you're married? You look too young to me. This 'as always bin a respectable place, I don't want nothing going on as shouldn't.'

'We told you, we've been married a month,' Carol said coldly. 'Plenty of people are getting married young these days. There's a war on.'

The landlady's sallow face flushed a dull, ugly red. 'And there's no call to be impertinent, miss. Or Mrs, if that's what you call yourself.' She looked pointedly at the ring on Carol's finger. 'Looks more like a curtain ring out o' Woolworths than a proper wedding ring. Still, if that's what you say . . . so long as you pays yer rent on time.' She stood with her hands on her bony hips. 'I come up to tell you about the bath. It's Friday nights, I 'as first turn, and you'll 'ave to 'elp fill it and empty it out after. An' it's an extra shillin' each.'

'A shilling *each*?' Carol said. 'All sharing the same water?'

'Take it or leave it,' Mrs Higgs said, turning to leave the room. 'I'll want 'elp whether you 'as a bath or not, can't manage it on me own. Oh –' She turned to Roddy '– an' you can make it yer business to keep me coal scuttle filled too. It's too 'eavy for me to lift.' Her small, muddy eyes dared him to object. 'My last lodger did it without a murmur. Lovely feller, 'e was. Got called up for the Army. I daresay you'll be goin' off soon too.'

'I've been turned down,' Roddy said, his voice trembling slightly. 'I won't be called up.'

'Turned down? Why? You look all right to me.'

'Flat feet,' Roddy answered, at the same moment as Carol said, 'Short sight.'

There was a long pause as they all looked at each other. Then Carol said, trying to make her voice sound convincing, 'Roddy's got flat feet *and* bad eyesight. That's why they won't have him. But he's really clever. He'll get a good job.'

'Hm,' Mrs Higgs said. She gave them another hard, suspicious stare and turned away, closing the door behind her. They heard her go down the stairs and Roddy sat down heavily on the bed.

'She doesnae believe us. She doesnae believe a word of it.'

'It doesn't matter,' Carol said. She went over to the door and pushed the bolt across, then came back to the bed and sat down beside him. 'It doesn't matter what she thinks. This is our room, our own private room, and we won't let her spoil it. Anyway, I feel just as much married as if we'd been in a church, don't you?' She pulled him close and kissed him. 'I'm your wife, Roderick MacPherson, whatever anyone else thinks, and I love you.'

They lay back on the bed together and, slowly, Roddy relaxed. Carol felt his body tighten against her, felt the hardness and the vigour in him and responded with her own softness. Their passion flared, and they forgot Mrs Higgs and the unlovely room with its cold linoleum and lumpy bed as they swept together into the new world they had discovered, their private world of delight that took them yet again to their own particular mountain peak.

The bed shifted and creaked beneath them. And as they reached the topmost pinnacle, they heard an echoing rhythm from below.

Mrs Higgs was thumping on the ceiling.

Gerald had succeeded in getting Jonas to start the tractor, and he and Erica began on the ploughing. Gerald sat in the seat, steering with his good arm, while Erica rode on the mudguard beside him operating the levers that worked the plough. They finished the first field at sundown and after the tractor had been put away they walked back so that they could admire their work.

'It looks beautiful,' Erica said, letting her gaze run down the rich dark earth of the newly turned furrows. 'Like dark brown corduroy. It's really satisfying to think we've done all that.'

'It'll be just as satisfying when we've sown the corn,' Gerald said, leaning over the gate. 'And when we first see it coming through like tiny green needles, and then when it's standing ripe and golden, waiting to be harvested ... That's what's so good about farming. You get so much satisfaction out of it – when it all goes right.' He grinned. 'It doesn't always, of course. The weather's wrong or you get pests or blight – there's always something to grumble about. Probably that's why Jonas is the way he is.'

'Your dad's not, though. He generally manages to look on the bright side.'

'Well, there are always two sides to look at, aren't there,' Gerald said thoughtfully. 'For a farmer, especially. I mean, in one field the weather's just right because you need a good downpour of rain, and in the next it's all wrong because you need sunshine and dry. You can choose whether to be pleased or fed up. The thing is to have as many different things on the go as you can, so there's always something to be pleased about.'

'Or grumble at,' Erica said, and he laughed.

'Well, that just depends on the sort of person you are.' He glanced at the girl beside him. 'You seem to take the rough with the smooth pretty well, Erica. I know you've had some pretty hard knocks but you keep smiling just the same.'

'I didn't to start with,' she said. 'I was really bitter. I took it out on everyone – specially Dennis.'

Gerald nodded. He had met Dennis several times, when the young Quaker had come out to the farm to see Betty and give a hand around the farm. Gerald didn't agree with either his politics or his religion, but he admired Dennis's courage.

'It must have been hard for you to understand, when your own fiancé had just been – well –'

'Oh, even before Geoff was killed,' Erica said, surprised that her voice could remain steady while she spoke of him. 'I took against him the minute I saw him. It was as if I knew there was something ... But you know, I had to work really hard not to like him! Daft, isn't it?'

'I don't think it was daft,' Gerald said gently. 'I don't think you could do anything that was daft.'

There was a brief silence. Erica was still staring at the ploughed furrows. She felt her cheeks grow warm and her heart begin to race. Then, slowly, she turned her head towards him.

Gerald was watching her. His eyes were quite dark. She met their gaze and felt her lips tremble and part.

'Gerald – I –'

'Don't say anything, Erica,' he said quietly. 'Let's just be here together. Just for a few minutes.'

'But –'

'Look,' he said, 'I know I can't be anything to you. You had this marvellous chap you were engaged to, and you wouldn't look twice at a bloke like me – a farmer's son.

And I'll be going away again soon, so I won't be around to cause you any trouble – any embarrassment or anything. But – just let me have this, would you? Please? Just a few minutes with you now and then, not talking, not doing anything, just being *with* you. That's all I'm asking.'

Erica gazed at him. He looked much fitter than when he had first come home. His thin body had filled out with muscle and his mother's feeding. His cheeks were no longer gaunt and a dirty yellow, but firm and slightly tanned. He was even beginning, very cautiously, to use his injured arm again.

'Gerald –'

'I've upset you,' he said contritely. 'Oh, blast it. I'm sorry, Erica. I shouldn't have said anything. Now you're fed up – you won't want anything more to do with me.' He straightened up and half turned away. 'Forget I said it, will you? I didn't want to put my foot in it.'

'No. Gerald, don't go –' Impulsively, she put out her hand and touched his arm. 'It's all right,' she said earnestly. 'I don't mind what you said, I don't mind it at all. I – I'm *glad* you said it. I – I like being with you, too.'

Gerald paused. He turned back to face her. The sun was disappearing now, leaving them in dusky twilight. His dark eyes searched her face.

'You don't have to say that, Erica.'

'I'm not just saying it.' She laughed shakily. 'It's true. I like being with you. I feel – sort of comfortable. As if we've known each other a long time.' She shook her head and laughed again. 'Doesn't make sense, does it.'

'Doesn't it?' Gerald asked. 'I think it does. I think it makes a lot of sense.' He moved closer and reached out with his good hand, laying it around her shoulders. 'I feel I've known you all my life, Erica. I feel I've been looking for you for years. It was like a miracle, that first time I saw you. As if a dream had come to life. I couldn't believe it. And all this time –'

'I know,' she said quietly, and moved into his embrace.

Their kiss was tremulous, like the first kiss of a boy and girl experimenting newly with love. Their lips brushed tentatively, parted and then brushed again. Then Gerald gathered her closely against him and his mouth became firmer, and Erica parted her lips for him and closed her eyes.

'Oh, my darling,' he murmured at last. 'My darling, I love you.'

Erica rested her head on his chest. Her thoughts and emotions fluttered together like butterflies, bright and uncatchable. But there was a dark one, too, a shadowy moth that hovered at the edge of the glowing light.

'I didn't think I'd love anyone again after I lost Geoff,' she said at last. 'I never even wanted to. I thought it would be disloyal. But now I feel – I don't know what I feel. Sort of guilty because I don't feel guilty, if you can understand.'

'I can understand. But it's not disloyal. You've got your whole lifetime to live. He wouldn't want you to go on by yourself, never loving anyone. Not if he really cared about you.'

'He did! We cared about each other.' She lifted her face. 'I still do love him, Gerald. But I love you as well.'

'Then that's all right,' he said. 'So long as it's me you marry and live with, and not a ghost.'

Erica gasped. 'Is that a proposal?'

'Well,' he said, 'it certainly sounded like one. Mind you, I didn't plan it. I wasn't going to say anything at all – didn't think there was a chance. But since the subject's come up – well, what d'you think? Could you bear to marry me?'

'It's so quick,' she said, half bemused.

'No quicker than a lot of other people. We don't know how much time we've got these days.'

'But you'll be going back soon – how can we possibly –'

'We'll apply for a licence straight away,' he said. 'I reckon I'm good for another month. We can just fit in a week's honeymoon. Or maybe we can get a special licence. I'll see about it first thing in the morning.'

'You can't. We've got two more fields to plough.'

'Bugger the fields,' he said, and caught her against him again. 'Us getting married's more important than a few fields. We'll let Jonas do them. Then everyone'll be pleased!'

They kissed again, this time with more confidence.

'Just a minute,' Erica said breathlessly, disengaging herself. 'You're forgetting something. I haven't said yes yet.'

'No more you have. And I don't reckon much to that for a proposal anyway.' Dramatically, he went down on one knee, laid his good hand over his heart and held out his other arm, still wrapped in its sling. 'Darling Erica, I love you with all my heart.' His voice had started out as if he were on stage, but as he spoke the words it shook and then became serious, almost imploring. 'Will you – will you *please* – be my wife?'

Erica looked down. His face, upturned, looked suddenly vulnerable. She thought of him going away again, back to the Africa desert. She thought of Geoff, riding the sky to his death.

'Oh, Gerald,' she said, her voice full of tears, 'of course I will.' And she lifted him so that he was standing once again, and put her arms around him to hold him closely against her heart. 'Of *course* I will.'

The moon was at three-quarters, showing a dim light through a haze of cloud on the night Micky and Desmond made their way to the airfield. They had been there twice before and Desmond had shown him the gap in the fence.

It was right on the outer perimeter of the field. You weren't even supposed to go this near without a permit, but there were places where the ground was wild and broken, and you could sneak between the hedges and gorse to the high wire fence. Even then, it looked insurmountable, with several strands of barbed wire stretched at an angle on top of the thick mesh. But to Micky's surprise, he saw that Desmond was right. There was a small place, surrounded by dense, prickly bushes, where the fence had been dragged loose and then roughly replaced. You could pull it up and wriggle underneath.

'Coo-er,' he breathed. 'That's smashing. Did you make it, Des?'

Desmond tilted his head and looked sideways. 'Might have.'

'You're not so daft as you look, sometimes,' Micky said. 'I bet you did, didn't you?'

Desmond looked sly but wouldn't answer. He scraped grass and earth away from the bottom of the fence and bent up the mesh. The gap underneath was just big enough.

'You go first,' he said, but Micky shook his head.

'I want to see how the land lays first. Reconnoitre. It ain't no good rushin' in and gettin' caught first time.'

By now, he had a very good idea of how the factory operated at night and had seen that the guard on the planes was minimal. So long as no unauthorised person came in through the gates, the whole area was deemed sufficiently protected. There were a couple of guards who walked round at night, but it was a good half-hour between each patrol.

The aircraft were on the tarmac ready to be transported to RAF airfields. Sometimes there were none, sometimes there was a whole new batch. That was the time, Micky decided, when he and Desmond should make their raid.

He looked at the gap under the fence, slightly nervous now that the moment had come. He knew that if they were found within the airfield they would be in serious trouble. But the thought of actually being in there – of being able to get near the planes themselves – was too tempting to resist. If he could just get hold of a gun . . .

He lay down and squirmed underneath the wire. Then he held it up so that Desmond could follow him.

Very, very cautiously, still flat on their stomachs, the two of them wriggled through the tussocks of last year's long grass. It seemed a long way, but at last they reached the edge of the apron, and looked out over a wide expanse of tarmac.

The planes were there. A row of them, lined up outside the big, camouflaged hangars. They looked bigger than

Micky had expected, like huge, resting birds in the silvery light, and he gazed at them in awe.

'Coo,' he breathed, 'don't they look smashing. I wish I could fly in one.'

They wriggled closer. The guard had walked past five minutes earlier and wouldn't be back for at least another twenty. Sometimes he stopped and had a smoke down at the far end. But you never knew who might be looking out from the buildings, and to get from the grass to the planes they'd have to run across the tarmac, in plain view of anyone watching.

'I don't reckon there's anyone else about,' Micky muttered, more to himself than Desmond. 'When I give the word, we make for the nearest plane, all right? Get right underneath it, so you're in its shadow, and stand still.'

He made sure that Desmond understood, then took one last, careful look around the airfield. It was silent. There was no one in sight. The guard was far away, down at the other end, probably having his cigarette.

'Go,' Micky breathed, and the two boys ran, half crouching, towards the shadow of the nearest aircraft.

Nobody shouted. Nobody ran. Nobody fired at them. They stood in the darkness, panting slightly, half scared by their own daring.

Desmond put up his hand and touched the belly of the aeroplane. 'It's big.'

'Yeah.' Micky craned his neck to stare up at it. He had never been so close to an aircraft before. 'I wonder if you can get inside. You'd have to climb up on the wing. I've seen 'em do it at the pictures.' He thought quickly. 'You stay here and keep a good look-out, tell me if anyone comes.'

Feeling very exposed, he scrambled up on to the wing and felt around the hood of the cockpit. He knew it would slide open, but could not find a catch. A sudden sound made him jump, and he cast a scared glance over his shoulder, but it was only the cry of an animal somewhere in the tangled undergrowth outside the perimeter fence. His fingers shook as he fumbled with the hood. If he couldn't even get *into* the blasted thing . . .

There was a click and the hood gave beneath his fingers. With a surge of triumph, he pushed it back and wriggled inside.

It was astonishingly small. There was just room for the pilot to sit, no more than that. In front of the seat was an array of switches, lights and dials. There was a wireless set, with earphones, and there was a gun, mounted on a turret.

Micky's heart gave a great leap. A wireless and a gun! That would make his army something to be reckoned with. And the RAF would never miss them. There must be heaps more in the stores. It would be far more use for him to have them.

The wireless set came out with a few tugs, leaving wires dangling from the gap where it had been fitted, but the gun was screwed in place. He leaned out of the cockpit and called softly to Desmond.

'I'm going to pass the wireless down to you. Is there anyone around?' He stepped out on to the wing and leaned over. The wireless was heavier than he'd expected and he almost dropped it before Desmond crept out from the shadows and stared up at him, eyes gleaming in the darkness.

'Coo,' Desmond said with awe, 'that's a wireless set.'

'I know that. Take it and get back under the plane.' The moonlight was brighter now and Micky felt as if he were standing in full sunlight, with the eyes of the whole of Portsmouth on him. His hands shook as he handed the heavy wireless to Desmond. 'Don't drop it.'

Desmond disappeared into the shadows. Micky looked after him, longing to jump down into safety, but he couldn't bear to leave without the gun. He turned back and fiddled again with the frame, his fingers trembling.

It was no use. The mounting was firmly fixed in place and refused to budge. And time was running short. Whoever was on patrol would be coming back this way soon, and they'd be sure to look specially at the aeroplanes.

The tarmac was a pool of darkness, lit by the uncertain half-light of the moon, but it was clear enough to see the deeper shadows around the grassy edges. Micky stared into the darkness, wondering if that was a movement he had seen, not too far away. The guard must be on his way back. The question was, how close had he got?

Feeling a sudden panic shake his legs, he scrambled down the wing and half fell under the plane. Desmond was still crouching there, the wireless in his arms.

'That erk must be coming back. You sure no one's seen us?'

Desmond shook his head. He was used to the concept of hide-and-seek. He sniggered, his voice loud in the silence. 'Coming, ready or not!'

'Shut up, you twerp. You want to get us caught?' Micky peered out. The sound of distant footfalls was little more than a disturbance of the air, but he dragged Desmond closer into the shadow. 'We'd better lay low till he's gone past again.'

The waiting seemed endless. They could hear the footsteps clearly now, coming closer. Micky's heart felt as if it were right in his throat, almost choking him. Would the guard look at all the planes? Would he look underneath? Thankful for the blackout, Micky knew that at least he wouldn't be shining any lights. As long as they stayed absolutely quiet in deep shadow, they ought to be safe.

He hoped that Desmond wouldn't do anything stupid. You could never be sure, with Desmond. He was quite capable of forgetting the danger of their position and making some daft noise, or start giggling and larking about. And if he thought the erk was a friend of his – one of the blokes he'd talked to in the hangars . . .

For the first time, Micky considered the consequences of being caught. It would mean prison, at the very least. Maybe even being shot, or hanged, for treason. Nobody would ever believe he was getting together his own army, to fight the Germans. By the time the guard had passed them, without so much as a glance underneath the aircraft, he was almost sick with fright.

The footsteps died away. Desmond drew in a breath, as if to speak, and Micky trod heavily on his foot.

'Shut up. He might still be able to hear us.' He listened. The airfield was silent again. 'Right, we got to get in the hangars, where you seen the planes and stuff. Where's the door?'

Desmond pointed towards the great sheds looming at the edge of the airfield. 'They got big doors. Where the planes go in and out.'

'I know that! But they must have small doors too – they don't open them big ones every time a bloke wants to go for a pee, do they? How d'you get in when you goes there?'

'There's a door in the side.'

'Bet it's locked,' Micky said, following the bigger boy cautiously across the open space, but when they finally reached the shadow of the building and he tried the handle, it gave under his touch. His heart leapt and he pushed the door open and slid inside.

For a few seconds, he stood quite still, gazing about him. The hangar was almost pitch black, but moonlight sloped in through a few gaps in the walls and the high roof. He could see the denser shapes of the aeroplanes, crouching like huge bats in the corners. When he flashed his torch, they shone in the thin light and threw weird, distorted shadows over the empty space.

'I don't like it,' Desmond said. 'Put the lights on.'

'Don't be daft!' Micky's voice was sharp as he fought down his own panic. He wasn't at all sure that all those queer shapes were planes . . . 'You'll get us caught. And don't make a noise. We got to keep quiet, see, like commandos. Where's these planes they're mending?'

'Over there.' Desmond pointed the torch towards a far corner. An aircraft stood half dismantled, with bits and pieces littered around it. Nearby was a wide bench, spread with tools, and as they approached it Micky gave a yelp of excitement.

'A gun! A proper gun! Look – it's just standin' on the bench, for anyone to pick up.'

He reached out and touched the weapon. It was smaller than he had imagined, its barrel not much more than eight inches long, but it was heavy for its size and felt solid in his hands. He put the rest against his shoulder and pretended to aim. 'D'you reckon it's loaded now?'

Desmond shook his head. He had never used any of the guns, only knew their shapes and sizes as he knew the shapes and sizes of aeroplanes and cars and other things that excited his mind. He knew that guns were dangerous, however, and backed away as Micky swung the heavy weapon around.

'You should never point a gun at anyone,' he said in the flat voice he used when reciting facts, or someone else's words. 'It might go off.'

Micky grinned. 'That's the idea, innit?' But he laid the gun down again and looked along the bench. 'Anything else worth pinchin'?'

There were no other guns, nor any ammunition. Micky slipped a few tools into his pockets. The light of the torch began to waver.

'We better get goin'.' He picked up the weapon and stuck it into the front of his jacket, hoping it wasn't loaded. But they wouldn't leave them standing on the benches with bullets in them. 'I'll carry this. You take the wireless.'

He followed Desmond to the small door and they opened it and peered out cautiously. Micky felt his nervousness return. If they were caught now, they'd be for the real high jump. And he had no idea when the patrol would come round again.

'Listen. When I say go, you get over to the fence as quick as you can. We got to get out of here fast.'

'Shall I take the wireless?'

'Of course you take the flippin' wireless! What d'you think we come here for?' Micky listened again. 'Right. Go.'

The two boys ran for the fence. There was a moment's panic as they searched for the gap, and then they were flat on their stomachs, wriggling through. Micky felt his jacket catch on the wire and pulled sharply, hearing the material tear. It didn't matter. He was out. He was safe.

'We still got to be quiet,' he said to Desmond. 'We got to stay quiet all the way home. An' we'll go a different way, a long way round, just in case there's anyone followin' us.'

By the time they finally reached home, their arms were aching from their burdens. He shifted the gun carefully, still not sure if it was loaded.

'Shall I take the wireless home with me?' Desmond asked. He was cradling it in his arms like a baby.

'No. I'm keepin' all the stuff. I got a special place for it.' Micky didn't want to risk leaving such valuable possessions in the den, where anyone might find them. He had prised up a couple of floorboards in his bedroom. There was plenty of room there, on the ceiling joists of the room below. 'You can put it down the bottom of our garden. I'll put the gun away first and then fetch it.'

Desmond looked regretful as he pushed the wireless set under a bush, but Micky gave him a friendly pat on the shoulder.

'You're a good soldier, Des. You're my best lieutenant. Tell you what, this is our secret, OK? We won't tell any of the others about it. It's just between the two of us.'

Desmond gave him a wide grin. Then he loped away up the alley, on his way home. Micky wondered how he would explain his absence. But perhaps, being Desmond, he wouldn't need to. His mum must be used to him doing queer things. She wouldn't think anything of it.

Micky hid the gun under the bush with the wireless. Then he went down into the Anderson shelter and curled up on the old mattress they kept down there. Mum would be out and Gran fast asleep in bed. If they wondered where Micky was, they'd just think he was in the tunnel shelters.

He imagined going out to Southsea beach when the Germans invaded, shooting them down with his gun. Using the wireless set to relay orders to his troops. Getting a boat to take him to France, right into the heart of enemy territory.

I might even learn to fly a plane, he thought, remembering

the aircraft lined up on the tarmac, ready to be flown away. That'd be better than any old boat. It can't be that hard.

Micky Baxter, world hero. Micky Baxter, air ace. Micky Baxter, VC.

CHAPTER FIFTEEN

'When's that *husband* of yours going to get a job?' Mrs Higgs asked, heavily emphasising the word husband, as she always did. She still doesn't believe we're married, Carol thought. Nosy old bat.

'He's been trying,' she said defensively. 'We've both been trying.' It had come as a shock to them both to find that jobs were not as easy to find as they had expected. People wanted to know so much about you. Who you were, where you came from, where you lived. When you were likely to be called up. And Roddy's excuse for not being in the Forces – that he was exempted on the grounds of being unfit – couldn't be used, not when he was looking for work.

'Well, I'd better get a job, then,' Carol had said at last, and they started to look in the local evening paper for jobs a sixteen-year-old girl could do. Serving in a shop, waiting in a restaurant, cleaning in one of Bournemouth's hotels. But women – especially young ones – weren't paid as much as men, and the sort of jobs Carol could do paid very little. Certainly not enough to keep two. And no sooner had she started to look than she began to feel ill, and they had a new worry.

'It must be a bilious attack,' she said to Roddy. 'I feel awful.'

He sat on the bed, holding her hand anxiously. She had been sick three times already that morning, running downstairs to the outside lavatory, and the third time she'd only just made it. Roddy had asked Mrs Higgs for a bucket, which she'd handed over with ill grace and a suspicious look, and he'd half expected her to charge extra for it. He brought it upstairs to find Carol back in bed, her face a pale greenish colour.

'It must be something you've eaten,' he said. 'D'you think it was those fish and chips?'

Carol shuddered. 'Don't talk about food. It makes me feel worse. Anyway, I was the same yesterday morning.'

'Well, we had fish and chips the night before too –' he began, but she turned her face away.

'We have them all the time. I'm sick of fish and chips. Ugh!' As if the word itself were enough, she sat up quickly and reached for the bucket. 'Roddy –'

He sat with his arm around her shoulders as she retched. He felt helpless. He had never had to offer comfort to anyone before, had always had it offered to him when he needed it. He wondered if Carol could be really ill, and remembered the time when one of his cousins had had appendicitis and had to be rushed into hospital. Suppose that was what was wrong with Carol?

Carol lay down again. She had brought up nothing but yellow bile but the effort had exhausted her. She groaned and looked up at him miserably.

'I feel as if I'm going to die.'

'No!' he said, panic sharpening his voice. 'No, you're not. You can't. It's just a bilious attack. The fish was off. I thought it tasted a bit funny myself.'

'So why aren't you ill too? Anyway, I was just as bad yesterday, you know I was. And the day before. There's something wrong with me, Roddy, something awful.'

'No,' he said again. 'You were all right in the afternoon. And it was the same the day before, you were only ill in the morning. It must be the fish.'

Carol closed her eyes, as if she hadn't the strength any more to hold the lids open. Roddy sat staring anxiously at her ashen face. He wanted very much to believe it was the fish. He could not even begin to think that it might be something else. He did not know what you did if someone were really ill; in his family, no one ever had been, apart from the cousin, and he hadn't heard about that until it was all over. He wished his mother were here, but his mother was far away in Scotland and did not even know where he was. Since he and Carol had run away, he hadn't written to her for fear of being caught.

'Are you feeling better now?' he asked carefully.

Carol moved her head, very slightly. It could have meant yes or no.

'I'll go and get a doctor if you want one,' Roddy offered, with no idea as to how he should do this. 'Mrs Higgs will know where the surgery is.'

'I don't want her in here. I don't want her knowing I'm ill.'

'But she already does. I had to ask her for the bucket.'

'I don't want her,' Carol said again, wearily.

Roddy didn't want Mrs Higgs in the room either. She took every opportunity to worm her way in as it was, her sharp eyes going everywhere. But she was the only person they knew in Bournemouth, and surely she would help if she knew how ill Carol was.

'Do you still feel sick?' he asked, still not sure what Carol's reply had meant.

'Oh, don't keep talking about it,' Carol said snappily, and turned over on her side.

A faint irritation touched Roddy's helplessness. He had only been trying to help. He did not know what else he could do. He bit his lip and stared out through the grimy window.

'I suppose you're wishing we'd never come here,' Carol said, without opening her eyes.

It was so nearly what Roddy had been thinking that he blushed. 'No! I've never thought that. I love you, Carrie. I just wish you weren't ill. I wish –' He stopped, unable to say all the things he wished, unable even to think them out clearly in his own mind. 'I wish there wasnae a war on,' he said miserably.

'If there wasn't,' Carol said in a small voice, 'we'd never have met each other.' There was a short, unhappy silence and then she sat up and put her arms round his neck. 'I'm sorry, Roddy. I'm sorry I'm such a misery.'

'You're not a misery,' he said, holding her tightly. 'You cannae help being ill. I'm the one who should be sorry, bringing you here.' He looked around the small, mean room with its grimy walls and tattered curtains and the gas fire they couldn't afford to light. 'It's no' what I meant it to be like.'

They sat close together, holding each other, resting their heads each against the other's shoulder, neither of them quite sure whether they were giving comfort or drawing it. Outside, heavy clouds were darkening the April morning to a reminder of winter, and a thin wind whipped a spatter of rain against the streaky window. In the room below, they could hear their landlady clattering with a broom and bucket, and knew that she would soon be on the stairs, making it apparent that they would be better off out of the house.

'What are we going to do, Roddy?' Carol asked at last. 'What's going to happen to us?'

The same April rain was spitting in Jess's face as she pushed Maureen's pram down to North End. Maureen was really getting too big for the pram now, but she couldn't walk all the way there and back, neither could Jess have carried the day's shopping as well as hold her hand. She put up the hood and strapped the waterproof cover over Maureen's legs.

'Want to get out,' Maureen objected. 'Want to walk.'

'You can't. It's raining.'

'Want to walk,' Maureen persisted, turning red. 'Want to walk.'

'I said no.' Jess pushed her hair back under her rainhat. Maureen had been getting very argumentative lately. She also asked incessant questions, driving Rose mad, and although Jess said that the questions must be answered because that was how Maureen learned, even she found them wearisome. And some of them couldn't be answered. Jess doubted if anyone could explain to a two-year-old how the sun stayed up in the sky, or what the sky was made of. But it didn't stop Maureen asking.

Maureen pushed down the front of the cover and started to climb out. 'Walk.'

'You'll get wet.' Jess pushed her back. 'Stop it, Maureen. Do as you're told. We're going to see Granny and Grandpa and I want you to be good.'

Maureen glowered at her. 'I am good. Want to walk.'

Jess sighed. The child was quite right, in a way. There was nothing naughty in wanting to walk. And as a baby, her wants had been attended to at once, without argument. It was difficult for her to accept now that they couldn't be.

Still, she had to learn. Everyone had to learn.

Jess pushed the pram along the road, ignoring Maureen's protests. After a few moments, she scarcely heard them. Her mind was too full of worries about her parents.

Arthur had been growing even more absent-minded lately. He would get up in the morning and dress, then decide that it was evening, undress and go back to bed. Or he would forget that he had just eaten breakfast and demand another one. Sometimes he was so persistent that Mary gave in and sat him down in front of another plate of bread and margarine, but when he had wolfed that down he went no more than a quarter of an hour before asking again.

'He's had three lots this morning,' Mary told Jess when she arrived with Maureen still complaining over not being allowed to walk. 'It don't seem to make a bit of difference. He's still saying he's hungry. I don't see how he can be. It can't be good for him, surely.'

'There must be something wrong with his digestion,' Jess said, lifting Maureen out of the pram. 'It's like he's got worms or something.'

'But he really doesn't remember having any food.' Mary pushed back her wispy grey hair. 'He gobbles it down like he's starving, hasn't seen food for days.' Her lips trembled a little. 'I don't mind telling you, Jess, I'm at me wits' end. I mean, it's bad enough seeing him like it, but when he starts to say I'm trying to starve him – well, it makes me want to weep, it does really. When I think what he used to be like . . .'

'I know, Mum. It's awful.' Jess put her hand on her mother's arm. She would have liked to hug her, to hold her in her arms like a child, but they hadn't held each other for years. 'Where is he now?'

'Out in the back garden. He's digging a hole for an Anderson shelter.'

Jess stared at her. 'But you've already got an Anderson.'

'I know. He's digging right beside it. It's like he doesn't even know it's there.'

Her heart cold, Jess followed her mother through the house and into the long, narrow back garden. It had been dug for vegetables and Ted had been up a week or two ago and sown some seeds. But now the plot was a mess of tumbled earth, and the two women could see Arthur's thin, frail body standing in a rough pit, shovelling earth with all his strength.

'Dad!' Jess approached the edge of the pit. It was almost waist deep. 'What on earth are you doing that for?'

He barely glanced at her. 'I 'aven't got time to stop. There's raids coming. I got to do me bit.'

'But you've already got a shelter. You don't need another one.'

'Bombs. They'll be dropping bombs on us. You'll see. You better get home and dig yourself one.'

'We've got one too. Frank dug it at the beginning of the war. We've had it nearly three years.' Jess stared at him helplessly. 'Dad, you'll make yourself ill, working like that. You'll tire yourself out. Why not come in and have a nice cup of tea?'

'Cup of tea? Ah, that's what she says.' He jerked his head at Mary, who was standing back, trying to keep Maureen away from the pit. 'Keeps on telling me to stop and 'ave some tea, but she won't never give me none, oh no, rather see me starve to death than spare a cup of tea for a poor old man.' He glared up at them, then his glance moved past Jess to Maureen. ''Ere. Who's that kid?'

'It's Maureen, Dad. You know Maureen.'

'Maureen?' His eyes narrowed suspiciously. 'I don't know no Maureen. Tell 'er to get out. I don't want no kids in 'ere, spoilin' things.'

'Dad!' Jess felt close to tears. 'Dad, this is your own grand-daughter. Our little Maureen. You must know her.' She reached behind her and took the toddler's hand. 'Maureen, come and say hello to Grandpa.'

Maureen leaned dangerously over the hole, beaming. 'Hello, G'ndpa. You dug a big hole.'

He stared up at her. 'It's my hole. Go away.'

'Dad!'

Maureen reached out her arms. 'Lift me down,' she commanded.

Her grandfather backed away, clutching his shovel to his chest. 'Get 'er out. I told you, I don't want no kids in 'ere. Take 'er away.'

Maureen stared at him, baffled, then her face screwed up and she began to cry. Jess gathered her up in her arms and turned to her mother in distress.

'Mum –'

'Bring her indoors, love. It's the best thing. He doesn't mean anything. He doesn't know what he's saying.' Mary drew her back into the house and they stood inside the kitchen door, facing each other. 'You see? You see what I've got to put up with?'

'What is it?' Jess whispered. 'What's happening to him?'

'What do you think? It's nothing to do with his digestion, I'm sure of that. It's his mind that's going.' Mary sat down heavily in an old kitchen chair that Arthur had painted green a year or two ago. 'I don't know whether it's this war, or what it is, Jess, but I don't mind telling you it's got me worried stiff. I don't reckon he's ever going to be the same again.'

'Senile dementia,' Jess said later to Frank, after Rose had gone to bed. 'That's what she's afraid of. Oh Frank, it can't be that, can it? I mean, people do go a bit funny sometimes and then they're all right again. Like Ted. A sort of nervous breakdown. It could just be something like that, couldn't it?'

'I suppose it could.' Frank was fastening new heels to a pair of his old shoes. He had cut the shapes carefully from a sheet of rubber and now he was tapping in brads. 'But it don't sound too good to me. Anyway, look how long it took Ted to get better, and he's a lot younger man.'

'I know, but ... senile dementia! It doesn't bear thinking of.' Jess wiped tears from her cheek with one hand. 'Poor little Maureen, she was really upset. And Mum's worn out with it all. I don't know how long she can go on managing. I mean, she's not that strong herself, and neither of them's getting any younger.'

'None of us are.' Frank finished the shoes and held them side by side, comparing the heels. 'Has she taken him to the doctor?'

'What's the point? They can't do anything, and she can't afford to spend money just to hear them tell her what she already knows.' Jess shook her head. 'It's so awful, seeing him like that. I mean, he used to be such a good father. And a lovely grandad. If you could have seen our Maureen's little face!'

'Better not take her down there any more.'

'But that means Mum won't see her either. And how can I go down, without Maureen? I'll have to leave her with Rose, and you know what she's been like lately.'

'Well, she'll just have to stop being like it,' he said sharply. 'She wants to be at home, she's got to help out. You've got enough to do without pandering to her whims and fancies.'

'Oh, you can't say she don't do anything, Frank. She's ever so good round the house, always ready to give me a hand and loves helping with the cooking. It's just the baby.'

'She liked looking after her all right before.'

'I know. But Maureen was just a baby then, you could pick her up and cuddle her and when you put her down you knew she'd stop there. It's different now, she's into everything. She opened that box Rose keeps her bits and pieces in the other day and upset it all over the floor. You can't blame Rose for getting fed up.'

'Well, she's got to learn. Babies aren't just dolls, to be played with just when you feel like it. You have to take responsibility for them.'

'I know. I tell her that. She says she will when she's got her own babies, but she's not responsible for Maureen.'

Frank put down the shoes. 'She'd better not say that when I'm around! Doesn't matter if it's her baby or not, we're family and families take responsibility for one another. And while she's under our roof and under our authority, she does as we tell her. Or maybe she thinks she's too old for that now she's nearly turned fifteen. They think too much of themselves these days, young girls.'

Jess was silent. She hadn't meant to make Frank angry. She'd come for comfort and support over her own parents. She thought of her father, coming in from the garden that afternoon, dirty and tired after his useless digging. He'd behaved quite normally then, telling her one of his Boer War stories, but all the time she'd been afraid he would turn on Maureen again, and she'd come away as soon as she could, and then felt guilty all the way home for having left her mother to cope.

It seemed all too easy to make Frank cross these days. It was the war, she knew. The constant strain, the work, the weariness. It was getting everyone down. Nobody talked about it much – there was no point, when everyone was in the same boat – but everyone was tired, tired of fear and grief, tired of hearing about death and killing, tired of the whole terrible shambles.

And there still seemed to be no end to it. After almost three long years, the tunnel was still as long, with not even the tiniest spot of light at its end.

She moved closer to Frank and he glanced at her and then put his arm around her shoulders and held her against him. She felt the steady warmth of his big body, like a rock that had been warmed by the sun.

'Don't say anything to Rose,' she said. 'It's as hard for her as it is for the rest of us. And she's growing up too, and

263

there's nothing we can do about that, either.'

'I know.' He bent and gave her a kiss. 'It's all right, Jess. It's just – when I think of the boys, out there in the country, and young Colin's ship being sunk, and Olive working on ack-ack guns – well, I feel as if everything's slipping away from me. I feel frightened, Jess.'

She stared at him. Frank, frightened? She had never thought it possible, never dreamed she would hear him admit it. She bit her lip, trying to stem the tears that stung her eyes.

Frank, frightened. And yet . . . Somehow, it made her feel a bit better, knowing that. As if he was just a bit more like she was, sharing her fears and anxieties. As if it would help him to understand hers just a little bit better.

'I'm glad you don't have to go away,' she said, putting her arms round him. 'I'm glad we can be together.'

Micky Baxter was enjoying the war again. For a time, after Cyril Nash was killed and Jimmy lost his leg, he'd felt fed up with everything. It wasn't his fault that the explosion had happened, it was the Germans', but everyone seemed to blame him, somehow. He couldn't walk down the street without people looking at him as if he was a murderer. And he'd had a lot of bad dreams too, when it all seemed to happen all over again, and sometimes he was the one blown up, or buried under a pile of rubble and knowing no one would ever get him out. For a long time he hadn't wanted to go out much at all, especially at night.

Of course, he never let on that he felt like that. He'd always been the big, bold boy of April Grove, swaggering along as if he was cock of the walk, and he wasn't going to let that go. So he forced himself to go out and march up the street as if nothing had happened, and never let anyone see that he was really quaking inside.

But now he'd got his gang together again and started to dream of winning the war, instead of being buried or blown to pieces, he felt better. And he felt better when he pulled up the floorboard in his bedroom and gloated over his hoard.

As well as the wireless and gun he and Desmond had stolen, he had a small rifle he had filched from a sentry hut near the Lines when Desmond had distracted the soldier's attention one night, and a pistol that young Martin Baker had pinched from an uncle. There was also a hand grenade that someone had found in the street – whether it was still live or not, nobody was sure – and a rusty old bayonet that Wendy had brought in one evening, as proudly as if she were carrying the very latest in tommy-guns.

'It was my grandad's,' she said. 'I found it behind his chest of drawers. It must've been there ever since he got run over.'

Micky stared at it jealously and stretched out his hand, but Wendy snatched the weapon out of his reach.

'It's mine. It's for our army. I only brought it to show you our army's as good as yours.'

'You can't have a bayonet,' Micky said. 'Girls aren't allowed to carry weapons.'

'Nor are boys,' Wendy said smartly. 'Not when they're under sixteen. You're not even old enough to join the Home Guard.'

'I wouldn't want to,' Micky sneered. 'Lot of old men playin' about with broomsticks.'

'They've got proper weapons now,' Martin said. 'Guns and stuff, left over from the big war. I've seen 'em. My uncle's in it.'

Micky gazed at him thoughtfully. 'An' he's got proper weapons?'

Martin nodded. 'He's in charge of them. He's got the key.'

'You mean he can get into the place where they're kept?'

'Any time,' Martin said, a little boastfully.

'So you could too, couldn't you? You could get the key and get in and pinch whatever weapons they've got.'

Martin looked at him nervously. 'I dunno. I dunno where he keeps it.'

'But you could find out,' Micky said. 'You could watch him and find out.'

Martin glanced at Wendy. 'But I'm not in your army. I'm in Wendy's. You said.'

'I can change me mind, can't I?' Micky demanded. 'I can have Wendy in if I want to. And then I'll keep the bayonet and you can get some more weapons off your uncle.'

'I dunno. I mean, suppose we got caught? My uncle can't half hit hard.'

'Anyway, it's stealing,' Wendy said. 'I never stole the bayonet. It was my grandad's.'

'Look,' Micky stated, standing in front of them with his feet planted wide apart, 'this is a war, innit? That means we can do what we like to win it. An' if the Home Guard ain't using the stuff, we got a right to take it. It's our duty to take it, 'cause we're a proper army an' they're just old men.' He gave them a triumphant look. 'We all got to do whatever we can to win this war, an' we'll show 'em we ain't just kids. You get the key to that hut, Martin, an' we'll show 'em!'

By the second week, Carol's sickness was no better and both she and Roddy were beginning to feel frightened.

'It must be something terrible,' she said, lying back after a bout of retching. 'I've never been bad like this before.'

'We'll have to get a doctor,' he said, stroking her forehead. 'You're like this every morning right up till dinner-time. You're getting thinner all the time.'

'It's evenings too.' Her face was the dirty grey of Mrs Higgs' sheets. 'What is it, Roddy? What's the matter with me?'

'I dinnae ken,' he said helplessly. 'I've never known anyone sick like this, only my cousin Moira when she was expecting her Alistair, and –'

'Expecting?' The last shred of colour drained from Carol's face. 'You mean she was expecting a baby?'

'Well, he wasnae a haggis,' Roddy said with a weak attempt at humour. 'Though he looked pretty much like one, the first time I saw him, all puny and whey-faced, but they said there was something wrong with him, jaundice or the like, but he was better in a week or two right enough, and my cousin Moira –'

'Roddy, will you please shut up about your cousin

Moira!' Carol struggled to sit up. 'You don't think that's what's the matter with me, do you? You don't think I could be – be expecting?' Her voice dropped to a whisper on the last word. 'Oh, Roddy . . .'

He stared at her. 'I've been careful every time. And we've been using the French letter –'

The first time they had made love, in Foster Gardens, it had taken them both by surprise and neither had known quite what was going to happen. After that, Roddy had asked one of his mates for advice and had pulled himself away from Carol at the crucial moment. But he hadn't been able to time it very well at first, so that sometimes he was too quick and sometimes too slow, and finally he had plucked up his courage and got a French letter from a barber. The rubber wasn't very thin, and neither of them liked it much, but it could be washed and used again and again.

'It doesn't always work, though, does it? If there's a tiny hole in it –'

'There cannae be,' he said. 'I look at it every time, to make sure.'

But Carol knew that Roddy's excitement sometimes overcame his caution. There had been times when he'd put it on almost too late, others when she'd been sure he'd taken it off too quickly.

She laid her hand flat on her stomach. There was no swelling there; she was hollow and empty.

'How soon does a baby start to grow?' she asked. 'How do you know when it'll be born?'

'Doesn't it take nine months?' Roddy said doubtfully. 'My cousin Moira –'

'I know it takes nine months. But nine months from when? How do you know when it started?'

He shrugged helplessly. 'I think the doctor tells you. We'll have to get a doctor, Carol. There'll be all kinds of things to arrange – a midwife, and napkins and a pram and –'

'Roddy, stop it!' The fear in Carol's voice and eyes shrilled into panic. 'I can't have a baby! I can't. How would we manage? What would we do? We're not even married.'

'Carrie, ssh –' Roddy cast a fearful glance towards the door. More than once, they had heard shuffling sounds on the landing and caught Mrs Higgs slinking down the stairs. After the first time, they had never spoken in the room unless it were in a whisper. But this time, their fears had driven all other considerations from their minds.

Roddy's caution was just too late. The door was flung open and their landlady stood there in her grubby flowered apron, arms akimbo, glaring at them triumphantly.

'I thought as much! I knew it, the minute I set eyes on you. There's something shifty about that young man, I said to meself, and that girl's nothing but a trollop. I'd lay a sack of gold they're not wed.' She advanced into the room, pointing her finger at them accusingly. 'You're nothing but a pair of liars, and shirkers too – all this talk about finding jobs, you've no more intention of working than flying to the moon. Parasites, that's what you are, and now you're in the family way and you'll be sucking even more blood out of your country in its hour of need.'

'I'm not,' Carol began desperately. 'I mean, we won't, we want to work, we –' A wave of nausea overcame her and she lay down, and then sat up again quickly and reached for the bucket. Mrs Higgs watched as she retched and heaved over it, with Roddy holding her shoulders, and when Carol had finished and lay back again she curled her lip.

'So you're not in the family way,' she said sardonically. 'Tell me that again when you've got a belly full of arms and legs. You won't be able to hide it when you're walking about like a barrage balloon.'

Carol was too exhausted to argue. Roddy looked at the landlady. Her face was grim, but she was the only possible source of help they had. He said, 'What can we do, Mrs Higgs? Shouldn't we get a doctor?'

'A doctor!' The woman gave an ugly cackle. 'It's not a doctor you oughter be looking for. There's other people can give you the sort of help you need.'

'What d'you mean? What sort of help?'

'Well, you can't tell me you want a brat round your necks,' she said witheringly. 'Couple of kids like you, and living in sin. On the run too, I wouldn't be surprised,' she added, looking at Roddy.

Roddy flushed scarlet and cursed himself as he saw the gleam of triumph in her eyes. They had been so careful not to confirm her suspicions and now he had handed her their guilt on a plate. 'I'm not, not at all,' he said quickly, but he knew it was too late. Mrs Higgs' face had settled into satisfied creases, and she was almost smiling. It was not a nice smile.

'I might be able to help you,' she said unexpectedly. 'I know one or two people. They charge, mind. And I'd need a bit for letting you know their names. It's a risky business and I wouldn't want to see my friends in trouble.'

Roddy and Carol stared at her blankly. Carol had no idea at all what she meant, and Roddy had only a glimmer, gleaned from half-heard stories some of the older sailors had told, and sniggering jokes. There was a song someone had sung once in connection with such jokes, and it came into his mind now.

> 'My uncle's a Harley Street surgeon,
> He uses a knife long and thin.
> He only does one operation
> And oh, how the money rolls in.'

'We're not doing anything illegal,' he said sharply, and laid his hand protectively on Carol's shoulder. 'Naebody's going to do anything to my Carrie.'

Mrs Higgs sneered again. 'Maybe you won't be so high and mighty when she's starting to show and folk start asking questions. It's not so easy having a bastard. But it won't be any good coming to me then, it'll be too late.'

'I don't care,' Roddy said firmly. 'It's dangerous. There was a girl in our street . . . She died.'

Carol gasped and caught at his hand. 'Roddy – you won't let them –'

'Naebody's going to hurt you, Carrie,' he said. 'Not while I'm around to take care of you. Aye, and the bairn too, if there is one.'

'Oh, there's a brat all right,' Mrs Higgs said. 'No doubt about that.' Her small eyes gleamed as she stared at them. 'Well, so what are you going to do?'

'What do you think?' Roddy returned. Before he had known the truth, he'd felt helpless and lost. Now that Mrs Higgs had confirmed their suspicions – and he had no doubt that she was right – he felt suddenly older, more in charge. The thought of becoming a father was both terrifying and uplifting. And it was up to him to take care of the mother of his child. 'We'll go to the doctor and ask him what we should do.'

Mrs Higgs scowled. She did not want Roddy or Carol to make contact with officialdom. Once they did that, questions would be asked – who they were, where they came from, why they had run away – and Mrs Higgs had a fair idea what the answers might be. There would be trouble, she was certain of that – trouble for Roddy as a deserter, trouble because of Carol's age, and – worst of all – trouble for Mrs Higgs for sheltering them. There would be reports in the newspapers, who loved a scandal like this, and her name would be spread all over Bournemouth. The police might even take it into their heads to look a little more closely into certain other matters she'd been at some pains to conceal from them.

'There's no need to do that yet,' she said in a conciliatory tone. 'Only cost you money, that will, and there's nothing he can tell you that I can't. 'Ad four of me own, I 'ave, not that there's one of 'em bothers to come and see me or give me an 'and now, but that's kids for you . . . Anyway, we'll just keep it quiet between ourselves for now, if that's what you want, and then if you changes yer minds about getting rid of it, you can just let me know, see? Only like I say, you'll 'ave to be quick, no one won't take the risk after about four months.'

'But how do we know when that is?' Carol asked. 'How do we know when it started?'

'Well, you must know when you was last *unwell*,' Mrs Higgs said meaningfully, with a glance at Roddy.

'I can't remember.' Carol looked frightened. 'I never even thought – I often miss – I was pleased –'

'Pity you never done something about it straight away,' Mrs Higgs said. 'Castor oil'll often shift it, if you catches it quick. Or you can try jumping off a chair. You could still give it a try.'

'I told you, we'll not do anything of the sort,' Roddy said at once.

The landlady shrugged. 'Please yourself. 'Ow long you bin being sick?'

'A fortnight, I think,' Carol said in a small voice.

'Well, you'd be about eight or nine weeks then. You got seven months to go. That's if you wants to.' She waited a minute. 'Like I say, anything you wants to know, just ask me. There's plenty of girls come to Martha Higgs for a bit of 'elp when they found themselves in trouble.'

'It's very kind of you,' Carol said. 'We didn't know what to do.'

'No, well, you wouldn't, would yer? Never bin told the facts of life proper, I daresay. Most girls ain't, and the boys is just left to find it out from their mates, an' they don't know nothing.' Mrs Higgs sniffed. 'Be a lot less girls in trouble and 'avin' to get married if they was taught a bit more about the birds and the bees, that's what I say. Anyway, that don't 'elp you now.' She gave them a speculative look. ''Ow much can you stretch yerselves to?'

Roddy gazed at her. 'How much? I don't understand –'

'Money,' the landlady snapped. ''Ow much you got?'

'But what do we need money for? There's nothing to buy yet, is there?'

'Rent,' she said succinctly. 'You wants to go on livin' 'ere, you got to pay a bit more. I ain't takin' the chance out of the goodness of me 'eart.'

'But we haven't got any money,' Roddy said. 'Our – our savings have almost gone. We won't have any more until we can get jobs.' He glanced at Carol. 'I mean, till I can get a job.'

'Well, you got to find the cash from somewhere. I ain't keepin' yer. And it'll cost you fifteen bob a week from now on, not ten.'

'Fifteen shillings? But we can't possibly afford that.'

'You wants me to keep quiet, dontcher? I could turn you out this minute if I wasn't so goodhearted. But I won't be taken advantage of. You told me lies already. 'Ow do I know you're on the square now? I could get run in, harbouring a deserter.' She glanced from one to the other, her eyes cruel little pebbles. 'Maybe you ain't found this out yet, but everything you want in this world's got a price, and you can only get it so long as you can pay for it.'

She gave them another swift glance and then marched out, banging the door behind her. Roddy looked down at Carol and then sank on the bed, laying his face on her breast. Carol slipped her arms around him and they stayed close, without speaking, for several minutes.

'She knows,' he said at last, hopelessly. 'She knows everything.'

'She can't. Not our names and where we come from.'

'It doesn't matter. She could go to the police and tell them I'm a deserter. They'd soon find out who I am.' He lifted his head. 'Carrie, they'd send me to prison. They might even shoot me.'

'No!'

'They could. They're allowed to.' He looked at her miserably. 'I don't want to go to prison, Carrie. I want to stay with you.'

'I want you too.' She held him more tightly, staring at the cracked ceiling. 'I wouldn't know what to do without you.'

For a few more moments they were silent, clinging to each other, locked in their desperate thoughts. Then Roddy said, 'D'you think it's true, Carrie? About the bairn? D'you think you're really – you know –'

'Expecting,' she said in a dull voice. 'Oh, I should think so. I mean, it's just the sort of thing that would happen, isn't it?' Her voice was bitter, uncannily like her mother's.

'I haven't never had no luck, not till I met you, and now even that's got to be spoilt.'

'Would it really spoil it?' Roddy asked after a minute or two. 'A bairn's not so bad, Carrie. My cousin Moira's wee one is a lot of fun. His name's Alistair and he –'

'I know all about your cousin Moira,' Carol said peevishly. 'You never stop talking about her.' She sat up. 'Roddy, this is me we're talking about. I don't want a baby – not for a long time. I know what they're like. Mrs Budd, next door to us had one just before the war started, and I could hear her crying every night. It was awful.'

'Mrs Budd was crying? Didnae she want a bairn either?'

'Not Mrs Budd! The baby. They went away to the country when the war started, but they came back at Christmas and the baby cried louder than ever. I could hear it through the walls.'

'Well, all bairns cry,' Roddy said reasonably.

'I know. That's what I'm saying. How would I manage, with a baby crying all night? I wouldn't know what to do. I don't know anything about babies, I don't know how you feed them or anything. It would die.'

Roddy could not think what to say. He remembered the pleasure in his own family when Moira had been expecting Alistair. His mother and his aunts had been busy for months, knitting tiny white garments and talking in hushed voices. And when Alistair had arrived, you'd have thought he was the only baby on earth. There had been no problem in knowing how to look after him – every female member of the family had been round to Moira's with advice.

'Och, you'll be all right once you're a mother,' he said. 'Mothers always know what to do.'

'How do they? How can they know what to do, if no one tells them?'

'It's instinct. We had a sheepdog bitch, and when she had her first litter she knew just –'

'Roddy, I'm not a sheepdog! People aren't like animals. They're humans. Do *you* know what to do?'

'No,' he admitted. 'But –'

'Well, you'll be a father,' Carol said. 'D'you think that's going to make a difference?'

There was a short silence.

'I wish we'd gone to Scotland,' Roddy said at last. 'My mother and father would tell us what to do.'

'Yes. They'd tell you to go back to the Navy. And where would that leave me?'

The door opened again and Mrs Higgs stood there. She glowered down at Roddy, still crouched by the bed, and demanded brusquely, 'Well? What's it to be?'

Roddy looked up at her. 'What d'you mean?'

'What's it to be?' she demanded impatiently. 'Are yer goin' ter pay me the fifteen bob or not?'

'I've already told you. We can't afford it.'

'You can't afford not to,' she said brutally. 'It's pay up or get out. I'm not 'avin' no trouble 'ere, I told yer before.'

'But we're not causing any trouble –'

Mrs Higgs held up her fingers and began to count. 'Livin' under my roof with no weddin' lines. Livin' with a girl what's too young to be away from her mother – that's abduction, young man, in case you don't know it. Puttin' 'er in the family way. *Desertin'*.' The last word was brought out almost with a flourish. 'I reckon they'll chuck the whole bleedin' book at you. They'll march you away so fast your feet won't touch the ground.'

Carol and Roddy stared at her. Then Carol said, 'Please, Mrs Higgs. Give us a bit longer. Roddy'll find a job soon, I know he will. We'll pay you as soon as we can –'

'That we'll not!' Roddy exclaimed. He leapt to his feet and faced the scrawny landlady. 'We'll not pay another penny. You might think you've got us right where you want us, Mrs Higgs, but I'm a Scotsman and proud of it, and I'll no' be browbeaten by the likes of you. It's my bairn Carrie's bearing, my flesh and blood, and I'll no' have it born in this rat-hole. I'll take her back home to Scotland with me, that's what I'll do, and you can whistle for your money!'

'Roddy, no,' Carol begged anxiously, but neither he nor Mrs Higgs took any notice of her. They stood facing each other with furious eyes, their bodies as taut as springs. In another moment, she thought, they would spring at each other like cats.

They did not. Instead, Mrs Higgs suddenly tossed her head, gave a snort like an angry bull and turned on her heel.

'We'll soon see about that,' she said from the doorway. 'Oh, yes, we'll very soon see about that. You're going to regret talking to me like that.'

She slammed out and they heard her feet go heavily down the stairs. There was a short pause and then the front door slammed and the footsteps rapped quickly away up the street.

'What's she going to do?' Carol whispered.

'God knows. She might do anything. He turned his head and looked at her. 'She might really go to the police.'

'Oh, Roddy.' Carol put her arms around him again and held him tightly. 'Oh, Roddy, what have you done?'

CHAPTER SIXTEEN

During the same week Portsmouth was throwing itself into an orgy of celebration and pageantry such as had not been seen since before the war began.

Warship Week, with a target of one million two hundred thousand pounds to buy a new cruiser, started with a spectacular parade through the streets. It was headed by the band of the Royal Marines – always the smartest of the lot, Frank declared – and included detachments from all the services. Already, the Mayor announced, over half a million pounds had been collected, and more was bound to come as people flooded to the King's Theatre for an all-star entertainment, to the Wessex Drill Hall for exhibitions and to a Tattoo in the Guildhall Square, with the steps being used for the first time since the blitz as grandstand accommodation.

'It's just like in peacetime,' Jess said but Cherry, who had come with them, gave her a comical look.

'What, with the poor old Guildhall standing there a ruin? And planes going over night after night?'

'Well, they are more often British ones than German now,' Frank said. 'We're giving Berlin and Hamburg a taste of what they gave us. Serve 'em right too, when you think what they're doing to poor little Malta.'

Malta was taking the brunt of the Luftwaffe's attention now. The bombing there was almost continuous and it seemed as if the people were almost permanently living in the catacombs and tunnels. But they fought back bravely, refusing to give in. They had been invaded too many times in their long history to allow it to happen again.

At home, news of the war was followed with a kind of eager desperation. For people like Frank, it was imperative to know its progress, to be able to carry a picture of the world as it plunged further and deeper into turmoil. It was as if, once he had let go of the threads, he would never be able to pick them up again and he would be lost in chaos. He listened avidly to the News on the wireless, questioned Jess about what she had seen at the cinema – her one afternoon a week there was her only relaxation – read the *Daily Express* and the *Evening News* from cover to cover, and plotted the changing events on his big wall-map.

For others, the war at home was more than enough. Everything seemed to be affected by the new 'Austerity' measures. The only crockery you could get now was white 'utility', with cups that had no handles, while luxury extras like soup spoons, butter knives and ornamental glassware were no longer made. And there was only one quality of a huge range of goods from sheets, carpets and kitchen utensils to pens, cigarette lighters and umbrellas. Even the few toys still being produced were not permitted to contain such materials as rubber or cork.

'Poor little scrap,' Jess said, watching Maureen playing with Keith's old coloured bricks. 'There's nothing for kiddies now. She's missing such a lot.'

'So am I,' Rose answered, rather sharply. She was getting tired of Maureen and the way everyone was sorry for her because there were no dolls or fluffy animals to be had. She had only ever had one doll herself, and not much more than Maureen had now, but nobody seemed to think of that. 'If it wasn't for the war I'd be able to go out for an evening to the pictures, or a dance. That's what most girls do when they're my age.'

'And look what happens to them,' Jess said. 'Mrs Glaister's half out of her mind with worry over young Carol. You don't think I want that happening to you, do you?'

'I wouldn't be so daft. I wouldn't go running off with a sailor.'

But Jess knew better than Rose how young emotions,

coming unexpectedly, could sweep a girl off her feet. And with all these sailors and soldiers about, far from home, you couldn't be too careful. There was talk of Americans coming too, now that they were in the war, and Jess had heard more than she liked about Americans.

'Utility' clothing began to appear too. The hemlines of skirts rose, to save on material, and there was a restriction on pleats or other designs that used more fabric than necessary. Men were forbidden double-breasted coats or turn-ups on their trousers. Already, they had lost pyjama pockets. Sometimes it all seemed so trivial that you had to laugh about it, but it was an aggravation all the same.

'They'll be measuring handkerchiefs next,' Cherry said.

'And what about ties?' Frank agreed. He had always hated wearing a tie. 'Think what we could save if it was against the law to wear ties. And peaked caps, they could save a bit there.'

'And you don't really need lapels on your jackets.' Cherry went on. 'Or –'

'Stop it, you two,' Jess said, laughing. 'You'll have us all in boiler-suits at this rate.'

'Well, why not? Winnie wears 'em all the time. He don't care what he looks like, he just does whatever's most practical. I reckon that's what we should all do, instead of wasting time on all these finicky little rules and regulations.'

'Well, we've all got to do our bit.'

'By handing in pyjama pockets?' Frank said. 'It's going to take more than a few inches of material to win this war, Jess.'

Jess nodded soberly. Like the rest of the family, she was still worried over Colin, who had not been heard of since the *Exeter* had been sunk.

'I can't bear to think of it,' Annie had said only yesterday. 'But I can't stop thinking about it either. Our Colin, drowning thousands of miles away from home. That's not what we had our children for, Jess.'

It wasn't. Jess and Annie had borne their children in times when a Great War had not long ended, a war which was to end all wars. They had hoped to see them grow in peace and prosperity. Instead, they had faced first the Depression and now this. A worldwide quarrel, none of their own choosing, that had got out of hand and looked like destroying everything they had lived for.

It was too much for some people to stand, and the newspapers began to carry more and more reports of suicides. Old men who felt helpless, old women too frightened to go on living, young lovers who were desperate at being parted. Sometimes Jess would look at these reports and think of Carol Glaister and her young sailor. Her heart ached for Ethel, little though she liked the woman, and she tried to express her sympathy.

'The little hussy!' was Ethel's response. 'Running off with all my savings. It just shows, you can't expect no gratitude from youngsters these days. Take all you've got to give and then turn round and stab you in the back. What am I supposed to do for a new summer outfit, with her living the life of Riley on what I've scrimped and saved for?'

Jess stared at her, shocked. She had always thought Ethel a coldhearted woman, but didn't she have any feeling at all for her daughter?

'Aren't you at all worried about her?'

'Why should I be? She'll be all right – always falls on her feet, that one does. Self, self, self, that's all she thinks about, never mind her poor mother.' Ethel looked down at her skirt and smoothed it self-consciously. 'What do you think of this, Jess? I got it in Bulpitt's, the last one they had before the utility stuff. You won't see pleats like this again. And if you'll take my advice, you'll get whatever you want now – there's to be no more lace or appliqué, not even a bit of embroidery. It'll probably be against the law to do anything to brighten yourself up a bit. I think it's a crying shame. Women need a bit of stuff to make them pretty, it gives 'em heart, and the men like it too.'

Jess turned and went indoors. She loved embroidery herself and liked to make Rose's blouses with a flower on the pocket, but she could never have put it before her own daughter's welfare. But perhaps Ethel was more upset than she let on. She'd always been a close one, never one to show her feelings, especially to Jess.

'If Carol was still home, she'd have to register for war service anyway,' she said to Frank. 'Not that they'd take her – they're trying to leave the young ones alone as long as they can – but she might be glad to get away from home. I reckon that's half the reason she's run off.'

'Princess Elizabeth's registered,' Rose said. 'I saw it in the paper. She went in her Girl Guide uniform, as soon as she was sixteen. There's been hundreds and thousands put down their names. Joy says she can't wait to volunteer.'

But however hard people tried to keep up their morale, the increasingly bad news was like a series of hammer blows. A simultaneous battery of raids devastated the cities of Exeter and Bath, closely followed by Norwich and York – all cities with three stars in the Baedeker guidebooks. Malta, awarded the King's own medal the George Cross, was immediately robbed by the Luftwaffe of thirty of the forty-six Spitfires delivered by the USS *Wasp* and was then abandoned, leaving the shattered island without ships and praying for a miracle. The last ship to leave, bringing back British personnel and their families, was HMS *Penelope*, which was hit so often during her zigzag voyage home that she was nicknamed 'Pepperpot'.

Yet, despite it all, there were still smiles to be seen on the faces of people in the streets. Still jokes to be cracked and laughter to be heard in even the grimmest of situations. And still bright spots to be found, little sparks of happiness and joy which brightened the days and gave hope that life was, even now, still worth living.

One was the wedding of Erica Jones to Gerald Spencer.

'I never thought I'd love anyone else, after Geoff died,' Erica said to Betty as the girls made themselves ready in the attic room at the farm. 'Sometimes I think I ought to feel guilty – but I can't. I'm too happy. But I did love Geoff, I did really.'

'Of course you did,' Betty said. 'And I bet you still do.

But you love Gerald as well. And you're going to marry him and be his wife and live happily ever after. And wherever Geoff is, I bet he's glad!'

'Yes, I think he would be,' Erica said slowly. She held up her arms and Betty slipped the white wedding dress over her head. It had been loaned to Erica by one of Gerald's cousins from Corhampton, who had got married a year or two before the war started, and with a little skilful sewing from Mrs Spencer it fitted Erica's slender figure perfectly. Betty arranged the skirt and stood back to admire the effect.

'It's lovely, Eric.'

Erica turned slowly. The dress was made of white satin and lace, the kind of dress you never saw these days, and it fell like a cascade of foaming water to the floor. The bodice was tight, drawn in to a tiny waist, and there were little pearl buttons down the front. The sleeves came to a narrow point at the wrist, held in place by a satin ribbon which looped around Erica's finger.

The door opened and Yvonne came in. She stopped and whistled.

'Whee-whew! You look a real stunner, Eric. It's like Cinderella – one day a Land Girl in muddy dungarees, the next a fairy princess!' She came forward. 'Let me put on the coronet.'

The coronet was a fragile creation of silver wire and pearls, with a few diamanté stones sparkling as they caught the light. Yvonne lifted it, holding the drift of net clear of Erica's face, and settled it on her pale gold curls. She stepped back to join Betty.

'You look smashing. Gerald won't be able to take his eyes off you.'

Erica grinned a little self-consciously. 'It's all thanks to you. If you hadn't lent me your new lipstick – and Betty didn't have a pair of stockings – and Maisie hadn't let me borrow this dress –'

'You'd have got married just the same, and Gerald would have thought you looked just as lovely in your old dungarees,' Betty said. 'I wish it was me and Dennis walking up the aisle today.'

'You'll have to be next,' Erica said. 'I don't know why you don't. You're mad about each other, anyone can see that.'

'Maybe today'll make him take the plunge,' Yvonne said. 'He is coming, isn't he?'

'If they don't get called out. He's got the leave arranged, but you know how much that means if a bomb's found somewhere.'

There was a knock from the bottom of the stairs and Mrs Spencer called up, 'It's time we were going, girls.'

'Whoops!' Yvonne said, bending to peer into the mirror. 'This is it. Your last chance to back out, Eric.'

'Anyway, you don't have to hurry,' Betty said. 'It's the bride's prerogative to be late.'

'Not likely,' Erica retorted, making for the stairs. 'Gerald's likely to be called back any day now – I don't want to miss a minute of being his wife!'

Laughing, they scrambled down the narrow stairs, Erica going sideways to avoid crushing her dress. They arrived at the bottom and found the Spencers standing there, both arrayed in the best clothes they wore only for going to church on very special occasions. Mrs Spencer looked almost regal in her dark green costume and hat with its tiny veil, while her husband was stiffly upright in a starched collar and black suit. They gazed at Erica for a moment and Mr Spencer cleared his throat gruffly.

'You look beautiful,' Mrs Spencer said at last. She lifted her veil and wiped her eyes with a small handkerchief. 'You look really beautiful.'

Erica laughed a little shakily. 'I feel scared stiff.'

'You'll be all right, my dear.' The farmer's wife shook her head. 'It's such a shame your own mother and father can't see you.'

Erica's parents had left Portsmouth a year ago and were now living in Gloucestershire. They had been invited to the wedding but sent a note saying that they could not possibly travel at such a time. Erica had shrugged and said it didn't matter, but Betty and Yvonne had felt sorry for her and indignant with the parents who showed so little interest in their daughter.

'Her mother's a cat,' said Betty, who had met Mrs Jones once. 'All she thinks about is herself. And our Erica was going the same way when she first came here. I reckon it was the best thing she ever did, joining the Land Army.'

The two girls and Mrs Spencer left to walk up the lane to the village of Bishop's Waltham, its little church already filled with people waiting for the wedding. Gerald had gone ahead with Maisie's husband Jimmy, who was to be best man. Mr Spencer was to give the bride away and the farm cart had been cleaned and scrubbed, and decorated for the occasion with primroses, daffodils, bluebells and all the bits of ribbon that could be found. Even Boxer, the horse, had an early rose tucked behind one ear.

'There you are,' the farmer said, helping Erica climb up into the cart. 'Lucky it's a fine day! Still, we could have used the car if it had rained.'

'I'd rather use this.' Erica sat on the narrow seat, holding a posy of flowers that Betty and Yvonne had picked for her that morning. She thought of the wedding she had planned with Geoff. It was to have been in Portsmouth Cathedral, with the bells and full choir, and the great church would have been filled with her parents' friends and relatives, all vying with each other to look the smartest and most fashionable. There would have been huge sheaves of flowers – exotic lilies, heavily scented freesias, roses like scarlet cabbages. Erica's dress would have been made especially for her and would have been the talk of the city, and after the reception in Southsea's grandest hotel, they would have driven away in Geoff's little sports car for a honeymoon in some romantic hideaway – they might even have gone abroad.

At the time, Erica had thought that was what she wanted. Now she knew that although she could have been happy with Geoff, the pretensions she had learned from her parents would almost certainly have damaged that happiness.

She looked at the primrose-studded banks and the burgeoning green hedgerows, and thought of Gerald, a farmer's son with none of Geoff's advantages, yet a man who would love and honour her through whatever life would bring them. And she felt a great, swelling contentment to be here, seated in a plain farm cart, jogging through the country lanes to her wedding in a little village church.

'I now pronounce you man and wife.'

The vicar's voice echoed softly through the small, crowded church. Almost everyone in the village was there, for the Spencers were known and respected for miles around and the three Land Girls had won the hearts of most of the local inhabitants. Even Jonas was there in the fourth pew, resplendent in a suit that had once been black and was now rusty with age, his ancient hat crushed against his chest as he grated out the hymns. He wore a rose in his lapel, and he glowered at Erica throughout the entire service. Only Betty, glancing at him over her hymn-book, noticed that his rheumy eyes were damp.

Erica was trembling as she made her vows. She looked up and met Gerald's eyes, terrified that she was about to weep, but when she saw the expression in his she hastily cast her glance away, for he looked as near to tears as she. In a shaking voice, she promised to love, honour and obey him, and heard him in turn vow to love, honour and cherish. '*With my body, I thee worship . . .*' Tonight they would lie together for the first time, unrestricted by convention or fear, and bring their love to its full consummation. Tonight, they would be truly married and nothing, not even the war, could part their entwined souls.

The service came to an end. The family party – Erica and her new husband, the Spencers and Betty and Yvonne – crowded into the vestry to witness the signing of the register, and then Gerald took Erica in his arms and kissed her gently on the lips. There was a hubbub of laughter and congratulations, with everyone kissing Erica and Gerald, and the sound of singing in the body of the church. And then out they came, with Erica radiant in the borrowed white dress and Gerald, proud and upright in uniform, his injuries healed and his face once more tanned from working outside.

At the door of the church, they paused. Only one person had a camera – the local doctor – and he had just one film, with eight exposures to be used. He took two, one of Erica and Gerald alone, one of the family group, and then he folded his camera again.

'I'll let you have the prints when I finish the film.' It might be weeks, months, even a year, for film was so precious he would take no more until another special occasion came along. But one day they would have them to look at, and meanwhile this day would live in their memories as a day of happiness that neither of them had expected.

'Come on,' Gerald said. 'Let's get into the cart and drive away. I want to kiss you properly, where no one else can see us. And – I've got something to tell you.' He looked grave, and a sudden fear clutched at Erica's heart.

'You're going away.'

'Come on,' he said again, and she scrambled into the cart, suddenly careless of the flowing dress, and looked at him with wide eyes.

'Your flowers!' Betty screamed from the crowd, and she turned guiltily, remembering where they were, and tossed the posy towards her friend. Laughing, Betty caught it and held it aloft while the others surged about her like waves. They were all in their best clothes, Erica thought, all arrayed to wish herself and Gerald well on their journey into marriage. But how short was that journey to be?

'When?' she said urgently as the horse trotted away. 'When are you going?'

For a moment or two, he didn't answer. His eyes were fixed on the horse's back and Erica looked at his strong hands, holding the reins, and laid her own on top of them.

'When?'

Gerald turned the cart into a narrow lane. It led nowhere but into one of the Spencers' fields. There had been three haystacks here, built last autumn to feed the animals through the winter, and now there was just part of one left.

Gerald drew the cart to a halt by the gate and then turned at last and looked down into Erica's face.

'Today. This afternoon.'

'*This afternoon?*' she echoed unbelievingly. 'But – you can't. We've only just got married. We haven't had a chance –'

'I know. I thought it would be at least another week. But there's something big on in Africa – they're getting back as many men as they can. There's nothing I can do about it.'

'I know.' The demands of the war came before anything else. It could not be escaped. 'But – this afternoon . . . Oh, *Gerald.*'

He held her in his arms, feeling her body tremble against him. His desire for her, which had begun very soon after he had first seen her, was almost overwhelming. He had never seen anyone so perfect as Erica, with her small figure so exactly proportioned, her hair like a golden nimbus about her head, her eyes so clear and blue. And as he had come to know her better, the desire had turned to love, and he had known that he must have her for his wife.

But to be snatched away at the very brink . . . !

'Listen,' he said. 'We've only got a few hours, and we don't have to waste them at a party with a lot of other people. We've got a honeymoon to have.'

Erica lifted her head and stared at him. 'A honeymoon? But how can we –'

'We'll have it here,' he said, and dropped over the side of the cart. 'It's all ready for you, my darling.' He lifted his arms and Erica leaned into them so that he could swing her to the ground. She stood in his embrace, staring in astonishment at the space between the haystack and the hedge, and then she began to laugh.

'Gerald! Behind a haystack!'

'There's not a better place,' he said, and bent to lay his lips upon hers.

He had turned the space into a room, with walls of hay, and furnished it with blankets and a pillow. There were two glasses and a bottle of home-made elderberry wine. There was a small picnic basket, and two plates laid upon the top of it with a silver knife and fork that Erica recognised had come from the Spencers' best service, handed down from Gerald's great-grandparents.

'A haystack honeymoon,' she said, half laughing, half crying as Gerald began to undo the tiny pearl buttons of her bodice. 'Oh Gerald, I love you . . .'

Nobody asked why Gerald and Erica took so long to come back from the church. Word had gone round quickly that Gerald had been recalled, and the reception continued without its central figures. Mr and Mrs Spencer received their guests, gave them each a glass of elderberry wine and sat them down round the long dining-table in the big room for a feast such as had not been seen for years. Betty, helping to serve slices of the huge baked ham and new potatoes she had helped grow herself, wondered what they would say at home if they could see all this. Butter, eggs, flagons of cider – it was like the black market! But this was a farming community and everyone had chipped in with something to help. No one was going to inquire too closely about where the ham had come from – or what had happened to the rest of the pig. The joke was that it was still alive, hobbling about on three legs somewhere.

It seemed queer to have a reception without a bride and groom, but everyone entered into the spirit of it and there were speeches, toasts and a lot of laughter and ribbing just as if Erica and Gerald had indeed been sitting in their chairs at the top of the table. Mr Spencer made a speech about how she had first come to the farm as a haughty townie, expecting her own room. 'She never did get one,' he observed. 'And now she's going to have to share with our Gerald.' There was a roar of laughter and cries of 'Shame!' but Betty, thinking of Erica even now facing the departure of her new husband, felt the tears prick her eyes.

'It's awful,' she said to Dennis. 'Nobody gets a chance these days. How can anyone get a start with all this going on? All the same, I wish it was us. Even if you do have to go away, I'd sooner we were married.'

'So would I,' he said, squeezing her hand. 'I think we

ought to fix it up soon. I wanted to wait till all this was over, just so that we could start properly – but we've waited long enough. We belong to each other, Betty – I want you to be my wife.'

Betty turned and looked up into his face. Her hazel eyes had deepened to a burning gold. She felt breathless, as if she had run a long way.

'D'you mean it? D'you really mean it?'

'Would I say it if I didn't?' he asked, smiling.

'Oh. Oh, Dennis.' The tears that had stung her eyes for Erica now welled up and brimmed over. She brushed them away, but more came and she gave up and let them stream down her face, laughing at herself, laughing with happiness. 'When? When shall we do it?'

'Do what?' Jack Spencer was at her elbow, laying his hand on her shoulder to turn her around. 'Here, Dennis, what are you doing to our Betty to make her cry?'

Dennis laughed and Betty shook her head. 'He's not doing anything. I mean, he's going to – we're going to get married, Mr Spencer. We're engaged – properly engaged. At least –' she turned and looked at Dennis again '– I suppose we are, aren't we?'

'We've always been engaged,' he said, and he reached out and drew her close against his side. 'We've always belonged to each other, Betty.'

They gazed into each other's faces, each reading the promise and truth that now shone out for all to see. And beside them, Jack Spencer banged loudly on the table and lifted his voice to silence the chatter that filled the room.

'Quiet, everybody! Quiet! Shut up a minute, will you!'

'Pray silence for his washup the mayor,' somebody called out, and everyone laughed then fell silent, waiting to hear what Jack Spencer wanted to say next.

'I've just heard a bit of good news,' the farmer announced. 'A bit of news we've been waiting for on this farm for a long time now. You all know young Betty here –' he laid his hand on her shoulder again – 'and you all know Dennis. Two of the finest young people you could wish to meet, and if you don't know why, I'll tell you. Betty came here not knowing one end of a cow from the other and now she can milk the whole herd and still do a day's ploughing at the end of it. She'll work at anything, any job you care to give her. And Dennis is the same, only now he's left us to join Bomb Disposal, and risk his life every day to save the rest of us. He won't fight, but he's no coward and I wish I could say the same for a lot of other people I know. We could do with more lads like Dennis.' There was a murmur of approval from his listeners. 'But that's not what I want to tell you,' Jack Spencer went on. 'The good news is that these two have decided to follow the good example set 'em today by our Gerald and young Erica – where've they got to, by the way –' he paused for the laughter to subside '– and they're going to get themselves wed, just as soon as it can be arranged. And I reckon we ought to congratulate 'em – even if it does mean we'll lose another Land Girl!'

The cheer nearly lifted the farmhouse roof. Betty stood blushing at Dennis's side, and he held her hand tightly and grinned at everyone. It was very different from when he had first come here, to face suspicion and hostility from many of the villagers. He knew that the change was largely because he had joined the Army, but he was also aware that much of the hostility had evaporated even before he'd left the farm. His own cheerful, steady personality had seen to that.

There was a sound at the door and everyone turned.

'Erica!'

She stood there in her white gown, her face radiant yet tragic at the same moment. Behind her, Gerald was sober, but his eyes too held a deep contentment. His hands were on her shoulders, his thumbs stroking her neck, very very slowly, very very gently.

'We just came in to say thank you,' Erica said, her voice trembling. 'Thank you for coming to our wedding. Thank you for all your good wishes and the presents and – and everything. And thank you for having the party without us.' Her lips quivered as she smiled around at them, and Betty's heart ached for her. 'I wish – I wish –' But she could say no more. The tears welled out of her eyes and she turned and laid her head on Gerald's shoulder as he closed his arms around her.

'Another drink, everyone!' Jack Spencer called, and began to move round the table, a bottle in each hand. 'Come on, now – there's got to be a toast to the happy couple. And they are happy, anyone can see that. And they'll go on being happy too, no matter how far apart they've got to be.' He handed a brimming glass to his son, and another to his new daughter-in-law, before planting a smacking kiss on her cheek. 'We're glad to have you in the family. And this lot won't last for ever, you'll see. You'll have years and years of being a farmer's wife.'

CHAPTER SEVENTEEN

At last it was time for the scholarship results to be announced. Tim went to school with a tight feeling in his chest that morning, and the whole class was unnaturally quiet and well-behaved. It was almost dinner-time when Mr Wain came in with a sheaf of papers in his hand.

The children stood up at once, as they always did whenever an adult came into the classroom. Tim felt his heart lurch and then seem to climb higher into his throat, beating uncomfortably. His legs trembled.

'You may sit down,' Mr Wain said. He looked at the papers in his hand. 'The following children, stand up when I call your names. These are the ones who have passed the examination for the grammar school.'

The class sat down again. Tim clenched his hands between his knees, pressing them firmly together to try to stop them shaking. It would be awful if he couldn't stand up when his name was called, and it was bound to be one of the first because it began with B.

'Rosemary Andrews,' Mr Wain read out, and a girl with yellow pigtails stood up, red with pleasure. 'John Antrobus. Michael Banks. Jennifer Collins. Robert Cook. Terence Granger. Peter Holliday –'

Tim listened, unbelieving, as the names rolled on. Jennifer *Collins*? Robert *Cook*? Peter *Holliday*? Where was his name? It ought to have been third on the list, straight after Michael Banks. *Tim Budd*. Before the Cs. What had happened?

The list ended. Twelve children were on their feet, looking excited, proud, self-conscious. The rest sat in various degrees of disappointment and resignation. Some had never expected to pass. Some hadn't even wanted to.

Tim stared at his desk. The ink-stained wood blurred and shifted under his gaze. His head seemed to be filled with a roaring noise and he felt sick and dizzy. He swallowed hard to keep from crying.

'As you know,' Mr Wain was saying, 'the grammar school and secondary schools have been evacuated to Winchester. That isn't very far away, but some of you may need to be sent to new billets. We'll be making arrangements during the summer, so there's plenty of time. And of course we'll be contacting your parents, but I expect you'll want to tell them the good news yourselves first, so there are some postcards and stamps here for you to use to write home today.' He smiled round the class. 'And those of you who haven't passed, don't be downhearted, the secondary school is very good and you'll learn lots of interesting things there.'

He nodded to Mr Hodges and went out. The children broke into a buzz of excited chatter. Tim bit his lips hard and dug his fingernails into his palms. It must be a mistake. It had to be a mistake. He must have passed. He was nearly a year older than most of the children in the class and he *ought* to have passed. He ought to have taken the scholarship last year, and passed it then, and he'd already be at the grammar school by now. He couldn't have failed.

Michael Banks was sitting next to him. He turned to Tim, his face glowing, and said, 'Gosh, isn't it smashing! I wish you were coming too, though, Tim. I'll have to sit next to someone else now.'

Tim got up abruptly and pushed his way past the crowded desks to the front of the class. Mr Hodges was talking to Rosemary Andrews and Jennifer Collins, who both sat at the front. Jennifer was the sister of Brian Collins, Tim's old enemy.

'What is it, Tim?' Mr Hodges asked. 'Do you want to be excused?'

Tim shook his head. He knew the tears were not far away, but he couldn't wait to get himself under control. He looked up at him, his lips turned down, his face crumpling.

'Why wasn't my name on the list, sir? Why can't I go to the grammar school?'

Mr Hodges looked embarrassed. 'Well, because you didn't pass the examination, Tim. But the secondary school is nearly as good –'

'But I ought to have passed,' Tim said, his voice turning liquid as the tears welled from his eyes. 'Everyone said I'd pass. *You* said I'd pass.'

'I thought you would. But your work just lately –'

'I did it all last year. I'd have passed then, I know I would.'

'But you didn't take the exam last year,' Mr Hodges said gently. 'You know that. A mistake was made somewhere and you got left off the list. And you know you haven't been doing as well this year.'

'I've had to do everything twice. I'm fed up with it. I'm fed up with school. I don't *want* to go to the secondary school.'

'I'm sorry, Tim,' Mr Hodges said, his voice hardening. 'You just have to accept it. That's where you're going. Now, you can go out to the lavatory and wash your face and then come back for prayers. It's almost time to go home.'

Tim glared at him and then stamped out of the room. He knew that he was likely to get into trouble when he came back, for being rude and slamming the door, but he couldn't help it. It wasn't *fair*. He *ought* to have passed.

He washed his face as instructed and then stood outside the lavatory door, in the little playground. It was the first warm day of spring. The sun was shining and he could see birds flying busily to and fro, building their nests. I'm not going back, he thought. They'll all see I've been crying. I'm not going back.

He turned his back on the school and, with tears once more streaming down his face, ran out of the playground, back to the vicarage and Mr Beckett.

To Tim, there seemed less point than ever in staying at the

village primary school. He was only doing the same things over again, he argued, and they hadn't done him any good the first time. And Mr Beckett couldn't help agreeing with him.

'He's got such a lively mind,' he said when Frank and Jess came to visit the boys. He had written to them, asking them to come specially because he was worried about Tim. 'He's getting bored and frustrated, and he's still resentful over what's happened. It's the kind of situation that makes bright little boys like Tim look for mischief.'

'Our Tim's never had to look far to find mischief,' Frank said grimly. 'Being at school's the best thing for him. At least he's under someone's eye.'

'But only for half the day,' Jess pointed out. 'And I think Mr Beckett's right. You know what boys are like when they're fed up. I don't want Tim roaming about getting into trouble. The devil finds work for idle hands, isn't that right, Mr Beckett?'

'It certainly can be,' the vicar agreed. He rubbed his hand across his face. He enjoyed having the children staying with him but there was no doubt it was a responsibility, and neither he nor Mrs Mudge were in their first youth. It was all very well to pretend to be a boy too and build snowmen or play cricket, but when it came to problems like this the parents had to make the decision.

'What do you think we ought to do?' Jess asked him, and he pursed his lips.

'What does Tim himself want?'

'You can't go by that,' Frank said at once. 'He's just a child.'

'It's his life, all the same,' Mr Beckett said. 'And he'll be much more willing to co-operate if he's happy. I'm afraid he hasn't been very happy for the past few months.'

Jess looked distressed. She turned to Frank. 'I don't want him to be miserable.'

'Nor do I. But he's got to learn to take the rough with the smooth, same as the rest of us. And I want him to have a decent education.'

'That's just it, though, isn't it. He ought to have passed that exam. He doesn't want to go to the secondary modern school. And he's just wasting his time at the village school.'

'What do you want me to do, then? Let him leave? He's only twelve years old. I want him to have a better chance than I had.'

'Frank had to leave school when he was twelve,' Jess told Mr Beckett. 'His dad died and he had to help support the rest of the family. They had a hard time – he's always wanted something better for our children.'

'I went to night school,' Frank said. 'For years. I kept my learning up. But there's nothing like that these days, with the war and all. If Tim leaves school now, he'll never be able to catch up. I don't want him doing labouring jobs for the rest of his life.'

'But he needn't,' the vicar said. 'Intelligent boys like Tim will always find a way to use their abilities. But they do need guidance as to the best way to use them.' He paused, then added, 'Suppose you let him leave the village school now and come home for a while? Then he might feel happier about starting at his new school after the summer holiday. He might be able to find some work to do in Portsmouth, to occupy him.'

'Come home?' Jess said. She looked at Frank. 'He could do, couldn't he? The raids aren't anywhere near as bad now.'

Frank shook his head. 'We're still getting 'em, though, and you don't know when they might start again. Look at the way they bombed Exeter and Norwich a few weeks ago. Anyway, even if we did let him leave – and I'm not saying we will, mind – he could still find work out in the country. There's always something to do around farms.' He glanced at Mr Beckett. 'Unless you don't want him here any more. If he's getting to be too much trouble –'

'Indeed not,' the vicar said warmly. 'I'm very fond of both your boys. I enjoy having them about the place. But it's Tim's interests I'm concerned with, and I think he would benefit from a spell at home. He needs something to take his mind off his grievances, and being back at home for a few weeks might be just the thing. Then he can come back fresh to start school again in the autumn.'

'Well, I won't say I wouldn't like to have him home again,' Jess declared. 'Both of them, come to that. But you're right, Mr Beckett, we've got to think what's best for Tim. Anyway, we can't talk any more about it now, I can hear them coming. Frank and me'll have a word and let you know what we decide.'

They discussed it later, on the way home in the train. Frank was still unwilling to consider letting Tim leave the primary school and come home, but the more Jess thought about it, the more she felt it was the answer.

'He's growing up,' she said. 'He's a year older than the boys and girls in his class. He's done all the lessons before, and he's missing his own friends. It's no wonder he's miserable about it.'

'That's all very well, but what's he going to do if he does come home?' Frank demanded. 'I don't want him at a loose end, roaming the streets with youngsters like that Baxter boy. There's going to be trouble there one of these days, you mark my words. That brat's going to end up in prison and I don't want our Tim mixed up with him.'

'Honestly!' Jess said. 'You talk as if Tim hasn't got a mind of his own. Who says he's going to get mixed up with Micky Baxter anyway? Don't you trust your own son? Don't you think we've brought him up to know right from wrong? Our boys might get into a bit of mischief, they wouldn't be boys if they didn't, but they've got their heads screwed on the right way. I think Mr Beckett's right. I think Tim's had a big disappointment, and he needs a bit of help to get over it, and if a spell at home will do that, we ought to let him come back. We're his mum and dad, after all, we're the ones that ought be helping him.'

Frank frowned and stared out of the window, saying nothing. Jess glanced at him and smiled inwardly. It might take a bit of time, but she was pretty sure he'd agree in the end. He'd probably announce it as if it was entirely his own decision – which it would be, of course. Nothing much happened in the Budd family unless Frank decided it would happen, but sometimes Jess had to do a lot of quiet work in the background to get him around to it.

'It'd be nice to be able to teach him a bit of woodwork,' she remarked casually. 'He's always been keen and he's getting to just the right age now.'

Frank gave her a quick look and she smiled innocently and looked out of the window. The train was passing a small wood, misted with green and blue.

'Look at all the bluebells!' she said. 'And the trees, just coming into leaf. They don't know there's a war on, they just go on living their own lives. It's lovely how the countryside just goes on, isn't it, Frank – it gives you heart to carry on somehow.'

Again, Frank said nothing. But he took her hand in his and held it as the train rattled on. And just before they got off at Copnor station, he said gruffly, 'All right. He can come home for a few weeks, till school starts. But that's all, mind. And if we get raids again, back he goes, like it or not. And he's not going to be running around with that Baxter boy. I'll find him a job, he can make himself useful.'

'Oh, he'll be all right,' Jess said. 'He'll be a great help.' But in her heart, she knew that she didn't care a scrap whether Tim was useful or not. It would be joy enough to have him at home, to see his cheeky face looking at her across the meal table, to hear his laugh and the jokes he was forever thinking up.

It was a shame Keith couldn't come home too. But perhaps once Tim had been back for a while and Frank saw that he was all right, she would be able to point out that the boys ought to be together. And then the Budd family would be complete again.

We've never really been a complete family, she thought. Little Maureen was only two months old when the evacuation started, and we've only been together since then at Christmas or for a week or two in summer. And now she's nearly three.

It was such a long time, to be missing your family life.

Roddy had found work. It wasn't regular, but he was paid

a few shillings a time for helping to hump boxes at a warehouse. He came home with two pounds at the end of the first week and paid Mrs Higgs a pound for two weeks' rent.

'I told you, it's fifteen bob now,' she said, staring at the handful of coins.

'And I told you we cannae afford that. You know the way we are. I've got to look after Carol and see she's properly fed and that.'

'Not much point, when she's throwing up all the time,' Mrs Higgs said cruelly. She had not yet carried out her threat to report them but they lived in a state of constant dread that she would. Carol was almost afraid to leave the house, even when she felt well enough, and Roddy could feel his back tingling all the time, expecting a heavy hand to land on his shoulder.

'We cannae stay here much longer,' he said when Mrs Higgs had gone muttering downstairs. 'Once the bairn's born the old besom will throw us out, sure as eggs is eggs. Anyway, I'll not have you and our little one living in a place like this.'

'What else can we do?' Carol asked. 'We can't afford anything better. And if we do leave, she'll report us anyway. She's got us just where she wants us, Roddy.'

'We can just disappear again. Go somewhere else, where they won't find us.' But he spoke without conviction, for they both knew now that it was not so easy to 'disappear'. There were papers that you had to have – ration books, identity cards, references. People were suspicious; you might be a fifth columnist or a spy. Only someone like Mrs Higgs, who was shady herself, would take them in, and then they might find themselves in even worse trouble. Better the devil you knew, Carol thought despondently.

'I'd like to take you home to Scotland,' Roddy said. 'My mother would take care of you right enough. And the bairn.' He touched her stomach gently. There was just a little round swelling there now, not much bigger than a grapefruit and only detectable because Carol had lost so much weight. 'Just think, Carrie, that's our little one in there. A real wee person, made just because we love each other.'

A real wee person they could do without, Carol thought, especially when she couldn't keep her food down. But the tenderness in Roddy's eyes caught at her heart and she could not say so. And when she wasn't feeling sick, there *was* something exciting about it. A real baby. Someone who hadn't existed before, ever, made as Roddy had said, just because they loved each other. It was marvellous and incredible and exciting – and frightening, too. A baby. Her baby. Someone who would depend on her, for everything.

'Roddy, I can't,' she said shakily. 'I won't be able to manage, I know I won't. I don't know anything. I'm not good enough.'

'You're good enough for me,' he said stoutly. 'And you're good enough to have my bairn. We'll manage together, Carrie.'

But they both knew that it couldn't really be like that. They couldn't live for ever on the fringes – one day, they would have to go to a doctor or a hospital, or someone at work would start asking questions about Roddy. Or Mrs Higgs would report them to the authorities.

All they could do was cling together for as long as possible and try to forget what might lie ahead.

Tim came home with mixed feelings. He had enjoyed his time in the country, looking on it as a long holiday and an adventure. Roaming the woods and fields, so different from the streets of Portsmouth, had made him feel like an explorer. I'd like to do that when I grow up, he decided. I'd like to explore the whole world.

Coming back to Portsmouth was an anti-climax. He knew every street around Copnor and many further afield. He was used to the harbour and the long ridge of Portsdown Hill, with the white chalk pits gaping in its side. A lot of the bomb damage, which had ripped the streets apart and turned them into a new kind of playground, had now been patched up and some of the houses demolished. The first excitement of the raids was over and a kind of dreariness had settled over the city.

But it was nice being home again. He hadn't realised how much he'd missed the familiar things, like Dad's armchair that he'd made himself, and the wireless he'd fixed together, and the rag rug Mum had made, which lay in front of the fire with Henry, the cat, curled on it. And he liked being up in the back bedroom with the window looking out over the allotments, which was as near as you could get to being in the country.

'Tim's not having the back bedroom, is he?' Rose demanded when she found him up there the first day. 'Me and Maureen sleep there.'

There were two iron bunks in the back bedroom. Maureen had recently been promoted to the top one, which she loved. She would clamber up the rail and sit there, surrounded by the assortment of animals Cherry had knitted for her – the grey elephant, the mauve donkey, a giraffe in a sort of yellowish tweed mixture – and tell herself stories. It was the only space she had to herself in the tiny house.

'A boy needs a room,' Jess said. 'He needs somewhere to keep his bits and pieces.'

'*I* need somewhere to keep bits and pieces,' Rose said. 'I don't see why I've got to move downstairs just for him.'

'You're not to talk like that. He's your brother. Aren't you glad to have him home?'

'Not much,' Rose said, but she said it under her breath and she made up the bed-settee in the front room with a bad grace. She didn't like sharing a bed with Maureen, who kicked in her sleep, and she didn't like not having a room of her own. But with only two bedrooms upstairs someone had to be down in the front room, and there was no use in arguing about it. And it was nearer to the back door and shelter, if the air-raid warning went.

Maureen was thrilled to have her brother home. Tim had always been ready to play with her and now he was here all the time. She followed him around like a puppy and he enjoyed the attention and let her go everywhere with him, even taking her up to the bedroom and tossing her up on to the top bunk to chat while he changed his clothes or sorted out his possessions.

They sang together. 'You Are My Sunshine, My Only Sunshine' or 'I went to the Animal Fair' were Maureen's favourites and she chanted them all around the house. '. . . *and what became of the monkey, monkey, monkey . . .*' until the rest of the family were sick of them. But Jess was too happy to have her family together again to object. She just wanted Keith home now, and everything would be perfect.

'Perfect!' Frank snorted. 'How can anything be perfect, when the world's tearing itself to bits? I don't reckon there's a country left that's not caught up in this war, one way or another.'

'You know what I mean,' Jess said. 'We're all in it together and we've got to make the best of it. Keep smiling through, like that song says.'

But it was hard for Frank to smile these days. He was up soon after five each morning, ready for the walk down through the battered streets to the Dockyard carrying his lunchbox, and often didn't arrive home, dirty and tired from a long day's heavy labouring, until eight or nine at night. And although there weren't as many raids now, you still had to be on the alert for the siren, and still had to take your turn at firewatching.

Saturday was often as long a working day as the rest, and then there was the garden or allotment to be tended, and jobs to be done around the house. It was only last thing at night, while Jess was putting together his meal for next day, that Frank got a chance to sit back in his armchair and read the paper. And then, as often as not, he'd fall asleep with Henry sprawled on top of him, his snores mingling with the cat's deep purr.

True to his word, once Frank had agreed to Tim's coming home, he had set about finding him a job. At not quite thirteen, there wasn't all that much Tim could do, but the chemist in September Street wanted a delivery boy and agreed to give him a chance. Frank was well known in the area for being steady and reliable, and Mr Driver took it for granted that his son would be the same.

'You can use this bike,' he said, taking Tim out to the shed in the back yard. 'It needs a bit of cleaning up – my last lad went into the Navy six months ago and it hasn't been used since. The wife'll give you some rags and a bit of cotton waste. Then come and see me and I'll show you what to do. I'll pay you five shillings a week.'

Five shillings! It was a fortune to Tim, who had never had more than a shilling at one time in his life. But his delight was soon tempered by Jess, who told him that she would expect him to hand over four shillings to her.

'A shilling's quite enough for a boy like you,' she said firmly. 'That bit extra will be a big help to us. Maureen's forever needing new shoes, and she's growing out of her clothes so fast I can't keep up with her.'

Tim handed the money over, slightly mollified by the thought that he was helping to look after Maureen. He took her out into the garden, jingling the coins that were left in his pocket, and taught her a new song.

'I've got sixpence, jolly little sixpence,
Sixpence to last me all my life.
I've got tuppence to spend and tuppence to lend
And tuppence to take home to my wife.'

But he didn't spend all his time with Maureen. As Frank had feared, he wanted friends of his own age, and inevitably he drifted towards Micky Baxter.

'Come 'ome from the country, 'ave you?' Micky jeered when they first met in April Grove. 'Didn't you like being away from Mummy any more? Ain't you scared of the bombs?'

'I'm not scared of anything,' Tim said, pushing away the thought of the crashed aeroplane and the pilot's hand, lying in the undergrowth. 'I've come home to work. I've left school now.'

'You 'aven't! You're not old enough.'

'Nor are you. Anyway, I've got a job, so that proves it.'

'Where d'you work, then?' Micky asked jealously. Nobody had given him a job, except for the few traders left in Charlotte Street, and he wasn't welcome there any more, since Ethel Glaister's accident.

'Up Driver's. The chemist's shop.'

'The chemist's shop?' Micky's eyes gleamed. 'You could get stuff, then. Stuff we need.'

'What sort of stuff?'

Micky debated with himself. To tell Tim what he needed, he'd have to tell him about the secret army and the growing arsenal. That meant trusting him. He wasn't quite sure if Tim could be trusted that much.

'Never you mind,' he said mysteriously, and then realised that he couldn't expect Tim to get 'stuff' if he didn't tell him what he wanted. 'It'd have to be secret.'

'I can keep secrets,' Tim said, immediately intrigued.

'I mean really secret. Not just games.' Micky looked at him speculatively. 'You'd have to swear not to tell a living soul.'

'Can I tell dead ones?' Tim asked, and then bit his lip. It was the sort of remark that nearly always got him into trouble, but he couldn't help making them. 'All right, what d'you want me to swear?'

'No. You'd have to come to our den to swear. And you've got to pass a test first.'

'What sort of test?'

Micky thought again. Here was a way of getting Tim to acquire what the gang wanted, without letting him in on their secret. And once Tim had done that, he wouldn't be able to give them away without getting into trouble himself. He grinned.

'You've got to get stuff to make gunpowder.'

'Gunpowder? What sort of stuff? Why d'you want to make gunpowder?'

'Never you mind. You just get some. And then we'll let you swear.'

'But I don't know what stuff you need,' Tim said. 'And how d'you know Mr Driver'll have any? He's a chemist, not a gunpowder maker.'

'I bet he will. You'll just have to find out, won't you? But you're not to ask him. You've got to get it secretly, so he don't know. That's the test, see? Otherwise it won't count.'

'What're you going to use it for?' Tim stared at him excitedly. 'Are you going to make fireworks?'

'Maybe.' Micky turned away. 'You just get that stuff and we might let you into our gang. But it's gotta be secret, see? Nobody's gotta know.'

Tim mounted his bike again and pedalled away up the road. His heart was racing. Fireworks! He hadn't seen fireworks for years. He thought of the ones his father used to buy before the war, ready for Guy Fawkes night. He'd start in the middle of October, as soon as they came into the shops, and bring home two or three a week – perhaps a roman candle and a rocket, or a catherine wheel, or – Tim's favourite – the zigzag of a jumping jack, which would leap all over the place when lit and make the girls squeal and hop about.

Frank would put the fireworks into a box which was kept at the top of the cupboard, and get it out every Friday evening to add the latest to the collection. Rose and Tim and Keith would gather round, stroking and admiring the coloured paper and longing for November the Fifth to arrive so that they could be set off in the garden. And during the last week, they would make a guy with a few old rags given them by Jess, and build a bonfire to be lit as soon as darkness fell.

There hadn't been any fireworks now since the war started, and nobody knew when they might be available again. Tim might be grown up before they appeared in the shops once more. And Maureen had never seen them at all.

Micky might let me make her some, he thought. If Mr Driver's got the right stuff, and I get some, he'd have to let me. A roman candle, she'd like that. Or one of those golden rod things that looks like a big spray of flowers.

The weather was growing warmer and although Carol was feeling less sick now, she was uncomfortable and almost always tired. The smell of stale cabbage that pervaded the house made her feel queasy, so she went out as much as she could, but there wasn't much to do. There were a lot of Servicemen in the streets and they whistled at her and several tried to pick her up. At one time, she would have answered them back and enjoyed it, but now she was embarrassed and ashamed.

'I saw you trying to get off with them Yanks,' Mrs Higgs told her one afternoon. 'I'd have thought you 'ad enough to think about, without playing the tart. Or maybe you thought you could earn a few bob before you starts to show.' Her small eyes gleamed dully as she stared at Carol's figure, still thin after her sickness. 'Don't you try bringin' men back 'ere, that's all.'

'I'm not,' Carol said furiously. 'I didn't even speak to them. I can't help it if they whistle at me.'

'Don't give me that! Any man knows when a girl's askin' for it. They can see what sort of a hussy you are just by lookin' at yer. They knows, right enough.'

'You're a filthy-minded old woman,' Carol said. 'I wouldn't bring anyone back here anyway. I'd be ashamed to admit I lived here.'

'Oh, would yer? Well, maybe you'd better find somewhere a bit more to yer taste, then. I'm sure I don't want to stand in yer light, Lady Muck. And if that feller of yours can't cough up a bit more rent, you'd better start lookin' for somewhere else anyway.' She turned and slopped downstairs in her down-at-heel slippers.

'Don't worry,' Carol shouted after her, 'we will. We can't wait to get away from you!'

She banged the door and flung herself on the bed, breathless with rage. She had reached the point now when the mere sight of Mrs Higgs made her angry. And the woman knew just how to taunt her. I'll kill her one of these days, Carol thought, I know I will. I'll push her down the stairs.

Half of her anger was fear. The thought of the baby growing inside her filled her with panic. She wanted to run, to get far away from it, but she knew there was no escape;

wherever she went, the baby would be with her, still growing. Once or twice she had thought about trying the landlady's suggestions of taking castor-oil or jumping off a chair. But she couldn't bear the thought of Roddy's disappointment if she did.

He really seems to like the idea of a baby, she thought in wonder. But he's not going to have to look after it, is he.

She couldn't look ahead at all. She and Roddy were fairly sure now that the baby was probably due in November. But November seemed a lifetime away. There was the whole of the summer to get through first.

Roddy too was having problems. The foreman at the warehouse was an old man who had been due to retire when the war started and had already lost his own son in the London blitz and his grandson at Dunkirk. He had been suspicious of Roddy ever since the young sailor had started work, and never tired of trying to catch him out.

'S'pose you're one of them bleedin' conchies,' he mumbled through his sandwich one morning. 'Too lily-livered to fight for your country. Bleedin' collaborator.'

'That I'm not,' Roddy answered angrily. 'It's none of your business anyway.'

'It is. It's everyone's business.' The rheumy eyes stared at him suspiciously. 'Told to look out for fiff columnists, ain't we? People with queer accents and that. I reckon you're about the queerest I've come across, no two ways about it.'

'I'm Scottish. Have you never heard a Scottish accent before?'

'Yes, I have, an' it didn't sound like yours. There was a bloke from Glasgow worked here once. Cut his accent with a knife, you could. Yours ain't anything like that.'

'I should hope not. I live near Edinburgh.'

'Hoity-toity!' the foreman mocked him. 'What's the difference – it's still Scotland, ain't it? You're still a Jock? That's if you really do come from there. Reckon you're a quisling meself. One of them spies.'

'Och, for goodness sake,' Roddy said in disgust. 'You don't know what you're talking about.' He finished his bait and got up. 'I'll get on with that new delivery.'

He started work again, but the old foreman scowled. He didn't like being talked to like that by a bit of a kid and he didn't believe that Roddy was as innocent as he appeared. There was something wrong about a lad of that age, miles from home, doing odd jobs in a warehouse. If he wasn't a 'conchie' he was the next worst thing – a deserter.

The old man thought of his grandson, not much older than Roddy, who had gone off to war as a fresh-faced young soldier and never come back. He thought of what he had heard about Dunkirk – the men standing in the sea, being strafed by German aircraft as they waited for rescue, the bombs, the blood.

'Lily-bleedin'-livered skiver,' he muttered, and shambled off towards the office.

The policeman had been thinking about retirement too. If the war hadn't started, he'd be in that nice little bungalow his missus had always wanted, growing roses and doing a bit of fishing. And his own grandson would be in the Force, instead of being sent out to Africa to fight in the desert. He had a lot of sympathy for the foreman.

'And you reckon there's something funny about this young chap, then?' he asked, leaning on the desk. 'I mean, just because he's Scotch don't mean anything. They're still English, after all, aren't they? They're on our side.'

'If 'e *is* Scotch,' the foreman said. 'Could be anything, couldn't 'e? I mean, 'ow're we supposed to know what 'is accent is? An' if 'e is all above board, why ain't 'e servin'? Whichever way you looks at it, there's summat queer. Any'ow, I thought it was me civic duty to come along and say me piece, so that's what I done. Up to you now.'

'You did quite right,' the sergeant said. 'It's information like this we're on the lookout for. You can't be too careful these days, not when there's a war on.' He drew a pile of forms across the desk and dipped his pen in the inkpot. 'I'd better take down a few details.'

The foreman wasn't the only visitor to the police station that day. Mrs Higgs had been in an hour earlier, complaining about her lodgers. She had spoken to a young constable who was waiting for call-up and his sympathies had been with the young couple she was grumbling about.

'It's not everyone can get into the Services,' he said. 'I bet he's tried hard enough. And if his missus is expecting –'

'Missus!' the landlady said scornfully. 'She's no more his missus than you are. Living in sin, that's what they are, and under my roof what's always been decent. I'd have thrown 'em out weeks ago if I hadn't bin so soft-hearted. But that's always bin my trouble. Fool to meself, that's what I am. "Martha," my late hubby used to tell me, "you're a fool to yourself and it'll get you into trouble one of these days." But there, I couldn't never stand by and see people suffer.'

'So why've you come here now?' the constable asked wearily. 'I mean, d'you want to report them for something or not?'

She stared at him. 'Well, that's for you to say, innit? If they're breakin' the law –'

'Yes, but I don't know that they are, do I? I mean, even if they're not married –'

'The boot'd be on the other foot if you 'ad it in for me,' Mrs Higgs said bitterly. 'Runnin' a house of disrepute, that's what you'd be callin' it. But when I comes all decent and honest and above board to report it, you're not interested. That's typical, that is. And what about 'im bein' a deserter? Ain't that important enough for you?'

'Well, there again, you don't *know* he's on the run.' The constable had recently attended a training course during which it had been impressed upon him that he must be sure of his facts before taking any action. 'Until we've got proof –'

Mrs Higgs' patience snapped. 'Well, ain't that what you're supposed to get, for Gawd's sake? You're the bleedin' police, ain't yer? Can't you investigate? Or are you too busy snoopin' round the shops to see who's getting stuff on the black market?' She glared at the young constable. 'Trouble is, there ain't no proper police these days, just old men and kids barely out of nappies. I dunno what the country's comin' to, I really don't.'

The constable tightened his lips and wrote down the

details Mrs Higgs gave him. He left the sheet of paper on top of the pile and the sergeant found it later when he was talking to Roddy's foreman.

'Here,' he said, 'there's another report here. Looks as if it could be the same pair. Scotch lad and a girl he says is his missus. She's in the family way.' He clicked his tongue. 'His landlady reckons they're not married and thinks he's a deserter. What's your chap's name?'

'Macintosh,' the foreman said. 'Some fancy first name – Rodney, would it be? They call him Rod in the warehouse.'

'That's what she says. Roddy, his young woman calls him. It must be the same ones.' The sergeant was beginning to feel excited. It wasn't often something like this happened in his quiet station. 'That's two complaints in the same afternoon. I'd better get round there straight away.'

'Shouldn't you get the authorities?' the foreman suggested. 'The military, I mean. If he is a deserter – he could cut up rough.'

'And if he isn't, I'm going to look a fool. And so will you. No, I'll go round first, ask a few questions.' The sergeant opened the desk to come through and bent to fasten his cycle clips round his ankles. 'You did right to come. I'll deal with it now.'

The foreman hung on, unwilling to miss the action, but he had walked to the police station and the sergeant was already fetching his bike from the passage. He couldn't trot behind him all the way to the street where Roddy lived. And it didn't look as if there was going to be an immediate arrest anyway. You couldn't bring a villain back to the police cells on the back of a pushbike.

'Will there be a reward?' he asked, without much hope. The sergeant gave him a reproving look.

'Helping your country's a reward, innit? Ain't that enough?'

He mounted his bike and pedalled slowly away along the street. The foreman stared after him for a moment or two, then shrugged and turned in the opposite direction.

He might as well call in at the Three Bells for a drink. Reporting a deserter was thirsty work.

Roddy had brought fish and chips home for supper. It was what they had most days – without ration books, they could buy little food and had to rely on the chip-shop and the local British restaurant, and they were afraid to go there too much for fear of being recognised. And buying any food at all usually meant standing in a queue for hours, and Carol had almost fainted when she tried that.

'I don't know why anyone ever has babies,' she said miserably, picking at the lukewarm chips. 'I feel like an old woman. And it's going to get worse. What's it going to be like when I'm fat and can't hardly drag myself about?'

Roddy shook his head helplessly. He had no idea what it was like to be pregnant. But women did have babies, lots of them sometimes, and survived. Surely it couldn't be that bad. He couldn't ever remember his cousin Moira being like this.

'Carrie,' he said, 'I think we ought to go to Scotland. My mother'll help us. She'll know what to do. She'll look after you.' He felt in his pocket and produced an envelope. 'I've written to her, see. I've told her all about us and the bairn. We'll save up for the fare and go as soon as we can.'

Carol took the envelope and stared at it. The address was a village a few miles from Edinburgh. She opened her mouth to ask how they could ever afford the fare for such a long journey, but the words were never spoken.

The bedroom door was suddenly flung open. Mrs Higgs stood there, meanly triumphant, and behind her on the landing was the large, portly shape of a police sergeant in uniform.

CHAPTER EIGHTEEN

Carol found the letter Roddy had written to his mother much later that night. It had slipped to the floor and got kicked under the bed. She picked it up and stared at the grubby envelope, marked with dust and traces of mud from someone's shoe.

It was too late now to ask Roddy how they could ever afford the fare to Scotland, and she didn't know if they would ever go there together anyway. She didn't know if they would ever go anywhere together again.

Roddy had been arrested. The big policeman had taken him away. It had seemed touch and go for a while whether he might take Carol herself away too, but eventually he'd decided that she hadn't actually committed any crime (thank God he didn't know about her mother's money, Carol thought), and in any case there wasn't any room in the cells. Instead, he had given her a good telling-off before reading out the long list of charges he had against Roddy, and marching him away down the smelly stairs.

'You're not taking him away!' she cried, catching at the dark-blue sleeve. 'It's not true, none of those things are true – Roddy never abducted me, I *wanted* to come with him. We were going to get married. It was *my* idea! And it's not fair to call him a deserter – he shouldn't never have been called up in the first place. He's clever, Roddy is, he was going to university, he didn't ought to be fighting, he –'

'And who are you to say who's to fight and who isn't?' the sergeant demanded. 'It's King and country, not bits of girls like you that we wants young men for. Anyway, that's not all. The whole case has got to be properly investigated. Why, he might be a spy for all we know. So might you, come to that.' He looked at Carol's white face and thin body. 'Here, how old are you anyway?'

'Sixteen,' Carol said wearily, and sat down on the bed. She was beginning to feel sick again.

'Sixteen when?'

'Just after Christmas. It's all right,' she said bitterly, 'I'm old enough to get married. And if we'd managed to get enough money to go to Scotland, I would've been by now.'

'Just after Christmas,' he said, staring at her. 'And how long have you and this young chap been going together, then, eh? Was there anything untoward going on before you was sixteen?'

'I dunno what you mean,' Carol began, and then caught his meaning and flushed scarlet. 'That's none of your business. You keep your dirty mind to yourself.'

'And you be careful of your tongue,' he retorted. 'It'll get you in trouble, it will, talking to a police officer like that. Well, I'll say no more about it now – but there'll be a thorough investigation, you mark my words, a very thorough investigation, and you and this young man might find yourselves in very serious trouble indeed.' He looked at Carol's bewildered face. 'It's rape if a man has carnal knowledge of a girl under the age of sixteen,' he said brutally. 'Statutory rape. And it don't matter if she *did* lead him on. It's a jail sentence.' He shook Roddy's arm. 'You'll be sorry you ever got yourself mixed up with this young woman,' he said. 'Prison's no rest cure, specially in the Services. After a couple of months in the glasshouse, you're going to wish you could be out there in the front line, mark my words.'

'Carol –' Roddy began, agonised.

'Roddy. Oh, *Roddy* –' She reached out both hands, but the sergeant was already shoving him on to the landing. She caught one last glimpse of his terrified face, and then the policeman's bulk filled the doorway.

'Now, you just stop here, young lady, and don't try running off,' he told her sternly. 'Your ma'll be along to fetch you, and if you've got any sense you'll be thankful to go home with nothing worse than a flea in your ear. You've had a lucky escape.'

'Escape!' she echoed bitterly. 'I escaped when I got away and came here.' She reached out again, pleading with him. 'Don't take him away. Please don't take him away. I'll die. I know I will. Please, please, *please* –' The tears were rolling down her cheeks now, and her words came with huge sobs that forced their way up from her chest like great, hard lumps. 'I can't live without Roddy. And I can't go home, I *can't*. It'll be like going back to prison. *Please* –'

Prison. The sergeant was turning away, his face stony. She heard Roddy's voice in her mind. *They'd send me to prison*, he'd said. *They might even shoot me*.

He was gone. All she could hear was the sound of his feet on the stairs, lighter, more stumbling than the sergeant's heavy tread. He was gone, and she might never see him again.

She reached hastily for the bucket and vomited.

The Portsmouth police came to see Ethel that same evening and gave her the fare to Bournemouth to go and fetch Carol herself. She arrived next morning, her immediate relief completely overshadowed by a furious temper, and her first action was to take her daughter by the shoulders and shake her.

'You little hussy! You naughty, *naughty* girl! Have you got any idea how worried I've been? I haven't slept a wink since you ran off, not a wink. I've been imagining all sorts of things – seeing you dead in a ditch, strangled or worse – I don't know how many times I planned your funeral. I thought I was never going to see you again. Don't you realise what I've been through? Don't you care?'

'You didn't care about *me*,' Carol said through her tears. 'You were always telling me off.'

'That's because I'm your mother. I wanted the best for you. I always did my best for you.' Ethel sat down in the battered basket chair and rummaged in her black patent handbag for a handkerchief. 'You don't know what it is to struggle to bring up your children right and then have it all thrown back in your face. You don't know what it is to be a mother.'

'Oh, don't I,' Carol muttered, and felt her face turn scarlet.

Ethel stared at her.

'What's the matter with you? Why've you fired up like that?' She got up again and looked more closely at her daughter. 'There's something funny about you. You're looking peaky. Are you all right?' She grasped Carol's shoulders again and Carol slid her eyes away. 'You're not going to tell me you're –'

'Expecting,' Carol said defiantly, meeting her mother's eyes at last. 'That's what you're going to say, isn't it? Well, I am, so there. I'm expecting a baby, Roddy's baby, and it's due in November, in nice time for Christmas. Won't that be a lovely present for you? You'll be a granny!'

Ethel gasped. She lifted her right hand and struck Carol hard across the face. Carol screamed and stumbled, and Ethel hit her again and then again, raining blows on her daughter's shoulders as the girl half fell, half cringed before her.

'You *filthy* little bitch! You trollop! Bringing shame on the family like this. I'll never be able to hold up my head again, never. I'll never be able to look that Jess Budd in the eye again. Everyone will be staring at us and sneering behind our backs. The whole street'll be talking. Oh, you hussy, you tart, you dirty, filthy little *slut*!'

'Stop it, Mum. Stop it. You'll hurt the baby.' Carol crouched on the floor, her arms held above her head. 'Stop it.'

The bedroom door opened. Mrs Higgs stood there, her arms akimbo, small eyes gleaming maliciously. 'That's right. That's what the little monkey needs. Pity she didn't get it before she got herself into this mess.'

'And you can keep your opinions to yourself,' Ethel snapped, turning on her. 'You ought to be ashamed, letting a bloke bring a decent girl to a place like this. Why, it's nothing but a slum. Filthy dirty windows, grease all over the floor, the stairs in a mess . . . My Carol's been used to something a sight better than this, I can tell you!'

'Well, you wouldn't 'ave known it from the way she's behaved,' the landlady said indignantly. 'Fish and chips every night, being sick in a bucket, stinkin' the place out . . . I'd 'ave thrown the pair of 'em out weeks ago if I 'adn't 'ad such a soft 'eart. They're lucky to 'ave 'ad anywhere at all to live, if you asks me.'

'I wasn't asking you,' Ethel said tartly. 'And I don't recall asking you in here neither, to shove your oar in where it's not wanted.' She turned to Carol. 'Get up and get your things together. We're going home.'

'Home? But –'

'You'll pay off the rent before you do,' Mrs Higgs said, planting herself firmly in the doorway. 'Three weeks behind, they were, and not payin' the full amount then. I give 'em a reduction to start with, to 'elp 'em along a bit, but it was fifteen bob a week after that, and that young scallywag never did give me the full amount. Three pounds they owes me.'

'Well, you'll just have to whistle for it.' Ethel snatched up the few clothes Carol had spread out on the bed and crammed them into her shopping bag. 'I'm not paying no rent.'

'But they *owes* me –' Mrs Higgs began, and then, as Ethel shoved her aside, 'I'll take 'em to court, that's what I'll do. I'll take the whole bleedin' lot of you to court. I'll see you in jail, see if I don't –'

Ethel ignored her. She grabbed Carol's arm and pushed her roughly past the landlady and on to the landing. Together, they stumbled down the dimly-lit stairs and out of the front door.

'Oh, Mum,' Carol said waveringly as Ethel dragged her along the street, 'what are we going to do? Suppose she does take us to court? I don't want to go to prison.'

'Don't be daft. She won't do nothing. I know her sort. She won't want the police nosing round, asking questions. I'm surprised she ever went to them in the first place.' Ethel's fingers were cruelly tight around Carol's arm as she hustled her round the corner, out of earshot of Mrs Higgs' furious yells. 'And now, my lady, we'll get you home and then you can tell me just what's been going on and what you think you're going to do about this baby you're expecting.'

Jess Budd had just come out of her front door when Ethel and Carol came round the corner by Mrs Seddon's shop. She stared at them in surprise and then hurried across the road, smiling with relief.

'Carol! Am I pleased to see you! We wondered whatever had happened to you. Where've you been? Are you all right?'

'Of course she's all right,' Ethel snapped. 'And it's none of your business where she's been. She's home now and that's all you need concern yourself with, and if you don't mind we'll just go indoors and have a cup of tea. We've had a long journey.'

'Hoity-toity,' Jess said as the door of number 15 closed behind the two. 'Well, I'm sure it doesn't matter to us where she's been, does it, Maureen. Wherever it was, if you ask me she didn't look all that glad to be home. I wonder what happened to that young man.' She took Maureen's hand and led her up the street to Annie's house, eager to share the latest scrap of news with her sister. 'Anyway, it's daft of Ethel Glaister to get up on her high horse – it only makes people talk all the more.'

Annie was interested to hear that Carol Glaister had come home, but she didn't have time to pay much attention to Jess's speculations. She had been down to North End that morning to see their parents and was soon telling Jess about Arthur.

'He's getting worse. He got up in the middle of last night and went out. Mum thought he'd gone to the lav – he's gone funny about using the po in front of her lately – but when he didn't come back she went downstairs and found the front door wide open. She went next door and got Mr Barrett out and they found him down near the Odeon in his pyjamas.'

'But that's terrible,' Jess said. 'He could have been run over in the blackout.'

'Well, it was getting light and there wasn't much traffic about, but you're right, anything could have happened.' Annie stirred her tea, frowning. She was looking thinner these days, Jess thought, and no wonder, with the worry over Colin hanging over her. 'I don't know what to suggest. I'd have them up here, we've got the room now, but he won't hear of it.'

'It'd be the best answer, though. We wouldn't have to keep running down to North End, and I could give you a hand with them. Perhaps we could get Frank to talk Dad round.'

'That's a good idea,' Annie said. 'Dad's always thought a lot of Frank. I'll get Ted to chip in too. He might take more notice of the men.' She rubbed her hand across her tired face. 'I dunno, Jess, it seems like this war just piles troubles on you all the time. Whatever would we have thought a few years ago if we could have looked ahead and seen all this happening, eh?'

'Maybe it's a good job we can't,' Jess said. 'I mean, it'd be nice to see into the future if you could be sure it would be good, but I'd be afraid to look now. There don't seem to be any end to it all.'

Together, they turned their heads and looked up at the mantelpiece, where Annie had stood a row of photographs. There were the girls, Betty in her Land Girl's sweater and breeches, Olive in her ATS uniform. And there was Colin, cheeky-faced and grinning, in his sailor's square rig.

There isn't even time to worry about it properly, Jess thought. When something as big as that happens, you need time to take it in, time to consider it all. But instead, there's all these other things – like poor old Dad losing his memory, and Olive risking her life on a gun battery, and Betty getting engaged to young Dennis, that Ted doesn't approve of. And rationing, and shortages, and nothing being the same as it used to be.

And we're supposed to *smile* about it all! Smile and

crack a joke, and look for the silver lining. *Turn the dark cloud inside out . . .*

She chuckled suddenly and Annie looked at her enquiringly. 'I never told you what Maureen said to me yesterday. You know how it rained in the morning. Well, I started singing that song, 'Pennies From Heaven', not thinking what her little mind might make of it, and she puzzled right up till dinner-time and then as we were sitting down, she said to me, "Do clouds have pockets, Mummy?" "Pockets?" I said. "No, of course clouds don't have pockets. Whatever makes you think they do?" And you know what she said? She said, "If they don't have pockets, where do they keep their pennies?" I had to think a bit, I can tell you, before I realised what she was on about.' Jess laughed again. 'The things she thinks of! You never know what she's going to come out with next.'

Annie laughed too, and picked up the little girl. 'You're a funny cuts, you are. You keep us all chuckling – I don't know what we'd do without you.' She held her niece close for a moment. 'I just wish they were all this small, so we could keep them safe at home,' she said quietly. 'But there it is, you can't stop the young ones growing up. And you can't stop the old ones getting older, either. You'll get Frank to have a word with Mum and Dad, will you? Perhaps we could all go down together, the four of us. Something's got to be done – they can't go on like this much longer. There's going to be an accident, one way or another.'

Joy heard about Carol's return from her mother. Jess Budd had been in for the *Evening News* and told her about it. Nobody knew much yet, but there was a lot of speculation and whispering in the shop.

'What's it all about?' Joy asked bluntly. 'Why are you all talking behind your hands? I suppose you think Carol's having a baby.'

'Joy! That's not at all a nice thing for a young girl to say. I don't know where you get such ideas.'

'Oh, for goodness sake, Mum. I'm not a little kid. I know how many beans make five.' Joy's restlessness was making her outspoken these days, and she was tired of being treated on the one hand like an adult – expected to do a day's work; and on the other like a child – being seen and not heard. 'Carol went off with a boy, didn't she? Everyone'll be watching her now.'

'I still don't like hearing you talk like that.' Alice frowned. 'And I don't want you seeing a lot of her, either. We don't know what ideas she's come back with. She was always a flighty little piece as it was, and you know what her mother's like.'

'That's right,' Heinrich said. 'Better to stay clear.'

Joy turned away. She had never been particularly friendly with Carol, until Rose had gone away and there hadn't been anyone else, but they'd had a few laughs then. And Roddy'd seemed a nice chap, and really keen on Carol. She wondered what had happened to him.

They all knew, soon enough. Ethel never said a word but it was in the *Evening News* a week or two later, the report of the young sailor who had deserted and run off with a girl who was barely sixteen. As the police sergeant had threatened, there was talk of abduction, and even rape, since Carol had been under age when they first began to go out together, but in the end that was dropped and Carol wasn't even called to give evidence. Roddy faced charges of deception and theft as well as the naval court-martial for desertion. He was dismissed from the Royal Navy and given a term of five years' imprisonment.

'Five years,' Joy said. 'That's awful. He'll be old when he comes out.'

'Twenty-three,' Alice said sharply. 'That might seem old to you, but he'll still be young enough to do plenty of damage. He's ruined that girl's whole life.'

'And at least he'll still have his life,' Heinrich added. 'Plenty of young men will never be twenty-three.' He gave her a hesitant glance, and said more gently, 'Joy, *liebchen*, you know that we only speak to you like this because we care about you. We don't want you to risk the same kind of trouble that Carol has got into. We know what it means, you see.'

Joy looked at him doubtfully. Her father's voice sounded almost as it had done before he was taken away, when he had been the mild, loving father she worshipped. She had not heard him speak like that for over a year. Her eyes stung a little.

Heinrich moved over to her and put his hand on her shoulder. For the first time in many months, she did not flinch away.

'I'm afraid it's true that poor little Carol may be expecting a baby,' he said. 'Her life will never be the same again. If she keeps it – and I cannot see how she can even think of such a thing – she will have a truly terrible time. Everyone will know, everyone will turn away. I am not saying this is right. I am saying it will be so. And how will she manage for money? She will live in poverty, for that mother of hers will never lift a finger to help.'

'And if she gives it away for adoption, she'll never forget it,' Alice added. 'She'll always wonder – every birthday, every Christmas, every *day*. She'll never forget.'

She was looking at her husband almost as if she'd never seen him before. For some weeks now, she had detected a softening in him, an easing in his bitter anger. But that it should take the plight of Ethel Glaister's daughter, of all people, to bring back the man he had been . . . ! She reached out her hand and touched him, feeling the tears in her own eyes, and so the three of them stood for a moment, linked. A family once again.

Joy met Carol in the street a day or two later. They hesitated and looked at each other for a minute, then Carol said, 'I suppose you won't want to talk to me now.'

'I don't mind,' Joy said awkwardly, trying not to look at Carol's waistline. She was wearing a loose frock, which made it difficult to tell if she was looking any fatter. But her face didn't look fat – it looked thin and unhappy. 'It's a shame about Roddy,' she said at last. 'I liked him. He was nice.'

'You needn't talk about him as if he was dead,' Carol said sharply. 'He's still nice.' Her lip quivered suddenly and tears filled her eyes and began to run down her cheeks. 'I hate thinking of him in prison,' she said. 'It must be awful. He never did anything to deserve that, Joy.'

'I know.' Suddenly, the awkwardness between them had gone and Joy could feel nothing but an immense sympathy for the miserable girl. She remembered what her parents had said, the sympathy they had shown. 'Here, I'm going down North End to do a bit of shopping for Mum. Why don't you come with me? I've got enough for the bus fare back.'

'Might as well.' Carol turned and walked beside her. She was silent for a few moments, then she burst out, 'Mum wants me to get rid of the baby. I can't. I've told her I can't. But she says she'll make me.'

Joy stared at her. 'Get rid of it? But – you haven't had it yet, have you?'

'Of course I haven't had it! It's not due till November. You know what I mean. She wants me to go away and have it and then get it adopted so no one round here'll know. She doesn't even want Dad or our Joe to know. It's supposed to be a secret – she'd kill me if she knew I was telling you. But I can't keep it all to myself, and I've got no one else to talk to.'

Joy didn't know what to say. She couldn't imagine Carol with a baby. 'But how would you look after it? I mean, you wouldn't be able to get a job or anything.'

'I don't know,' Carol said hopelessly. 'I don't know what I'd do. But I can't give it away, Joy. It's Roddy's baby. I've got to keep it, for him.'

The whole story poured out now, as the two girls walked along September Street. All the time in Bournemouth, lying on the creaky bed in Mrs Higgs' room, being sick and thinking she was ill. The search for jobs. The frightening realisation that she was pregnant, and Mrs Higgs' suggestions about an illegal abortion. And Roddy's love, shining steadfast throughout all their anxieties.

'He didn't know what to do. He tried so hard to do his best. And now he's in prison, and he didn't even do the things they said. He never stole any money, Joy – I did that.

I took my mum's savings. But he swore it was him, just to keep me out of trouble.'

'He got you into trouble, all the same,' Joy said. 'I mean, you're going to have this baby, aren't you. My mum says he's ruined your life.'

'Well, he hasn't,' Carol said fiercely. 'You can just tell her he hasn't. He's made my life special. Nobody ever loved me till Roddy came along – not really. Even my dad . . . And now I'm going to have his baby, and that'll love me too. And I'll love it and look after it till Roddy comes out of prison and we can get married.'

The determination to have her baby had come almost as soon as she'd arrived home. Until then, she had been terrified, ready to give anything to have the baby magically spirited away. She didn't want an operation, such as Mrs Higgs had suggested, she just wanted it never to have happened. But once home, with Ethel ranting at her, her feelings had changed. She had clasped her hands protectively across her stomach and defied her mother.

'It's my baby! Mine and Roddy's. He wanted me to have it, and I will.' And she had felt a sudden surge of love for the little person growing within her, the person that she and Roddy had made through loving each other. 'You can't force me to give it away.'

'Oh, can't I? And just how do you expect to manage on your own, eh, tell me that. Because you won't get no help from me.'

'I bet Dad'd help me. He wouldn't make me give it away –'

'Your Dad's not going to know nothing about this,' Ethel said sharply. 'Why, it'd break his heart to think his daughter had gone to the bad like this. You're not to tell him, see, nor our Joe, nor no one else. There's no need for anyone to know.'

'Of course they'll know,' Carol said. 'They're not blind.' And she listened in dismay as Ethel outlined her plans. A mother and baby home, full of girls waiting to give birth. Somewhere out in the country – 'far enough away so no one from round here'll know,' Ethel said. And then the baby handed over to strangers, taken away, never to be seen again.

'No,' she said. 'No. Roddy'd never forgive me.'

'*Roddy!* It's nothing to do with him.'

'He's its father,' Carol said. 'He was pleased about it –'

'*Pleased?* The very idea –'

'He wanted us to have it. He'd hate me if I gave it away.'

'He probably hates you anyway,' Ethel said shrewdly, 'for getting him into such a mess. Not that it wasn't all his own fault.'

Carol stared at her. Roddy, hating her? 'It's not true,' she said shakily. 'We love each other.'

'And how long's that going to last?' her mother sneered. 'Five years he's been put away for. Five years. That little bump you've got there'll be at school by then. D'you think he's still going to want you, after he's been in jail for five years? Why, you won't even recognise each other!'

It's not true, Carol thought, squeezing her eyes shut and trying to conjure up Roddy's face. But to her horror, she couldn't do it. She couldn't see him.

She could see his hair and, if she concentrated hard, she could see his hands, long and knobbly, the hands that she'd loved to have caress her. She could catch a glimpse of his eyes – just briefly, for a moment – and then his mouth. But she couldn't put it all together and see *him*.

I can't remember what he looked like, she thought in panic. I've lost him already.

'See?' Ethel said cruelly. 'See?' She waited a moment, then went on, 'We'll have no more argy-bargy about this. You'll do as I say. I'll find out about these homes first thing tomorrow, and we'll see about getting you in one. I'll put it out that you're going down to Devon to be with our Shirley. And then when it's all finished with you can come back here and get yourself another job. It's going to cost me enough as it is, this lot, and I'm not going to keep you in luxury a minute longer than I have to –'

Carol opened her eyes. She stared at her mother and then came abruptly to life. She jumped up from her chair, her hands balled into tight fists, her face scarlet with sudden rage.

'No!' she shouted, so loudly that Jess Budd next door heard her through the wall. 'No, no, *no*! I won't do what you say. I won't go away and have my baby and pretend I'm in Devon. And I won't give it away – I won't. You can't make me. *Nobody* can make me.'

She ran out of the room and up the stairs. Ethel sat quite still, listening to the slam of the bedroom door and the storm of weeping that followed it. Then she shrugged and began to gather up the tea-things.

'Can't I, my lady?' she said to herself. 'We'll see about that. We'll soon see about that.'

CHAPTER NINETEEN

Babies were more happily in the air out at Bishop's Waltham, where Erica had settled back into life as a Land Girl almost as if she had never married the farmer's son. There were small differences – she had the embarrassment of trying to remember to call Jack and Ada Spencer 'Mum' and 'Dad', and they tried hard to behave as if she were now their daughter rather than a Land Girl. But since they had never had a daughter, and there was still work to be done on the farm, neither of them was quite sure what difference it should make.

'You'll move down into Gerald's room, of course,' Mrs Spencer said. 'I'm sure he'd expect you to.'

Erica hesitated, looking at Betty and Yvonne. 'I don't know – I think I'd rather stop up in the attic now. At least till he comes home – I'll move down then, of course.' She blushed as the others laughed. 'I've got used to the company,' she confessed.

'Well, there's a turn-up,' Betty said. 'First time we came here you looked at us as if we'd got fleas.'

'Mind you, I probably did have,' Yvonne added with a grin. 'We all did, in Rudmore.'

The awkwardnesses soon disappeared. Within a week, Erica had stopped calling her parents-in-law anything at all, and they had returned to their normal behaviour. And up in the attic, it was easy to believe that nothing had changed.

It was about a month after the wedding when Erica first confided her suspicions to the other two girls.

'But we all miss from time to time,' Betty said. 'Specially

when something exciting's happening. I never saw my period once, when we went on holiday one summer.'

'I've always been regular as clockwork,' Erica said. 'I'm nearly three weeks over now. And I felt a bit funny yesterday morning, when I bent down to do the milking.'

Betty looked at her. 'But you and Gerald hardly had time. I mean – I never thought you went together before the wedding. I thought –'

'We didn't,' Erica said, blushing. 'But that afternoon – well, we didn't know when we might see each other again. And we *were* married. You couldn't expect us not to –'

'Well, we didn't think you were picking flowers all that time,' Yvonne observed. 'But d'you really mean to say it was only that once?'

Betty remembered her sister Olive, telling her it hardly ever happened the first time. 'How d'you feel about it?' she asked curiously. 'If you really are – you know. Are you pleased?'

Erica looked nonplussed. 'I haven't thought about being pleased or not. I've only just started to wonder if I *am*. But – I don't feel upset. Actually, I think I feel quite excited, really.'

'A baby,' Yvonne said, looking almost as excited as if it were her own. 'That'll be smashing. I bet the guvnor'll be pleased. And Mrs Spencer.' She grinned wickedly. 'Here, you'll be able to call 'em Granny and Grandpa now!'

'You ought to find out if you really are expecting,' Betty said. 'There might be things you shouldn't be doing round the farm. I mean, you want to take care of yourself.' She thought of Olive, losing her baby during an air-raid. 'Isn't there something about not lifting your arms above your head?'

'That's an old wives' tale,' Yvonne said. 'My mum's had six and she never did anything different with any of us. How could she? I mean, she couldn't stop hanging out washing just because there was another one on the way, could she.'

'Well, you ought to see about it anyway,' Betty insisted. 'You're doing a lot of heavy work. You ought to tell Mrs Spencer. She'll know.'

Erica felt shy about telling her mother-in-law the news. For one thing, it made it so obvious what she and Gerald had been doing on the afternoon of their wedding – not, as she had said to Betty, that there was any reason why they shouldn't. But it couldn't be hidden for ever, and Betty was right, there might be things she should be careful of. So one evening, when the other two girls were cutting down some old cotton frocks to make blouses, she went downstairs to where Mrs Spencer was topping and tailing gooseberries in the farm kitchen, and listening to *ITMA* on the wireless.

'I'll do some of those,' she offered, and sat down at the kitchen table with a pair of scissors. The gooseberries were from Mrs Spencer's kitchen garden and would be bottled or made into jam to last the family through the winter. The farmer's wife made other jams and preserves too, with plums and apples from the orchard, and the jars gleamed like precious jewels in the cupboard.

'You'll have to teach me to make jam,' Erica said, when the wireless programme had finished to the music of *It's That Man Again*. 'I want to be ready to be a proper farmer's wife when Gerald comes home.'

'You're doing well enough,' Mrs Spencer answered. 'You can milk a cow as if you'd been brought up to it, and do most of the other jobs around the place as well. But you're right – you ought to be learning a few of the other sorts of skills – they'll be more use to you when you've got a family round your skirts.'

Erica blushed. She'd been wondering how to introduce the subject, yet now that the opportunity had been handed to her she still couldn't find the right words. There was a short silence, and then Mrs Spencer gave her a quick glance and said casually, 'Was there something you wanted to tell me?'

Erica took a deep breath. She knew her face was fiery and she felt almost guilty, as if she were about to confess to some minor sin. We were *married*, she told herself fiercely. There was nothing wrong in what we did, even if it was behind a haystack . . . She looked up and met her mother-in-law's eyes, and then blurted out, 'I'm having a baby. At least, I think I am. But we never – I mean, I don't want you to think . . . It was only that one afternoon . . .'

Mrs Spencer gazed at her. Her eyes were suddenly bright. She blinked and reached across the table for Erica's hand, holding it tightly.

'My dear child! I never thought for one moment – not for one moment that you and Gerald . . . My Gerald wouldn't . . . A *baby*. Oh, that's lovely, that really is lovely. Our first grandchild. Oh, I must tell Jack.' She got up and hurried round the long table to hug Erica. 'I had an idea there might be something – I can always tell, there's something about a girl's skin – but I thought no, it couldn't be, it'd be a miracle . . . Just that one afternoon – oh, I'm so pleased, you can't *think*!'

Erica clung to her, her own tears flowing suddenly. Half laughing, half crying, she said, 'I didn't know how to tell you. I mean, I don't know for certain. And I don't really know what all the signs are. I really wanted to tell Gerald first, but I can't say anything unless I'm sure. I don't want to raise his hopes if it's a false alarm.'

'Of course you don't.' Ada Spencer gazed at her fondly. 'We'd better wait a week or two more before we mention it to anyone else. And then you'd better go and see the doctor. They can tell at about eight weeks.' She hesitated and then said, 'I daresay you'll want to go and see your mum and dad, to tell them.'

Erica looked away. 'Well, some time, I suppose. To tell the truth, I don't think they'd be all that interested.' She glanced down at the bowl of gooseberries. 'I mean, they never came to the wedding, and they've got all their own friends down in Gloucestershire. I don't think they're bothered about me now.'

'Not bothered about their own daughter, not even when she's expecting her first baby? Oh, you poor love.' Mrs Spencer enfolded Erica in her arms again. 'Well, I hope you're wrong about that. I hope you'll find they're as pleased as I am. But if not – well, you know you've me and Jack to look after you. *We're* your mum and dad now, and this is your home for as long as you and our Gerald want it to be.' She let go of Erica to mop her eyes with the corner of her apron. 'And I hope it'll always be your home, and that you'll have a lot more kiddies to bring up here for us to love.'

'So do I,' Erica said shakily. She looked around the big, cluttered kitchen, remembering how scornful she had been when she first walked in two years ago, and how haughtily she'd demanded a room of her own. Now, it appeared comfortable and homely, a place where she could be her true self – the Erica who had almost got lost in the pretensions of society.

She looked at her mother-in-law. Ada Spencer was small and plump, with grey hair that she cut herself, curling in wisps around her plain, round face. Perhaps she had been pretty once, but it was honest kindness that shone from her eyes now and that, Erica knew, was worth more than any surface beauty.

'Oh, Mum,' she said, and the name came as naturally to her tongue as if she had been using it all her life, 'I *am* glad I came here.'

Carol held out for another week, but Ethel's continual haranguing and her own shaky health added up to a misery that she could fight no longer. She was still being sick several times a day – some young mothers-to-be were, the doctor said, examining Carol with some sympathy, and it could last right up till she was delivered – and as she lay on her bed, listening to her mother's diatribes it began to seem as if anything must be better than staying at home.

'All right,' she said at last. 'All right, all right, all *right*. I'll go. I'll go tomorrow if that's what you want. Then I'll be out of your way and you won't have to be ashamed of me. You won't have to keep looking at me to see if my belly's getting fat so that everyone'll know. You can forget all about me.'

'Forget about you!' Ethel said, but her eyes gleamed triumphantly. 'It'll take a long time to forget the dance you've led me these past few months. A proper little madam you've turned out to be, and I hope they make you see sense where you're going. You'll be putting it up for adoption, mind. I'm not having you come back here with a bundle in your arms.'

Carol's eyes filled with tears, but she was too exhausted to argue any more. And she knew that it would be impossible for her to keep her baby if her mother refused to accept it. Impossible for her to manage alone, either. A sixteen-year-old girl couldn't earn enough to keep herself, let alone a baby, and how would she be able to go to work anyway? She had no choice.

'You'll thank me for it in the end,' Ethel told her. 'You'll be grateful when you look back on this. You've got your whole life in front of you – you don't want to start off saddled with a mistake you made when you were barely out of your own pram.'

'Oh yes,' Carol said with a weak attempt at sarcasm, 'and you'll be telling me next you're doing it all for my own good.'

'Well, so I am! I'm your mother, ain't I? Of course I'm doing it for your good.' Ethel prepared to leave the room. 'I'll go and write to the Home straight away. They said they could take you this week. We'll arrange to go on Friday, after my hair appointment – I don't want them thinking you come from a poor home or anything like that.'

She went downstairs. Carol lay for a few minutes staring at the ceiling. Then she felt under her mattress and drew out a grubby, creased envelope. It was the letter Roddy had written to his mother. Carol had never opened it. She'd kept it exactly as it was, the traces of mud still smeared across it, and at night she fell asleep with it clutched between her fingers. It was the only thing of Roddy's she had, the only souvenir by which to remember him.

Since his court-martial and imprisonment, she had heard nothing from him. Ethel had forbidden her to write to him, but in any case Carol did not know which prison he was in. She had thought of writing to the address on the envelope and asking his mother to send on a letter, but she was afraid that such a request would be refused. Roddy's mother must hate her for what had happened to him. Even if she sent the letter he had written, Carol didn't think Mrs MacPherson would take any notice of it. She would simply tear it up. And then her last shred of comfort would be gone.

'It's no good you hanging about waiting to hear from him,' Ethel had told her, noticing that she spent a lot of time waiting for the postman. 'They don't let prisoners write letters. And if anything came to this house with a prison postmark on it, I'd put it straight in the fire.'

Carol pressed the crumpled envelope against her cheek, and then turned her face to the wall and closed her eyes. Oh Roddy, Roddy, she thought, I'm sorry. But what else can I do?

By the end of the week, Carol had gone again. Sent down to relations in Devonshire, Ethel said, to be with her little sister Shirley. It was the best thing for her, after what she'd been through, poor kid. Maybe she'd come home again after a few months.

The other residents of April Grove took this with a pinch of salt, not least because Ethel had never in her life been heard to express sympathy for her daughter.

'She hasn't gone to Devon,' Rose said scornfully. 'She's gone to a Home, where they take girls who're going to have babies.'

'Whatever are you talking about?' Jess demanded, shocked. 'How do *you* know she's expecting a baby?'

Rose gave her an exasperated look. 'Everyone knows, Mum. We're not kids any more. Anyway, she told Joy.'

'Well, I don't want you talking about it all the same. Especially when our Tim's here.'

But Tim wasn't interested in Carol Glaister. He was off on his bike every morning, up to Mr Driver's, where he collected his errands and cycled all over Copnor delivering medicines. He enjoyed being in the open air and getting to know the customers, and he whistled cheerfully as he zoomed round the corners, practising riding with no hands or with his feet on the handlebars.

He had not forgotten his desire to be in Micky Baxter's secret army, however, and when he saw Micky and Jimmy Cross coming along September Street, he rang his bell and skidded to a halt.

'I got that stuff you wanted.'

Micky stared at him. 'What stuff?'

'To make gunpowder with. It's saltpetre.' Tim handed Micky a screw of brown paper. 'That's what you want for gunpowder. I looked it up in a book.'

'You never said nothing to old man Driver, did you?' Micky asked suspiciously.

'Cross my heart I never.' Tim was still feeling guilty over this. He had looked in his father's encyclopaedia first and then in one of the chemist's books when the shop was full of customers. He'd found the saltpetre in a jar under its name of potassium nitrate, and scooped a few teaspoonsful into the brown paper, screwing it up quickly, terrified of discovery. Afterwards, he'd found it difficult to meet Mr Driver's eye and had scurried out of the shop as soon as he could.

Micky unwrapped the brown paper and examined the white crystalline powder. 'You sure it's the right stuff? It looks like sugar to me.'

'I wouldn't put it in your tea,' Tim said. 'It'll blow your head off. It's saltpetre, like I said. And I'm not getting any more. There's enough there to blow up all Pompey.'

'In this little bit?' Micky stared at it unbelievingly. 'Garn! You're having us on.'

'It'd take a bomb as big as a ship to blow up Pompey,' Jimmy Cross chipped in. 'Bigger. The one that blew my leg off, it was six foot long, and that never blew up no more than a couple of old houses.'

'Well, it probably didn't have saltpetre in it,' Tim said. 'There's all sorts of different kinds of gunpowder. I'm not getting any more, anyway.' He looked at Micky. 'I've done what you said, I've passed the test. Now you've got to let me come to your den and tell me your secret.'

'All right. But you've got to swear utter secrecy, mind. Otherwise we tells old man Driver about the saltpetre.'

He took Tim to the den that evening. He had brought his collection of souvenirs with him, and Desmond had added a few more bits and pieces that he'd collected from the wrecked planes in the corner of the aerodrome. Tim stared in fascination at the growing display, lit by the flickering glow of an old paraffin lamp.

'Where d'you get all this? That looks like a proper wireless. And that's a real bayonet.'

Micky gave him a contemptuous glance. 'Course they're real. We're a real army. This ain't a kids' game. And if you want to be in it, you'll 'ave to get your own weapon. A gun'd be best. We got guns too, only I didn't bring them tonight.'

Tim looked at him. It sounded like one of his boasts.

'I don't believe you. Where could you get guns?'

'We got 'em from the Home Guard shed. Martin got the key.' They had gone there late one night, he and Desmond with the key Martin had filched from his uncle's kitchen, and come out with half a dozen assorted weapons, some British, some German, to add to their arsenal. They were all at least twenty-five years old but the Home Guard had cleaned them and they were ready for use. They were special, Martin had said proudly; some of the Home Guards in the country were still using broomsticks, and hardly any had an armoury like this. 'We'll bring 'em along one night and show you. We gotta do some shooting practice, anyway.'

'I bet you don't know how to shoot them,' Tim said jealously, still only half believing him. 'You've got to know what you're doing with guns.'

'Garn!' Micky scoffed. 'What d'you know about it? I bet you ain't never even touched one.'

'I have. Reg Corner used to take me and Keith shooting when we were out at Bridge End. He let me fire it and I shot a rabbit. We had it for supper,' Tim said proudly, but Micky sneered again.

'Rabbits! We're goin' to be shootin' *Germans*. You can 'ave them for supper if you want!' He picked up Wendy's bayonet. 'This is from the last war too. It was Wendy's grandad's. He killed about a hundred Germans with it, didn't he, Wen?' He stroked the rusty blade with some reverence. 'You can still see the blood, dried on.'

'What else have you got?' Tim asked, looking at the pile on the old table.

'Coupla gas masks. A wireless set – we're goin' to get it to work and listen in to the pilots when they're goin' on raids. Three unexploded incendiaries –we're goin' to dismantle them and use the stuff for our own bomb. And two grenades.'

'Aren't you scared they'll go off?'

'Nah. Safe as houses.' Micky waved his hand around the ruined cellar. 'An' look what we got over here.'

He shone the lamp into a dark corner, where almost no light could filter down through the cracked ceiling, and Tim felt the skin lift at the back of his neck.

'Crikey! What's that?'

'It's part of a German plane,' Micky said proudly. 'Des got it. It's a pilot's seat and the lid off the cockpit. We're makin' our own plane, see?'

Tim stared at it. In the dim corner, it looked very much as if a complete aircraft were there, nosing out of the shadows. He could see the dome of the cockpit bubble, a patchwork of cracked Perspex glinting in the unsteady light. And something else, something black and shifting.

'There's someone in it,' he whispered. 'It's not – it's not a *dead pilot*, is it?' The image of a hand, encased in a leather glove, rose in his mind, and he felt his flesh crawl.

'Yaaargh!' The bubble lifted suddenly and the shadowy figure came terrifyingly to life, leaping out with arms outstretched, fingers clawing the air. 'Yaaargh! Got you – yaaargh! You're dead!'

Tim screeched and fell backwards, tipping the lamp out of Micky's hand as he did so. There was immediate panic as the boys scrabbled to save the light. Wendy yelped as someone trod on her hand, and Desmond scrambled down from the cockpit and began to laugh.

'That scared you. You all thought I was a dead pilot. Hooo-hooo-hooo, that scared you.'

'You stupid twerp,' Micky said furiously, steadying the lamp and setting it on the table. 'You coulda got us all blown up. You won't be allowed to be in the army if you can't 'ave a bit more sense.'

'That's right,' Jimmy Cross said. 'I dunno what my mum'd say if I went home without my other leg.'

Tim spluttered, but there was an edge of fear to his laughter. He looked at the heap of bits and pieces on the table, his eyes drawn to the grenades and incendiaries.

'Where d'you keep them? You don't leave them here, do you?'

'Don't be daft. They gotta be locked away. Anyway, never you mind, it ain't none of your business.' Micky planted himself firmly in front of the table. 'It's secret, understand? Everything here's secret.'

'Can I be in your army, then? Can I help make fireworks and things?'

'Fireworks! We ain't makin' fireworks. That's kids' stuff, that is. We're makin' *bombs*. Proper bombs. We're goin' to blow things up. We're an army.' Micky narrowed his eyes and gave Tim a hard look. 'I'll talk it over with the others, all right? We might let you in – and we might not. You can come back tomorrow and we'll tell you then. Now you can scram.'

Tim shrugged. He felt annoyed at being sent away, but he wasn't sorry to scramble up the broken steps and out into the fresh air again. He knew that Micky was just playing with him, pretending that he might not be allowed to join them, when they obviously needed everyone they could get. By tomorrow, he was confident that he would be a member of the secret army, perhaps even a Lieutenant.

They'll have to let me in now, he thought, now that I've seen the den and the bits of plane and everything. And then he remembered that with all the fuss over Desmond's prank, Micky hadn't made him swear to secrecy after all.

Whistling, he climbed on to his bike and pedalled off along the road. It was one of those that had been bombed early on, and some of the ruined houses had been cleared and static water tanks erected in the spaces. Their grey galvanised steel sides were scrawled with messages to Hitler and chalk pictures of him in undignified postures, and children were clambering on piles of bricks to peer in. They made good swimming pools on hot days, though there was trouble if a warden or policeman caught you.

Tim rode down to North End. He had promised Jess he would go to see his grandparents and he was keen to see if Arthur had any relics of the Boer War that he could take with him to tomorrow's meeting. Micky had said that any new member of the gang had to provide his own weapon – he thought of their faces if he turned up with a real rifle, or even a musket. He was fairly sure his grandfather had used a musket.

Arthur had been a little better just lately. Since Frank and Ted, accompanied by their wives, had been to see him and discuss the idea of him and Mary moving into Annie's house, he had been quiet, even a little subdued, and had hardly stirred from the house. He hadn't even gone into the garden to dig the hole for the new shelter, and he hadn't once complained that Mary was starving him. She was relieved but as she'd told Jess, she still wasn't really happy about him.

'It's as if he's not there half the time. He just sits in his armchair, staring at the fireplace, and doesn't seem to hear me, nor the wireless, nor nothing. It's like he's lost all interest. All he keeps on about is that he's not doing his bit for the war. He says he's useless.'

'Poor Dad,' Jess said. 'I still think he's had a sort of breakdown. Like Ted did. And look at Ted now – right as ninepence, except that he drinks a drop too much beer these days. I'll send our Tim down, see if he can cheer him up a bit. He's always had a soft spot for Tim.'

Tim leant his bike against the front wall and knocked on the door. His grandmother opened it, her face anxious.

'Tim! I thought it was your grandad. You haven't seen him, have you?'

Tim shook his head. 'No, I thought he'd be at home. I came down to see him. I wanted to ask him something.'

Mary drew him indoors. She looked up and down the street and then shut the door. 'I'm worried stiff, Tim, I don't mind telling you. He went out after tea, said he was going for a drink up the Star. I didn't want him to go, not the way he's been just lately, but he started to get his dander up a bit and I didn't want to upset him, so I didn't say no more. I had half a mind to walk up there myself after a bit, make sure he was all right. Did you come past that way?'

'Yes, but I never saw Grandad. He must have been inside.'

Mary pulled worriedly at her lip. 'I don't know. He's been gone two hours now, and you know he's not a drinking man, not really. I don't suppose he goes to the pub more than half a dozen times a year. I think I ought to go and have a look, only I'm frightened to go out in case he comes back a different way and wanders off again.'

'I'll go,' Tim offered. 'I can go to the Jug and Bottle and ask if Grandad's there. I'll get him to come home, shall I?'

'Oh, Tim, that would be a help, it really would. Then I can stop here so that if he comes home I won't miss him. I don't know what he'd do if he came in and found the house empty, he might go off anywhere. You go and find him, Tim. He'll come home for you.'

Tim cycled off up Stubbington Avenue again. He wasn't really worried about his grandfather, but he knew that the old man was supposed to have been ill lately and Jess always said you shouldn't stay out late in the evening if you'd been poorly. The night air could give you a cold.

It was light until late in the evening now and there were plenty of people about in the street. The air-raid warnings had been fewer lately and weren't generally expected until after dark anyway. It gave everyone a bit more time to do their gardens, or just visit each other for a talk.

Tim was almost at the top of Stubbington Avenue when he saw his grandfather. He was coming down the street between two young soldiers, each rather red in the face and holding on to his arms.

'Come on, old feller,' one of them said as they drew nearer to Tim. 'Not so far now, and then we'll all sit down for a cuppa, eh? That's the ticket.'

'Cuppa?' Arthur piped. 'Cuppa? You'll be lucky, mate. My missus won't give nobody no cuppas, she never even gives me one. Starves me, she does. I 'aven't 'ad no tea for weeks. Just plain water, that's all I gets.'

'Shame,' the other soldier said. He had red hair and his cap was stuffed into his pocket. 'You'd be better off in barracks along with us.'

'That's where I'd like to be. 'Elpin' with the war, that's what I oughter be doin'. I bin in two wars already, the Boer War and the last lot, what was supposed to be the war to end all wars.' Arthur snorted. 'There'll never be no war to end all wars. But it's blokes like me they wants, blokes who's seen it already, got a bit of experience. I could tell 'em what to do. I could give old Rommel a bloody nose.'

'That's right, old chap. You tell 'em.'

'I would, too. But they won't take no notice. They don't want to listen to blokes like me, what knows a thing or two. Just chuck us on the rubbish heap, that's what they does.' Arthur's face crumpled and he began to sob. 'We ain't fit for nothing else. Rubbish, that's what we are, just useless rubbish.'

Tim could bear no more. He stopped his bike in front of the staggering trio and said, 'That's my Grandad. I've come to take him home.'

The soldiers stopped. 'Your Grandad?' The red-headed one looked at Arthur. 'That right, mate? This kid belong to you?'

Arthur peered blearily and Tim held his breath, wondering if the old man would recognise him. Then he saw the wavering eyes clear a little.

'It's our Tim. My Jess's boy,' he explained to the soldiers. 'Bin out in the country, he has, refugee or whatever they call 'em. I didn't know you'd come back,' he said to Tim.

Tim had seen him three times since his return but he said nothing. He reached out and touched his grandfather's arm. 'Come on home,' he said gently. 'Grandma's waiting for you. She's been worried.'

'Dunno why she should be,' Arthur said resentfully. 'She don't 'ave no time for me nowadays. Won't even give me a cuppa tea for me breakfast.'

The soldiers looked at Tim, who shook his head.

'He doesn't remember. He forgets everything. She gives him everything he wants.'

'Poor old sod,' the red-headed soldier said. 'He's been in the Star and Garter, asking for drinks and carrying on about the war. Only he didn't seem to know whether we were fighting the Germans or the South Africans. The landlord thought we'd better bring him home – if he could remember where that was.'

'Well, I'll take him now,' Tim said. He touched his grandfather's arm again. 'Come on, Grandad.'

Arthur was leaning against a low wall, crying softly, his old face tired and hopeless. Between his sobs, only a few words could be made out, and as he listened Tim felt his heart move oddly, as if it were twisting in his breast.

'Rubbish,' Arthur whimpered. 'Useless rubbish . . . no use to no one . . . nothing but rubbish . . .'

'Come on, Grandad.' Tim was near to tears himself. 'Come on home. Grandma's waiting for you, with a cup of tea.'

But the words seemed to mean nothing to his grandfather. Shrunken now from the man he had once been to a trembling shadow hardly bigger than Tim, Arthur allowed himself to be led down the long street to the house where he and Mary had lived for so many years. Once again, he was lost in his own world. A world where the spectres of war pressed unbearably about him, where fear and misery stalked, and despair cast a fog over his bewildered mind.

The soldiers came all the way to the front door and then slipped away, not waiting for Mary's thanks. Between them, Tim and Mary got Arthur up the stairs and into bed, with a cup of tea which he seemed unable to taste and finally left to go cold on the table beside him.

Tim went home, subdued and miserable. His grandmother got into bed beside her husband and lay wakeful for several hours before finally falling into a deep sleep.

Arthur fell asleep quickly, but woke an hour later. For a while he lay in the darkness, puzzled, unable to remember where he was. His mind was filled with images of war – of war in Africa, in the Crimea, in the trenches and fields of Flanders. He heard the ear-pounding rattle of gunfire, the scream of bombs, the drone of enemy aircraft and the incessant, tormenting wail of the siren. And at last he got out of bed and went downstairs and out into the back garden. He opened the door of the old washhouse and found a coil of washing line, and hanged himself from the pulley in the ceiling.

CHAPTER TWENTY

Arthur was buried a week later, after an inquest which concluded that he had taken his own life 'while the balance of his mind was disturbed'. Mary, who was exhausted, did not attend, and her daughters stayed at home with her while the men saw him to his resting place. Tim and Rose were sent over to Gosport to spend the day with their Uncle Howard, and Keith stayed out at Bridge End with Mr Beckett.

Olive and Betty both got leave for the day and busied themselves unobtrusively about the house, getting a few sandwiches ready for the men when they came back. They took a pot of tea into the front room, where their mother and grandmother and Auntie Jess were sitting, but didn't stay. The atmosphere in the living room, with the table laid with Annie's embroidered tablecloth and the best teacups, was more comfortable.

Like the rest of the family, Olive was very shaken by her grandfather's death, but at least it brought Derek home for a couple of days' leave and they were able to have some time together in their bedroom at Annie's house. They lay close together, reluctant to waste even a moment in sleep, each treasuring the beat of the other's heart.

'Sometimes I think this is all we're ever going to have,' Olive said. 'A day or two here and there, a couple of nights. We never have time to get used to each other.'

'I don't want to get used to you.' Derek moved his hands gently up and down her back. 'I want to feel like this about you for the rest of my life. I don't want to stop feeling excited because we're together.'

Olive laughed softly and nuzzled her face into his neck. 'Nor do I. I don't want to get like a lot of old people, just living in the same house and hardly bothering about each other. But I'd like us to be together all the time. I'd like to know that you'll be home for your tea every night and you'll be in bed with me every morning when I wake up.'

'I'd like to know that too. Specially the bed bit.' He held her hard against him. 'Oh, Livvy, I miss you so much when I'm away. And now you're in the ATS and working on that gun . . . I hate thinking of you there at night, and not in this bed where I can imagine you.'

Olive sighed. 'We've been through all this before, Derek. I told you then, I wouldn't volunteer if you didn't want me to. But even if I didn't, I'd be called up. At least this way I got a bit of choice, and I *am* back in Pompey.'

'I know, I know. It just feels queer, that's all. You doing things I don't know about. I mean, if you were still in Dad's office I'd know where you were every minute, I could picture you walking up the street and sitting down at your desk and doing your typing and invoices and things . . . Now, I just don't know where you might be, and all the time I'm scared you're going to get hurt.'

'I could get hurt just as easy in the office. We don't always get proper warnings – one of these hit-and-run raiders comes over, and half the street's flattened before anyone knows a thing about it. Anyway, don't you think it's the same for me? I don't know what you're doing. I've never even seen the camp, only from outside when I've come down to see you on a few weekends. And you could be bombed just the same.'

'I know. I'm sorry, Livvy. It just takes a bit of getting used to, that's all – knowing you've got a whole life that's nothing to do with me.'

'I tell you about it,' she said, feeling a little hurt. 'Maybe you don't really like me having it – is that what it is? Or maybe it's because I enjoy it. You don't think I should.'

'I never said that.' He held her more closely. 'That makes me sound really selfish. I'm glad you're doing something you enjoy. But – well, a man *likes* to know what his wife's doing. It doesn't seem right, that's all, you doing things I don't know about.'

'You think I'm not telling you things I ought to tell you. You think I'm keeping secrets from you. But they're only war secrets, Derek – things we all have to keep quiet about. There's nothing else.' She looked anxiously into his face. 'You do believe that, don't you? You do trust me?'

'Of course I do.' But they both knew that, in a strange way, she was right, and Olive was silent. It was true that there were things she didn't tell Derek. And the main thing was that, although he knew she enjoyed her work, she was always careful not to let him know just how much she enjoyed it.

She had found something in the Ack-ack team that she had never known before, and she liked it. She liked the sense of urgency, the knowledge that she was doing something real in the war effort, and she liked the company of the rest of the team. She had never before experienced the camaraderie of a group of people who forged special bonds through working closely together. It gave her a special glow that she took pains to conceal from Derek, knowing that he might be hurt by it.

And concealing anything from Derek added to that tiny gulf and made it just a little wider.

She clutched him fiercely against her. 'I love you, Derek. I *love* you. Nothing's going to come between us – nothing. I won't let it. I won't let anything happen to us.'

'Of course it won't.' He spoke gently, comfortingly. 'We're special, Livvy. We'll come through this and we'll be together always, sleeping in the same bed every night. Don't sound so frightened. Everything'll be all right one day.' He ran his hand down her spine and she shivered and pressed closer. 'Everything'll be all right,' he repeated. 'Nothing's going to happen to us.'

Everything will be all right.

Dennis and Betty told each other this too. It was what everyone said – it *won't happen to us, nothing can come between us, we're special*. Yet even as they spoke the words, they knew that it couldn't be true for everybody. It's true for us, they insisted, it's got to be true for us. You couldn't go on, day after day, if you didn't believe that.

'The more experience I get, the safer I am,' Dennis said. 'I know every bomb now like the back of my hand. I could defuse them with my eyes shut.'

'Well, don't try to prove it,' Betty said. 'The Germans are tricky devils. You know they keep changing things so that you'll be taken by surprise.'

'That's what makes the job so interesting,' Dennis said with a grin. 'Never the same from one day to the next. Keeps you on your toes.'

'Stay on them, then, ready to run. Don't forget, we've got a wedding to have.'

They had not yet decided where to have their wedding. At first, Betty had wanted to be married in church, like her sister Olive, but Ted was still against their marriage and she was afraid he would refuse to give her away. And the serene gentleness of the Quaker way was becoming more and more attractive to her.

'Come to Meeting with me,' Dennis said. 'You'll see what it's like then, and you can choose. I'll do whatever makes you feel happiest, Betty.'

They went to Portsmouth and stayed with Dennis's parents. Betty had been there several times now, and grown accustomed to the quiet house and the serenity of the two elderly people who lived there. Robert and Cecily Verney had married in their thirties and Dennis had been born five years later, the only child they were to have. Now Robert was seventy years old, a tall, rather thin man with silver hair and kind grey eyes, and Cecily was a small, bright little wren of a woman, always busy yet never harassed. They welcomed Betty as if she were already their daughter, and she found herself in the kitchen with her sleeves rolled up, making scones as if she'd lived there all her life.

'I love getting my hands into a bowl of flour,' Cecily said, bustling about the old-fashioned kitchen. 'It seems such a natural thing – something women have been doing for thousands of years. Making a home and family, feeding people you love – it's what life is for, isn't it?'

Betty had never thought of it like that. Doing household chores and cooking meals had always seemed to her to be something you had to do but would rather not. Something you got out of the way as soon as possible so that you could go on to more interesting things. And even though her own mother took great pride in the whiteness of her step, the crispness of her curtains and the quality of the food she served, it was more a matter of pride itself than as a service to her family.

Everything Cecily did, from cleaning the lavatory to polishing the furniture, seemed to be done as a gift, either to her family or her God. It didn't matter that it would soon all have to be done again – that simply gave her the chance to renew her gift. And if she didn't have time to complete all the tasks, or if something went wrong, she accepted it as the way of the world, and felt content that she had done all that was possible.

'We're all human beings,' she said to Betty. 'We can't work miracles. Yet we all have the seed of God within us, which can help us to achieve so much more than we think is possible.'

Betty was getting used to these ideas now. At first, she had been embarrassed by Dennis's references to God – although her mother was a churchgoer, there was seldom any 'religious' talk at home – but she was coming to appreciate the certainty they all had of their beliefs, and the tolerance that they had for others.

'Of course we *think* we're right,' Robert Verney said with a smile. 'But nobody can know for certain. And there are many paths to the top of a mountain. The view may be the same for all of us, once we reach it.'

As Dennis had suggested, Betty accompanied them to their Sunday morning Meeting. She felt rather timid about it, knowing that the entire hour might be spent in silence unless someone felt compelled to speak, but the rest of the people there welcomed her smilingly and drew her into their circle. She sat beside Dennis, listening to the silence and slowly feeling herself relax.

There was no form of service, no prayers or hymns. A few children sat on the benches, most holding a toy of some sort, and after twenty minutes they all got up and went out with a dark-haired young woman who was carrying a book. Betty supposed she would read to them, or let them play or draw pictures. The adult members sat on, their eyes closed or fixed on the floor or the ceiling. She wondered what they were thinking of.

You weren't really supposed to think about anything, Dennis had said. You were supposed to empty your mind and let God speak through you, if he wished. You weren't supposed to come with anything prepared, because that would be 'you' speaking and not God. You weren't supposed to know what you were going to say, or even that you were going to speak at all.

'You're just a mouthpiece,' he said.

'Like a sort of loudspeaker, or megaphone?'

'That's right,' Dennis said with a grin, 'but not so loud.'

It seemed to Betty that anything that broke this silence would sound unnaturally loud. She wondered if anyone would dare to get up.

The meeting was almost three-quarters over before anyone stirred. And then Robert Verney rose to his feet and laid his hand lightly on Betty's shoulder.

'Something very good has happened in our family this week. Our son Dennis has told us that he is planning to marry Betty and make her our daughter. It has shown us that even in these dark and terrible days, good may come out of evil, for if it had not been for this war these two might never have met. And how many others are meeting and finding love through the chaos that the world is in today? How much love is growing out of the ruins of our cities and our countries, as plants and flowers are growing on the places where bombs have fallen? Let us all look around us and see the good that is proving triumphant each day, and thank God for the brightness of his love.'

He sat down again. Nobody moved or spoke, but Betty felt a breath of warmth stir the air, as gentle as a sigh. She felt Dennis's hand touch hers and let him fold her fingers in his palm.

After a while, a woman rose to her feet, and then another man, each to give their own example of love coming out of the war. And as they stood chatting afterwards in the little garden that surrounded the Meeting House, Betty felt that she had been touched by the serenity that she had noticed both in Dennis's parents and the other members of the Meeting. It was something like the feeling of 'goodness' that she'd had after church as a child, yet it went deeper than that. As they walked home, she was thoughtful, and later she asked Dennis what happened at a Quaker wedding.

'Well, it's something like a Meeting,' Dennis said. 'But of course everyone knows they're there for the wedding, so there's more preparation. But we all sit quietly until the bridegroom feels that the right moment has come, and then he stands up and says that he wants to marry the bride and she says she wants to marry him, and really that's all there is to it.'

'That's all?' Betty said. 'It doesn't sound much.'

'Well, they do make their vows. But they make them in their own words, not just repeating what someone else is telling them – and it seems to mean more. It's really very moving.'

'But suppose they can't think what to say? I mean, they might miss out something important.'

'Well, they do have the Certificate on the table in front of them, so they can read it if they need to,' Dennis said, 'and don't forget that God is there to help.'

Betty was silent. She wasn't sure that she believed that God was inside her, a part of her, telling her what to say. If he was, the devil must be there too, she thought, because all too often she said the wrong thing.

'I always thought I'd get married in church,' she said. 'With a white dress and veil and everything. You don't have them at Quaker weddings, do you?'

347

'No, we don't really believe in dressing up. But if that's what you want, Betty, that's what we'll do. Whichever way we choose to get married, it won't make any difference to me because as far as I'm concerned we're married already. This is just a sort of declaration to all our friends. And a legal certificate, of course!'

Betty laid her head against his shoulder. She wanted to say that it didn't matter to her either. But it still did, a little, and she knew that she could not pretend. There had to be real honesty between herself and Dennis.

'Let's think about it a little while longer,' she said. 'Let me have some time to get used to the idea.'

For a few weeks it seemed as though there was a brief respite in the tribulations of the war. Bomber Command was making heavy attacks on Germany – a thousand aircraft at a time were sent to bomb cities like Cologne, Essen and Bremen, reciprocating the blitz on London and other British cities. The fires were seen almost two hundred miles away and although many like Jess thought of the innocent lives – children and old people – that were being lost, the general opinion was that it was a just reprisal and essential in the conduct of the war.

'Serves 'em right,' Ethel Glaister said viciously, and even Tommy Vickers shook his head and said, 'It's got to be done. You can't hold back when you're fighting someone like Hitler.'

In Portsmouth, Stay-at-Home Holidays were the fashion. Few people would have gone away anyway, unless they had relatives to visit, but now the local authorities took some trouble to arrange entertainment for those who had to stay in Portsmouth. A Naval and Military Tattoo was staged at Fratton Park, and the Royal Marine and Naval bands gave performances every week at Hilsea Lido, Milton Park and Southsea Common. Jess and Frank went out to a few, but for the most part Frank worked on the allotment, using his week's holiday to get the ground ready for the next crop of vegetables.

'There were a few funny things in the paper last night,' Cherry remarked as she ate Sunday tea with Jess and Frank. 'It said that since the year 1400 BC, the world's had three thousand, one hundred and twenty years of war and only two hundred and ninety-one years of peace. How do they know that, I wonder? I didn't think history went back that far.'

'I suppose they use the Bible,' Frank said. He was feeding the cat Henry with small triangular pieces of bread, spread with fish paste. 'That's full of wars. I dunno why they have to print that sort of stuff though – supposed to cheer us up, is it?'

'There was another bit. D'you know, the Isle of Man's been in a state of war with Germany for the past twenty-eight years! They forgot to invite them to Versailles after the last war, so they never signed the peace treaty. It's like not inviting one of the fairies to the Princess's christening, isn't it.'

'What fairies?' Frank asked in bewilderment. 'And which Princess? Are you talking about Princess Elizabeth or Margaret Rose?'

'No, of course I'm not, you daft ha'porth. The Sleeping Beauty and that sort of princess. *You* know what I means, don't you, Jess?'

'Of course I do,' Jess said, laughing. 'But Frank's mind doesn't run much on fairy tales.'

'Anyway,' Frank said, trying to redeem himself with his own touch of humour, 'if they've been at war with Germany all that time, it's a pity they didn't do something about Hitler before. They could have saved us all this trouble.'

'Oh, they've always been an independent lot,' Cherry observed. 'It comes of having three legs.' She winked at Rose and Tim. 'Did you know that? About people in the Isle of Man having three legs?'

'Of course I did,' Tim said. 'That's why they turn cartwheels instead of walking. And people from Portland have got tails, I bet you didn't know that. And if you take polar bears to the Antarctic, the penguins kill them.'

The three adults stared at him. 'The penguins kill them? How?'

'They get stuck in their throats,' Tim said, and went off into a peal of laughter while Jess and Frank groaned and Rose rolled her eyes.

'It's just one of his stupid jokes. He's always making jokes.'

'Well, I think it was a right funny one,' Cherry declared, her small, round body shaking. 'You're a star turn, you are, Tim, and no mistake. My godfathers, I wish I could think up jokes like that. The penguins kill them! Eh, I'll have to remember that to tell 'em in the boiler-shop tomorrow.'

'D'you often tell them jokes?' Tim asked curiously.

'Well, we have to do something to pass the time along. No use going around with our faces down to our knees. That's not going to win the war.'

'You mean telling jokes helps win the war? You mean it's patriotic?'

'Don't encourage him,' Jess began, but Cherry was already nodding her head.

'Of course, Anything that keeps a smile on people's faces is patriotic. Look at Tommy Handley and Arthur Askey and Charlie Chester. And George Formby, going out to entertain the troops. And I bet it does people good to see your cheeky face coming round with their medicines.'

Tim strummed an imaginary banjo. '*You should see the things I see, when I'm cleaning windows . . .*' He caught his father's eye and stopped hastily, though not without muttering something about 'being patriotic', and sniggered behind his hand.

'You'll make him worse,' Jess told Cherry. 'He's getting above himself lately. Thinks he's grown up because we've let him have a few weeks off school and he's got a job. You know you've got to go back to Bridge End after the holidays,' she said to Tim.

Tim made a face. 'Do I have to? I like being at work.'

'Yes, you do have to,' Frank said severely. 'You're only just coming up to thirteen. You're not leaving until you've got a good education behind you. I want you to have the chances I should have had.'

'But I don't see what good learning History and stuff like that does. I'm going to be an explorer.'

'You'll need to learn Geography, then,' Frank said smartly. 'Or you won't know where to explore. You don't know much about the world as it is. D'you know where the Galapagos Islands are? Or New Guinea?'

'I know where Japan is,' Tim said. 'And Burma. And Java, and Malta, and the Yangtse River. I bet you didn't know those places when you were thirteen.'

'That's enough, Tim,' Jess began, seeing Frank's face darken, but for once her husband wasn't about to tell Tim off for being cheeky. He looked at her and shook his head.

'All places that are caught up in the war. You're right, Tim. I didn't know about all those places when I was your age. I didn't need to. But all the same, I want you to go back to school and learn as much as you can. Things are going to be different once this lot's over. We're going to need people who've had an education. And I want you to have a better chance than I did.'

'Your dad's right,' Cherry said. 'It's a hard life doing the sort of work he does. I wouldn't like to see you having to slave like he does in that boiler-shop.'

Jess looked at her. It was strange that Cherry knew so much about Frank, things that Jess herself had never known and would never see. It was as if he had two lives and Cherry was allowed into them both, whereas Jess was shut out.

But there were no feelings of jealousy or envy in Jess these days. She felt secure and comfortable in Frank's love, and knew that whatever relationship he might have with Cherry, it could never threaten her. Indeed, she felt now that Cherry was almost as much her friend as his.

She'd been even more her friend since Arthur's terrible death, coming round at once to offer whatever help might be needed, sitting and listening as Jess wept, even managing to offer some comfort to Tim and Rose. It was funny that a little woman without any looks, who'd never been married herself or had children, should seem to know just what to say. And it wasn't empty comfort, either. It was down-to-earth common sense.

Jess knew nothing of the words Dennis's father had spoken at the Quaker meeting. But dimly, she felt the same wonder that, out of a war that had brought about so many terrible things, there were still bright new spots of friendship and love to help them on their way.

Perhaps Tim was right. Making jokes *was* patriotic. Anything that kept a smile on people's faces had to be good.

I just wish we could have Keith at home too, she thought wistfully. Then there really would be something to smile about.

CHAPTER TWENTY-ONE

The Home Carol Glaister was taken to by her mother was at Godalming, near Guildford. She wasn't likely to run into many Portsmouth people there, and in any case the house was right out in the countryside and it didn't look as if the girls left it very often, especially as their condition began to show.

It wasn't at all what Carol had expected. She'd thought it would be like a hospital, with rows of beds, or perhaps like the boarding schools she'd read about. Instead, it was just a big house with a lot of bedrooms and three or four large rooms downstairs. One of these rooms was private – she and Ethel went in there when they arrived, to be interviewed – and the rest were for the girls' use. There was a dining room with a big table, a sitting room with a lot of rather shabby armchairs, and a sewing room with a few treadle machines and some trestle tables spread with material and half-made baby-clothes.

It was all rather bare, with no carpets on the wooden floors, and the decorations looked as if they'd been done a long time ago and needed renewing. There were some girls, all in different stages of pregnancy, sweeping and dusting in the big rooms and sitting at the machines and tables in the sewing-room. The glanced at Carol with automatic curiosity, running their eyes expertly over her body.

The woman who ran the Home was called Mrs Whiting. She was middle-aged, with a big bust, and wore a tweed suit. She spoke in a posh voice, as if she were just finishing a toffee. She offered Ethel and Carol a cup of tea and told them to sit down.

'Now, let me see, you're expecting delivery some time in November.' Her voice was as brisk and matter-of-fact as if she was talking about a parcel, Carol felt a sudden urge to giggle. 'Well, I don't usually take gels quite this early, but I understand there are special circumstances in this case. A rather unpleasant court case . . . yes, I think you're quite right, Mrs Glaister, it will be a good idea to have Carol away from home. Less to remind her.'

But I want to remember, Carol thought. However, she did not have the energy to say so. Since agreeing to come here, she had been sunk in a state of lethargy and couldn't raise the strength to object to anything. All she could think of now was that at least she'd be free of her mother. Just go away and leave me, she begged Ethel silently. Just leave me alone.

Mrs Whiting was asking a series of questions now, all of which Ethel answered, and again Carol had no energy to make any objection. Roddy didn't 'take me away', she thought, and he didn't take advantage of me. And he never took that money, Mum knows that. But whatever Ethel might say to Carol in private, she was not going to let anyone else think ill of her daughter. That was too much a reflection on herself as a mother.

'Well, I think that's all very satisfactory,' Mrs Whiting said at last. She had been making notes in a folder and now she closed it and gave Ethel a polite smile. 'I think Carol will get along very well with us.'

'I don't want her mixing with any rough girls, mind,' Ethel said. 'She's been brought up nice. Just because she's in this trouble now –'

'I quite understand. And I can assure you we have no "rough" gels here,' Mrs Whiting said coldly. 'I'm very careful who I take, and any gel who doesn't know how to behave is sent home at once.' She gave Ethel a stern glance, as if to say that she would know just who to blame if Carol didn't behave herself. 'Of course, you understand that Carol will have to work while she's here. I don't believe in giving these gels the lap of luxury to live in. Some of them will have to be fending for themselves when they leave here, and some actually choose to keep their babies. I give them all a good grounding in housework and cooking, and they make all their own maternity clothes and a *layette*, whether they're keeping the child or not.'

'Well, that's something,' Ethel said. 'It's costing enough as it is. At least she'll be learning something useful.'

'Most of the costs are met by charity,' Mrs Whiting pointed out with a touch of acid in her voice. 'We're asking only that you pay what it would normally cost you to keep the gel at home. And to provide her with a small sum as pocket money for personal necessities and so on.'

'Pocket money!' Ethel grumbled. 'Ought to be out earning her own living, that's what she ought to be doing. Shouldn't be costing me a penny by now.'

But Mrs Whiting refused to be drawn into any argument. Instead, she pressed a button in the wall beside the fireplace and after a few minutes the door opened and a girl came in. She looked about nineteen, and she was heavily pregnant.

'Show Carol the bedroom, Susan,' Mrs Whiting ordered. 'Carol will be in Room Three with you and Ann and Mary. Then you can take her to the kitchen. I daresay there'll be a job there she can do.'

She stood up and offered her hand to Ethel. 'We think it's best for the girls to feel part of the establishment at once. I expect you'll be wanting to catch your train. I believe there's one soon after two o'clock. It's a pleasant walk back to town, and you've got plenty of time – you'll be able to have a snack lunch in the little cafeteria on the station.'

Ethel stared at her. She opened her mouth and then closed it again. Once more, Carol had the urge to giggle, but she was afraid that if she did she might cry instead. Now that the moment had almost come, she felt an unexpected reluctance to be left here alone.

I wish all this had never happened, she thought miserably, but that would mean that she would never have met Roddy, and that was a thought she couldn't bear. Pushing it from her mind, she followed Susan out of the room, aware of her mother close behind.

'Well!' Ethel said as soon as the door was closed. '*She* won't stand for no nonsense, you can see that. You'll have to mind your p's and q's here, young woman, or you'll be back on the doorstep so fast you won't know what's hit you – and you won't be getting no welcome from *me* if that happens, I can tell you. I'm not going through all this caper again.'

They stood in the hall, looking at each other uncertainly. I suppose we've got to say goodbye now, Carol thought. That Mrs Whiting didn't say anything about Mum coming upstairs. She darted a quick glance at her mother's face and then looked down at the floor.

'Cheerio then, Mum,' she mumbled, and half turned away.

'Well, is that all you can say?' Ethel exclaimed. '*Cheerio?* When we might not see each other for months, and by then you'll – you'll have had –' She seemed unable to say the words. Instead, she reached out both hands and grabbed Carol by the arms, dragging her closer. 'Don't I even get a kiss? I am your mother, after all.'

Carol submitted to the awkward kiss bestowed upon her – the first she could remember for years – and stepped back thankfully when it was over. Ethel produced a small, lace-edged handkerchief from her handbag and touched it to her eyes.

'You be a good girl, mind. Write to me regular. And I won't say but what I might not try and get up to see you some time – before it's all over. But you know how it is these days, I'm so busy, what with your father and Joe and little Shirley . . .' Her eyes flickered sideways and Carol realised that she was keeping one eye on the door to Mrs Whiting's room, and one eye on Susan, who was standing by looking bored. Of course, she thought. Mum wouldn't want to give them the impression she didn't care about me.

'Yeah, all right,' she said, and turned away again. 'Cheerio.'

She didn't wait to see Ethel go out of the front door. She followed Susan up to the large, bare bedroom, nodded silently as she was shown her own iron bed with its brown blankets, and listened as she was told which chest of drawers was hers and where she could hang her clothes. Then she went down to the kitchen.

There were several girls there, all preparing vegetables or making pastry. Carol was given a pile of potatoes to peel. She started to scrape at them with a knife, misery weighing like a lump of lead on her heart.

Roddy doesn't even know where I am now, she thought. And I don't know where he is either. We might as well be in different worlds.

Out at Bridge End, Keith was feeling miserable. He missed Tim and was fed up with being with Stella and Muriel. He resented being the only member of the family who was still evacuated – as if he were a baby, he thought, kicking at stones as he mooched through the country lanes. But Maureen was a baby, and *she* wasn't evacuated, It wasn't fair.

'I think it was a lot better before the war started,' he grumbled to Mrs Mudge. 'We used to go out to the beach at Southsea and stay all day. We'd get the bus from Copnor and take sandwiches and lemonade and Dad would swim right out deep and take us on his back. One at a time,' he added, not wishing Mrs Mudge to imagine a picture of the three of them sitting on Frank's back in a row, like Indians paddling a canoe. 'And there were sweets in the shops, loads and loads of sweets in big jars. Me and Tim used to go and look in the window and choose what to buy.'

'What sort of sweets did you buy?' Mrs Mudge asked, only half attending. She was making a casserole with corned beef and haricot beans. A bowl of dried egg, mixed with water, stood on the table beside her, ready to be used for a cake. 'I used to like a nice toffee myself, with nuts in, but since I had my plate I can't manage them, they get stuck. It's like figs, the pips get right underneath. Not that you see a lot of figs these days,' she added with a sigh.

'We couldn't afford toffees,' Keith said. 'We only got threepence a week. I used to get sherbet balls mostly, the pink and white ones. They go all fizzy in your mouth. Tim used to get mint humbugs – they had little ones, you'd get quite a lot in two ounces. Or liquorice bootlaces.'

'Well, you can still get your sweets,' Mrs Mudge said. 'You're allowed two ounces a week.' But Keith knew it wasn't the same. The few sweets that were still available were rationed now and you had to give up 'points' for them. And there wasn't any fun in choosing any more – Mrs Mudge had the ration book and she did the shopping and just gave the children whatever she'd managed to buy.

'Nothing's any fun any more,' Keith said glumly. 'We're not even getting a proper holiday this summer. School's going on all through August. It's not fair.'

'Well, you'll just have to learn to be thankful for what there is,' the housekeeper said a little sharply. She was sorry for the children, but she was too busy looking after the rambling vicarage and trying to make meals out of almost nothing to be very sympathetic towards Keith – he might miss his brother, but he hadn't lost anyone, after all. And she was anxious about Mr Beckett, who was looking more and more tired. 'Go and play outside. It's too nice a day for you to be sculling about indoors.'

Keith went out, but he was no longer interested in fishing for sticklebacks or picking blackberries. He kicked idly at stones and threw sticks at birds and wished he could go back to Portsmouth too.

'But you've always got along so well with Stella and Muriel,' Mr Beckett said later, when Keith refused to go swimming with them. 'You'll hurt their feelings if you keep behaving like this.'

Keith shrugged. 'So are my feelings hurt. Nobody cares about that.'

'Of course they do,' Mr Beckett was beginning, when the door from the kitchen suddenly burst open and Mrs Mudge erupted into the room, her face scarlet and wet with tears, and her lips working. She was waving an orange telegram envelope and trying to say something, but her words were drowned by sobs.

'My dear Mrs Mudge! What is it? Whatever's happened?' The vicar caught at the envelope and tore the flimsy sheet of paper from inside. 'Is it your son? Has something happened –?' He stared at the sheet, and Keith saw his face go suddenly grey. 'Oh, how dreadful. How perfectly dreadful.'

Keith felt a moment of panic. He knew very well what a telegram meant. They hardly ever brought good news. They came to say when people had been killed, or taken prisoner of war. And everyone stopped what they were doing when they saw the familiar red bike of a telegraph boy come spinning along the street. Everyone had the same moment of fear, dreading that it might be for them, dreading what news it might contain.

Mrs Mudge's son Stanley was in the Army. He'd been away ever since the war began and Keith had never seen him. He stared at her now, trying to imagine what it must be like to hear that your son had been killed thousands of miles away.

But she was shaking her head. 'It's not my Stanley. Thank God, it's not him. But oh, those poor little girls, those poor, dear little girls –'

'Stella and Muriel?' Keith asked, his voice high with fear. 'What's happened to Stella and Muriel? They were all right just now, I saw them in the garden –' He realised that the telegram couldn't possibly concern them and his thoughts flew to the only other two girls he could think of in that moment. 'Is it our Rose and Maureen? What's happened to them? What is it?'

Mr Beckett turned his head and looked down at him. For a moment or two, his eyes were blank, almost as if he didn't know who Keith was. At last he spoke, his voice remote, as if it were coming from a great distance.

'It's not Rose and Maureen,' he said quietly, and laid his hand on Keith's shoulder. 'It's not your sisters.' He paused and then said, 'Keith, I'm going to ask you to be very brave and very kind. You see, we're going to have to help Stella and Muriel quite a lot.' He looked again at the telegram, as if to make sure that it really did say what he thought it said. 'Mr Simmons – their father – has been killed. His ship was on convoy, taking essential supplies to Malta. It was hit by

German bombers and sunk.' His voice shook a little. 'This is going to make them very unhappy indeed.'

'You mean he's dead?' Keith repeated. 'He's not coming back? Not ever?'

'Not ever.'

'But they haven't got a mum,' Keith argued, as if the Germans would surely have taken this into account. 'That means they're orphans. Won't they be able to stop here any more?'

'Of course they'll be able to stop here,' Mr Beckett said sharply. 'And you're not to say anything to them to make them think they can't. I told you, we've got to be very kind.' He paused. Keith was only a child, he had no real comprehension of what it all meant. Or had he? Children were forced to grow up so quickly these days . . . He turned to Mrs Mudge. 'Call them in, my dear. I'd better tell them at once. Keith, why don't you go out for a little while. And when you next see the girls, just tell them how sorry you are. There won't be any need to ask a lot of questions.'

The news left the two little girls stunned.

'But we haven't got anybody now,' Muriel said in a bewildered voice. 'We haven't got Mummy, or our baby, *or* Daddy. Who's going to look after us?'

Mr Beckett shook his head. It was almost unbearable to try to imagine what must be in their minds. They'd already been through the blitz, seeing their own home bombed twice and their mother and baby brother killed. They'd had to wave goodbye to their father, knowing he was going into danger, and now they had to face the fact of his death. All this, and they were still at an age which ought to be concerned with nothing more worrying than how to dress their dolls. It was quite inhuman.

And we're doing the same thing, he thought heavily. In Germany, there are little girls just like this, and boys like Tim and Keith, facing just the same tragedies. What *is* the world about, to allow it all to happen?

'Mrs Mudge and I will look after you,' he said gently. 'This is your home – at least until someone says there is another home for you to go to. And try to remember that whatever your father suffered, it must have been very quick –' he hoped that was true '– and it's all over now. He's at peace, with all the other brave men and women who have died in this war.' This cruel and terrible war.

'Daddy . . . ?' Muriel said, still in the same bewildered voice. 'Daddy's not coming home? But we *waved* to him. We waved really hard.'

'No,' Stella said in a hard, unchildlike voice, 'we didn't wave to him, Mu. We waved to some other daddies. We just pretended it was him.' She moved away and stared out of the window, her eyes blank and hopeless. 'I don't suppose there was anybody who waved to him, not really.'

'You mean it was *our fault*?' Muriel said, her voice breaking, and before either Mr Beckett or Mrs Mudge could speak, the tears were pouring down her cheeks. She cried loudly, sitting quite still in her chair, her mouth a square hole in her crimson face. It was almost like an animal in pain, Mr Beckett thought despairingly, like a dog howling at the moon. He looked helplessly at Mrs Mudge, and the housekeeper gathered Muriel against her bosom, stroking her hair and murmuring in her ear. But nothing, it seemed, would stop Muriel's weeping.

'It's natural,' Mrs Mudge said quietly, under cover of the sobs. 'She needs to let it out.' She reached out an arm to Stella. 'Come here, Stell. You need a good cry too. It'll make you feel better.'

'How will it?' the older girl demanded. 'Mum and Dad will still be dead, won't they? And our Tom? Crying's not going to bring them back to life.'

'Nothing's going to bring them back to life,' Mr Beckett said quietly. 'But there isn't anything we can do about that now. We have to think about you and Muriel, and you have to think about yourselves. It's quite right to cry at times like these. Mrs Mudge is right. It helps to mourn.'

'Like when we were bombed out,' Stella said in the same hard voice. 'Like when Mum and our Tom were blown to bits. And now Dad –' She stood up, looking away from Mr Beckett and Mrs Mudge. 'I'm fed up with crying. It doesn't do any good.'

'Stella –' Mr Beckett said, reaching towards her. But she backed away, like an animal afraid to be touched, and looked at him with stony eyes.

'I'm going upstairs,' she said, and was out of the room before anyone could move.

Mrs Mudge looked at the vicar. She was still holding Muriel, who was sobbing now against her chest. 'I suppose we'd better let her go. Perhaps she'll cry when she's alone. But I don't like to think of her, grieving all by herself. She needs some comfort.'

'We all have to grieve in our own way,' Mr Beckett said. 'And I daresay we'll have plenty of chances to help poor Stella. It's been a terrible shock for her – for them both.' He moved across and stroked Muriel's hair. 'Poor little souls. It's a cruel, cruel world.'

'The poor little scraps,' Mrs Mudge said later. Her eyes were red with crying. 'Haven't they got any other relatives at all?'

'Only Mike's mother, and she's in a mental hospital. She doesn't recognise anyone. And poor young Mrs Simmons lost her parents when she was a child. She was brought up by her grandmother and an aunt, but I believe they're both dead now.'

Mr Beckett sighed and reached for his cup of cocoa. It had taken Mrs Mudge all evening to get Muriel to go to sleep, and even now she was likely to cry out and wake again. And Stella was still lying stiffly in her bed, refusing to speak at all.

'What's going to happen to them, then?'

Mr Beckett shook his head. 'It's up to the authorities. I hope they'll leave them with us for the time being – there's no point in taking them away. We're all the family they've got.'

'It's a shame you can't adopt them,' Mrs Mudge said thoughtfully.

'I'd like to. But – I don't know. I'm an old man, Mrs Mudge. I'll be getting on for eighty by the time those two are grown up. What I'd like is to see them settled with some nice family. The Budds would be ideal – Mrs Budd's a motherly little body and Mr Budd's a decent man. And they get along well with the boys and Rose. But all they've got is that tiny terraced house, with two bedrooms. I don't know how they fit their family in as it is.'

'They couldn't afford it, anyway,' Mrs Mudge agreed. 'Two extra children on a dockyardman's wage . . . And I don't suppose there'll be much coming to the girls from their dad.'

'Well, we must just carry on as we are.' The vicar stood up and stretched his thin, spidery body. 'Everyone's so busy these days, I daresay they'll be glad to leave the girls with us.'

It wasn't just the girls, he thought, making his way upstairs. It was Keith as well. He knew the boy had been frightened and unsettled by the news of Mike Simmons' death. He didn't know how to cope with it. He had only met Mr Simmons once, so couldn't feel any grief, and Stella and Muriel's despair frightened and embarrassed him. His mind was mixed up with a blur of reality and fairy-tales – the word 'orphan' came straight out of the Brothers Grimm and conjured up visions of children wandering lost in everlastingly bleak landscapes. He pictured Stella and Muriel, setting off hand in hand on a journey that had no end.

'Where *do* people go when they're dead?' he asked Mr Beckett when the vicar came in to say goodnight. He'd been asking this question for years and nobody had ever been able to answer it satisfactorily, but now it seemed even more urgent to find an answer. 'I mean, there's so many people dying now, Heaven must be getting ever so crowded. Suppose there's not room for them all? What happens then?'

'There's room for everyone,' the vicar said, but even he had begun to wonder lately. 'Heaven is infinite.'

'I don't know what that means,' Keith said a little sulkily. He didn't like it when people used words he couldn't understand.

'Without end,' Mr Beckett said, feeling on surer ground

now. 'Like the sky. Think of the stars at night, Keith, going on for ever and ever, further than we can see. Millions and millions of them, stretching out in space for millions and millions of miles.'

'But they must come to an end,' Keith argued. 'Even millions and *millions* of miles have got to come to an end sometime.'

'Not in infinity. And not in Heaven.' The vicar placed his hand on Keith's shoulder. 'Don't worry about it, Keith. Don't even try to understand. None of us can, our minds aren't able to take it in. Just have faith.'

But it wasn't easy to have faith, when you were living with two little girls who had no mother or father, no uncles, aunts or grandparents, and who didn't seem to believe in anything any more.

Stella lay in bed, staring into the darkness. In the garden, under her window, was the shaggy patch of grass where nothing else would grow, the patch where she and Muriel had been playing the day Daddy had come to see them. She could see him now, tall and sunburnt, watching them over the gate. She could feel the joy leap in her breast as she jumped up and ran towards him. And now he would never stand there again, and she would never feel his arms around her or see that broad smile which lit up his eyes and made even his curly hair look as if it were laughing.

Daddy, Daddy . . .

The tears made her throat ache. But she'd cried before, when they'd come out of the Anderson shelter, right back at the beginning of the war when the raids had begun, and seen their house no more than a ruin. She'd cried for her dolls and her toys, for the little bedroom she and Muriel had shared, that Mummy had made so pretty with flowery curtains and pale green wallpaper. She'd cried when she saw the house they were to live in in October Street, bare and damp and stinking of cats' pee.

Daddy . . .

And she'd cried again when the bomb had hit that house, and they'd told her that Mummy had gone for ever, and her baby brother Thomas. Stella had seen Thomas being born, she'd helped look after him, she'd held him and bathed him and changed his nappies. She hadn't been able to believe that he was dead. He'd only been a few months old. What was the use of being born at all, if that was going to happen to you?

The crying had hurt. It had hurt her chest and her throat and made her nose swell and her eyes sore. And it hadn't done any good. It wouldn't do any good now.

She lay with her face to the wall, her hands clenched, her anger building inside her like a hard, jagged lump, refusing to cry, refusing to sleep.

But she could not stay awake for ever. And when she slept at last, the images in her brain grew larger and darker, their shadows looming over her like menacing ghosts. She heard the roar of the aircraft, the thunder of exploding bombs, the crash of falling houses. She heard the screams and the shouts, the panic and the sobs, and she could no longer refuse to cry, no longer refuse to understand that her father was dead, that he had died like her mother and brother, blown apart by a German bomb as he did what his country had required him to do in a quarrel that was not of his own making.

She knew, and she understood, and her understanding welled up in a searing nightmare of grief and anger, of fear and despair.

She sat bolt upright in bed, and her screams rang through the silent house.

'*Daddy! Daddy! Daddy!*'

CHAPTER TWENTY-TWO

The bombing began again in August, and Portsmouth suffered its first air-raid for over a year – the fifty-eighth raid of the war. Eight high-explosive bombs were dropped around Cosham, on the railway embankment and in the grounds of the mental hospital. Four failed to detonate and Dennis and his team were called out to deal with them.

'The trains have been stopped,' Captain Anderson said. 'One of the bombs is sticking out of the embankment, one's in the hospital grounds, the others have buried themselves. The thing we've got to decide is which one to deal with first.'

They examined each site. The bomb sticking out of the embankment had a clockwork fuse-pocket in plain view on top of it. The Pioneers were already digging carefully down to its mate, at the bottom of a deep crater about twenty yards away. The third had landed much too close for comfort, and the fourth had dug itself a pit in the middle of the hospital gardens. It had been cordoned off, but the hospital windows were crowded with curious faces.

'You'll have to get all those people away from there,' Captain Anderson said sharply to the matron. 'If that goes off, it'll probably shatter every window and they'll be cut to ribbons.'

'It's the patients. They're fascinated by anything different.'

'Well, they'll have to be fascinated somewhere else. Get 'em round the back of the building.' He turned to Dennis. 'Which d'you think we'd better deal with first?'

'This one's nearest to civilians. But the others could cause a lot of damage to the railway, and it's the main line from Portsmouth to the West Country. They'll take longer to deal with, too, the three of them.'

'During which time this little beauty might blow up and take the hospital with it.' The Captain frowned and pulled his lip. 'Get the men over here. They'd be halfway down if they'd started straight away.'

The officer in charge of the Pioneers wasn't too pleased to have his decision countermanded, but he brought his men across and they began to build a shaft down to the bottom of the crater. The bomb could be seen nose-down in the chalk, its tail sticking out – one of the least attractive propositions a bomb disposal team could work on for, until the earth was scraped away from its sides, its type and condition couldn't be assessed, and nobody knew how long any time-fuse might have to run. All those personnel not actively engaged upon the work moved away to what was considered a safe distance.

'Let's have a look at that clockwork toy,' Anderson said, and they walked back to the embankment. 'We could make a start on this one while they're digging.'

Dennis clamped his stethoscope to the side of the bomb. He could hear the steady, measured ticking that meant the bomb was alive and timed to explode. It might be at any time – from the very next minute, to several months.

You always assumed it was due to go off at once. It might lie there ticking until Christmas, but you always acted as though it had only minutes to run.

'Bloody hell,' Anderson said. 'We're not supposed to touch it.'

Dennis raised his head and stared at him.

'That new order from DBD. We're not supposed to deal with clockwork fuses until they've sent one of their bods down to make some experiments. We're supposed to report to them and then wait.'

'*Wait?*' Dennis echoed. 'But that's madness. We don't know how long it's got to run. And once we've started work on it, it's our responsibility.'

'Mine,' the Captain said. 'My sole responsibility. Not yours, Verney.'

Dennis ignored this. He knew Anderson wasn't trying to pull rank, simply stating the facts as laid down by military orders. But they worked so closely together now that he took almost as much part as the Captain in making the decisions.

'We can't leave it now,' he said. 'It'll take at least two hours to get anyone down from London. We'll be lucky if it lasts twenty minutes.' He thought for a moment. 'Anyway, we've started – we've used a stethoscope on it. That makes it our bomb.'

Anderson grinned faintly. 'I doubt if DBD will take that view. But let's go ahead anyway. I agree with you – we can't take the chance. And we've got three other bombs, a railway line and a hospital full of patients to think about too.'

With the bomb in such a convenient position, stopping the clock and removing the fuse was as simple as such a task could ever be, with the menace of an explosion still hanging like a shadow over everyone's head. But Dennis did not allow himself to think of that. He had schooled himself to think of the job as just a job – something that needed the utmost care, but held no danger whatsoever, at least to himself. Yet he never forgot the other men who were compelled to work close to him, listening on their headsets or helping with the delicate work of scraping away mud or keeping the right tools at the ready.

As always, immediately before he began work, he thought for a moment of Betty. She was like both a prayer and a beacon in his mind and his heart, a reminder that he had the world to live for. He held the thought of her and then pushed it gently away. There was no room for distraction in the task he was about to begin.

The fuse was out. The team breathed a sigh of relief and began the work of removing the bomb to the truck for safe disposal. The clock stopped just as they were strapping it down.

'So much for waiting for the boffin from London,'

Dennis remarked. He and Captain Anderson looked at each other and grinned, and Dennis wiped the sweat from his brow. 'Well, that's one down. Three to go. Let's go and see how they're getting on with the one at the hospital.'

The shaft was almost completed now, its walls lined with close boarding. It was almost a crime to build so well and then dismantle it all again, Dennis thought. But any of the Pioneers would be able to set up as a builder and joiner after the war – if they survived.

'It's keeping all the pressure equal that's the skill of it, sor,' the Irishman in charge told him. 'There's a whole lot of strain on the sides, don't ye see, especially when ye get down deep, and ye have to be sure that it's properly distributed or ye'll get a collapse. And there's water down there too, so we'll have to be putting the pump on it before ye can start work.'

Flannery was a good workman, an expert on timbering and excavation, and Dennis knew that he took as much pride in his work as if he were building a house for the Queen. He watched as the pumps were installed and the water began to gush up from the depths.

'There's a lot down there. How much will this pump extract?'

'Quarter of a million gallons a day, sor. But we can put another one in if that's not enough.' They looked at the stream of the water that was now finding a channel across the garden. 'They should be gathering that up for the vegetable gardens. It'll be a gift, after the drought we've had.'

With the pit relatively dry at last, Dennis and Captain Anderson climbed down the long ladders to the bottom, their headsets fastened on so that they could talk to the men above. They stared at the bomb, now standing on its nose supported from above by strong webbing straps.

'Looks straightforward enough,' Dennis said.

'Hmm. It *looks* straightforward. But we never take anything for granted in this job.'

Once again, the bomb had begun to tick, and the big clock-stopping magnet was clamped to the side and switched on. Time was now less of a problem, but the bomb was still filled with explosive and in an unstable state. And there was always the chance that the clock would start again, or a second fuse come into operation.

Captain Anderson settled himself at the other end of the bomb with his stethoscope. They took turns at this job, working together as smoothly as a machine. It didn't matter who finally defused the bomb; as Anderson had told Dennis on his first operation, there was no place for heroes in this job.

Dennis inserted his chisel gently into one of the notches on the base-plate. He tapped his hammer against it.

The hammer refused to move away from the chisel.

'Christ,' he said softly, 'the whole lot's stuck to the magnet.'

He pulled and prised, struggling to free the tools, but the magnet was too powerful. The entire bomb had become a magnet. He wondered what that was doing to its electrical fields, and whether there would be any change in the explosive. Was this a new German device, or merely a freak?

The tools came away in his hand. He tried again, jerking the hammer away after a sharp tap, and this time managed to loosen the plate slightly. The bomb seemed to give a tiny sigh, and Dennis felt his flesh crawl.

Betty, he thought. Betty. I'm coming out of this alive and we're getting married. As soon as possible. In a church or a Meeting, or at the back of one of the pigsties, I don't care which.

He pushed the thought of Betty away and concentrated again. The chisel slid in and out of the second notch, then the third and the fourth. The plate came away in his hand.

Now for the fuse-pocket.

Dennis switched on his torch and shone it inside the bomb. It was oddly hollow, and it took him a moment or two to realise why. Instead of being cast-filled, as most of the German bombs were, this one had been filled with powder. The powder had begun to deteriorate and liquefy to pure nitro-glycerine which had settled into the nose of the bomb, leaving the tail end, which was uppermost, empty.

That was why it had magnetised the hammer and chisel, he thought. But the important thing now was to get the fuse-pocket out. And the fuse-pocket was low down in the bomb, half submerged in a pale brown fluid which could detonate at the slightest vibration.

Very gently, Dennis reached down the inside of the casing. The slightest ripple caused by his fingers could cause an explosion, and in the confines of the narrow shaft it would be devastating. But there was no other choice. He felt the touch of liquid against his fingertips and almost physically forced his heart to remain steady. Even an increase in the beat of his pulse could do it . . .

Slowly, gradually, he let his fingertips drift deeper into the syrup. He remembered once, as a boy, being taught to catch trout with his hands by 'tickling' them. You did it almost casually, letting your fingers relax and whisper along their bodies so that they noticed it no more than the flowing of the stream. The slightest suspicion of anything more, and they were off.

Tickling a bomb was a hundred times more delicate than that.

He had his entire hand in the fluid now. His fingers were closing round the fuse-pocket. It was loose, making the bomb even more unstable than they had supposed, and he felt the weight of it – a steel casing which held almost two pounds of picric explosive, itself highly sensitive to movement or disruption. A bomb in miniature, a bomb within a bomb.

Moving with infinite care, he withdrew it from the nitro-glycerine and squatted for a moment holding it in both hands, still trying to quell the thudding of his heart. He had only to breathe a little too fast . . . But with ordinary care, it ought to be safe enough now.

'I'll get it out of here,' he said quietly to Captain Anderson, and began to climb the ladder.

It was a job he had done dozens of times before. It ought, as he had said, to have been straightforward. Safe. But somewhere on his way to the far end of the hospital grounds to destroy the fuse, something went wrong. Perhaps he tripped. Perhaps he stumbled. Perhaps the explosive had simply become so unstable that nothing would have prevented it going off.

Dennis's last thought was of Betty, and the wedding they had been looking forward to so much.

Chapter twenty-three

'They don't know if he'll pull through or not,' Betty told the Spencers as she sat in the farm kitchen, white and exhausted, after her first visit to the hospital. Mrs Spencer had put a cup of tea in front of her the moment she walked in, but she hadn't touched it and there was a thin scum forming on its surface. 'He's all bandaged up like one of those Egyptian mummies, and they've shaved off his hair and he's got tubes and things sticking into his arms. I don't think he even knew I was there. It's horrible.'

'Poor Dennis,' Erica said soberly. Her waist had begun to thicken now and she had taken out the seams of her breeches until they could be stretched no further. But she had suffered almost no sickness, and her hair and skin glowed with health. 'He's really brave, Betty. I'm sorry I was such a pig to him when we first came here.'

'Don't you insult my pigs,' Yvonne said, but there was no heart in her banter. She took Betty's cup and emptied it down the sink. 'Here, have a fresh one. It'll do you good. And take lots of sugar.'

'I don't like sugar,' Betty said drearily, but she lifted the cup and sipped it, and a little of her colour began to return to her cheeks. 'I wish I could stop in the hospital all the time. I wouldn't be in the way. I'd just sit there beside him, and be there if – if he wakes up. But they won't let anyone stay for more than an hour.'

'They never do,' Mrs Spencer said. 'Goodness knows what they're doing all the time, but it's like a secret world. Especially Army hospitals. They'd keep you out all the time if they could.'

'Oh, they're nice enough, it's just that those are the rules.' Betty set down her teacup and it rattled against the saucer. 'I want to be *with* him. He needs me. And suppose – suppose anything happens. I mean, he might *die* and me not there.'

Her voice rose dangerously, and Mrs Spencer reached out and laid a firm hand on her arm. 'Now, you're not to talk like that. Dennis isn't going to die. He's stayed alive three days, he'll not give up now. I'm sure he knows you were there and he's making up his mind this instant that he's going to get better so you can get wed. In fact, if you ask me it might be a good time now to start sewing yourself a wedding dress. I've got some nice white muslin laid by, we could use that unless you want to borrow the one Erica had.'

Yvonne looked scared. 'I don't think we ought to do anything like that. It might be unlucky. Like buying a pram before the baby's born.'

'Rubbish,' the farmer's wife began robustly, but Betty shook her head.

'I'm not having a wedding dress. We're getting married the Quaker way, without any fuss. We ought to have done it straight away – I'd have been Dennis's wife by now, instead of just his fiancée. It'd be me the doctors talked to, and I'd be allowed to see him more often.'

Erica nodded. 'You can't afford to wait these days. You just don't know what's going to happen. None of us does.'

She looked down at her lap. Gerald knew about the baby now, and had written to express his delight, but it hurt that he'd never been able to tell her to her face how pleased he was, that he'd never been able to take her in his arms and give her that special kiss. She wondered if he would be able to come home before the baby was born, or if it would be sitting up, perhaps even walking and talking, before he saw it. Or if he would ever see it . . .

The fighting in North Africa and the Western Desert was still serious and Churchill himself flew to Cairo to see what was going on. General Auchinleck had done well at El

Alamein, he said, but it was imperative to deal with the Germans, who were even now only sixty miles from Alexandria. An offensive was needed. He appointed 'Strafer' Gott as commander of the Eighth Army.

The new leader never had the chance to prove his own capabilities. His transport aircraft was shot down within twenty-four hours by German fighters and he was killed. Someone else had to be found quickly, and that someone was Bernard Law Montgomery.

Montgomery was an unknown quantity. He was small for a soldier, his face as sharp as a ferret's, with bright eyes and an arrogance that suggested not so much that he looked to God for help, as that God looked to him. He had fought in the Great War – now beginning to be called the First World War – and won the DSO, and he had been in France before Dunkirk. Now he strutted into North Africa, under the cynical eyes of an army which had already suffered heavy losses, and declared that only he could defeat the Desert Fox.

'Thinks a lot of himself,' Frank remarked. 'Let's hope it's not another lot of hot air. I'm beginning to wonder if any of them knows what they're up to.'

'They've been having nothing but rows in Parliament,' Ted agreed. 'And by all accounts, Winnie and that General Auchinleck had a stand-up row right there in the desert – the general saying the army was exhausted and had to have better tanks and stuff, and Churchill shouting him down and saying nothing mattered but beating Rommel. How can he say that? They've got to have the right equipment, haven't they? They can't fight a war without guns.'

'That's right. And it was Churchill himself who said "Give us the tools and we'll finish the job". I don't suppose anyone dared remind him about that, though.'

There was a lot of grumbling these days, about the way the war was being managed. All the authorities came in for their own slice of people's disapproval, from the government downwards. Portsmouth City Council received its own barrage of complaints.

'What's the point of having their offices all the way out at Southsea? It's all right for them, in a nice hotel on the front, but it's a day's march to get there. And that new Citizen's Advice Bureau office, it's just snowed under, when you can find it at all. It took Annie hours to track it down when she wanted to find out about clothes for that family down Kendal Street, and there's only two women running it, you know, two sisters, and half the time they can't find out what you wants to know, any more than anyone else, not that it's for want of trying.'

'You can't blame the Council for everything,' Jess said. 'I saw Uncle John the other day and he said they're working all the hours there are to keep things going. I know a lot of people moan about the Mayor, but I reckon he does his best. None of them expected to have to run the city during wartime, after all, when they put up for election, and nobody knew what the war would be like. Nor how long it'd last.'

That was the trouble, really. Nobody had expected the war to last this long, and there was still no end in sight. In fact, it seemed to be going from bad to worse, with the whole world sliding into chaos. Sometimes it seemed that it never *could* end. It was like a huge tangle of wool that could never ever be unravelled.

Betty came home to see her mother one afternoon, before she went to the hospital. She had timed it so that her father would be out, saying she couldn't bear to see him, knowing how he felt about Dennis.

'You ought to give him a chance,' Annie said. 'Your dad's not a monster. He wouldn't have wanted anything like this to happen.'

'That's not the impression he's given me. Struck me he'd think getting blown up was too good for Dennis. Anyway, even if he did change his mind he'd be too bloody obstinate to say so.'

Annie opened her mouth to object to her daughter's language, and then closed it again. Betty was having a bad enough time as it was, without starting a row about something that didn't really matter. She was obviously

376

worried out of her mind about Dennis, sitting there at the kitchen table, her face streaked with tears, fiddling with a cup of tea.

'You can't go in to see Dennis looking like that,' Annie said. 'You wants to look cheerful, put a bit of heart into him. He's got enough to put up with, without seeing you with a face as long as a fiddle.'

'I've told you, he can't see me at all. His face is all bandaged up. And he's still unconscious.' Dennis had made little visible progress, though the doctors told Betty that some of his injuries were beginning to mend. 'Oh, Mum, what am I going to do if he never wakes up? He could stop like that for months – years. People do. I can't bear seeing him like that, lying there so helpless.'

'I know, love.' Annie put her arm around Betty's shoulders. 'It's a dreadful thing. But there's nothing we can do about it except hope for the best. I'm sure he knows when you're there. He must be able to feel you holding his hand and loving him.'

Betty sniffed and rubbed her eyes with the heel of her hand. 'I try to talk to him. I tell him I'm getting ready for our wedding. I'm going to marry him, as soon as he's fit, you know. I don't care what Dad or anyone else thinks. But I never know if he can hear me or not.' Her sobs began again. 'He just *lies* there like a – a statue.' She had almost said 'mummy'. But mummies were dead, and Dennis still had a spark of life in him. She spent her visiting times praying that the spark would ignite again.

The back door opened suddenly and Ted came into the kitchen. He stopped short in the doorway and the two women looked up at him, startled.

'Ted! You're early. I never expected you until six o'clock.'

'We've changed shifts. I forgot to tell you.' His eyes were on Betty. 'I suppose that's why you came round, you thought I wouldn't be here.'

Betty shrugged and didn't answer. Her father sat down heavily opposite her.

'Don't tell me it's not true. I'm not a fool. You've been

avoiding me for weeks. Just because you can't have your own way –'

'You've been drinking,' Betty said coldly. 'Spent the rest of your shift in the Keppel's Head, have you?'

'Now, look here, my girl –'

'Stop it,' Annie said loudly. 'Stop it at once, the pair of you. Ted, you know what our Betty's going through. Whether you like Dennis or not, he's been badly hurt and no one knows if he's going to live or die. Just think of that. And if he does die, it'll be because he was trying to save folks like you and me from getting blown up. I can't see what you've got against him, I really can't.'

'Who said I had anything against him?' Ted muttered. 'He's all right. It was only when he was a pacifist –'

'Don't make any mistake, Dad,' Betty said at once. 'He's still a pacifist.'

'Well, all right, but at least he's doing something now, ain't he? Or he was, until –' Ted stopped and scowled, then looked up at Betty from under his brows and reached his hand awkwardly across the table. 'Look, girl, I don't want to make things worse for you. I know you think a lot of the chap. And maybe I was a bit hasty, taking against him the way I did. Anyway, all I want to say is – well, I hope he gets better soon, that's all. He's a decent enough young man, even if he does have some funny ideas, and if you still want to get wed when he's on his feet again – well, I'll not stand in your way.'

He finished gruffly, and Betty's face crumpled as she took his hand. He had not touched her in this way since she was a little girl, and she felt the warmth of his strong fingers with a strange sense of familiarity. The tears blurred her eyes, but she gave him a wavery smile.

'Thanks, Dad. I really do love Dennis, you know. And he loves me.'

'I know. And it's for you to work out your life. You're twenty-one, after all, old enough to make your own decisions. All I'm saying is, me and your mother will back you up, whatever you decide. We just want you to be happy, ain't that right, Annie?'

378

Annie nodded. She'd suspected for some time that Ted might be changing his mind, but as Betty had said, he would find it difficult to admit it. But now he'd done so, and only she knew what it had cost his pride.

'You're a good man, Ted,' she said. 'A good husband and a good father. Have I ever told you that?'

'Not nearly as often as you should,' he answered with a grin. 'And I'd say you were a good wife too, only I've been in the house ten minutes already and I'm still sitting here at this table without a cup of tea in front of me. Is that the way to treat the head of the household, I ask you?'

'Oh, you . . . !' Annie jumped up and fetched his cup from the dresser. She poured a stream of strong brown tea into it and placed it before him. 'There you are. Head of the household, indeed! I'd just like to know where we'd all be if *you* had the running of the house, with all the rations to sort out and the cooking and washing to do, instead of spending all your time on a boat going backwards and forwards across the harbour!'

Ted lifted his cup. He winked at Betty and she grinned back. Suddenly, the atmosphere in the house was lighter than it had been for many months. And when she set off an hour later to visit Dennis in the hospital, she knew that her gnawing anxiety had been eased by the relief of being on good terms with her father once more.

But all relief fled when she walked into the ward and saw that the screens were standing around Dennis's bed. Her knees shook as she approached and she looked fearfully at the nurse who emerged from behind the screen. The girl gave her a small, sympathetic smile.

'I don't know how long you'll be able to stay,' she murmured. 'He's not at all well. The doctor thinks –' She hesitated, and Betty saw with shock that there were tears in her eyes. She was a very young nurse, no more than eighteen or nineteen, and she hadn't had time to get hardened yet. The ward was full of young soldiers, and every day one or two of them died.

Simultaneously, the two girls put out their hands and touched each other, each wanting both to give and receive comfort. They stood close for a few seconds, and then a patient called out in sudden distress from the far end of the ward and the young nurse disengaged herself and hurried off.

Betty tiptoed quietly through the screens and looked down at the bed. Dennis was lying very still. He was still heavily bandaged and looked thin and flat under the white sheets. He had lost two fingers from one hand, the doctor had told her, but the other was miraculously undamaged. He might easily have lost both.

Tubes emerged from beneath the covers, one attached to a bottle that hung from the bedhead, another disappearing under the bed. His chest rose and fell very slightly with his faint breathing.

'Oh, Dennis . . .' Betty whispered, and sank on to the chair that stood beside him.

Dennis's uninjured arm lay across him, on top of the sheets. She laid her hand on his, very gently. It felt cold.

'Dennis, my darling, don't leave me. Please don't leave me.'

The words were no more than a thread of sound in the tiny oasis of silence. Beyond the screens, she could hear the sounds of the busy ward – people crying out and groaning, visitors walking in and chatting to someone two or three beds along, the brisk clack of the nurses' shoes. They seemed to have nothing to do with this little space where only she and Dennis existed, where two lives that should have been shared were threatened with the final parting.

'Dennis . . .'

Only his mouth and nose were visible amongst the bandages. His lips were pale and slightly parted. There was a tiny bubble of moisture in one corner. If that bubble bursts, he'll die, Betty thought irrationally. In sudden panic, she began to talk to him, her voice a whisper though she wanted to shout through the thick, muffling bandages. She talked to him about Erica and Gerald and the coming baby, about Yvonne and the pig which had pinned her to the wall of the sty, about the weather and the winter mud and the sale of last spring's lambs, about every detail of life on the farm. She talked about herself, how she was missing him, how she longed to feel his arms about her again. She talked about the days when they had begun to fall in love, the first Christmas they had spent together, the night she had slipped down from the attic room to be with him, and the glory and delight of their lovemaking.

'Don't leave me, Dennis,' she begged, stroking his unresponsive hand with trembling fingers. 'Don't go away. I need you. We belong together. We've got to be together. We're getting married, remember? A Quaker wedding, just as you wanted. It's all I want – just to be your wife. To be together for the rest of our lives. Till we're *old*, Dennis – till we're really, really old.'

There was a slight movement behind her and she sensed the nurse's presence at her side. She could not look up. She kept her eyes fixed on the bandaged face, on the pale lips and tiny bubble of moisture. It hadn't burst. It wasn't going to burst. He had to stay alive.

'Dennis, I love you,' she whispered.

The nurse touched her shoulder. Reluctantly, Betty turned her head and glanced up, meeting the tired young eyes. There was sympathy there still, but there was also a resignation, as if already Dennis had slipped away too far to be called back. No, Betty thought, *no*.

'I'm afraid he can't hear you,' the nurse said quietly. 'He's very near the end.'

He's not. He's not. Betty turned back to the bed, her fingers tightening on Dennis's hand. She felt a sudden wave of outrage, a pure, clear anger, like a knife slicing through her breast.

'No,' she said, in the same anguished whisper. 'No, Dennis. You mustn't. I need you. I love you. You're not to die. *You're not to die.*'

'It's no use –' the nurse began, but Betty lifted her free hand in a gesture of restraint. She was staring at Dennis intently, her heart beating fast. There had been a movement. She was certain there had been a movement. An almost imperceptible stirring in the cold, still fingers. A shiver across the parted lips.

'He's different,' she breathed, staring at the muffled face. 'He's breathing differently.'

'They do when –' The nurse's voice was still quiet, but there was a detachment in it now, as if she had accepted the fact of Dennis's death and was already seeing him as just another ex-patient, a bed to be emptied and remade for the next young soldier. Again, Betty felt a wave of anger. He's not a 'they', she thought, he's Dennis and he's mine and he's not going to die.

She bent her head so that her face was close to the swathe of bandages. Very gently, she touched her lips to his, felt their dryness against her skin, let the tip of her tongue move lightly across them. Dennis, Dennis . . . She hardly knew whether she uttered his name or simply thought it. But she knew that the strength of her longing, of her determination, was reaching him. She knew that he could hear her with his mind.

And if he could hear her with his mind, his heart would listen too.

'Please,' the nurse said anxiously. 'Please, you mustn't –'

But Betty did not hear her. For a fraction of a second, she had felt Dennis's lips move in response to hers. For the briefest instant of time, he had shared her kiss.

'He knows I'm here,' she breathed. 'He knows. Oh, Dennis – *Dennis* . . .'

And under her hand she felt his fingers stir, felt a trace of warmth creep back into the chilly flesh. She flashed a swift glance of triumph at the nurse's face and saw her stare as Dennis's hand moved, shakily and unsteadily, and the fingers curled beneath Betty's to turn his palm to hers.

'Look,' she said softly, 'he's smiling.'

It was the faintest of smiles. A mere quiver of the parted lips. But for Betty, it was a sunburst, and she knew that Dennis was going to live.

The bubble of moisture had disappeared. But it didn't matter any more.

CHAPTER TWENTY-FOUR

It seemed as if the Germans had suddenly remembered where Portsmouth was. In the next raid over a hundred buildings were damaged, though nobody was killed.

'We're getting our own back, though,' Frank said with grim satisfaction. All day the wireless had been giving news bulletins of a massive raid on France. The French had been told that it was not the invasion itself, and were advised to keep out of the way for the time being and wait to be told how they could help. 'The biggest air battle since the Battle of Britain, they're calling it. That'll keep 'em busy.'

It did, but the next news was worse. A huge contingent of commandos, mostly Canadian, were killed during an attempt to seize the port of Dieppe. Of the six thousand men who had departed from ports in the South of England – including Portsmouth – only two thousand returned, and of the RAF air cover, over a hundred planes were lost. It was, the newsreader reported in a sober voice, one of the worse disasters since Dunkirk.

'And now the Duke of Kent's been killed,' Jess said sadly a few days later. 'Flying on active service over Scotland. They say a shepherd found the plane on fire. And the baby Prince Michael only two months old – that's awful.'

'It's the same for a lot of other people,' Frank remarked. 'But that doesn't make it any easier for the family, I know. Royal or not, it comes down to the same thing in the end.'

'I saw him when he came to Pompey last year,' Jess said. 'Me and Annie went down to the Guildhall Square. I thought he was lovely. He looked so much like the old

King. He said he'd never seen so many cheerful people anywhere. Not that everyone's managing to keep smiling,' she added. 'Ethel Glaister next door's had a face like a wet weekend for the past fortnight.'

It was the sort of remark that made Frank smile and the children giggle. But Jess was right. Ethel Glaister had nothing to smile about these days, nothing at all.

'You're nothing better than a lodger these days,' Ethel said tartly, as she and George finished their supper of fried potatoes with a bit of scrambled dried egg. 'Off playing soldiers for weeks on end, leaving me with all the responsibility, then coming back for a couple of days just when you feel like it. It's been a godsend to you, this war, hasn't it? Given you a taste of freedom. Think you're a single bloke again.'

'For God's sake, Ethel, don't start,' he said wearily. 'It's not my fault I don't get home often. Can't I have a bit of affection?'

'Affection! So that's what you call it. A bit of a fumble in bed and you snoring like a pig straight after. Not much affection in that.'

George looked at her with distaste. Now that she'd mentioned it, he didn't think he wanted that kind of 'affection' either. Once upon a time, when they were young, Ethel had been really attractive with her blonde hair nicely done, a bit of make-up on her face and her neat little figure shown off just right in the smart clothes she wore. He'd only had to look at her to feel the stir of desire, and she'd been as ready as he was, laughing and giggling and egging him on. They'd had a lot of fun together.

But now she looked hard. Her painted fingernails were more like talons and her hair was set in rigid waves, as if it were a metal cap. The colour didn't look so natural either – it was brassy, and sometimes it even looked a queer sort of green when the light shone on it. And her clothes were a bit tight, though they were still very smart – too smart, somehow. She was forever fussing about them and you couldn't touch her for fear of creasing something or leaving fingermarks.

And he didn't want to touch her. When he looked at her now he felt nothing – only this faint repugnance, this little shudder of loathing. And he wasn't even sure he could manage it now, not after the way she talked to him. A man needed to feel his wife looked up to him a bit, after all. He didn't want to feel treated like dirt.

You've gone too far, my girl, he thought. You've pushed just that little bit too far.

It was a sad feeling, but it was also liberating. He felt suddenly free – free of Ethel, free of the hurt she could deal him, free of her nagging tongue and bitter sarcasm. He felt as if he had grown suddenly taller.

'No,' he said, 'there isn't any affection in it. And you don't have to worry, Ethel. You can have your bed to yourself tonight. In fact, you can have it to yourself for the rest of your life.'

Ethel stared at him, her mouth open. He noticed that her teeth were beginning to go yellow with nicotine, and her skin looked coarse under the powder. Her fingertips were yellow too.

'What do you mean? What are you on about?'

'Oh, come off it, Ethel. You've been nagging at me about my snoring and using up half the bed for years. Well, I'm telling you I won't be any more. From now on, it's your bed. I won't be bothering you again.'

'Well, I know you're away most of the time, don't I. There's no need to be nasty about it.'

'I'm not talking about being away,' he said. 'Not like I'm away now. I'm talking about not coming back.'

'Don't be daft. There's nothing happening where you are. You'll be coming back, turning up like a bad penny. After all, you don't fight anyway, you just build a few tin huts.'

George took no notice. Not so long ago, her words would have pricked him with humiliation. Now, they just didn't matter.

'I'm not coming back at all, Ethel. I mean, I'm not coming back to you. To this house.'

Her jaw dropped even further and her face whitened, leaving only the rouge standing out like red blotches on her cheeks. 'You're not coming back? You mean you're *deserting* me?'

'If you want to put it that way, yes.' He pushed back his chair and stood up. 'I've had enough, Ethel. Enough of being treated like an intruder in my own home. I've had enough of listening to you going on and on at me all the time. I've had enough of *you*. More than enough.'

Ethel's mouth closed and then opened again. She looked like a fish, he thought, one of those cods you used to see on fishmongers' slabs, lying there with their cold eyes staring.

'Well, aren't you pleased?' he asked. 'You can't pretend you want me here. You've been making it pretty plain that I'm in the way. And now you've got your house to yourself. I'm off and I'm not coming back.'

Ethel found her voice. 'What about money? How am I going to manage? What about the children? You're not thinking of them.'

'They'll be all right. Our Shirley's in the country, she'll be safe and happy enough there. And Joe's finding his feet in the Navy. As for Carol –' He stopped and gave her a glance of pure loathing. 'Well, you ought to be proper proud of yourself over Carol.'

'What do you mean? Our Carol's all right. She's safe and happy down in Devon. If it wasn't for me going and fetching her back from Bournemouth, she'd be in a fine pickle. As it is –'

'As it is, she's not in Devon at all like you've given out, she's in a home for unmarried mothers up near Guildford,' he broke in, and saw Ethel's face redden. 'For God's sake, Ethel! You didn't really think you were going to keep it a secret from me, did you? I told you before, Carol's my daughter and I've got a right to know what's happening to her.'

'How did you find out? Who told you?'

'Carol did, of course,' he said scornfully. 'She can write, you know. She wrote me a letter and told me all about it.

You shouldn't have sent her to that Home, Ethel. She's miserable there.'

'She don't deserve to be anything else. Bringing trouble on the house. And what d'you expect me to do? Keep her here? I'd have died of shame.'

'Well, I don't reckon she'll ever come back, not now she's got away,' George said. 'We'll probably never see her again – and never know our own grandchild.'

'I don't want to talk about Carol,' Ethel said coldly. 'She's no daughter of mine.'

'You're wrong there. She's your daughter through and through. You could have been in the same position as her if I hadn't held back till we were married. You were panting for it. And I don't reckon it was just me, neither. There was plenty of other boys after you, and you didn't do much to put 'em off.' He paused for a moment, then added quietly, 'I always had a bit of a suspicion about our Joe.'

Ethel flushed scarlet. 'That's a filthy thing to say!'

'So it is,' he agreed. 'It's not very nice thinking it, neither. Most of the time I put it out of me head and took him as my son. But there's a look about him at times – puts me in mind of that Will Barlow you used to be pally with.'

'I'm not going to listen to this,' Ethel said, getting up and clattering the plates together. 'I don't know what's got into you, George Glaister, I don't, honest. It must be the strain of going away.'

'It's the strain of being here with you for over eighteen years,' he said. He buttoned up his tunic and looked around for his hat. 'Well, I don't see much point in hanging about here any longer. I've told you I'm leaving you, and that's all there is to it. I might as well go straight back to the camp now and get a good night's sleep.'

'A good night's sleep! And just what d'you suppose *I'm* going to get?' Ethel slammed the plates back on the table. 'I won't be able to sleep a wink, not a wink. My own husband, deserting me – why, I'll never be able to hold up my head again. What are all the neighbours going to say? What's that Jess Budd next door going to say? I'll be a laughing-stock, that's what I'll be, a laughing-stock.'

'Well, that's your business.' George glanced in the mirror that hung over the fireplace. He had grown a moustache since he'd been in the Army, and he looked different – stronger, somehow, more upright. It might have been the square-bashing and the outdoor life, but he felt that it had a good deal to do with his own attitude. His attitude towards himself, and to Ethel. 'I'm not interested any more. And I don't suppose anyone else is, not all that much. They've got their own lives to live. You'll be all right.'

'But how am I going to manage?' Her shrill voice had turned into a whine. 'What about money? How am I going to live? You've got to look after me, George, that's the law, you've got to provide for me.'

'Oh, you'll get your money,' he said. 'You don't have to worry about that. It'll be sent through, same as always. But don't expect it to be as much. I'm allowing a bit to our Carol as well.'

'*Carol?* You're sending money to that little hussy? *My* money?'

'No,' he said, 'my money. I've taken off what I spend on beer. It won't make no difference to you. But it'll make a lot to her, what with the baby coming and all.'

'You can't. If there's any spare money, you ought to be giving it to me. I'll take you to court.'

'You do whatever you want,' he said, turning away. 'I've made up my mind and now I'm off. You won't be seeing me here again, Ethel.' He looked at her and hesitated for a moment. Even now, it didn't seem quite right to walk out without a goodbye kiss. But Ethel hadn't kissed him in years, not properly. Not more than a peck on the cheek. And the way she was looking at him now, she was more likely to bite his ear off.

'Goodbye,' he said quietly, and went out of the door.

Ethel stood quite still. She heard the front door open and close. She heard his footsteps march quickly away up the street. And then she ran after him, jerked the door open and yelled into the darkness.

'George Glaister! Don't you dare walk away like that.

You come back here this minute. You're not to go, d'you hear me? You're not to leave me. You're *my husband*, you promised to look after me till death us do part. You're *not* deserting me, you're *not*!'

Her screams grew louder and more frantic, penetrating the closed doors and windows of almost every house in April Grove. Jess Budd heard them as she sat sewing sailors' collars in her back room. The Shaw family heard them as they sat playing cards. Mrs Seddon in the corner shop heard them as she sat at her table with a pile of ration coupons before her, struggling with the everlasting paperwork.

George Glaister heard them as he marched away up October Street. But he never turned his head, and his steps never faltered. He felt as if he were marching away from a dark shadow and into a world that was new, a world that was just for him. He could be himself at last, he thought, and it didn't matter what discomfort or hardship he might have to face, he could face it as himself, standing tall and upright with his head held high.

George Glaister had become a man again.

'It's time we done something,' Micky declared. 'The Jerries are gettin' worse. And we ain't doin' nothing to stop 'em. That raid on Dieppe was stupid. They practically *told* the Jerries they were comin'. What they wants to do is go over secretly, so no one don't know nothing about it, and get at the headquarters. Shoot old Hitler, that's what they wants to do.'

The secret army had gathered in Micky's den. He had brought a few of his trophies – some fragments of shell and shrapnel, Wendy's bayonet, the wireless set, and a handful of Desmond's bullets. He had left the guns he and Desmond had collected in his bedroom, some hidden under the floorboards, the rest in the old fireplace with a bit of plywood fixed over it so that his gran wouldn't go nosing.

'Shoot Hitler,' Desmond said, aiming an imaginary gun. 'Kill Hitler. Kill. Rat-tat-tat-tat-tat.'

'Shut up, Des.' Micky looked round the den at the little group. 'What I'm sayin' is, *they* won't do it, so we got to. The war's never goin' to finish otherwise. It's up to us.'

'You'd never get near him,' Tim said. He shared Micky's dream of defeating the enemy single-handed, but couldn't rid himself of the suspicion that it simply wasn't possible. 'I mean, if it was that easy, someone would've done it already.'

Micky shook his head. 'They don't do it that way. They don't kill the leaders. They just sets the soldiers against each other. But it's Hitler what's in charge, and if he was out of the way the rest'd chuck it in. I mean, I've seen him on the pictures, he's barmy.'

It sounded reasonable enough. Most people believed that Hitler was not only evil but mad as well. With him gone, perhaps the others would return to sanity. And soldiers only fought if they were ordered to. With no leader to egg them on, they would probably just put down their guns and go home.

'So what are you going to do?' Tim asked. 'How d'you reckon you're going to get to Hitler?'

'I'll get a boat. We'll row across the Channel and land in France at dead of night. We'll get to Berlin and find out where he is. They won't take no notice of us. That's our advantage, see. Nobody bothers about kids. We can get into his hideout easy and then –' Micky waved his arm '– it'll be curtains for Adolf.'

Tim pursed his lips. It couldn't be that easy.

'Berlin's hundreds of miles away from France,' he said. 'How are you going to get there – walk? It'll take weeks. And you can't speak French, or German. They'd rumble you straight away and you'd finish up in one of those concentration camps.'

Micky scowled. 'Think of a better idea, then.'

Tim shrugged. He had never been convinced that Micky's army would be a success. 'You haven't got any guns.'

Micky gave him a sideways glance. He had been wary of taking Tim into his confidence over the weapons he had collected, suspecting that Tim might draw the line at stealing guns from the airfield. Taking the enemy's weapons as trophies was one thing – stealing them from your own side quite another, even if they weren't using them to good effect. But he couldn't resist the opportunity to boast.

'We have got guns, so there.'

'You haven't. What sort?'

'A Lewis gun,' Micky said proudly, not entirely sure that he was right. He had to go by Desmond's knowledge, after all, and Desmond might easily be wrong. Anyway, it didn't matter . . . 'And a Vickers K. And some tommy guns.' These were the ones they had filched from the Home Guard shed when Martin had managed to 'borrow' the key from his uncle.

'I don't believe you,' Tim said. 'Anyway, you don't even know how to shoot.'

Micky jumped up. 'I do! Desmond's got the ammo, haven't you, Des. And he knows how to load 'em. He's been learning all about it in the ATC on Sunday mornings. He's been on the ranges, shooting. He's a crack shot. And so am I. I'm *better*.'

'Oh, yeah?'

'Yeah.' Micky squared up to Tim, his fists clenched. 'Want me to prove it?'

Tim stared at him. He and Micky had known each other since they were five years old. Each a natural leader, they had vied to be top dog in the street. But Micky had never been tied down by a strict father or anxious mother. He had always been allowed to roam freely in the streets, doing as he pleased and coming home when he felt like it. The other children, made to go to school regularly and called indoors at bedtime, were fascinated by his wildness.

Lately, with his secret army and his den, his power had been absolute.

Tim envied him. It didn't seem fair that Micky should be the one to be able to shoot, to have his own guns, to be leader of the army. It didn't seem fair that he should be able to talk about going to Berlin and shooting Hitler, being a hero.

But being at home with his father and mother had brought home to Tim some of the realities of the war. He listened to the news more than he had out in the country. He heard the bombers flying over every night. He read the newspapers and saw the headlines about the disastrous raid on Dieppe. He saw his cousin Betty with her eyes reddened with weeping over Dennis, and his aunt grey-faced with worry over Colin. He thought of Stella and Muriel, with no mother or father now to love and look after them.

'I don't care whether you're a crack shot or not,' he said to Micky. 'You'd never get anywhere near Berlin. You're just a lot of hot air, like a barrage balloon.'

Micky took a swing at him, but Desmond came out of the shadows and thrust himself between them. Micky's fist caught him a glancing blow on the shoulder, but the bigger boy took no notice. His face was white and there was a pinched look around his nose.

'*We're* real soldiers,' Desmond said pugnaciously, standing in front of Tim. 'We're Micky's army. Kill Hitler.'

'That's right,' the others joined in. 'Kill Hitler!' They leapt up and down, waving their arms and jeering. 'Kill, kill, kill.'

'Oh, for cripes' sake,' Tim said, turning away, 'you're all as barmy as he is. I'm fed up with this army. It's not an army at all. You're just a lot of stupid kids. I'm not going to be in it any more.' He gave Desmond a push. 'Get out of my way.'

Micky started to speak again, but his voice was drowned as Desmond gave a sudden bellow and made a lunge for Tim, his big fists windmilling wildly. His eyes glittered in his white face, and Tim felt suddenly scared. There was something inhuman about Desmond when he got into this mood. He was like a machine running out of control. Tim backed off, looking round for support.

'Get him off. Stop him.' A swinging fist caught him on the ear and he spun back against the wall. 'He's gone mad!'

Desmond was coming after him. His eyes looked red – like a mad bull, Tim thought – and his lips were drawn back so that his teeth were exposed in a snarl. They were dirty, yellow teeth that looked as if they might poison you if they bit you. His hands were enormous.

Another smack caught Tim on the shoulder. He raised his fists and lashed out, hardly knowing where his punches would land. One of Desmond's blows landed on his eye and he let out a yelp of pain, staggering as the cellar walls spun round him in a blur of red and black and bright, jagged white light. Desmond gave a roar of triumph and grabbed his arms, wrestling him to the ground. For a few more moments they flailed at each other and then Tim felt his knuckles connect with something hard. A vicious pain shot up his arm.

'*Ow!*' Desmond hopped backwards, holding his nose. Tim peered up at him. Blood flowed between the bigger boy's fingers and he was starting to cry. Tim felt pleased and triumphant and guilty all at once.

Micky grabbed Desmond's arm. 'Pack it in, Des. *Pack it in.* Or I won't let you be my Lieutenant no more.' The bigger boy hiccuped a couple of times and then stopped crying and stood still, like a chastened dog. Micky gave Tim a contemptuous glance.

'Go on then, if you want to. Get out. I always knew you were a cissy anyway. I only let you in so we could get some saltpetre to make bombs with. And don't come here no more, see?'

'Don't want to,' Tim said defiantly. He scrambled up the cellar steps and stood looking down at them. Micky watched him.

'And don't go blabbin' our secrets round, neither. You've sworn an oath of secrecy, remember.'

'I didn't. I never did. I never swore anything.' The swearing-in ceremony had been forgotten. 'I can tell anyone I like.'

He saw Micky start up the stairs after him, and turned and ran. Within seconds, he could hear the whole gang in hot pursuit – but the derelict street was a jungle of overgrown weeds and garden plants run riot, with broken fences and holes making booby traps everywhere. Soon, he had left them behind and was able to make his way home through the maze of alleyways and back paths without being seen again.

It was a daft thing to do, telling Micky they'd forgotten that oath. Now the captain of the secret army would be on the lookout for him all the time.

And although Tim told himself he wasn't really scared, he still couldn't hide a small quiver of apprehension. Suppose they really did have guns . . .

Betty visited Dennis in hospital as often as she could. Since the day he had turned the corner, he had improved steadily, the wounds caused by the flying fragments of shell as the bomb exploded healing well. Nothing could put back the two missing fingers, of course, and his head was still bandaged, but he could talk and Betty liked to be there even if he was asleep.

'You don't have to keep coming so often,' he said one day. 'You've got enough to do on the farm. You'll wear yourself out.'

'What else would I do with my spare time?' she asked mockingly. 'Just sit about and watch the wheat grow? Oh, Dennis –' her voice broke '– I don't want to be anywhere in the world but with you. You must know that. I can't manage without you.'

'But we have to be able to manage without each other,' he said gently. 'None of us can rely on having the right person with us all the time. We're all alone in the end, you know.'

Betty stared at him. 'What do you mean? I don't like it when you talk like that.'

'It's the truth. One day, however hard we try to be together all the time, one of us is going to leave the other one alone. You know that's true.'

'But not for a long time,' she said on a note of desperation. 'Not till we're really old.'

'Betty, how can you say that? Face the facts, darling. Life

is never certain, and it's more uncertain these days than ever.'

'But you won't be going back to bomb disposal. You can't.' She touched his hand, the one with the missing fingers. 'You've done your bit, Dennis. Nobody can call you a coward now.'

'I was never worried about being called a coward,' he said. 'I didn't go into BD because of that.'

'I know . . .'

'I joined because I wanted to save some of the lives that are being wasted. And I know I can't go back. But that doesn't mean I can't do something else.'

'The farm. You could come back to the farm. Mr Spencer would be pleased to have you. He'll need someone soon – Jonas is getting slower every day, only he won't admit it. There's plenty you could do on the farm.'

'Yes,' Dennis said with a little sigh. 'Perhaps.'

Betty looked at him. Only the lower half of his face was visible under the helmet of bandages. She knew that the doctors had been afraid that his head injuries might have affected his brain. They didn't seem to have done, but Dennis had never talked quite like this before, about being alone and uncertain. He had always shown such cheerful optimism – such faith.

'Dennis,' she said timidly, 'you don't feel different about – about, you know, Quakers and – and God – do you?'

His mouth smiled. 'I don't think so. Why d'you ask?'

'Because you seem different. As if you *see* things differently now. I wondered if – well, people do lose their faith when something terrible happens to them.'

'Then it wasn't much of a faith in the first place,' he said. 'How can anyone look around and see the appalling things that happen to others and expect to be immune? If you're a human being, you share in the human condition and you don't expect your God to look after you at the expense of others. No, I haven't lost my faith, Betty.' He paused, his smile wry. 'But perhaps you're right. Perhaps I am seeing things differently.'

The nurse came along the ward then and told Betty she must go. A new doctor was coming to see Dennis. Disturbed and reluctant, Betty laid her cheek against Dennis's and he turned his face to press his lips against hers. She felt a wild desire to hold him fiercely in her arms, to feel the length of his body against her, his limbs entwined with hers in the act of love they had shared so deeply and fully together. But a kiss – hardly more than a peck – was all she was allowed in this public place.

'I'll see you again in a few days,' she said softly. 'Oh Dennis, I love you so much.'

'I love you too, my darling Betty,' he said, but there was a note in his voice that disturbed her even more. If I didn't know better, she thought, I'd think he was saying goodbye.

And as she walked, with slow, dragging steps, out of the ward and through the hospital she felt as if she were leaving a part of herself behind.

It was impossible for Tim to avoid Micky and his henchmen for long. For a few days, he went straight up to the chemist's shop early in the morning and spent an hour or two in the back room, amongst all the bottles and carboys, helping to make up the medicines. This amounted mostly to counting pills and labelling the bottles, but once or twice Mr Driver let him mix some of the coloured fluids and explained to him what was happening. He was gratified to find a boy so interested in his work, and toyed with the idea of offering Tim a permanent job.

Frank had been angry when he saw Tim's black eye, though somewhat mollified when he heard that it was Micky Baxter's gang he'd been fighting with. At least, he said to Jess, that meant the boy wasn't getting mixed up in any of their scrapes. He decided to teach Tim to box, and gave him several lessons in the back garden.

Tim cycled round the streets doing his deliveries, keeping a sharp eye open for the secret army. Not that he was scared of them, he assured himself, but he didn't want to get into any more fights. In fact, he was rather regretting his action. Micky and the others were the only children around, and he missed the company of the others out in the country more than he'd realised. And even if he hadn't really believed in the secret army, it had been something to think about – something exciting to be part of.

Accordingly, when he saw Martin Baker wandering along September Street, he pulled on the brakes and skidded to a halt beside him. He wasn't scared of Martin anyway. Nobody could be scared of a little kid like Martin.

'Shot any Germans yet?' he asked with a touch of scorn in his voice.

Martin looked at him. 'Micky says you're a traitor to your country.'

'I'm not!'

'You are. He says the secret army was made to win the war, and if you won't be in it you're a traitor.'

'That's daft. It's not a proper army. He can't say I'm a traitor to my country just because I won't be in his stupid gang.'

'It's not stupid,' Martin said. He had been completely won over by Micky's glamour, and would have followed him anywhere. 'It's a proper army.'

'Oh yeah,' Tim sneered. 'With proper guns and all. Only he never shows them, does he. They're all under the floor in his bedroom. Have *you* ever seen them?'

'Yes, I have. And Micky's bringing them tonight so we can learn to shoot.' He paused and glanced at Tim. 'You could come too if you want.'

'I can't. I've left.'

'You could join again. Micky says you could join again.'

'Don't want to,' Tim said, struggling with a desire to see if they really did have guns.

'Go on,' Martin said coaxingly. 'It's a good army. And Micky reckons he knows where he can get a boat, to go to France. With an engine.'

'He couldn't –'

'He knows the boat. It's already been to France. It was at Dunkirk.'

'My uncle went to Dunkirk,' Tim said. He leant on his handlebars. He had finished his deliveries for the day, there was nothing good on the wireless that evening and he'd already read that week's *Hotspur* from cover to cover. The evening stretched ahead of him.

They didn't really have any guns, of course. It was just a pretence. But it wasn't a bad game, pretending to be a secret army. Better than sitting at home playing Ludo with Rose, or listening to her and Joy nattering on about clothes.

'All right,' he said. 'I'll come after tea. But you tell Micky to make sure that Desmond keeps off, see?'

The secret army was in the cellar in full strength, waiting for him – Micky, Martin Baker, Jimmy Cross, Wendy and Alan. And Desmond, skulking sullenly in a corner, fiddling with an old pilot's cap. He stared inimically as Tim came cautiously down the steps, letting his eyes get used to the dimness.

'Well, get an eyeful of this,' Micky said as Tim reached the bottom step. 'The wanderer returns. I s'pose you think we ought to kill a fatted calf or whatever it was.'

'You must have learnt that at Sunday School,' Tim retorted and saw Micky flush. The Sunday afternoons he had been forced to spend in the schoolroom, listening to Bible stories and colouring in pictures of Jesus carrying a small lamb, were still a sore point.

'Look, we don't *'ave* to 'ave you in the army,' Micky began, but Tim's eyes were on the table. He stopped, then took a cautious step forward, staring.

'Those are guns. Real guns.'

'Well, I told you we 'ad 'em, didn't I. Now perhaps you'll believe me.'

The guns lay spread out as if on display. The sort of guns Tim had seen illustrated in *Hotspur*. They were, quite obviously, not toys.

'Coo,' he breathed. 'They're smashing.'

He reached out and touched one gently with the tip of his finger. The other children were watching him. Beside the guns, he saw a pile of bullets and his eyes widened again. Suddenly touched by panic, he stepped back.

'Where did you get them?'

'Never you mind. We bin issued with 'em, see. We're a proper secret army, and if you don't join in you're a traitor.'

'I'm not. You can't make me join.' His eyes strayed back to the guns.

'We can. It's conscription. You got to be in it. So's anyone else, if I says so. And you got to swear an oath.'

Tim hesitated. It didn't really seem likely that Micky Baxter would have been entrusted with the task of forming a secret army. But it wouldn't have seemed likely a few years ago that girls would be firing Ack-ack guns, like his cousin Olive, or driving ambulances like Gladys Shaw. You didn't know what they'd decide to do next.

A thought struck him. 'You haven't got uniforms. If you're a proper army, you ought to have uniforms.'

Micky rolled his eyes. 'Give me strength! We wouldn't be a secret then, would we? Now look, are you going to be in this army and swear this oath or not?'

Tim stared at him and then looked at the guns again. He made up his mind.

'No. I don't believe you. You've pinched those guns from somewhere.' A memory stirred in his mind, something his father had read out of the *Evening News*. 'I bet they're the ones that got took from the Home Guard shed. You pinched them from there. Didn't you?'

Micky glanced round at the others. His eyes narrowed and he took a step forward.

'I told you, it's none of your business. Anyway, you got to be in the army now. You know too much.' He'd heard the phrase at Saturday morning pictures and kept it ready in his mind. 'You got to swear the oath.'

'No,' Tim said. 'No, I won't.' He turned to go.

Micky grabbed his arm. 'You got to. You got to swear secrecy. We don't want no one else knowing about this.'

Tim shook Micky's arm off angrily. 'Let go.'

Micky grabbed him again. 'You're our prisoner, then. If you're not in the army, you've got to be kept prisoner. We can't take no risks of you telling the coppers. We'll keep you here. We'll torture you.'

'Don't be daft,' Tim said, trying not to feel scared. The cellar was a grim place, with black, damp-streaked walls and dark recesses that might hold anything. 'You can't keep me prisoner.'

'Can't we, then?' Micky sneered at him. 'Who's to stop us, eh?'

'If I don't go home tonight, they'll look for me. My Dad'll get the police out.'

'They wouldn't find you,' Jimmy Cross said. 'This place is secret.'

'They would. They'd look everywhere.'

Micky sneered again. 'Garn! They'd just think you'd got blowed up. Or run off. There's plenty of people disappears these days and no one never finds out where they've gone.'

'Kill him,' Desmond said suddenly. 'He's a traitor. Kill him.'

There was a sudden, cold silence. The other children glanced at each other uneasily. Wendy Atkinson shifted her feet and reached her hand out to her brother, who crept close to her, his eyes big and fearful.

'You can't do that,' Tim said. 'That's murder.'

'It's execution,' Desmond said. 'Kill. Kill Hitler.' He picked up one of the guns.

Micky looked at him, then turned his eyes back to Tim.

'He doesn't know what he's saying,' Tim said. 'You know that. He says things and he doesn't know what they mean. He's round the twist.'

Desmond took a handful of bullets from his pocket and began to load the gun.

'Stop him,' Wendy said in a high, frightened voice. 'Stop him.'

'It's all right,' Micky said. 'They're not the right ammo. It won't work.' But his glance was uneasy. He held out his hand. 'Give us that gun, Des. It ain't yours.'

Desmond held on to it. 'It is mine. I got it. My gun. My bullets.'

'Give it here.' There was an edge to Micky's voice now. 'I'm captain of this army, I give the orders. You give it here.'

Desmond did not answer. He turned away and went on forcing the bullets into the gun.

'He's barmy,' Wendy said. 'He'll kill us. Come on, Alan. We're going home.'

Alan held tightly to her hand. He was whimpering softly, like a puppy which had hurt its paw. Together, they sidled round the wall to the steps. Martin Baker gave Micky a quick look and followed them.

'Stop here,' Micky said. 'Nobody's goin' out till I says so.'

'You can't stop us.'

'I'm the captain. This is my army. You got to do what I say.'

'Not if we don't want to,' Wendy said boldly. 'It's not a real army. It's only pretend. Go on, Alan.' She pushed her brother up the steps.

'No!' Micky said roughly. 'No. Nobody's to go.' He looked at Desmond, still struggling with the gun. 'Give us the gun. Give it here.'

For answer, the older boy hefted the weapon against his shoulder and pointed it at Micky, squinting along the barrel as if taking aim. Wendy gave a scream, and pushed Alan harder up the steps. Martin Baker scrabbled close behind them, sobbing with fright. Tim backed into a corner, thinking of bullets ricocheting around the tiny basement and wishing he'd never got involved with Micky Baxter and his secret army.

'Don't do that, Des,' Jimmy Cross said. 'You know you're not supposed to point guns at people.'

'Kill,' Desmond said in the monotonous voice that meant he was retreating into his own private world, hardly aware of other people. 'Kill Hitler. Kill, kill, kill.'

'I'm not Hitler,' Micky said. His voice had roughened to fear. 'Give us that gun.'

'Kill. Kill. Kill.'

'For Christ bloody Jesus' sake,' Micky said. 'Give us it.'

'He's gone off his rocker,' Tim muttered, and slid along the blackened wall. 'He's gone right round the bend.'

There was a sharp spike of sound as Desmond cocked

the gun. Jimmy Cross made a faint noise, almost a gargle, and Tim almost cried out. He knew that the gun was now armed and might go off at any minute. If only Desmond hadn't got his finger on the trigger. *Please*, don't let him have his finger on the trigger . . .

He slid further round the wall, coming close behind Desmond, who was still aiming the gun at Micky. He felt sick with fright. He could hear Wendy's voice, in the ruined rooms of the house above, and wished he could have escaped as well. His hand trembling, he reached out and grabbed Desmond's arm.

'Let go. Let go of the gun, Des. *Let go, or you'll kill us all.*'

Desmond jumped violently and sprang backwards, knocking Tim to the ground. He was screaming and clutching the gun to his body, his hands tightly squeezed around it, and it was pointing at the ceiling and firing, over and over again, the explosions shattering the crumbling walls, the bullets ripping through the lath and plaster above. Tim heard Wendy cry out in terror somewhere overhead. There were shards of brick and splinters of wood flying everywhere, and he felt a sudden searing pain as something stabbed into one of his legs. He screamed at Desmond – '*Let go, let go, let go!*' – but his voice went unheard and Desmond's eyes were shut, his face horribly distorted as he flailed with the gun, clutching it like a lifeline rather than the instrument of death it really was.

He heard Micky yell, and then Desmond crashed to the floor with a long, thin scream that sounded exactly like the rabbit Tim had shot with Reg Corner out at Bridge End.

CHAPTER TWENTY-FIVE

'He's really done it this time,' Frank said grimly. 'I always said that boy'd bring trouble. And I told *you* to keep away from him,' he added to Tim. 'You'll be lucky if you don't end up in prison.'

'He's lucky he's still alive,' Jess said. She had been crying most of the night and her eyes were red and swollen in a pale, puffy face. 'Oh, Tim, how could you be so stupid? Getting mixed up with guns – secret armies – I thought you were a sensible boy. I thought you could be trusted.'

'I can,' Tim said, but he didn't sound too sure about it. 'I never stole anything. I didn't even know they had guns till last night. I thought it was just a game.'

'A *game*!' Frank echoed. 'Funny sort of game, when two boys end up in hospital. You ought to have known that Baxter boy would be up to something. Look at what happened last time – young Cyril Nash blown to bits and the Cross boy with only one leg. You'd have thought he'd have known better than to go back for more.'

'More legs?' Tim said, and immediately wished he hadn't. He knew as well as his father that this was no time for jokes – he just hadn't been able to help it. He saw Frank take a deep breath, his angry face darkening even further, and added quickly, 'I didn't mean that. I didn't even know I was going to say it.'

'Your tongue's going to get you in trouble one of these days,' Frank told him. 'It's about time you learnt to control it. Time you learnt a few other things as well.' He turned to Jess. 'I told you he'd be better off out in the country. If he'd stayed out at Bridge End, this would never have happened.'

'Yes, it would,' Tim said. 'I just wouldn't have been there when it did. *Ow!*'

Exasperated beyond words, Frank had lashed out and cuffed him sharply on the ear. Tim retreated to a corner and sat miserably rubbing his head. His dad was right. He did have too much to say, and usually at the wrong moments. And it wasn't even that he found the situation funny. He was scared and upset, and his legs and arms still shook when he thought of the gun going off and everybody yelling and scrambling to get out of the way. It was a miracle someone hadn't been killed, the policeman had said.

Tim thought of it all again. It was like remembering a nightmare. There were gaps in his memory where he couldn't recall anything clearly, and flashes when everything seemed to be happening at once. And the noises – Micky's voice, harsh with panic, bawling out orders, Desmond screaming like that shot rabbit, the sharp rattle of the gun, going on and on as if it had taken over and couldn't be stopped . . . It was horrible. He didn't think he would ever be able to forget it.

Mum was right. They were lucky nobody had been killed. As it was, Tim had got away with a big splinter of wood in his leg and a few grazes, but Micky had almost bled to death and they thought Desmond would lose one of his eyes. And the police had been up in number 10 half the night, tearing the place to bits if what Nancy Baxter said was true, and Tim had been told to stay indoors until they came to talk to him too.

'That's a day's work lost,' Frank grumbled. 'I can't go in the Yard till they've been. I just hope you're proud of yourself.'

Tim said nothing. Of course he wasn't proud of himself. He felt humiliated and ashamed and frightened. Suppose he did end up in prison. His father would never want to speak to him again. And Mum wouldn't be able to show her face in the street again. They'd probably have to move, and they might not even tell Tim where they'd gone, for they surely wouldn't want him back at home when he came out.

I might be there for years, he thought, and saw himself sitting alone in a bare cell, living on nothing but bread and water, until he was an old man.

There was a sudden loud knocking on the front door, and Tim almost jumped out of his skin. Jess gasped and put her hand to her mouth, turning to Frank, who got up and stood for a moment in the middle of the room.

'Now you answer his questions properly,' he said sternly to Tim. 'Tell him the truth. It won't help you to go telling lies to try to get out of it.'

He went through the passage and they heard him open the door. There was a murmur of deep voices, and then he came back, followed by a policeman carrying his helmet. If he hadn't taken it off, Tim thought, he wouldn't have been able to get through the door. As it was, he seemed to fill the room with his huge body in its dark blue uniform.

The policeman nodded to Jess. 'I'm sorry about this, missus. It's a bad do. I'll have to ask your boy a few questions.' He glanced at Tim. 'This the young man?'

'Yes, this is Tim. He's our oldest boy.' Jess's voice was quick and nervous. 'He's a good boy, really, he's never been in any trouble before. It's only that he's got into bad company . . .' Her voice trailed away. Mothers always said those things. The policeman must have heard them a hundred times before. Probably Nancy Baxter herself had said exactly the same about Micky.

The policeman nodded. He put his helmet down on the dining table and pulled out a chair. He sat down, his hands on his knees, facing Tim. His big face was serious.

'Now then. You were one of the boys involved in the incident last night in the basement of number 24 Turkey Street, is that right?'

Tim nodded miserably.

'Tell me exactly what happened. In your own words.'

Whose words would I use, Tim thought, but there were no jokes left in him now. In a small, hesitant voice, he described what had taken place in the ruined den.

'I wanted to leave. I was fed up with it – I couldn't see we'd ever do any good. And I was fed up with Micky ordering me about. He just wants to be in charge all the time.' A faint note of indignation crept into his voice. 'He thinks he's boss of the whole street.'

'All right, I know all about Micky Baxter,' the policeman said. 'So you wanted to leave, did you? Why didn't you, then?'

'I tried. I told Micky I was going. He said I couldn't go, I'd sworn an oath of secrecy. I hadn't,' Tim said, turning his eyes towards his father. 'I never swore anything. But Micky said I knew too much and I'd have to be kept prisoner down there. He said nobody would ever know what had happened to me. He said people would just think I'd run off, or – or got blown up or something.' Tim's voice shook and ended in a whisper. He hardly dared look at his mother.

'Oh, that awful boy,' Jess said, almost in tears again. 'He's a wicked, wicked boy. We might never have seen our Tim again.' She covered her face with both hands and Frank put his hand on her shoulder. But he was looking grimmer than ever. He nodded curtly at Tim.

'Go on, then. Tell us what happened after that. How did they come to start shooting?'

'That was Desmond.' Tim strove to be fair. 'I mean, I don't think he really knew what he was doing. He'd gone all funny, you know, like he does – his voice went sort of flat. He said I ought to be killed. But he was talking about Hitler too. That was what Micky wanted to do – get over to Germany and kill Hitler. That was why he was getting the guns. But I think Desmond had got muddled up and maybe he thought we were there, or we'd caught Hitler or something – I don't know.'

'So was it him did the shooting?'

'Yes. He picked up the gun and aimed it at Micky. I tried to get it off him but he must have already had his finger on the trigger.' Tim's voice was thick now, as if he were trying not to be sick. 'It went off and just kept on going. Desmond was sort of jumping about – it was like he couldn't let go – and the bullets were hitting the walls and bouncing . . .' He shook his head, trying to go on, but his voice refused to work and the tears were streaming down his face. 'I thought we were all going to be killed,' he whispered at last.

The three adults stared at him, then turned their eyes to each other. Jess was as white as snow, and even the policeman's face had lost its ruddiness. Frank cleared his throat.

'You're lucky you weren't,' he said gruffly. 'You're all lucky you weren't. You were bloody silly, the whole lot of you.'

Tim nodded. There was a brief silence, then Frank turned to the policeman.

'So what happens now? Are they going to be charged?'

The policeman shrugged. 'That's not up to me, sir. I'll have to go back to the station and make a report. The super will decide what to do about it. It's obvious that the Baxter boy was the ringleader – a proper little arsenal we found, up in his bedroom. Grenades, bullets, a bayonet – you never saw anything like it.' He glanced apologetically towards Jess. 'And I'm sorry, missus, but we'll have to have a look around here too. See if your boy's been hiding anything.'

'Oh, no, he wouldn't –' Jess began, then stopped and looked at Tim. 'You haven't got any – any guns or anything, have you?'

'No. I never had anything, only a couple of bits of shrapnel for souvenirs. Everyone has that.' For a moment, Tim was afraid that it was against the law even to collect shrapnel. He met his mother's eyes and she stared hard at him.

'Tell the truth, now. It won't do you any good to tell lies.'

It was almost the worst moment of all, to know that his mother no longer trusted him. Cheeky and mischievous as Tim had been, he had never lied to Jess – well, only about things like whether he'd cleaned his teeth or eaten the last apple, things that didn't really matter. He gazed at her, trying to find the warmth he had always been used to seeing in her eyes, but all he could see was doubt and disappointment.

'I haven't got anything. I really haven't.' He turned back to the policeman. 'You can look anywhere you like. Under my bed – in the drawers. I haven't got anything at all.' He thought suddenly of the white powder he had slipped out of the jar in Mr Driver's shop and felt his skin scorch with colour. 'I mean –'

'Yes, Tim?' Jess said sharply. 'What? You'd better tell us.'

He wriggled miserably on his chair. 'It's just – well, I thought it was for fireworks. We haven't had fireworks for ages and Maureen's never seen any at all. I was going to make a her a golden shower.'

'Fireworks?' Frank said. 'You were going to make fireworks? How? What with?'

'Saltpetre,' Tim whispered. 'That's what Micky said we needed. He said I had to get it.' His eyes were agonised as he looked round at the three adults. 'I didn't think it was stealing, not really. I mean, there was a whole jarful and I only took a couple of spoons. And hardly anybody ever asks for it.'

'Let's get this straight,' Frank said. 'You took saltpetre from Mr Driver's shop? You took it for Micky Baxter to make fireworks?'

Tim nodded. Frank tightened his jaw and looked at the policeman.

'I can guess what sort of fireworks that young ruffian was going to make. He's a menace, that boy is, always has been. If ever anything went wrong in this street, that Micky Baxter was at the bottom of it – broken windows, stuff pinched off the allotments, you name it . . . Why, look what he did next door in Mrs Glaister's house, practically wrecked the place. And he's been up in court more times than I've had hot dinners.' He glowered at his son. 'If I've told you once to keep clear of him, I've told you a hundred times. And now you're in it as deep as he is. Fireworks! Stealing saltpetre from Mr Driver! And what's *he* going to have to say about it, eh? Tell me that. He gave you that job as a favour to me. How'm I going to go in there and tell him you've been stealing stuff off his shelves?'

Tim shook his head. There was nothing he could say to defend himself. He'd known he was doing wrong, taking the saltpetre without asking. And he *had* known Micky had guns. He'd never actually seen them – he might pretend he'd thought Micky was spinning a yarn – but he'd half-known it was true really.

'I'm sorry,' he said wretchedly. 'I didn't think it'd matter. I never took anything else. I just wanted to make a golden shower for Maureen.' He looked at his mother. 'She's never seen a firework.'

Jess felt her heart move with sudden pity. Poor Tim, she thought. He really didn't mean any harm. He'd got led astray by young Micky, and he'd been silly, but he'd never done anything really serious. He'd just wanted to do something for his baby sister.

'It's hard on boys like Tim,' she said to Frank after the policeman had gone. 'I mean, they've had their childhood taken away from them. Look at fireworks. Tim and Keith used to love Bonfire Night, with you bringing home a couple of fireworks every week and making a bonfire in the back garden. And everyone in the street watching each other's displays, and seeing rockets going up in the sky all over Portsmouth. And then all that stopped, and they weren't allowed to go to the beach any more, or fly their kites, and then they got sent out to the country, away from home. I don't think we realised just how bad it was for them.'

'Bad? It's been like a holiday! They were as happy as sandboys with Mr and Mrs Corner, you know that. Spoilt, they were. And that vicar's not much better, what with playing cricket and building snowmen with them half his time. They've been allowed to run wild, that's the trouble. They haven't been disciplined as they should.'

Jess sighed. Tim had been sent upstairs to tidy his bedroom after the policeman had gone. The room had been thoroughly searched – even the floorboards had been lifted up – but nothing had been found, apart from an old pocket-knife that Frank had lost years ago and a marble that Keith had once forced through a knothole. But the policeman hadn't been able to tell them what would happen next. He would have to go to each boy's house, and then he'd have to go and see the chemist.

'I'll take that young man up to see Mr Driver myself,' Frank decided. 'I know it won't make such difference – we can't ask for special treatment – but at least young Tim can tell him what's happened and apologise. I feel proper ashamed, I do. I always thought we'd brought our boys up to be trusted.'

'We have,' Jess said. 'I honestly don't think he realised how serious it could be.'

'Well, he should have done. He's almost thirteen – quite old enough to know the difference between right and wrong. Anyway, he's old enough to take responsibility for his own actions. I'm not going to apologise for him – he's got to do that for himself.' He went to the door at the foot of the staircase and shouted. 'Tim! Come down here. That's his job finished, anyway,' he went on as they heard Tim's footsteps come slowly down. 'Mr Driver won't want a thief working for him.'

Tim arrived just in time to hear the last words, and Jess saw him turn scarlet. She looked at his tear-filled eyes and once again felt overwhelmingly sorry for him. Poor Tim. He'd been silly, but that was all, and he was certainly getting his punishment now. She was sure he'd never do anything like it again.

She watched as Frank led his son up the street. Even standing at the door, she felt exposed, as if all the neighbours were peering out of their windows and talking about it. And this was only the beginning. If Tim had to go to court, everyone would know about it. It would be in the *Evening News*. She'd never be able to hold up her head again.

Jess shut the door and went back to the kitchen. She dumped a pile of washing on the wooden draining-board beside the sink and started to run some hot water out of the Ascot. The green soap she used to scrub clothes was almost finished; when she'd done this lot the scrap that was left would have to go in the jamjar with the rest, to be melted down into one lump so that none would be wasted. You couldn't afford to waste anything these days – string, greaseproof paper, tiny stubs of pencil, it was all carefully saved so as to get the most use possible.

She worked automatically, carrying out her chores without thinking about them, doing the things she did every day almost without being aware of it, her mind fixed entirely on Tim and what had happened in the bombed house.

She'd been as angry and upset as Frank. But although she'd been hurt by the fact that Tim had taken stuff from Mr Driver, and by his allowing Micky Baxter to lead him into trouble, she knew that a good deal of her anger – and Frank's too – stemmed from their shock at what *could* have happened. It was frightening to think of Micky Baxter, hoarding guns and grenades in his bedroom, carrying them through the streets, letting the other children play about with them. And that Desmond – why, the boy was simple, there was no knowing what he might have done. Almost had done . . .

We might never have seen our Tim again, she thought, and the tears that she'd thought must have all been cried during the night began to flow again. Tim, hopping about on one leg like Jimmy Cross. Tim, torn to pieces in an explosion like Cyril Nash . . .

Jess left the washing and went and sat down at the table. She felt sick and giddy. She laid her head on her arms and wept.

Mr Driver listened with a grave face to what Tim had to say.

At first, it had been hard for Tim to say anything at all. He'd tried frantically to think what words he could use to tell the chemist what he had done. They jangled about in his head, a great tangle of them jostling and bumping into each other, not making any sense at all. Some of them repeated themselves and echoed in the hollowness that seemed to have replaced his brain, hammering against the inside of his skull and making his head ring.

'Just tell me simply what it is, Tim,' Mr Driver said gently, and he put his hands on Tim's arms and shifted him slightly, so that he was looking straight into his face.

The chemist's eyes were brown and mild. Short-sightedness had etched a little frown between his brows, but it didn't make him look cross, only slightly puzzled. Tim had never seen him look angry.

'Just tell me one word,' Mr Driver said. 'And then another one. Let's piece it together gradually, shall we?'

But once Tim had got out one word, the rest came tumbling after it, like the litter of piglets Reg Corner had once shown him at the farm. To Tim's ears, his words seemed just as muddled, but Mr Driver listened patiently and seemed to understand.

'So you thought Micky Baxter wanted to make fireworks, and he asked you to get some saltpetre for them. But why didn't you ask me, Tim?'

'I don't know. Well, you might have thought it was dangerous.'

'So I should hope,' Frank began, but Mr Driver shook his head.

'Boys are bound to want to make experiments, but it's best if they have a little bit of guidance so that they don't take unnecessary risks. If you'd asked me, Tim, I would have told you what saltpetre was and how it should be used. And I would probably have suggested that you bring your friends along here one evening, so that we could experiment together. Then we wouldn't have had any accidents.'

'I'm sorry,' Tim whispered.

'Well, is that all you can say?' Frank exploded. 'The young hooligans had guns and ammunition that they'd stolen from the Home Guard. They had a couple of hand grenades, a bayonet and God knows what else, all stashed away in that Baxter boy's bedroom. And you can't tell me they wanted the saltpetre to make fireworks. It was gunpowder they were after making. Bombs. Why, they could have blown up the entire street!'

Tim was crying now, his shoulders shaking with great, retching sobs that seemed to force their way up from deep inside his chest like hard, rough lumps. He coughed and spluttered, and felt his father's angry disgust trickle down through his fingers.

'No. We wouldn't. It was *Hitler* . . . We wanted to *help* . . .'

'Micky Baxter never wanted to help anybody but himself,' Frank stated grimly.

Mr Driver frowned thoughtfully. 'But you say you thought it was to make fireworks. Did you really believe that, Tim?'

Tim hesitated. He badly wanted to say yes. He wanted to pretend he'd never known anything about the guns or Micky's plans, that he'd thought it was just a game. But he looked up and met Mr Driver's mild brown gaze, and knew that he couldn't do it.

'I tried to,' he said at last, reluctantly.

Mr Driver smiled a little. 'You tried to. I expect you thought you'd succeeded too, didn't you? So long as you didn't think about it too much.' He glanced up at Frank. 'I don't think you need to worry too much about this young man, Mr Budd. He's always struck me as a very honest and open lad. I think he's just got himself into rather a muddle with this secret army and plans to kill Hitler – all very laudable, after all – and lost sight of things a bit. I don't think I shall be taking the matter any further.'

Tim stared at him. He turned his eyes up to Frank. His father was looking bewildered.

'But the matter's already gone further,' Frank said. 'It's a police matter. It's out of our hands.'

Mr Driver shook his head. 'As far as what happened last night, you're right, of course. But nothing can be done about the saltpetre unless I press charges.'

'You mean you'll not tell them he took the stuff? But –'

'Oh, I won't hide anything from them. And I don't

advise you to try either, Tim. But they can't charge him with theft without my agreement. And I don't propose to ruin the boy's life because of one foolish error.'

'Well,' Frank said after a moment, 'that's very generous of you, Mr Driver. And a damn sight more than you deserve,' he said to Tim. 'You ought to be very grateful.'

'Yes,' Tim said humbly. 'I am. Thank you, Mr Driver. And – and I really am sorry.'

'Yes, I believe you are,' the chemist said. He gave Tim a kind, rather tired smile and said, 'I haven't forgotten what it is to be a boy. I was always fascinated by chemistry, always mixing substances together to see what happened. One day, perhaps, I'll tell you about some of them. But for now –' he glanced at the Roman numerals on the clock hanging on the wall '– there's work to be done. I've got a lot of deliveries waiting to be made.'

'Yes,' Frank said, 'and I daresay you're looking for a new delivery boy now, to take 'em round. You'll want a boy you can trust.'

'Oh,' Mr Driver said, 'I think I can trust Tim. Can't I, Tim?'

Tim felt as if his heart had leapt into his throat. He gazed at the chemist, scarcely able to believe his ears. He opened his mouth, struggling once again for speech, and finally managed a sort of gargling, 'Yes. Oh, yes –'

'Mind, I shall want your promise that you will never again take anything from any of my jars or boxes without permission,' the chemist said warningly. 'I shall have to have that. But if you can promise me that, then I see no reason why you shouldn't start work again straight away As I said, there's a lot to be done.'

The door opened and Mrs Driver put her head into the room. 'Old Mrs Brannigan's out here, asking where her medicine is. She says it ought to have been sent round this morning, first thing. And there's a queue halfway down the street with prescriptions to be made up. I'm sorry to interrupt, but I think you'll have to come –'

'It's all right, my dear. I'm coming now.' Mr Driver indicated a pile of packages and bottles standing on the bench. 'There they are, Tim, all ready for you. And it sounds as if there'll be some more when you get back. It's going to be a busy day.'

CHAPTER TWENTY-SIX

'Well, I don't know as I'd have done it,' Annie said. 'Giving him a responsible job like that. I mean, you don't know what else he might be tempted to do.'

Jess stared at her. 'Annie, this is our *Tim*. He's as honest as the day is long. Of course he wouldn't pinch the medicines.'

'Well, he'd already pinched something,' Annie said reasonably. 'Who's to say? You know what boys are. Once they start –'

'Tim'll never do anything like that again,' Jess said positively. 'He's been silly and he's learnt his lesson. He's not a bad boy, you know he's not – not like that Micky Baxter.'

'Look, he's been away from home for two years,' Annie pointed out. 'He's been out of your care. How d'you know what sort of children he was mixing with out in the country? How d'you know what sort of ideas they have out there?'

'For goodness sake, Annie, he wasn't on the moon!' Jess could not remember ever having felt so exasperated with her sister before. 'And he was staying in a vicarage. I don't suppose Mr Beckett taught him to steal. Or Reg and Edna Corner, where he was before. A more decent couple you couldn't wish to meet.'

'Well, he got it from somewhere,' Annie said and went out to the kitchen in a huff.

Jess walked back down April Grove almost in tears. Her own sister, painting Tim black like that – Tim, the favourite of the family, always smiling and ready with a joke.

'I thought I'd get some sympathy from Annie, of all people,' she said to Frank when he came home from work, bringing Cherry with him for a game of cards. 'But all she seemed to want to do was make it worse. I've never known her like it before.'

'I daresay she's worrying about Colin,' Cherry said. 'She still hasn't heard anything, has she? It must be terrible not to know what's happened to your boy.'

Jess looked at her, feeling ashamed. 'You're right. She must think I'm lucky to have Tim safe. And then to have to listen to me whining about a bit of boys' trouble –'

'You can't help that,' Cherry said. 'You're upset too, and no wonder. It was a bit more than "boys' trouble" after all. Someone could have been killed.'

'I know. That's the awful part. I feel sick every time I think about it. Even if it hadn't been Tim –' She shuddered. 'It doesn't bear thinking about.'

Frank got out the cards and began to shuffle them. Rose, who had been reading in a corner, got up to join them at the table. Tim was upstairs, chipping away at a model aeroplane. He'd been quiet and subdued since the accident, spending a lot of time by himself. Keeping out of Frank's way, Jess thought, knowing her husband was still angry, but she felt sorry for her son all the same. Yet now that Cherry had pointed it out, she knew that Annie needed her sympathy and support just as much.

'There's Mum, too,' she said. 'Annie does much more for her than I do. She goes down North End nearly every day to do a bit of work and cook her some dinner. It'd be a lot easier if Mum would agree to come and live with her, but she won't – says all her memories are in that house and she won't leave it.'

And even that wasn't the extent of Annie's worries. There was Olive as well, and Betty. Ted seemed to have come round about Dennis, but he still wasn't out of hospital and Annie had told her Betty seemed to be worrying about him more than you'd expect, now he was recovering. But people did sometimes act a bit funny after a bad accident. It took time to get over it.

I'll go up and see her first thing in the morning, Jess decided. I'll leave Rose to get the dinner and go down to Mum's with her. She needs a bit of company just as much as I do. We ought to share our worries, not upset each other over them.

She looked across the table at Cherry, who was fanning her cards out in her hand. It never ceased to surprise her, how Cherry could put her finger on things. Funny how she'd so quickly become such a member of the family.

Even funnier, when Jess thought back to her first impression of 'Cherry' – the saucy little flirt, wiggling her bottom round the boiler-shop and turning all the men's heads.

Betty was at the hospital. When she had come into the ward, she'd been pleased to find Dennis sitting up in bed. His eyes were still bandaged but he turned his head and smiled when she came into the ward. He held out his hand.

'I knew it was you. I know your footsteps. And that nice scent you wear.'

'It's Ashes of Roses.' She kissed him and then sat down beside him, holding his hand. 'How're you feeling today, Dennis?' She felt uneasy. There was something different about him today – a tightness in his lips, a brittle hardness in his voice.

'I'm all right,' he said, but he didn't sound all right and Betty looked at him more closely. She saw the creases on his forehead, the lines around mouth and nose. Some of them were scars, but others looked more like bitterness and anger.

Dennis had never been a bitter or angry man. And those lines had not been there the last time she came in.

'What is it, Dennis?' she asked. 'What's happened?'

'Nothing. Nothing I can't deal with myself.'

She was shocked. 'But you don't have to deal with *anything* yourself, Dennis. You've got me. We share things. Everything.'

'There are some things,' he said, 'that nobody can share.'

'I don't understand. What are you talking about?'

He was silent for a moment, playing with her fingers. Then he said quietly, 'I've been thinking, Betty. I think maybe we made a mistake. Well, not a mistake – I know we loved each other –'

'We still do.' Her voice was edged with panic. 'Nothing's changed, Dennis. I haven't changed. I still love you as much as ever. More.'

'I know. But – I can't hold you to the promises we made, Betty. Not any more. Things have changed. I've changed. Nothing will ever be the same again.'

'I don't know what you're saying.'

'I'm trying to tell you –'

'No!' she cried. 'I don't want to hear it! Don't say it, Dennis – please, *please* don't –'

'I have to. I must.'

'No. No. *No*.' She was in tears, clutching his hands, staring into his face. But he couldn't see her, couldn't see her anguish. 'Dennis, no –'

'Betty, don't make this hard for me –'

'What else can I do? I can't let you –'

'And *I* can't let *you*,' he said with sudden strength. 'Betty, do you know what they told me today? Do you know what the doctors say? They say I'm blind.' His voice shivered and dropped. 'I'm never going to see again. I'm going to be like this all my life – useless. How can I marry you? How can I be such a burden?'

Betty stared at him, at the scarred face and the bandaged eyes that would never see again. Blind eyes, that turned Dennis into a different man.

But that wasn't true. He was the same Dennis. Nothing could change the Dennis who lived inside.

'You'd never be a burden,' she said shakily.

'I would. What could I do? What can a blind man do? Tune pianos?' His voice was bitter. 'That's what they do, isn't it. How many pianos are there going to be to tune after the war – and how many blind men to tune them?'

'Dennis, don't talk like that,' she begged. 'There must be other things – people do all kinds of things.'

'What sort of things?'

'I don't know.' Betty had never known anyone who was blind. 'But there must be things. Anyway, what does it matter so long as we're together?'

'I'll tell you how much it matters,' he said. 'I'll tell you what it means. It means I'll never be able to do anything useful again. I won't be able to read or write or even walk down the street. I won't be able to ride a bike or drive a tractor or plough a field. I won't be able to do my job. I won't be able to go back to BD. I'm useless.'

'BD? But of course you can't go back to BD – and I'm thankful for it. D'you think I want you going back to that? You've done quite enough. You've saved any amount of people from being blown up. You've risked your life over and over again. You were lucky not to be killed that last time. I think you've done as much as anyone could expect.'

'I haven't done as much as *I* expected –'

'You expected too much, then. Who do you think you are, Dennis Verney? Who said you had to do it all by yourself? What is it makes *you* so special?'

'But there's still bombs out there,' he said restlessly. 'They're finding more and more every day. And the raids haven't stopped. They reckon we'll be getting a fresh lot soon. This has just been a lull.'

'Well, I'll be just as glad if you're not out there,' Betty said robustly. She moved closer and put her arms round him. 'It was bad enough before, knowing what you were doing – but seeing you like this, knowing that you were almost killed – I'd never have a minute's peace.'

'Nobody's getting any peace,' he said. 'That's what all this is about.'

Betty was silent. Since Dennis had been in hospital, she had come to realise even more strongly that there was a thread of steel running through him that was unbreakable. It had been there when he refused to abandon his principles and join up, when he had gone to prison, when he had worked on the farm. She had recognised it again when he left the farm and joined BD. When she had first seen him lying in the hospital bed, unconscious, unmoving, his broken body swathed in bandages, she had feared it was gone. But it had been there still, keeping him alive, bringing him back to consciousness, forcing him to recover.

'There are times when you have a choice,' he'd said to her when he'd been able to talk again. 'It's like standing on a high diving-board, trying to decide whether to jump. You can choose whether to live or die. I was tempted to die – but then I heard your voice, telling me about the farm, talking about the times we'd spent together . . . I couldn't leave you, Betty. I had to come back.'

She reminded him of that now. 'It was me you wanted to come back to, Dennis. Not BD. It was *us* – our life together. That's what's important. You've done your bit for the war.'

'I didn't do it for the war,' he said wearily. 'I did it for the peace. Aren't you *ever* going to understand?'

Betty bit her lip. She was acutely hurt by his words, and even more so because he'd spoken to her in a way he'd never done before. And because he was putting a gap between them – a gap in their understanding, their closeness. She felt a sudden panic, as if he were drifting away from her all over again.

'Of course I understand,' she said gently. 'I'm sorry – it was the wrong word to use. But I can't help the way I feel, Dennis. I can't help wanting to keep you safe.'

'And I can't help the way *I* feel.' He sat silent for a moment or two, then burst out, 'I feel so bloody useless, sitting here all day, Betty. It was bad enough when I thought I'd get better and be able to go back. But now –' He shook his head. 'Look, I'm trying not to be sorry for myself. I keep telling myself there must be a reason why I'm still alive – there must be work still for me to do. But I've got to face it myself. I can't hide behind your skirts.'

'You wouldn't be,' Betty said, still hurt. 'It wouldn't be like that.'

'It would. Of course it would.' Dennis shook his head again and let go of her hand to run his fingers through his hair. 'Look, I won't be able to do a *thing*. You'll have to do it all. Everything around the house, every little job – all the things a man ought to be doing. You'll have to do the lot. And how can we have children? What use is a father who can't see? No, you'll be better off without me. Better off finding someone else.'

'No! I couldn't do that. There'll never be anyone but you, Dennis.'

'Yes there will.' He spoke as if he had spent a long time convincing himself. 'You're young, you're pretty – you're everything a man could want. They'll be queueing up for you, Betty.'

'Then they'll be disappointed,' she said sharply. 'The shop's shut. I'm not interested in anyone else, Dennis, nor ever will be.'

But she could not convince him. And in the end, the nurses sent her away and she walked out of the hospital feeling as though she had left her heart behind.

Over the following week, she visited him as often as she could. But he would not change his mind, and on the seventh day she arrived to find a strange young soldier in the bed that had been his. Dennis had been moved to another hospital, they said, a hospital about sixty miles away, where he would be taught to live life as a blind man.

CHAPTER TWENTY-SEVEN

The secret army appeared in the Juvenile Court halfway through November. Micky was out of hospital now, but Desmond had been kept in for several operations on his damaged eye. He was also very confused, and there was talk of moving him to St James', the mental hospital, when he was better.

Frank and Jess went to the court with Tim, all dressed in their best clothes. Frank wore the dark suit he'd got married in and Jess had her brown hat and coat with one of Annie's scarves in the neck. She had debated wearing the spray brooch Frank had given her one Christmas, gold wire with coloured stones that looked like flowers, but decided in the end that the magistrates might think it looked too flashy for such a sober occasion.

'Why don't you put a bit of lipstick on?' Rose suggested. 'You look ever so pale.'

But Jess shook her head. She had never worn make-up and knew Frank wouldn't like it. And she didn't want to look common.

The court was a gloomy place, all dark panelled walls and flaking distemper. There was a long table for the magistrates, with three high-backed chairs behind it, and there were seats like church pews lined up in front of them.

The magistrates came in through a side door. There were two men and one woman, all dressed in dark colours. The men looked between sixty and seventy, one with silver hair and rimless spectacles, the other with a short dark beard like Edward the Seventh's. The woman was short and plump, with heavy glasses and dark hair. She looked about fifty and reminded Jess of a schoolmistress.

The boys stood in a row, their parents and the police close behind. Micky's probation officer was there, and Granny Kinch had persuaded Nancy that she had to come too. Nancy wore her red coat, buttoned neatly except where one had come off, and a black scarf wound round her head like a turban. Granny Kinch wore the herringbone tweed she had had ever since Jess had known her. She looked odd with her curlers out, her sparse grey hair sticking out from under a shapeless brown felt beret, and she kept chobbling her mouth at the unfamiliar feeling of having her teeth in.

Mr Beckett had come down from Bridge End. He was at the court when Jess and Frank arrived, tall and solemn in his dark clerical suit. He shook their hands and murmured a few words of reassurance before the magistrates entered, then sat down beside Mr Driver.

'I never thought we'd have to come to a place like this,' Jess whispered to Frank as they took their seats. 'I mean, our Tim of all children! He's not a bad boy, not really.'

'He got led astray,' Frank allowed. 'And I don't think he ever really believed in those guns. But you can't expect to get into bad company and not be tainted, that's what it boils down to. He's been silly and now he's going to have to pay.'

In fact, Tim hadn't been charged with much at all. Micky bore the brunt of it, and the charges against him – breaking into Home Guard premises, stealing weapons, possessing those weapons – were very serious. Desmond too had been charged with the same offences, but the other children – Jimmy Cross, Tim, Martin Baker and Wendy and Alan – had been accused merely of 'being accessories' which didn't seem so bad. And Martin and Alan were both too young to appear in court, while Wendy had been let off because she hadn't actually been in the house when the gun was fired.

The four boys made a sorry little line in front of the magistrates. Desmond had been allowed out of hospital for the day and stood swaying slightly, his head still bandaged. He had lost weight and his old jacket hung loosely from his bony shoulders. He stared blankly about him with his one eye and didn't acknowledge any of the other boys; most of the time he mumbled to himself in a slurred undertone.

Micky stood cockily with his legs apart, glowering under his heavy brows and trying to look as if he didn't care. His grandmother had forced him into a relatively clean shirt and tried to brush his jacket, but his shoes were scuffed and grimy and one of his socks was already falling down. His hair had been cut last night, with a pudding-basin over his head, but the scissors hadn't been sharp enough and it looked ragged round the edges.

Jimmy Cross stood on his wooden leg, leaning on his crutch. As soon as the magistrates saw him, they called for a chair, and he was allowed to sit down, the false leg sticking out in front of him. He looked a bit pale, as if he was scared of what was going to happen. His mother hadn't let him out of the house since the night of the accident and he was bored, fed up and frightened. He'd decided he wasn't ever going to speak to Micky Baxter again.

Tim stood on the end of the row. His face was white, but he looked clean and tidy. Jess had washed his hair last night and brushed it this morning until the fair curls shone. His face had been scrubbed pink, and he wore a new shirt made from a yard and a half of grey flannel that Jess had been saving, and his best grey jacket and short trousers. Frank had lent him one of his own ties, and his shoes had been polished until he could see his face in them.

The magistrates listened while the policeman read out a report on what had happened, and then they looked severely at the boys and started to ask questions.

'Why did you want to collect the weapons? What was the purpose of this "secret army"? Where did you get the weapons? Who actually broke into the store? What did the rest of you know about this?'

Gradually they got all the truth and heard the story of the shooting. Then they moved closer to each other and talked in low voices for a while. From time to time, they all turned and stared at the boys, examining their faces and looking them up and down.

Thank goodness I smartened Tim up a bit, Jess thought. He looks a nice little boy. That Micky Baxter looks a real little villain, and anyone can see Jimmy Cross has just been led astray. And as for Desmond – well, he doesn't seem to know what's going on. You can't help feeling sorry for him really.

She turned her eyes to the other adults. Mrs Cross was looking pale and frightened, and Desmond's mother looked worn out. Poor soul, she'd had a terrible time, what with her hubby getting killed when Desmond was a baby and having to struggle to bring him up, as well as run the shop all by herself. But you couldn't be sure that the magistrates would take any notice of that. They might just lump all the boys in together and send them off to an approved school as an 'example'. Breaking into Home Guard premises and stealing guns *was* serious, and even though Tim hadn't been involved in that he'd still been there that night. And he had taken the saltpetre, although Mr Driver had been as good as his word and never pressed charges.

At last the magistrates seemed to come to a decision. They drew apart, nodding, and faced the court again. The one who looked like the old King leaned forward and addressed the boys sternly.

'You're all aware that this a very grave matter. Breaking and entering is always serious, and stealing is more serious still. Stealing weapons such as guns and explosives such as hand grenades, even in times of peace, must be dealt with harshly. At the present time, with the country at war and in need of all its defences, it borders on treachery.' He paused and looked at them solemnly. Tim was crying and Jimmy Cross was staring at his feet. Only Micky met his eye with an attempt at bravado, and then gazed at the ceiling.

Jess turned quickly to Frank and grabbed his hand. Treachery! The magistrate was calling them traitors. Her Tim, a *traitor*. She felt the tears, which hadn't been far away all morning, come hot to her eyes.

'We shall take into account the fact that you say you were trying to form your own so-called army in defence of your country and that you had no other purpose in collecting these weapons.' The magistrate stroked his short grey beard. 'It seems that you may have been driven by misguided motives rather than criminal ones. Nevertheless –' his heavy brows drew together in a frown and Tim shrank visibly '– you must realise the seriousness of your actions. Guns are not toys. They're lethal weapons, to be used only by qualified men in very special circumstances. We cannot and will not have gangs of children setting themselves up as soldiers and risking their own and others' lives. The country has troubles enough, without mischievous boys adding to them.'

He paused. The courtroom was silent. All eyes were fixed on his face. Even Micky had removed his gaze from the ceiling and was watching him. After a few moments, he went on, speaking slowly and impressively.

'The youngest boy, Timothy Budd, has shown that he did not fully understand the actions of the rest of the group. He was unaware that his friends possessed authentic weapons. He had already decided to leave the group. Moreover, he has never been in any kind of trouble and has been vouched for by his employer, neighbours and by those with whom he has been billeted with in the country, as a decent, well-behaved and quiet youngster from a good home.'

The magistrate's eyes rested for a moment on Jess and Frank, and then on Mr Beckett and Mr Driver. Jess tried to meet his gaze without flinching, but felt her colour rise. Frank, still holding Jess's hand, looked steadily back at him.

'James Cross.' The glance moved on to Jimmy, sitting on his chair with his wooden leg stuck out in front of him. 'I must confess I find it difficult to understand why a boy who has already been in danger of his life, and suffered severe injury at the hands of this same gang leader, should want to take further such risks. James, you have already lost a leg. What in heaven's name possessed you to allow yourself to get involved in such danger again?'

Jimmy shrugged and said nothing. There was nothing to say. It would be impossible to explain to this man what it was like to be a boy at home alone in Portsmouth while your friends were mostly out in the country and war raged all over the world. You took what friends there were, and what excitement you could get. And Micky *was* exciting – there was no question about that.

The magistrate sighed and turned his attention to Desmond. 'Desmond Cook. Now this I find a very sad case. A boy who is clearly backward, with very little understanding of what is happening around him, easily led and easily used. Desmond, I understand you are still receiving hospital treatment, is that correct?' He leaned a little closer and looked into Desmond's face, but Desmond looked blankly past him. The magistrate glanced towards Mrs Cook.

'Yes, sir, he is,' she whispered. 'In fact, they think – they think he'll have to stop there all his life.' She lifted a handkerchief to her face and began to cry.

'Yes.' The magistrate looked down at the papers on his desk. 'Yes, I see that here.' He cleared his throat and shuffled the papers about. He looked from under his brows at Micky.

'Michael Baxter.' His voice had deepened. 'Michael Baxter, you've been before this court before, more than once. You've been charged with breaking and entering a neighbour's house, with shoplifting, with a number of petty offences. You are already on probation. Now you come before us on much more serious charges, charges which cannot be overlooked or dealt with by a probation order.'

He's going to send him away, Jess thought. And if he does that, he'll send them all away. Jimmy, and Desmond and my Tim. Oh God, *please* don't let him send my Tim away . . .

'Whatever your motives were – and we'll suppose that they were as good as you claim – you have broken into

Government premises and stolen Government property. You've been in illegal possession of dangerous weapons and because of this possession others have been harmed – could easily have been killed. You might have been killed yourself.'

He looked as if he didn't think that would have been such a bad thing, Jess thought. But he didn't say so. He went on, still speaking in that deep, stern voice.

'As it is, Desmond Cook has lost the sight of one eye and may have to spend the rest of his life in hospital care. And all this despite the fact that another of your friends, James Cross, is here with only one leg owing to an earlier escapade, while another young boy, Cyril Nash, lost his life during the same incident.

'It seems to us that you do not have the ability to learn a lesson from events. We have a duty to the rest of the community to ensure that you learn this lesson – and others too which seem to have passed you by. You're a dangerous young man, the clear and self-confessed ring-leader in this unhappy affair, and the community is entitled to be protected from you. We therefore have no choice but to send you to an approved school for a term of two years, with a recommendation that you be treated as the criminal you are and given no privileges until you can prove yourself worthy of them. I hope this will have the effect of making you think about where your errors are leading you, and helping you to become a decent and upright citizen.'

There was a snorting sound from further along the pew. Granny Kinch was sobbing noisily, her face smothered by a stained and crumpled handkerchief. Nancy was staring stonily in front of her. Micky shrugged and looked at the ceiling again, but his face was pale and his jaw was clenched.

'As for the other boys,' the magistrate continued, 'we take the view that they were led astray by Michael Baxter and that no useful purpose would be served by sending them away. Desmond Cook has many more months, if not years, of hospital treatment to face anyway, and James

Cross must surely have learned his lesson by now. As for Timothy Budd, I'm surprised he was ever brought in front of this court. It's quite clear that he merely strayed into the fringe of Baxter's activities and was withdrawing from them. He strikes me as a child who does know how to learn a lesson, and who has learned this one well. I do not think we shall see him before this court again.' He paused, while Tim stared at him. 'We are therefore sending you, Timothy Budd, from this court without a stain on your character – but we do warn you that if we see you here again, *for whatever reason*, the penalties may be very heavy.' He turned to the other two boys. 'Desmond Cook, you will return to hospital with no further action taken against you. James Cross, you will be put on probation for eighteen months and given the same warning as Timothy Budd. We do not wish to see any of you in this court again.' He stacked his papers together and stood up. The three magistrates filed out.

Tim stood uncertainly for a moment or two, then turned and ran into his mother's arms. She clasped him against her, laying her wet face against his hair, while Frank stood by, one hand on her shoulder, the other gripping his son's arm. His face was tight, almost angry, but Jess knew that he was as near to tears as he was ever likely to come.

'Oh, Tim,' she said. 'Oh, *Tim . . .*'

CHAPTER TWENTY-EIGHT

November was a month of both sadness and celebration.

Field-Marshal Montgomery – known by now to all as 'Monty' – had scored an emphatic victory at El Alamein. Rommel's army had fled, defeated, leaving Monty a hero, and in honour of the occasion Churchill declared that the church bells could be rung throughout the land.

They rang in Portsmouth, at the Cathedral and at St Mary's, while the chimes were struck at the Guildhall by four volunteers who climbed ladders into the tower which stood so proudly above the gutted building. Jess and Frank walked down with Rose and Maureen to watch, Jess thinking sadly of the day in October 1938 when they had come to celebrate Mr Chamberlain's announcement of 'peace in our time'. It was then that she and Frank had decided to try for one last baby to complete their family. Later, filled with dread of what was to come, she had regretted that decision, but as she looked at Maureen's rosy face now, she could not wish it any different. I'm glad we've got her, she thought. I'm really glad.

But the world was still at war. The French fleet was scuttled at Toulon, seventy brave ships – which it had been hoped would be able to join the Allied forces – sunk rather than submit to seizure by the Germans. Such a waste, Jess thought, adding to the waste the war had already caused – a waste of ships, a waste of aircraft, of buildings and, most of all, a waste of lives.

'And they tell us not to waste a thing,' she said, thinking of the old biscuit tin with all the bits and pieces – string, buttons, little strips of sticky paper from the edges of stamps – carefully stored there. 'It doesn't seem to make sense.'

Tim and Keith were delighted to have the bells ringing. Tim was back at Bridge End and he went to the church tower to help Mr Beckett untie the clappers, and watch as the ringers raised the bells 'open' for the first time since the war had begun. Their music sounded over the fields and woods of the countryside, bringing people out of their homes to listen with misty eyes to a sound that spoke to their hearts of peace.

'Let the youngster have a pull,' one of the old men said, and Tim took hold of the rope, trembling a little with excitement and praying that he could keep his bell in its place, sounding sweetly amongst the others. He pulled off behind the treble and heard the creak of the ropes, followed immediately by the tumble of notes, from the highest to the lowest, like a cascade above his head. I'm doing that, he thought exultantly, I'm making that noise. And a huge grin broke out over his face as he pulled the rope, catching and releasing the sally, stretching his arms high on the rope's end.

It was the best thing that had happened since he'd come back to Bridge End soon after the court case. He was at the secondary school now, but it was an awkward journey each day on the bus, and when he got there he found all his old resentment returning when he was placed in a class of boys all at least a year younger than himself. And the secondary school didn't do the subjects he'd been looking forward to – French, Latin, the interesting maths. He was bored and irritated, and the shock and misery of the gun episode and the court case were still weighing on his mind.

The atmosphere at the vicarage was depressing these days, too. Stella and Muriel were still suffering from the shock of their father's death. Muriel had constant nightmares and was afraid to go to sleep, so made excuse after excuse not to go to bed. And Stella had completely withdrawn into herself. She had lost interest in school-work, in learning to cook with Mrs Mudge, in playing and reading – in everything, it seemed. And she had even drawn away from her sister, which upset Muriel even more.

'Why won't you give your sister a kiss and cuddle?' Mr Beckett asked in despair. 'Don't you see how unkind you're being? You're all she has now.'

Stella gave him a withering look. 'I know that.'

'Then why –?' He gazed at her helplessly. 'Stella, look at me. Look at me properly.'

She turned her head, but her gaze slid past him. He wanted to shake her, but he knew it would do no good. She was as unhappy as Muriel, and no wonder. But he couldn't let her freeze into her misery.

'We have to love each other,' he said gently. 'There isn't any point in life if we don't.'

'There isn't any point anyway,' she said in a small, hard voice. Her eyes met his for the first time, and he was shocked to see the depth of her desolation. 'What's the use? People just get killed if you love them.'

'Stella, you mustn't say that!' He stopped himself, wondering just why she shouldn't say it. In her short experience, that was just what did happen. 'It doesn't happen to everyone,' he went on, praying for the right words. 'And it doesn't happen *because* you love them. We live in dreadful times – nobody can deny that – but we still have to go on loving each other. Whatever happens. In fact, it's more important now than ever before.'

'I can't,' she said, still in the small, desolate voice. 'I can't. I'm afraid that if I love Mu, something will happen to her. It happened to Mummy, and Thomas, and now Daddy, and if it happened to Mu as well . . . It would be my fault.'

'*No!*' He could not let her go on thinking this. 'Nothing's going to happen to Muriel. Nothing. Your family has had enough tragedy. Nothing more will happen to you.'

She looked directly at him. 'You can't promise that.' But there was a very faint note of hope in her voice as she added, almost as if against her will, 'Can you?'

He knew that he could not. He could make no promises. If he did so, and something did happen, Stella would never regain her lost trust . . . But the chances were that nothing would happen to Muriel. Out here in the country, she was as safe as any child. And he couldn't let Stella go on suffering in this way.

'I promise,' he said steadily, lifting his eyes only momentarily towards the ceiling. *If You are really there, hear this prayer* . . . 'Nothing is going to happen to Muriel.'

He watched her carefully. There was only the slightest change in her expression – little more than a minute relaxation of the muscles. But it was a start, he thought. A corner turned.

Already, he prayed every night that nothing would happen to the children in his care. Now he must pray even harder for the two girls. That they would stay safe in his care for as long as they might need. That they should, somehow and however slowly, eventually regain their faith in the life they had been given.

That nothing more would harm their damaged hearts.

Carol Glaister's baby was born in the middle of November. Ethel was notified by telegram. She stared at the orange envelope for a few minutes, wondering what it contained. Telegrams these days were usually the bringers of bad tidings, and she had both a husband and a son serving in the Forces.

Jess Budd was at her front door when the boy came skidding round the corner on his red bicycle, and she hesitated, not wanting to go in and leave Ethel to face bad news on her own.

'What is it?' she asked uncertainly.

'Well, I don't know, do I,' Ethel snapped. 'I haven't got X-ray eyes.' She tore the envelope open with one finger. 'I hope to God it's not my Joe. But I daresay it's just George gone and got himself wounded. I just hope they're not thinking of sending him back here to be looked after.'

The woman doesn't have any feelings at all, Jess thought. She had heard the screeching that had gone on the night George left, and was pretty sure they'd had a bust-up, but that didn't mean Ethel had to be utterly callous. But you never really knew with Ethel. She was the sort who kept her feelings tightly buttoned up. And she really had been upset when she'd thought her little Shirley had been drowned.

She waited while Ethel read the brief message. Then, to her astonishment, she saw her neighbour's face darken with fury. With a swift movement, Ethel screwed the paper up in one hand and flung it into the gutter.

'The nerve! The sheer bloody nerve! How dare she send me a telegram, for those nosey parkers up the Post Office to see and laugh over. Why couldn't she write a letter, decent and private? I never heard such cheek.'

'What is it? What's happened?' Jess asked anxiously. 'Is it your Shirley? Is she ill?'

'Shirley? No, of course it's not Shirley. It's that little hussy Carol, that's who it is. Can't write to me herself, oh no, has to hide behind someone else's skirts. As if I was interested anyway. As if I *cared*.'

But you do care, Jess thought, watching her. You wouldn't be making such a song and dance about it if you didn't. Though I'm not sure whether it's Carol you care about, or yourself.

'Has she had her baby?' she asked tentatively, still not quite sure whether she was supposed to know about Carol's 'trouble'. 'Is she all right?'

'All right? That little madam will always be all right. Fall down a sewer and she'll come up smelling of roses. Not that it's any business of yours, Jess Budd, and I'll thank you not to go discussing our business with the rest of the neighbourhood, if you don't mind.' Ethel turned to go indoors. 'I suppose she'll be expecting me to write and say how pleased I am. Well, she'll just have to wait. Pleased! I've never been so ashamed in all my life.'

The front door slammed behind her and Jess looked at it for a long moment. I hope I never feel like that about my

Rose, or Maureen, she thought. I hope I'll be able to bring them up not to get into trouble.

She glanced at the ball of paper lying in the gutter. I shouldn't, she thought. It's private, even if it is a telegram. But Ethel had thrown it down there for anybody to pick up, so she couldn't really care. And after a moment or two's indecision, she bent and picked it up, smoothing it out quickly and guiltily, half afraid that Ethel might be watching her through the window.

It was from someone called Elizabeth Whiting, and it had been sent from Godalming. The message was brief and, to most mothers, would have been an occasion for joy.

17 NOVEMBER CAROL GLAISTER GAVE BIRTH TO BOY 6LB 2 OZ BOTH WELL WRITING.

So that was that, Jess thought, turning to go into her own house. That poor young girl was a mother now, and still not seventeen. And not likely to get any help from her own mother, by the look of it.

I suppose she'll give him up for adoption now. A sad business. They weren't much more than babies themselves, either of them. They'd done wrong, there was no denying that, but who hadn't made a mistake at some time during their life?

Fall down a sewer and come up smelling of roses, she thought with a wry smile, and remembered the day when Ethel herself had fallen down a drain in Charlotte Street and come up smelling of something very different.

For the families in Portsmouth, one of the darkest moments of November was the departure of 698 Unit for North Africa. They came home for a few days' embarkation leave and it was almost like a miniature Christmas, with the pain of separation like a shadow in the background.

'We've done nothing but say goodbye ever since we were married,' Olive said to Derek as they lay in bed on their last night. 'Are we ever going to be able to have a proper married life, d'you think?'

'We'd better,' he said grimly. 'Soon as we've fixed Adolf. It can't be long now, Livvy. We've been at it three years – he's bound to crack soon.'

'I don't know. He's as stubborn as ever, it seems to me. He'll never give in. And he's got all the rest of the world at each other's throats – I mean, it's going to take years to sort it all out.'

Derek didn't reply. Until now, he had managed to keep the worst of his fears at bay. The Unit had been lucky not to be sent overseas again after Dunkirk, and he'd hoped to see the war out without having to go abroad, although there had been times of frustration when he wondered just why he was in the Army at all, if all they were going to do was build tin huts . . . But like most married men, all he really wanted was to get home and live his own life.

'Don't worry about it,' he said at last, kissing her. 'Us worrying about it isn't going to make a scrap of difference. Let's just enjoy what we've got now.'

Olive lay in his arms. The family had given them a real party tonight, just like Christmas, with a meal as good as any Annie had cooked in peacetime – well, almost as good – and games and a sing-song till gone midnight. They'd all given Derek presents – mostly things like bars of chocolate from their own ration, or cigarettes, shampoo or Bryl-creem – and he had given them gifts as well. There had been a lot of laughter when it was discovered that his gifts too were mostly bars of chocolate or cigarettes, for the Army received better rations than civilians, and everyone had remarked that it was the thought that counted after all, and the children had unwrapped their chocolate immediately and eaten it as fast as they could.

Olive had given Derek a new mouth-organ. He had grown quite proficient on his old one, but this one was chromatic, with a slider so that he could get double the notes, and he started to play it at once, to accompany the sing-song. He gave his old one to Jess, to pass on to Tim at Christmas.

'It's a shame Betty's not here,' Jess said to Annie. The sisters had patched up their difference, agreeing that everyone was a bit short-tempered these days, and Annie had given Tim a bar of chocolate from her own ration when he'd come home from the court. 'She was looking proper peaky when I saw her last week.'

'I know. But she's working hard on the farm, making up for all the time she had off when Dennis was in hospital. And trying to keep her mind off him, I wouldn't wonder.' Annie sighed. 'Worrying herself stiff, she is, and there don't seem to be anything she can do about it. I don't know how to advise her, I really don't.'

'Is he still saying he doesn't want to marry her?'

'Well, it's not that he doesn't want to, that's the trouble. I mean, if he just didn't feel the same way, she'd have to accept it and look round for someone else. But she says he loves her as much as ever. In a way, that's *why* he won't go on with the wedding – he says he won't burden her with a blind man. He doesn't think he can give her a good life.'

'He's right, in a way,' Ted said. 'I mean, a husband who can't see isn't much of an asset to a young woman.'

'But if they'd already been married when it happened –' Jess began.

'That's what Betty says. She wants to stick by him. She says she doesn't want anyone else, and she doesn't want to live without him.'

'So why doesn't she just go up to this place he's at and tell him?'

Annie sighed. 'Oh, it's this Quaker business. She won't try to persuade him. Says she's just got to wait until he comes around to it of his own accord. I dunno how she's got the patience.'

'Well, I think they want their heads knocking together,' Olive declared. 'I know what I'd do if it was me.' She wound her arm round Derek's. 'I wouldn't want to give up the chance of being married.'

'I don't think Betty wants to give it up either,' Annie said a little sharply. 'But she can't force Dennis to walk up the aisle, can she.'

'Maybe Dad could though,' Olive suggested wickedly. 'You know – shotgun wedding!'

'*Olive!*' Annie was outraged, 'I never thought to hear such things from a daughter of mine. Why, if you were a bit younger I'd send you to the kitchen to wash out your mouth.' She glanced at Jess as Olive and Derek moved away, grinning at each other. 'I don't know what young people are coming to, I'm sure. It's being in the ATS, that's what it is. They mix with all sorts.'

Now, at last, the party was over and everyone had gone home or to bed. The house was quiet. Olive lay in Derek's arms, feeling him stroke her body with an intense concentration, as if trying to memorise every tiny contour, every minute crease. She breathed deeply, inhaling the scent of him – the real scent of him, not the sharp, medicated smell that came off a bar of soap, but the scent that was Derek alone, warm and faintly musky. Sometimes, when he was away, she would go to the cupboard and bury her face in his civvy clothes, just to remind herself of that scent.

'Oh, Derek,' she said, 'we've said goodbye so many times. And now you're really going away. *Africa* – I can't even imagine it.'

'I'll be thinking of you all the time, Livvy.' He didn't say everything would be all right, or that it would all be over soon. People didn't say those things any more. They were so obviously not true. All he could say were the things that were true. 'I love you. There'll never be anyone else for me. And when we get back, we'll do all the things we've always planned to do. Get the car out again. Have our own house. Start a family.'

'If only we hadn't lost the baby,' Olive said sadly. 'It would have been born by now. We'd have been a real family, before you went away.' She looked at him suddenly. 'Derek – shall we try again? For a baby, I mean? It might – it might –' She stopped and turned her face away, the tears brimming in her eyes.

'It might be our last chance,' he said quietly. 'I know, Livvy. I know.'

'I'm sorry,' she whispered. 'I didn't think – I didn't realise I was going to say that.'

'But it's true,' he said. 'And you know what? We've got to face the truth. We can't pretend, not any more. Not tonight.' He stopped his caressing and held her hard against his body. 'It might be the last time we'll ever hold each other like this.'

They lay tightly entwined, as close as if they were trying to merge into one, so that no one, nothing, could ever separate them. Olive buried her face in his neck, feeling the pulse against her lips. She did not know whether the tears that flowed against her cheeks were Derek's or her own.

'There must be thousands of people who feel like this,' she whispered. 'Millions. It's got to be the last time for some of them. Oh, Derek – suppose – suppose –'

'I'm going to do my damnedest to make sure it isn't,' he said forcibly. 'I'm not ready to chuck in the towel yet, Livvy, not by a long way. What, when I've got you to come back to? And maybe our baby as well? I tell you, they'll have a job to kill *me* – I came back from Dunkirk, remember!'

'I just couldn't bear it if anything happened to you,' she whispered, and he put his hands on her shoulders and shook her gently.

'I wouldn't think so much of it myself! Now –' he smiled down into her eyes and brushed the tears away from her face with tender fingers '– how about getting on with the matter in hand, eh? Didn't someone say something about a baby? Well, there's only one way of getting one that I know of.'

He bent to lay his lips on hers, and Olive closed her eyes. She pushed all other thought out of her mind, concentrating entirely on Derek, on his kiss, on the feeling of his body next to hers, his skin touching her skin, on the length and hardness of his thighs, the strength and tenderness in his arms.

In a few hours, he would be back in his rough khaki uniform, swinging his kitbag on to his shoulder and marching away up the street. Marching away from Olive. Marching away for goodness knows how long. But for tonight, he was naked and he was hers.

CHAPTER TWENTY-NINE

Tim and Keith came home for Christmas, even though only ten days beforehand there had been German hit-and-run raids all over southern England. Twenty houses had been wrecked in Henderson Road and a further two hundred damaged. German aircraft had swooped low over the city, machine-gunning people in the streets. Frank had been all for making the boys stay out in the country, but Jess was adamant.

'We have this argument every year,' she said. 'And the Germans always drop a few bombs just before Christmas. They do it just to spoil things for us, and I'm not having it. In fact, if I had my way the boys would come home for good.'

'You don't have to tell me that,' Frank grunted. 'And I don't have to tell you that they're better off at Bridge End. Look what happened when Tim was here in the summer.'

He'll never let us forget that, Jess thought, but she won the day and Tim and Keith came home on the train two days before Christmas.

'Can't I stop here?' Tim had asked, almost as soon as he came through the door. 'I don't like it at Winchester. It's horrible. I liked working for Mr Driver. He was teaching me science.'

'You do science at school,' Frank said.

'Not proper science, with experiments and things. We don't get all the stuff like Mr Driver has. Anyway, he knows more about it than the teacher does.' Tim looked at his mother with his large, hazel eyes. 'I could help you look after Maureen. I bet she misses me.'

Jess sighed. It was true, the little girl did seem to have been pining for her brother. She roamed the house looking for him and asked for Timmy when she went to bed. And she'd stopped singing 'You Are My Sunshine'.

She was curled up on the floor with him now, leaning against his legs and humming softly to herself. She looked happier than Jess had seen her since he'd gone back to Bridge End.

'You've got to stay at school, Tim,' she said sadly, but to Frank, when the children were in bed, she said, 'Couldn't he come home? He really doesn't seem to be settling. And there *are* schools open in Portsmouth – he could go somewhere, surely.'

'I don't want his education messed about with any more. He's got to get down to it and learn whatever he can.'

Jess said no more. She was pretty sure that Tim was learning very little, but it was no use harping on about it. Frank would only get annoyed. And she'd learned that if you left him to think things through himself, he very often came round in the end.

1943 started wet and windy. It wasn't really cold, but drying clothes was a constant problem and the coal ration was barely enough, even if you only lit the fire at teatime. The Budds' small room was continually festooned with damp washing, either ranged on the wooden clothes-horse in front of the fire, so that no one could see the flames, or draped around the picture-rails. And Frank's coat never did seem to dry out. It was soaking when he came home in the evening and still damp when he put it on next morning.

'It's not healthy,' Jess said worriedly. 'You'll be getting pneumonia.' But there was nothing to be done about it, and he still went to work early every morning, even when he was streaming with a cold.

'There's a war on,' he said. 'You've just got to carry on.'

Most people did, with dogged persistence. They hadn't got this far just to be beaten. Hitler had given them nearly four years of hell and the longer it went on the more determined they were not to give in. And to keep a smile on their faces while they did it, too.

At least there was plenty of entertainment to help them. You could go to the pictures every week, two or three times if you had the time and the money, and see stars like Joan Crawford and Bette Davis in *Stage Door Canteen*, or Ingrid Bergman in *For Whom The Bell Tolls*. Betty Grable was the most popular star of all, and there was a new girl called Veronica Lake, who had lovely rich hair that hung half across her face.

The wireless was good too. All the comedy shows were still running, together with newer ones like Charlie Chester's *Stand Easy*, and there was lots of music. The big bands were popular – Tommy Dorsey, Harry James, Artie Shaw, Woody Herman and, most of all, Glenn Miller. Glenn Miller's music seemed to express the feeling of the war, somehow, especially when he volunteered for military service and started to modernise the American army and air force music with numbers like 'Blues in the Night', 'American Patrol' and 'In the Mood'. And there were crooners like Bing Crosby and Frank Sinatra singing 'You'll Never Know' and 'My Heart and I', and the lovely young Anne Shelton who recorded the German favourite 'Lili Marlene' and made it a British hit.

The raids went on, sometimes during the day, sometimes at night. A church was bombed in the Isle of Wight during a children's service. Planes swooped low over the streets, gunning down people walking or cycling. There was a stream of advice as to what to do – don't run, lie down wherever you are – but it was hard not to run when an enemy aeroplane was roaring overhead and you could hear the spatter of machine-gun bullets all around you.

The *Evening News* said that the war was costing fourteen million pounds a day. Fourteen million pounds! It seemed unbelievable that there could be that much money in the country. And all being spent on killing people.

A pilot from Southsea was awarded the BEM. His bomber had crashed into the sea, and he and the sergeant had swum for over three hours with the injured gunner before being picked up, while the navigator stayed with the broken plane, supporting the wireless operator who had a fractured spine. All three men were rewarded with medals and commended for their courage.

Halfway through the month, a violent gale swept Southern England, accompanied by thunder and vivid lightning. Maureen thought it was an air-raid and asked Jess persistently why they didn't go to the Anderson shelter. In the end, she became so anxious that Jess took her down there until it was over. It wasn't that she was frightened, exactly, she told Annie later, it was just that that was what they always did in an air-raid, and the baby was worried when they didn't. She didn't really know what there was to be frightened of, poor little scrap.

After that the weather turned cold and there was a heavy snowfall, followed by a gale so severe that it was almost classed as a hurricane. Trees were uprooted, roofs torn off, seaside promenades battered almost to pieces and roads subsided in the floods caused by the heavy rain and swollen seas. Buildings that had already been damaged or shaken by the bombing collapsed and strewed rubble across the roads. And in the Dockyard two men were killed when the howling wind smashed the roof they were working on.

'I'm thankful January's over,' Jess said as they surveyed the mess the gale had left behind. 'Perhaps February'll be a bit better.'

'Elsie and Doris Waters are coming to the King's again,' Frank remarked. Elsie and Doris were his favourite radio characters, with their comically wry discussions on war-time life. They seemed like real people, people like himself and Jess with the same kind of lives and problems. 'We'll book up and go. It'll do us good to have an evening out. Rose can stop with Maureen, she can have young Joy down to keep her company if she likes.'

The boys were back in the country, but Mr Beckett had written to say that he still wasn't happy about Tim. It was difficult for him to get to the secondary school and he didn't seem to be settling down there. The lessons didn't suit him and he didn't even seem to be making any friends.

'Our Tim, not making friends! But he's always been a popular boy. Everyone likes Tim,' Jess said with some indignation.

'I'm afraid it's partly due to his own attitude,' Mr Beckett said when they went to see him. 'I don't mean he's being deliberately obstructive, but he really does deeply resent not having taken the scholarship examination at the right time and being forced to stay at the primary school for an extra year. And he seemed so much happier being at home during the summer and having a job – despite the spot of trouble he got into. I'm sure that wouldn't happen again.'

'Are you saying you think Tim ought to come home again?' Frank said bluntly.

'I think it's something we ought to consider. Well – it's your decision, of course, not mine. I don't want to interfere in any way –'

'But you know a lot about Tim,' Jess said. 'You can see what's happening to him. We only see him when he's happy at home.'

'That's quite true. And he *is* happy at home, isn't he? There's no doubt about that.'

'No,' Jess said, glancing at Frank, 'there's not. But he's been happy here too.'

'I know, but that was when it was all a game, an adventure. A lot of things have happened to Tim in the past year. Finding that pilot's hand – seeing his friends shoot each other – realising what the war is all about. Seeing what's happened to Stella and Muriel. It's all had its effect.'

'Those poor little girls,' Jess said, momentarily diverted. 'What's happening about them now, Mr Beckett?'

The vicar sighed and rubbed his tired face. He had been like a boy again when the children first came to the vicarage. But the shocks they had suffered, not to mention the troubles and difficulties of his own parishioners, had taken their toll. A year or two ago, he'd had to remind himself that he was almost seventy. Now, he needed no reminder that he had passed the allotted threescore years and ten and was living on what some would call borrowed time. He was too old at last for snowball games and cricket, but he felt a greater sadness that somehow the children in his care had grown too old too.

'I'm afraid the authorities have decided to take them away. They're no longer official evacuees, you see – they're orphans. They'll be going to a children's home as soon as places can be found for them.' His old eyes blurred. 'I pray that they will at least be able to stay together.'

Jess stared at him in horror. 'They'd never separate them! Why, it would be criminal. They've only got each other.'

'I agree, Mrs Budd, I agree. But the authorities see things rather differently. I doubt if I shall be given any say in the matter at all.'

'I don't see why they can't stop here,' Frank said gruffly. 'You've given 'em a good home, Mr Beckett. None better.'

There was a short silence. Then the vicar shook himself and said, 'But you came here to talk about Tim. He's no longer a little boy, Mrs Budd. He's growing up. He isn't satisfied with games of cricket or building snowmen any more.'

Jess nodded. She felt near to tears. Her Tim, growing up, no longer a little boy. I've missed the last three years of his childhood, she thought, and they'll never come back again. And if this war goes on much longer, he'll be called up himself and have to go right away – and maybe never come back . . .

She thought of Sella and Muriel, being sent to yet another strange place, perhaps even separated. Their childhood had been ruined – perhaps their whole lives. They needed each other. They needed their mother and father. Families ought to be together, she thought again.

'I want him at home,' she said abruptly, turning to Frank. 'I want them both at home. This has gone on long enough.'

'You know what I think about that –' Frank began.

'Yes, I do know. You've told me over and over again. But I've got a right to say what I think, too, and I don't reckon it's doing Tim any good to be here now. You've been good to him,' she said to Mr Beckett, 'and so were Reg and Edna Corner, but you're right, evacuation is for children, not boys growing into young men, and that's what our Tim is now.'

'He's only thirteen years old –'

'I don't care what he is, he's growing up. This war's making everybody grow up. Don't you realise, he could be in the Army in three years' time. They're making sixteen-year-olds register now, you know that. It could be fifteen-year-olds next – *fourteeen*-year-olds. Who's to say? I want my boys at home. I want to be a family while we've got the chance.'

Frank stared at her. He had seldom heard Jess speak so forcefully, seldom seen that look of determination on her face. He wanted to argue, to tell her that he was head of the family and they'd do what he said, but he couldn't do it. She really meant it this time, he could see that, and she wouldn't let go.

'All right,' he said at last, 'we'll think about it. Perhaps he can come home and go to the secondary school in Pompey. There's still one or two open, like you said. But not Keith. He's still at the village school and he's doing well there. I don't want him unsettled.'

Tim came home a fortnight later. But he didn't start at another school. He didn't want another change, he said, and he hadn't been learning anything anyway. He wanted to go back and work for Mr Driver. He wanted a proper job.

'Well, he could get an apprenticeship in a year or two,' Frank allowed. 'Fitter, or toolmaker, or something like that. He's a bright enough boy and he likes making things. I'll see if there's a chance for him in the Yard.'

'What about the ferry?' Ted suggested. He and Annie had come down for Sunday tea. 'We've got a lad just coming up to his last year. A good engineering apprenticeship'd

447

stand him in good stead. I'll put his name forward if you like, when the time comes.'

That seemed a good idea, and they discussed it for a while. But to Jess, none of it seemed all that important. She had him home again, she could look across the table and see his cheerful face, she could listen to his everlasting jokes. And the main thing was that he was happy again. She had her old Tim back.

I don't know how she's got the patience, Annie had said.

Betty didn't know how she had the patience either. A year or two ago, she thought, I wouldn't have been able to bear it. But she knew now that she had to give Dennis the time and space to work out his own problems. Persuading someone to do what they really felt to be wrong never worked. It would only bring trouble later.

All through January, she worked on the farm in the wind and rain, coming in soaked of an evening to the big, warm kitchen, stripping off her wet clothes in the attic and rubbing herself dry with a towel before coming downstairs in her pyjamas and the old coat she used for a dressing-gown, to sit by the range with Erica and Yvonne. Erica was heavily pregnant by now, for it was almost exactly nine months since her May wedding, and she did no work outside but stayed indoors with Mrs Spencer, learning to cook and sew.

'I never enjoyed sewing at school,' she confessed. 'It didn't seem much use – making silly little aprons and doing patchwork. But I don't mind doing something useful.'

'Oh, I like doing patchwork and embroidery too,' Mrs Spencer declared. 'You get fed up with the everyday stuff. Turning shirt collars and doing sheets sides-to-middle – well, it's something and nothing, isn't it. I mean, you can't really look at it and think you've done something worthwhile, even if you have. But a nice patchwork quilt – why, that's a work of art. I've still got my grandmother's, that she made when she was a girl. It's an heirloom, that is.'

They spent a lot of time making clothes for the baby. Erica learned to knit and made several little matinee coats in fine white wool. Mrs Spencer unravelled an old blue jumper and made leggings and a coat.

'Suppose it's a girl?' Yvonne said when she saw them.

'Well, she'll just have to wear blue, won't she,' Mrs Spencer said tartly. 'Even a baby can't be fussy in wartime.'

But the baby turned out to be a boy and arrived with the minimum of fuss. He was born at the beginning of February in the middle of the night, keeping the whole household awake ('the first time of many' the doctor said wryly). By daylight he was wrapped in a soft white shawl knitted by Mrs Spencer, and lying beside his mother in the bed in Gerald's room. He had a fuzz of golden hair, just like Erica's, and brown eyes like his father.

'He's gorgeous,' Yvonne said, bending over and touching the soft cheek with the back of her finger. 'And he's not even wrinkled! I thought all babies looked as if they'd been badly packed. How d'you do it, Eric?'

'Easy,' Erica murmured, half dozing on her pillows. 'Easy as shelling peas.'

'That's not what I've heard! You're a lucky one, you are.'

'She is,' Mrs Spencer said. She had been hovering by the bed ever since the baby had been born, unable to tear herself away from her first grandchild. 'She's a natural mother. And he's a beautiful baby. Let's hope there'll be plenty more like him.'

Betty gazed down at the small red face. She felt a confusing variety of emotions. Delight that Erica's baby had been born, relief that he and his mother were both well. Sadness that Gerald wasn't here to see his son. And a huge, overwhelming grief for herself and Dennis.

She had not seen Dennis since he had been moved. He had written to her once, telling her that the move had been sudden and there hadn't been time to let her know. But on the whole, he said, he felt it was for the best. Coming to see him had been hurting her more and more each time, and hurting him too. He loved her as much as ever – too much to put her through a life burdened by a blind, helpless husband. He had nothing to offer her now, and he wanted her to be happy with someone else.

Betty knew that he was wrong. But she also knew that once Dennis had made up his mind to take a course of action, nothing would sway him. He had already been to prison for his beliefs. He had risked his life. He would not give in if he really felt he was doing the right thing.

'Wait a while,' Mr Verney had counselled her when she had gone to see him and his wife. 'He may come round, when he's more accustomed to the idea of blindness. It's a very great shock, to lose your sight. He needs time to regain himself.'

'He needs me, too,' Betty said, but there was nothing to be done about it and she kept away from the hospital and restricted her letters to two a week, telling him about the farm and the village doings, but making no effort to persuade him to change his mind. She signed her letters *from your loving Betty* and left it at that.

Now, she looked down at Erica's baby and felt an overwhelming sense of loss, a despair that she would never hold Dennis's baby in her arms like this. Never hold any baby, for if she couldn't have Dennis's she would never have one at all. And, following the despair, there came a rush of furious anger.

You've no right to do this to me, she thought. You've no right to take away everything I want. What's a pair of eyes compared with a lifetime? What does it matter if a father can't see his children, so long as he has them?

'He's gorgeous, Eric,' she said in a shaking voice, and turned swiftly away to walk from the room.

She would go to the hospital straight away. She'd beg the money for her train fare or hitch-hike the sixty miles. She would see Dennis and tell him that she could not, *would not*, accept his decision. He had no right to make it alone. It was her life too. They must at least talk about it, she must make him see that life was possible again, that it was there to be shared whatever the difficulties, that there was still so much to be enjoyed.

She must make him see that their promises, and their love, held as strongly as ever.

There was no need for Betty to hitch-hike to the blind hospital. As soon as she told the Spencers what she meant to do, they gave her their full support and insisted that she take enough money to keep her there for as long as necessary. 'I know you've got your savings,' Mrs Spencer told her, 'but you don't know how long you'll need to stop, and you've got to find somewhere to stay. We can't have you sleeping in a ditch.'

'That's right,' Yvonne chimed in. 'And you'll want warm clothes too. You can borrow my new jersey.'

Yvonne's new jersey had been knitted from two old ones, unpicked and washed and the best bits of wool rewound. ('We threw away the holes,' she said with a grin.) The colours were oddly merged but it was thick and warm, and Yvonne had worn it every day under her old jacket. Betty was reluctant to take it, but her own clothes were wearing thin and she hadn't got enough coupons for new wool.

'I'm leaving you with all the work to do,' she said awkwardly, knowing that to be honest she shouldn't be leaving at all. The Land Army worked under the same conditions as the Armed Services, after all, and you weren't supposed just to march off and leave it. But Mr Spencer shook his head.

'We'll call it compassionate leave, if anyone asks. But I don't suppose they will. Got too much else on their plates. And there's not much we can be doing outside in this weather.'

Betty set off early one morning, taking the train from Winchester to London. The hospital was on the other side of the city, out towards Essex, and she had to cross from Victoria Station to Liverpool Street. She sat on the bus, looking out at the bombed streets.

It was even worse than Pompey. Row after row of shattered houses, some patched up with boards and tarpaulin, others just left to rot. Big shops with gaping windows. Churches with their roofs open to the sky, their interiors filled with rubble. Damage that had obviously been done three years previously, during the worst of the blitz, and fresh damage that must have occurred only weeks or days ago. It was a wonder there was anyone left.

The hospital was on the edge of a quiet village, about ten miles from the centre of the city. It was a big house, surrounded by gardens that had been mostly dug up to grow vegetables, and Betty carried her small suitcase up the long drive, her knees trembling as she wondered what Dennis was going to say when she arrived. I won't let him send me away, no matter how hard he tries, she told herself. I won't give him up. I *know* we belong together.

It was a fine, dry morning and there were a few people walking around the grounds and some working on the vegetable beds. They must have other patients here as well as blind people, she thought, and then noticed that most of them were tapping the paths with white sticks. And others were sitting on benches, chatting as if they'd just met in the park, their heads turned towards each other. Surely they could see.

'Dennis Verney?' the nurse said in the front hall of the big house. 'Yes, he's here. He's out in the garden somewhere. He spends a lot of his time outside. He used to work on a farm, you know.'

'Yes,' Betty's throat felt tight. She wanted to say *He taught me to milk a cow*, but the words wouldn't come and anyway the nurse was already turning away to deal with a man who was fumbling his way down the stairs, his eyes blank and sightless. Betty murmured her thanks and went out again through the front door. She stood for a moment or two, looking across the quiet garden and wondering where to start looking.

She came upon him quite suddenly, at the far corner of the grounds, working on a fence. It had been damaged, probably by animals forcing their way through, and he was painstakingly snipping off lengths of new wire, tacking them to the post and winding them in with the existing mesh.

Betty stood still. He looked much better than when she'd seen him last, in hospital. He had filled out a little, so that he was no longer gaunt, and his skin had regained some of its colour. His hands worked methodically with the wire, and except for the fact that his fingers seemed to stroke the post as he felt for the right place to fix the new strand, it would have been hard to tell that he couldn't see what he was doing.

Dennis, she thought, Dennis, and her whole body seemed to melt and yearn towards him.

She was never sure what made Dennis pause suddenly and turn his head towards her. Perhaps she made a small sound. Perhaps he knew, by a slight alteration, a shift in the atmosphere, that he was no longer alone.

'Hullo?' he said enquiringly. 'Who's there?' And then, as Betty took a tentative step towards him, his nostrils flared a little and he narrowed his blind eyes. 'Who is it?'

Betty could not speak. She took another step, saw the suspicion dawn slowly on his face. He tilted his head slightly, as if trying to identify something, and then he said slowly, 'Ashes of Roses. *Ashes of Roses*. Betty, is it you? *Betty . . .?*'

Lots of girls wore Ashes of Roses. But Dennis had told her once it smelt different on her than on anyone else. More natural. More true. He had said he would never forget it.

'Dennis,' she whispered, and walked straight into his arms.

'I thought I was never going to see you again,' Betty wept against Dennis's shoulder. 'I thought you were going to go away and forget all about me.'

'I'd never forget you.' He held her tightly. His own tears were soaking into her hair. 'If you knew how I've wanted you, how I've lain awake at night just aching to hold you again –'

'If it's half as much as I've wanted you, I do know,' she whispered. 'Dennis, it's been awful . . . I'm not going away, you know. I'm not leaving you, and if you try to leave me again, I'll – I'll – well, I don't know *what* I'll do!'

He laughed shakily. 'Marry me.'

Betty lifted her head and stared at him. '*What?*'

'Marry me,' he said. 'That's the best way of making sure I don't leave you again.' The shake in his voice deepened to an unsteady throb. 'I mean it, Betty. Marry me, before I can change my mind again. Not that I will. Not now. I want to be with you. I want to be safe.'

She understood what he meant. It wasn't danger he was afraid of, it was loneliness – her loneliness as much as his. And the waste of a precious love.

She felt her strength returning and stood more firmly against him. It didn't matter that he was blind. It didn't matter that life might be difficult for them. What mattered was that they would face it together, that they would be an ordinary couple, man and wife, with an ordinary family.

'I'm not letting you go,' she said. 'Tell me what we have to do to get married.'

CHAPTER THIRTY

The last few days of March were blustery as the month went out like a lion, but spring was around the corner and the lighter evenings brought new heart. And at the end of the first week of April, two events brought great pleasure to the residents of April Grove and its surrounding cluster of streets.

'Proper funny do, this is going to be,' Ted Chapman grumbled as he and Annie got off the bus near Fratton Station and walked with Olive and the Budds through the streets to the Meeting House. 'No hymns, no prayers – not that I've ever been one for kneeling down and spouting a lot of mumbo-jumbo – and your mother not even allowed to wear her best frock. Too bright and gaudy, if you please! I thought it was supposed to be a wedding, not a funeral.'

'Well, it's Betty's choice and I think she should have what she wants,' Olive declared. 'Anyway, you ought to be pleased. It's not costing you much!'

'That's not the point,' Annie said. 'The point is every mother wants her girl to have a nice wedding, and this looks as if it's going to be a proper dismal affair. Your dad's right. Them Quakers don't know how to enjoy themselves. No proper invites, no wedding breakfast, no bridesmaids. And our Betty not even wearing white – I thought I'd die of shame when she told me.'

'It doesn't mean anything, Mum,' Olive said, though privately she thought it probably did. 'Not what you think, anyway. They just don't do it that way. They like things to be quiet.'

'Well, a white frock don't make a lot of noise,' Annie

said. 'And I do think she could've had little Maureen with a few flowers.' They walked in silence for a few moments and then she added, 'Well, I'm glad I've asked a few people back home after. At least our friends'll know it's not our doing.'

The whole family had been in and out of Annie's house for the past two days, bringing contributions and helping to prepare a spread that was almost as good as pre-war. Tins of spam had been produced, jellies made and piles of sandwiches cut and filled with jam or fish paste. It was too early for much in the way of salad but Annie had opened a jar of beetroot and some of her pickles, and done a big bowl of new potatoes. There were fresh carrots too, from Frank's allotment, and bottles of cider and jugs of lemon squash.

And there was a cake. Everyone had given eggs, butter, sugar and fruit from their rations and Annie had baked it in her biggest tin. You weren't allowed to make icing now, but she'd made a sort of marzipan and put on a few plaster roses, saved from someone else's wedding several years earlier, to decorate it. It didn't look anything really, when she thought of the beautiful cakes she'd made and decorated in the past, but it was the best she could manage and Betty was delighted with it.

'It's the thought that counts,' she said, giving her mother a hug. 'And it'll taste smashing.'

Betty and Dennis were coming together, from his parents' house. That was another thing that seemed wrong to Annie and Ted. A girl ought to be married from her own home, not her bridegroom's. But everything was upside down at this wedding, and there didn't seem to be anything you could do about it. And the Verneys were such nice, kind people – even if they were really a bit above the Chapmans' class – that you couldn't argue. Anyway, Betty said Quakers didn't argue.

'What, never?' Annie had asked sceptically, and Dennis grinned.

'Well, hardly ever! They do sometimes,' he added fairly. 'They're not angels or anything.'

'I still don't know about our Betty marrying that young man,' Ted said to Annie privately. 'When all's said and done, they're different to us. I mean, his father works in the library, doesn't he? That's not our sort of people. And with all these funny ideas – and then to top it all, him being blind – well, I dunno how our Betty's going to settle to it, I really don't.'

'They love each other. You can see that. And our Betty's been a different girl since they fixed the date. They'll be all right, Ted. It isn't easy for anyone these days.' She sighed. 'Look at our Olive.'

Derek had been away for four months now and Olive had lost weight. She looked pale and miserable, and though she tried to keep a smile on her face, Annie could tell that it was hard for her. It was just as well she had her job to keep her mind occupied, and the rest of the gun crew sounded a nice bunch.

The Meeting House was in Claremont Road. The little group reached the door and hesitated.

A number of people were going in. They wore ordinary clothes, mostly in quiet, neutral colours though there was one woman with a bright feather in her hat. They looked at the little party and smiled, and as Annie paused on the step a small man in a dark suit and spectacles came forward and held out his hand.

'Mrs Chapman? You must be Elizabeth's mother. Welcome to our Meeting. Come inside. My name's Oliver Bradshaw. I'm one of the elders.'

'Thank you,' Annie murmured. It had taken her a moment to realise that it was Betty he meant when he said 'Elizabeth'. 'Er – this is my husband – um, Edward.'

Ted's eyebrows shot up, but he put out his hand and shook the other man's. 'Ted, they call me. Pleased to meet you, Mr Bradshaw.'

'Oliver, please,' the little man said, smiling. He had a nice face, Annie decided, a bit ugly but kind. I don't think I could call him Oliver though, not till I knew him a lot better.

He led them into the meeting room. It was a large,

square room with seats like church pews all around – not in rows, like in a proper church, but against each wall, in a square. There were three rows on each side, and in the middle was a large, low table with a small jug of primroses on it and a couple of Bibles.

There were already a good many people in the room. Annie looked at them in surprise. It seemed as if the whole congregation had come. Yet Betty had told her that they wouldn't be inviting anyone. 'It'll just be announced at the meeting for a week or two before,' she'd said, 'and people will come if they want to.'

They must have all wanted to. There was hardly a seat left in the place. But Oliver Bradshaw led them to one of the empty pews in the front row and told them to sit there. 'We've been saving these places for you,' he said with his kind smile.

Annie sat down, with Ted on one side of her and Olive on the other. Jess and Frank took the rest of the pew, with the boys and Rose between them. Tim was starting to grow now and his legs looked lanky in his short trousers. He'd started to pester for long ones, but Jess said he'd have to wait till he was fourteen and took no notice of his complaints.

Now that they were settled, Annie could see quite a few familiar faces. The Spencers were here, from Bishop's Waltham, and Yvonne and Erica with the baby. Frank's brother Howard and his wife had come over from Gosport, and there were two or three cousins and their families. Uncle John Bellinger, who was on the City Council, was here in his dark suit and he winked at her. Annie frowned at him. It might not be a proper church, but you ought to behave with a bit of respect all the same.

It was a shame Mum couldn't have come. But ever since Dad had died, she'd seemed to fade away. She hardly went anywhere now, and although Annie had persuaded her at last to come and stop with them, she didn't have the life in her that she used to have. She just sat in a chair all day, shaking her head and grieving. It almost broke Annie's heart to see her.

Mr Bradshaw and three other men came in and closed the door behind them. They sat down on the empty pew opposite Annie and folded their hands in their laps. She realised that one of the men was Mr Verney.

The room was quiet. Annie glanced at Ted, who was looking uneasy. She peeped sideways at Olive, and past her towards Jess. Her sister glanced round and their eyes met, each asking the same question. What was supposed to happen now? Where were Betty and Dennis?

Mrs Verney was sitting behind her husband. She was wearing a brown skirt and jacket, not exactly a costume but looking very neat, with a white blouse underneath. She had a matching brown hat, quite plain, no feather or veil or anything to make it pretty. She caught Annie's eye and gave her a friendly smile.

Doesn't anybody say *anything*, Annie thought. Are we all going to sit here, staring at the floor and not saying a word, for the rest of the morning? If our Betty was here, she'd be getting the giggles. But our Betty *should* be here. Where on earth has the girl got to?

The silence went on. Annie felt Ted fidget beside her. He was getting impatient, she thought, and besides that he'd never liked being in confined spaces ever since his 'trouble'. If something didn't happen soon he'd be just as likely to drop something, just to make a noise.

There was a soft click as someone turned the handle of the door. Annie looked round and breathed a sigh of relief. They were here at last, Betty and Dennis, standing in the doorway and smiling. Betty had her hand in the crook of Dennis's arm and he was holding his head up high. His scars were almost healed, his eyes were open and you wouldn't have known he was blind.

The Quakers stood up, looking towards the couple and smiling. Annie and Ted and the rest got hastily to their feet, glancing sideways to see what to do next.

Dennis and Betty came forward side by side. Betty turned him gently so that he could sit on the last empty pew. She was wearing a frock Jess had made for her in soft grey wool, some material she'd got in Bulpitt's with coupons from half the street. It wasn't a wedding dress, but at least she'd be able to wear it afterwards. And even though grey was a funny colour for a wedding, Annie had to admit she looked well in it, with her hair brushed into a soft, red-gold halo of curls and her skin healthy from the outdoor life she led.

Betty looked across the little space at her mother, and Annie smiled at her. Now, at last, the wedding could begin.

Betty felt the warmth of Dennis's hand in hers. She'd been afraid she would be nervous, here in this crowd of people who were mostly strangers, for she'd only attended this Meeting about half a dozen times. Instead, she felt wrapped and comforted by their silent peace.

She caught her mother's eye and smiled back. Her father was looking stiff and uncomfortable. Poor Dad. He must wonder what on earth was going on. So must Auntie Jess and Uncle Frank and all the others who had come along to this plain room, so different from the churches they were used to. But she was sure that by the end of the morning they would all be feeling the peace that was in her heart, the peace she had always sensed in this quiet company. Then they would understand.

She sat very still. Her father shuffled his best black shoes and she heard him sigh. Annie touched him reprovingly, but when she glanced at Betty again there was bewilderment in her eyes and Betty knew that she was wondering when something was going to happen. Wasn't anyone going to get up, say a prayer, read a service of some kind? Wasn't there anyone to lead it, as a vicar or priest would have done?

I've tried to explain, Betty thought, but they just couldn't understand. They couldn't really believe how anyone could get married without some stranger in a white frock reading a lot of words over them. They couldn't believe that you could use words you had chosen or even made up yourself, and that you could decide for yourself when and how to say them.

'I've heard people ask each other which priest or minister married them,' Dennis had said. 'We Friends don't say that. We say we marry each other. It's our own business. We don't involve anyone else, except as witnesses.'

'But doesn't there have to be a registrar?' Betty had asked. 'There always has to be a registrar, surely.'

'Not at a Quaker wedding. Quakers and Jews are the only ones allowed to marry without. One of the elders acts as registering officer.'

Quakers and Jews. An odd combination, and yet it seemed peculiarly appropriate for weren't both persecuted, in their different ways, during this war?

'We consider it a privilege,' Dennis added with a smile.

'Well, I'm glad you've got some privileges. And the Jews as well.' There had been increasing concern over the treatment it was said the Nazis were meting out to the Jews. Some people refused to believe rumours of slave labour and death camps; others swore they were only too true.

The silence had grown very deep. It was as if the souls, the spirits, the essential *beings* of all the people in the room, had gathered into one, as if there were just one entity present, a benign and loving presence that enfolded and absorbed everyone here. Betty felt almost as if she had been lifted slightly above her body, as if she had drifted just outside herself to join that unity; and as if the same thing had happened to them all, so that they met and touched in a space that was neither physical nor even of the mind, but of something else entirely.

Dennis's fingers tightened about hers. She felt his movement and rose to her feet alongside him. They turned to face each other and he held her hands closely in his. His voice was deep and steady. The big white certificate lay on the table before them, and Betty glanced at it, prepared to whisper the words, but Dennis had no need of a reminder.

'Friends,' he said, 'I take this my friend Elizabeth Anne Chapman to be my wife, promising, through divine

461

assistance, to be unto her a loving and faithful husband, so long as we both on earth shall live.'

There was a pause. Betty looked up into his face. If she had not known he was blind, she would have believed that his eyes smiled into hers. Then she caught the glint of tears in them, and knew that she was not far from weeping herself.

'Friends,' she said, and her voice was low yet clear, with just a hint of the tears which were building so strongly in her, 'I take this my friend Dennis James Verney to be my husband, promising, through divine assistance, to be unto him a loving and faithful wife, so long as we both on earth shall live.'

They stood very still, facing each other, their fingers entwined. And then Dennis felt in his pocket and took out the golden wedding ring. Betty held out her shaking hand and he slipped it on, pushing it over the knuckle. She stared at it and a tear dropped on to the back of her hand and ran down to touch the gold, magnifying it so that it blazed with sudden light.

Dennis bent and kissed her lips. Then they sat down together, still holding hands very tightly. Betty was shaking.

I'm Mrs Verney, she thought. Just those few words in front of these people, and I'm Mrs Verney. And I don't feel a bit different. Not a scrap.

But that, she realised, was because she had been feeling like Dennis's wife for a very long time. Ever since that Christmas two years ago, when she had crept down to his room and slipped into his waiting arms. Ever since she had first said she loved him.

It was several minutes before anyone else spoke. And then Oliver Bradshaw rose to his feet. He looked at the newly-weds kindly.

'Friends, we have come here today to witness the marriage between these two young people. I know we all wish them well, all the happiness that they deserve. And there will be those amongst us who know these two young people, who will have kind and generous things to say about them. Forgive me if I ask to be the first.'

He paused, then went on quietly, 'I've known Dennis and his father Robert for many, many years. Indeed, I think I can say I've known Dennis all his life, for he first came to this Meeting in his pram as a small baby, only just able to sit up. He would be wheeled into that corner there and allowed to sleep or to play, whichever he preferred. He was not always quiet. I can remember one occasion when his mother took him out, and she might as well have let him stay, for his screams could be heard as clearly through the windows as they could when he were still in the room.'

There was a quiver of laughter in the air. Oliver Bradshaw smiled and waited a moment, then continued.

'Since then, I've watched – many of us have watched – Dennis grow into the fine young man he is today. We've seen his belief and determination match that of his father's as he faced the tribunal as a conscientious objector and quietly accepted their decision. We've seen his strength as he endured a prison sentence and his cheerfulness and willingness as he worked on the land. And we have seen his courage as he took the decision to risk his life in the service of others.'

Not in fighting the war, Betty thought. In the service of others.

'Finally,' Oliver Bradshaw said, 'we see the greatest evidence of all of courage as he faces the future without sight. And we see the fortitude and love of our friend Betty, who stands beside him today as his wife. Friends,' he said, turning to Betty and Dennis, 'this Meeting wishes you great happiness in your union. We are glad to have been here today to witness it.'

He sat down. Again, nobody moved or spoke but the atmosphere in the room was filled with a tender lovingness and after a few moments, someone else got up and spoke of knowing Dennis, recounting a story of Dennis's exploits as a boy that made them all laugh. And then, as if a spring had been released, one after another the members of the Meeting rose and made their own contribution so that the good wishes and the stories went on and on and the gathering began to seem more like a celebration. And at the very last, when it seemed that there was no more to be said, Ted Chapman cleared his throat and came to his feet, twisting his hat in his hands, big and awkward in the crowded room.

'I don't know if it's proper for me to do this,' he began gruffly. 'I never been to one of these sorta weddings before. It ain't what I'm used to, and standing up like this and speechifying in public, that ain't what I'm used to neither. But it gotta be said, and I'm the one that's gotta say it.'

The Quakers listened attentively, and Oliver Bradshaw nodded. Annie, who had been about to tug at Ted's sleeve, glanced anxiously along the pew at her sister, who shrugged. He was on his feet now. There was nothing to be done about it.

Ted lowered his head. It was an almost belligerent movement, like a bull about to charge, and the glowering look he sent about the room added to the impression. But Annie knew that he was simply nervous. Oh Ted, she thought, don't make a fool of yourself.

'When I first met young Dennis here,' he said gruffly, 'he was working on the farm with our Betty. She brought him home to Sunday dinner one weekend. We knew there must be summat special about him, but she hadn't said nothing else. She never told us why he was on the land. Why he wasn't in the Services.'

He's going to put his foot in it, Annie thought. He's going to offend them all. Oh, *Ted*.

'I asked him that dinner-time, straight out. I could see there was summat funny about it. *If* you'll pardon me. And he told me, just as straight. He never tried to hide nothing, I had to give him that.'

He paused again. The Meeting Room was totally silent. You could have heard a hair drop.

'Well, I dunno if you can imagine what I thought about *that*,' Ted said, his tone leaving no room for doubt as to what he'd thought. 'I don't mind telling you, I was proper disgusted. And I said so. Called him a coward and I dunno what else. I told him to get out of my house. And I told my daughter not to bring him back, neither.'

Annie had heard of people wishing that the ground would open up under their feet. She stared at the wooden floorboards, praying to see them suddenly part. She dared not look at Betty.

'Course, he told me he was joining the Pioneers,' Ted said. 'And maybe I oughter've backed down a bit. But I'm a stubborn old devil – pardon my language – and I couldn't forget that I had a lad in the Royal Navy – a lad whose ship's bin sunk off Japan and we've never heard whether he's still alive or not – nor that I'd got a girl in the ATS. And I couldn't forget Dunkirk, neither, and going over in the old *Ferry King* to pick up the poor bug – the poor devils – pardon me again, but me feelings are a bit too strong to watch me words, as anyone who'd been there would understand. Anyway, what I means to say is I thought of all that and I looked at this bloke, fit and healthy and refusing to fight, and I don't mind telling you, it stuck in me craw to have him sitting there at me own table.'

'*Ted*,' Annie whispered agonisedly. 'Ted, for heaven's sake sit down . . .'

He flicked his hand in a gesture of silence. 'I'll sit down when I've had me say, and not before. I haven't finished yet, not by a long chalk.' He surveyed the room again. The Quakers were still sitting with eyes downcast, showing almost no reaction to his words, although one or two were looking flushed. The rest of the guests, the Budds and the Shaws and their other friends and neighbours, were looking as embarrassed as Annie.

'It's all right,' he said. 'You don't need to look so flummoxed. I didn't come here to cause no unpleasantness. What I'm working up to is this. I've come to realise I was wrong. I've watched this lad – well, *heard* about him, more like, through the wife and our Betty – join up and do just about the most dangerous job there is. He still won't fight, and I can't pretend I understand why when you looks at what's going on in the world, but he's no coward. He's proved that, over and over again. He's risked his life and he's lost his sight, and all I want to say is this.' He looked over towards Dennis and then stepped across the little space and held out his hand. 'I'm proud to know you, Dennis, and I'm even prouder to have you for a son-in-law. I hope you and Betty has a long and happy life together. And if you can see your way to overlooking what happened before, I hope you'll come down April Grove and see us as often as you can. You're welcome in the Chapman family.'

Dennis came to his feet. Betty nudged his right arm and he lifted it so that Ted could take his hand. They clasped each other's palms firmly and Ted gripped Dennis's forearm and then clapped him on the shoulder.

'Oh, *Dad*,' Betty said, and flung herself into his arms, tears streaming down her face.

There was a collective sigh of relief and pleasure. Annie got up and hugged Ted's arm, then kissed both Betty and Dennis. The Verneys joined in, followed swiftly by Jess Budd and then Frank. And everyone, Quakers and guests alike, turned to each other, smiling and holding out their hands or kissing. The quiet room was suddenly filled with hubbub and laughter.

The Meeting never did return to order. Dennis had told Betty that after everyone had said all they wanted to, there would be a final period of silence and meditation before the elders shook hands to signify that it was over. But once they were all on their feet, the silence broken, there was no chance of settling down again. They moved to the table to see the registering officer – another of the elders – fill in the big Certificate of Marriage, which set out the words that Dennis and Betty had used, and was then signed by everyone present. While that was being done, he completed the more usual certificate and handed it to Betty.

'Be happy, my dear,' he said, smiling, and she took it and thanked him. But it was the big Quaker certificate, rolled into a long cardboard tube, that she held most tenderly. This was the complete record of the day.

They left the room. In one of the other rooms, someone had made tea and they stood about, drinking and chatting and nibbling biscuits. It wasn't much of a wedding feast, Annie thought, thankful that she'd prepared something more festive at home, but somehow it didn't seem to matter after all. And neither did the fact that there were no bridesmaids, nor that she'd been denied the chance of wearing her best pink frock or that Betty wasn't in white.

What mattered was the radiance on Betty and Dennis's faces. The sheer joy that shone like an aura all around them. The ecstatic happiness that vibrated in the air and filled the room from wall to wall, from corner to corner.

And it didn't matter, either, that they had to go home in a bus. The one that came along had the whole top deck empty and they all climbed up the stairs and sat chattering and laughing, drawing the conductor into the fun. When he heard that they were a wedding party he put away his ticket-machine and went back downstairs.

'I've never seen yer,' he said as his head disappeared. 'Never saw no one up there. Bin the quietest run of the morning, this one 'as.'

'Wasn't that nice,' Annie said to Jess when they were back in April Grove, in the house with the turret. 'You know, I thought it was going to be a bit of a washout, but it was lovely. I mean, there wasn't hardly anything to it, but somehow or other it seemed to mean such a lot. I don't know how to explain it. Everyone seemed to be part of it, in a way, even all them people we didn't know.'

'I know,' Jess said thoughtfully. 'I felt it too. Like as if everyone was together – not just sitting in a room, but in a different sort of way. Close.'

There's only two things missing,' Annie said, glancing through the open door into the other room. Betty and Dennis were there in the middle of a laughing crowd, but Olive was sitting with her grandmother near the window, looking out into the sunlit street. Her face was abstracted and sad.

'I know. Olive must be missing Derek badly today. And we all know who else ought to be here.' Jess reached out, her face filled with concern for Annie's lips were quivering and her eyes were suddenly filled with tears. 'Colin. Oh, Annie, I don't know what to say –'

She stopped abruptly. Olive, sitting by the window, had suddenly leapt to her feet. Pushing past Dennis and Betty, she thrust a way to the door. She jerked open the front door just as the bell began to shrill, and snatched at the orange envelope that was being held out by a boy in dark blue uniform.

'A telegram! She must've seen him coming down the street.' Jess lifted her fingers to her mouth. 'Oh, Annie, if something's happened to Derek, today of all days –'

But Olive, her face as pale as ashes, was staring at the envelope and making no attempt to open it. Moving stiffly, as if in a trance, she turned and looked across the crowd towards her mother.

'It's for you,' she said in a strange, creaky voice. 'Mum – it's for you.'

'For *me*?' Annie gaped at her, then stepped forwards. 'A telegram for me? Oh, my goodness. Oh, Ted –'

He was beside her, taking the envelope from Olive's fingers. While everyone fell silent, he pulled out the sheet of paper and read it. They saw his face whiten. They saw Annie's unbelieving stare, the slow shake of her head as if refuting the news it had brought. They saw her turn her head and gaze up at her husband as if asking him if it were really true.

Jess found Frank beside her, and felt for his hand. 'It's Colin. It must be Colin. Oh, poor Annie.'

But Annie was smiling. Her white face had regained its colour in a rush and she was smiling, even beginning to laugh. It's hysterics, Jess thought, it's shock, reaction. She stepped forward, ready to fold her sister in her arms.

Annie turned to her. 'Look at this, Jess! Look at this! He's *safe* – our Colin's safe. Look! It says he's in Japanese hands – in a Japanese prisoner-of-war camp. He's been alive, all this time. Oh Jess, Jess, *Jess*!'

The tears were cascading down her cheeks now and she was laughing and crying at the same time. It was hysteria, right enough, but no one had the heart to do anything about it. Let Annie laugh or cry all she liked. She'd kept her feelings to herself long enough.

Jess took the envelope and the sheet of paper and read it carefully. Then she turned to Frank and smiled, and the tears were in her eyes too.

'It's true,' she said. 'Colin's still alive. He's a Japanese prisoner of war. He's going to come home again, Frank. He's *all right*.'

'Thank God for that,' Frank said quietly. 'And let's hope it's not too long before the war's over and he's back again, eh, Jess? Nearly four years it's been going on. That's as long as the First War lasted. It's got to come to an end soon.'

The wedding reception had become a party, the quietness of the Meeting forgotten in a sudden burst of jubilant celebration. And in the midst of it all, Dennis and Betty stood close, their arms wound about each other's waists, unwilling to part even for a moment.

'I love you, Betty,' he whispered in her ear, and she smiled back at him.

'I love you too, Dennis. And everything's going to be all right now. Uncle Frank's right – the war can't last very much longer. Derek'll come home and make Olive happy again. And best of all, our Colin's safe.' She smiled. 'D'you know something? I feel as if today's a turning point for us all. From now on, everything's going to get better. Just you wait and see.'

'Like in the song,' he said with a grin. 'And what's the other one? "Keep Smiling Through"? D'you know, Betty, I can hear your smile when you talk. And it's just as lovely as when I could see it. So you will keep doing it, won't you? Smiling through, I mean. It's what keeps everyone going.'

He was right, Betty thought as they went out for a breath of air a little later and wandered hand in hand across the moonlit path over the allotments. Smiling did keep you going. It had kept Olive going while Derek was away, it had kept her mother going through all the anxiety over Colin. It had kept Betty herself going when Dennis was taking those terrible risks. It had kept them all going through raids and sleepless nights and the grinding despair of the days.

Four years. It *couldn't* be much longer.

All Orion/Phoenix titles are available at your local bookshop or from the following address:

Mail Order Department
Littlehampton Book Services
FREEPOST BR535
Worthing, West Sussex, BN13 3BR
telephone 01903 828503, *facsimile* 01903 828802
e-mail MailOrders@lbsltd.co.uk
(Please ensure that you include full postal address details)

Payment can be made either by credit/debit card (Visa, Mastercard, Access and Switch accepted) or by sending a £ Sterling cheque or postal order made payable to *Littlehampton Book Services*.
DO NOT SEND CASH OR CURRENCY.

Please add the following to cover postage and packing

UK and BFPO:
£1.50 for the first book, and 50p for each additional book to a maximum of £3.50

Overseas and Eire:
£2.50 for the first book plus £1.00 for the second book and 50p for each additional book ordered

---

BLOCK CAPITALS PLEASE

name of cardholder ....

address of cardholder ....

delivery address
(if different from cardholder)
....

postcode ....

postcode ....

☐ I enclose my remittance for £ ....

☐ please debit my Mastercard/Visa/Access/Switch (delete as appropriate)

card number ☐☐☐☐☐☐☐☐☐☐☐☐☐☐☐☐

expiry date ☐☐☐☐   Switch issue no. ☐☐

signature ....

prices and availability are subject to change without notice